T0168408

After the Western Reserve

After the Western Reserve:
The Ohio Fiction of Jessie Brown Pounds

edited by

Sandra Parker

Bowling Green State University Popular Press
Bowling Green, OH 43403

Copyright 1999 © Bowling Green State University Popular Press

Library of Congress Cataloging-in-Publication Data
Pounds, Jessie Brown, 1861-1921.
    After the western reserve : the Ohio fiction of Jessie Brown Pounds
/ edited by Sandra Parker.
        p.   cm.
    Includes
    ISBN 0-87972-787-X (cloth : alk. paper). -- ISBN 0-87972-788-8
(pbk. : alk. paper)
    1. Ohio--Social life and customs--Fiction. 2. Frontier and pioneer
life--Ohio--Fiction. 3. Christian fiction, American. I. Parker, Sandra
(Sandra A.)
PS2649.P78A6   1999
813'.4--dc21   98-48224
                                                                      CIP

Cover design by Dumm Art

Dedicated to

Agnes Schiltz Parker (1910-1958)

Warren Howard Parker (1898-1976)

CONTENTS

Bijah Morrison believes he "orto hev" ten acres "o'pastur
notches right out o'my farm" and schemes for its acquisition.
His two neglected sons don't share his values; "botheration,
father" Matt asks, why not paint the house or buy mother a
sewing machine? The boy becomes a miser, while his brother
Sammy dies as a drunkard with brain fever. Matt marries the
snippy Melia Riggs; his dispirited mother dies, and savings are
again spent on a funeral. The farm is deeded to Matt, and a "veritable reign of terror" follows for Bijah who villagers say "is
gettin' his pay . . . for the way he's brought up his children."
When the village decides to buy the ten-acre lot to extend their
burial ground, Bijah becomes its first occupant.

In the twenty-five years between two visits of the German
settler Peter Hartmann to the New England immigrant home on
the Western Reserve of the Ellsworth family, the reader learns of
the 1834 adventure of the 14-year-old daughter Abbie who
became a school teacher. Her success with 30 unruly farm children hinges upon the insurgency of August Baughman who is
won over when he understands her motivation, earning money
for her sick older sister's medicine. Hartmann's second visit 25
years later happens because the thrifty German colony in the
south part of the township again needs a teacher, but Abbie's
teenage daughter is still a student, so he must wait and put up
with a "deacher [who] vas a man, an' der poys locked him up in
der wood-gloset."

Cheerful, old Miss Melury Haines tells the story of the village's first Children's Day which was proposed by Libbie
Barnum. The narrator explains the reluctance of Uncle Sile to

participate because of his anger with Zack Minor, a trader and jockey, who sold him a "balky old animal." But after his grandson Carl begs him to attend the event and Uncle Sile sees the boy perform with Zack Minor's son, Johnny, he repents his anger—then Zack Minor finally apologizes, takes back the balky horse and repays Uncle Sile.

Mr. Cornwell is invited to Western Reserve village from the city; he is to serve as pastor and is told to "get on the right side of Colonel Bristow," a community leader who refuses to become a member of the church. The new pastor urges everyone to give to a foreign mission collection. Squire Morrison struggles with the demand for one day's wages, which he calculates to be $25.00 but ultimately decides to "quit hiding behind Colonel Bristow's back" and makes the offering. Ingleside finally accepts Bristow's intransigence and becomes proud of its foreign missionary support.

Dexter Center is unhappy with "the sign of a low groggery" which exists opposite the "little white 'meeting-house' where the various denominations represented in the village were wont to worship." Community leaders call a council of war, and the "village oracle" Deacon Briarly makes a potent speech about whisky being like "snakes and the lizards an' the creepin' things of the airth." Urged to greater caution in his speech, Briarly comments that he is "losin' all my gift for public speakin,'" but at the next civic meeting he threatens cramming "brimstone down their throats with a red-hot poker." His enthusiasm leads the residents to drive out the saloon-keepers, and all attempts to reform the Deacon cease.

Father Winniston is a seventy-four-old settler of Craydock's Corners who has grown into a charming patriarch. Young pastor Reid is attracted to his granddaughter Sabrina, but is warned by the old man against "speritualizing" on the scriptures. Winniston is especially opposed to the possible acquisition of an organ in the church, which is desired by Mrs. Squire Seakin. A friend of Mr. Littleton, Reid visits, also preaches and admires Sabrina Winniston, a "disguised princess." An organ is brought to the

church and Father Winniston rages. He attacks Littleton for "des-
ecrating the altars of the sanctooary," and the church members
respond by putting Winniston out of the eldership. The old man
falls ill and is seen by Littleton to be—"honest, narrow, loving
and intolerant, with the habit of giving the name of conviction to
his prejudices, and of preserving them to his own and others'
hurt." On his deathbed the old man hears music, the harp and
psaltery. Some claim the old man repented his anti-music position, but Littleton is content to marry Sabrina and be quiet about
whether or not Father Winniston experienced a change of heart.

Hillsbury Folks
        Forty years ago Hillsbury was a "type" of village near
a "Great City" which has since swallowed the village,
except for its graveyard. Before the factories were built on
the village common, the village consisted of two stores,
each led by a representative of the two political parties.
Three churches existed—Methodist, Congregationalist and
Disciples. The "graded school" was a source of pride and
employed three schoolma'ams. Miss Fanny was primary
teacher who was called "Miss Stuck-Up." Miss Emily was
tall, fair, and hero worshiped, despite her being a
Methodist. Mrs. Caroline More was principal and a Calvinist disciplinarian. Conrad Wetzel or "Cooney" played
hookey and was returned by his father to be punished by
Mrs. More's long black ruler, which takes two hours and
causes Miss Emily to weep. The reader learns that Cooney
Wetzel becomes the village's only rich man—manufactur-
ing glue. So much for tribulation.

        Dr. Meecham is young, sincere, single minded, but
ignorant. He administers lots of cod liver oil, iron, and
whiskey. He hates cold water and fresh air and accidentally
extracts the wrong tooth from Joe Wetzel. Then the doctor
says his services were free. Meecham leaves Hillsbury in
disgrace after killing a patient with anesthesia.

        The narrator remembers growing up in the Disciples'
mission in Hillsbury but attending the Methodist and Con-

gregational Sunday-schools. The comparisons of the two churches include their services, spirit and music. Brother Baxter is the Methodist pastor, a "roar'ah" in the church but genial with children. Facing a dispirited revival meeting, Baxter is ashamed when Bully Hedding, the town's scalawag, offers to be a "decoy duck." James Burdick is the Congregational minister, with side-whiskers and written sermons. His hold on the people is loosened by a woman, when he secretly marries Mary Corwin, the "giggling organist of the Methodist church." He then resigns and goes to the West.

IV The Drunkard   70
     The village's drunkard was served by two saloons, one kept by Jake Shaeffer, who was prayed over by the Woman's Temperance Crusade, and another by Old Leech. Neither saloon liked to serve Old Bill Higley who became picturesque during his carouses. His ability to talk while drunk is "One drop o' grace in my heart," and his companion is a scotch terrier called Fan. Higley goes to pray with Brother Baxter and then drunkenly chastises pompous Sam Slatterly. Illness and poverty force sobriety on Bill Higley who is visited on his deathbed by Brother Baxter. Here it is revealed that the dying man was a Methodist minister who became an unreformed alcoholic. Without hope, Fan remains his only mourner and dies a week later.

V The Scalawag   74
     Bolinbroke Hedding or "Bully" says he has traveled and served in the war with the Army of the Potomac. He is a villain and village clown who sits on the pork-barrel at Wetzel's store telling lies. He surreptitiously gets an army pension and calls his business butter and eggs. The "pursoot of your livin' by means of your wits" is illustrated by his selling spoiled butter to suburban housewives in the city. As he grows old, drinking takes its toll; his children leave, his wife dies. Deserted and unmourned, Bully's death in effect abolishes the loafer's seat at the village store.

Rachael Sylvestre, A Story of the Pioneers   78
     In 1882 Joseph Arrondale, aged 76, writes the story of his family's early days on the Western Reserve fifty years ago. He

traces the childhood he shared with his admired older brother Stephen and the entry into Blue Brook from the East of the Sylvestre family whose two daughters interest the neighborhood. The contrasts between the two families grow as the Arrondales become followers of the Disciples of Christ, while the Sylvestres are supposed to be atheist rationalists. However, the younger Sylvestre daughter, Martha, converts and is repudiated by her patriarchal father, and eventually the older daughter, Rachael, converts too. The Sylvestre patrimony is dissipated by fire and ill judgments, especially after the father urges Martha to marry a visiter named Charles Easton who turns out to be Benjamin Redding, a bigamist and ner do well. Redding dies while trying to escape retribution in Blue Brook, and later Martha dies from grief, leaving her baby Rachael to her sister who marries the ever devoted Stephen Arrondale. Joseph becomes a school teacher and surrogate family member, helping to raise his brother's and Rachael's children while cherishing their genesis on the early Western Reserve.

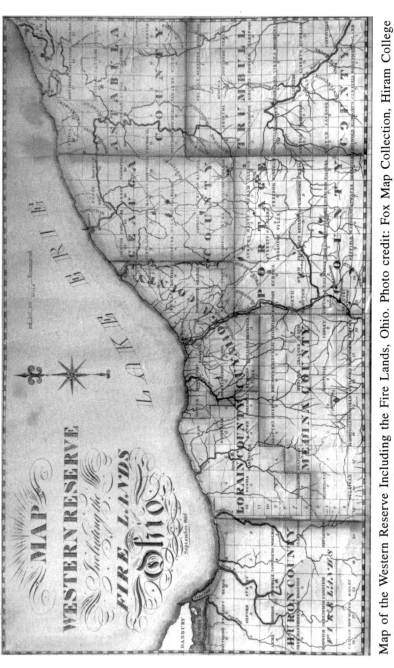

Map of the Western Reserve Including the Fire Lands, Ohio. Photo credit: Fox Map Collection, Hiram College Archives. Reprinted with permission.

Jessie Pounds. Reprinted with permission from Disiples of Christ Historical Society, Nashville, Tennessee.

ACKNOWLEDGMENTS

I am grateful to Hiram College's Archivist, Joanne Sawyer, for introducing me to the writing of Jessie Brown Pounds and encouraging my study of her texts. Also, Archivist David McWhirter of the Disciples of Christ in Nashville was instrumental in providing access to additional resources, namely Pounds' periodical fiction.

Several Hiram College colleagues have encouraged and assisted in this project, in particular, David Anderson, director of the 1982 National Endowment of the Humanities program called "Regionalism in the Humanities," which initiated my interest in "lost" regional authors like Pounds. Joyce Dyer, the college's writing director, has also unstintingly offered loyal encouragement and wry critical judgments. My expressions of gratitude for collegial support must include Hiram College itself, which has supported my research through several sabbaticals.

Ultimately, my inspiration for persevering in the evolution of this anthology comes from Jessie Brown Pounds herself, a woman whose idealism and hard work have given me renewed faith in the boundless elasticity of the human spirit.

INTRODUCTION

This anthology attempts to enfranchise a voice excluded from America's literary canon. It provides a historical overview of the career of Jessie Brown Pounds (1861-1921), emphasizing her regional fiction that begins with early short stories in 1889, continues with material published posthumously in 1921 and concludes with the historically based novel *Rachael Sylvestre* (1904). These stories are chronologically selected and preserve the author's original punctuation and spelling. The purpose of this collection is to present the best writing of an excellent but little-known author and to acquaint the general reader with the life, era, and work of Pounds by tracing her development as a regional writer and supplying a context for her work and its position in American literature. Jessie Brown Pounds' significant narratives illustrate how a comparatively isolated Ohio woman, committed to writing regional fiction, became part of a distinguished American literary tradition that culminated at the end of the nineteenth century.

Pounds' books, anthologies of fiction, and novels were published in Cincinnati by the Standard Publishing Company between 1886 and 1901; her serialized novels and stories were published in: *Disciple of Christ* (1885), Isaac Errett's *Christian Standard* (1886-1918), James H. Garrison's *Christian Evangelist* (1910-1913), and Charles Clayton Morrison's *Christian Century* (1919-1921). She also had stories published by the Christian Women's Board of Missions. Pounds' books have been unavailable and out of print for over a century and were never reviewed by non Disciples of Christ media.

There are several reasons for her disappearance from America's literary canon, including problems faced by other nineteenth-century women writers. Pounds has been less fortunate than writers like Harriet Beecher Stowe, Louisa May Alcott, and Alice Cary who have been reassessed in the past quarter century. Pounds wrote within an indigenous Protestant tradition in the nineteenth century that battled for its place among Christian denominations. Little interdenominational literary support occurred, and Jessie Brown Pounds only submitted her fiction to Disciples' publications, effectively limiting her reputation. Furthermore, a significant proportion of her writing was designed for children, a nineteenth-century literary convention; women writers turned their hands to children's texts, sacred and secular, and such distinguished authors as

Louisa May Alcott have been belittled because of their emphasis upon the edification of the child reader. Furthermore, critics have often ignored nineteenth-century authors who wrote within a middle-western popular culture tradition in Ohio, a state not widely acknowledged for regional writing. For all of these reasons, Jessie Brown Pounds' writing has gone out of fashion. Pounds' eclipse is a result of a process Louise Bernikow has described: "which authors have survived time and which have not depends upon who noticed them and chose not to record the notice" (3).

Nonetheless, Jessie Brown Pounds makes excellent reading, informs the reader about an interesting and valuable slice of Americana, and provides an example of the quality of regional writing done by women during the last third of the nineteenth century. The stories included in this anthology substantiate the claim that the genre of short fiction elicited some of the best work of America's women writers.

This country's vastness has meant that its literature reflects wide geographical and ethnic diversity. The conception of regionalism was recently redefined by Judith Fetterly and Marjorie Price in their book *American Women Regionalists, 1850-1910.* They describe regional writers as those who write from within a culture and cherish its locale and people. Women's values like stability, love, and domesticity counterbalance the threats of frontier life. Character becomes more significant than plot because action is generated from within. Regional sketches and stories describe the environment, how it influences people, and what messages it embodies; they are told by a narrator who avoids condescension by sharing the point of view of the people who live within the culture. Therefore, the reader is invited to share the community experience of the region, which is realistically depicted in such forms as its dialect, customs, daily practices, and landscape.

The history of America's attitudes toward regional writing goes back to such innovators as the eastern author Sarah Josepha Hale, famous for her contributions to *Godey's Ladies Book,* the first publication in America to pay women authors and promote their original material, who in 1828 called for literature that is a "record of conjugal and maternal love" (72). Four years later in 1832 regional Ohio editors of the *Western Monthly* magazine pleaded for "kindling a national feeling in favor of indigenous talent" (188). Even foreign visitors, like Harriet Martineau in her 1837 *Society in America,* claimed that the best literature in America is its "tales and sketches in which the habits and manners of the people of the country are delineated" (325). In the 1840s, America's famous female transcendentalist, Margaret Fuller, deplored "the absence of compositions founded on regional history and relevant to pioneer experience" (130). Her contention was repeatedly supported by western intellectuals like William D. Gallagher, who mentored Ohio's first generation of women writers, Julia L. Dumont, Pamilla W. Ball, Harriet Beecher Stowe, and Alice Cary. Gallagher's staunch support of regional writing appears, for example, in 1844 when he calls for authors in his *Western Literary Journal and Monthly Review* who will diffuse a knowledge of the region and thus further its prosperity.

After the Civil War, intellectuals' demands for regional literature had a new basis—it would heal the nation's wounds and preserve its vanishing traditions. In this spirit, Ohio's famous man of letters, William Dean Howells, initiated his editorship of *Harper's New Monthly* in 1889 by saluting regionalists' powers of "honest observation." His friend Hamlin Garland labeled the central task of American literature the creation of an "authentic national product." Today, a century and a half later, support for regional writing continues to come from writers like Pulitzer Prize-winning Ohio author Toni Morrison, who situates three of her novels in the region. In 1985, western author Louise Erdrich in the *New York Times Book Review* articulated the regionalist credo: study of place, "its people and character, its crops, products, paranoias, dialects and failures . . . ." She adds, "truly knowing a place provides the link between details and meaning. Location, whether it is to abandon it or draw it sharply, is where we start" (23).

Jessie Brown Pounds was born on August 31, 1861, in a Greek Revival home in Portage County, Ohio, 30 miles southeast of Cleveland. The historical and cultural place that shaped her life was originally Connecticut's Western Reserve, eight, later twelve, counties in northeastern Ohio that covered three and a half million acres. Explored and surveyed by the Connecticut Land company late in the eighteenth century, in 1803 it was absorbed into the Union and lost its legal entity when Ohio claimed statehood. Nonetheless, during the entire century people continued to identify with the region's unique and homogeneous spiritual heritage, originally defined by its New England settlers, like the pioneer family of Jessie Brown Pounds, whose lives resonated with the Western Reserve's ethos of religion, community organization, education, and even architecture.

Connecticut's Western Reserve was her neighborhood; here were the farms and houses later transformed in her fiction into Craydock Corners, Hillsbury, Eden Valley, and Blue Brook. Jessie Brown's forebears came to America on the Mayflower, fought with the Minutemen, and migrated to the West from New England after the 1787 opening of the Northwest Territory. She was the fifth child of Yankee parents, Holland Brown and Jane Abel. Her relationship with her schoolteacher mother was close, since she was the spoiled youngest child, and her mother taught in their home. Her father was a farmer and follower of Alexander Campbell, the Scottish founder of America's new religious movement first called Campbellism and then the Disciples of Christ. Holland Brown converted at Wadsworth before his marriage and served as a preacher on horseback for the impassioned religion. As a liberal Campbellite, he moved his family in 1852 to Hiram, Ohio, which was the location of their educational institution, founded in 1850—the Western Reserve Eclectic Institute which by 1852-53 served 529 students, 458 from Ohio. Holland Brown became friends with the Institute's intellectual leaders and was an Abolitionist who entertained Sojourner Truth in his Hiram home. From her father and his intellectual friends, like James A. Garfield, B. A. Hinsdale, and Isaac Errett, all connected with the Western Reserve Eclectic Institute, Jessie received unusual encouragement for her early literary ambitions.

The child Jessie was empathetic to her parents' idealism and committed herself to a lifetime of emulation. From her mother, Jessie learned the joy of books and the art of storytelling. Pounds' favorite early reading included the Bible and Shakespeare, Charles Dickens, and Walter Scott. Later she enjoyed Lord Alfred Tennyson, George Eliot, and Elizabeth Barrett Browning and American contemporaries like Harriet Beecher Stowe, James Russell Lowell, and John Greenleaf Whittier. In 1884 she dedicated two sonnets, one to Lowell's sense of "place" and another to Whittier's "grace that lies in common things."

In the 1870s, after the Civil War with its legacy of anger, loss, and nostalgia, Holland Brown moved his family from the rural Western Reserve countryside to the environs of nearby Cleveland. He shifted from being a Portage County farmer to Disciple of Christ minister in various towns in Cuyahoga County, including the west side of urban Cleveland; for instance, he worked at the Franklin Circle Christian Church, in an area teeming with emigrants, over 40 percent of whom were from Germany.

Thus, Jessie Brown's background provided her with distinct advantages. Her Yankee-bred family valued education, tolerance, discipline, hard work, and social responsibility, a heritage central to her fiction. Her youth provided the girl with the observation of conservative, provincial settlers in isolated village settings. The village of Hiram again served as her home while she attended classes for two years as a teenager at Hiram College, which in 1867 had changed its name from the Western Reserve Eclectic Institute. At the college, Jessie Brown was influenced by the spirit of intellectuals like Almeda Booth, James A. Garfield's friend and mentor, who left the Western Reserve Eclectic Institute in 1867 after instilling high standards for women who prized academic achievement and selfless commitment to others' betterment. Jessie Brown's early fiction, like "Janie," depicts town and gown conflicts, and later she mined as well as the third scene of her youth, Cleveland's urban setting. Each of these three different milieus can be traced in her narratives about how different people in the Western Reserve viewed human experience. Throughout the next four decades of professional writing, Jessie Brown Pounds drew upon these adjacent locales within northeast Ohio to show how they differed widely in such terms as psychology, social class, environs, and values. Each setting provided her with ideas for stories, though no locale ever interested Jessie Brown as much as Hiram's rural countryside.

Her career as a writer began with religious juvenalia. Jessie Brown began writing poetry at a very early age, and by 1873, at age 12, her poems were being published. Soon her poetry and lyrics made her famous among members of the Disciples of Christ; called their "sweetest singer," she composed over 800 hymns, including "The Touch of His Hand," "The Way of the Cross Leads Home," and "Beautiful Isle." Late in her career in an essay called "Concerning Hymns," she expressed disappointment about the limits of the lyric form. Though she began as an unpaid literary contributor, she quickly evolved into playing a significant role in Disciples' literary establishment; as the years went by, Jessie Brown continued to publish in a variety of newspapers and periodicals that represented the range of Disciples' liberal philosophy. For example, in 1885 when she was 24, *The Disciple of Christ* launched the beginning of her serious literary career when it printed her short story "Janie," and between 1884 and 1887 she edited the *Disciple of Christ*. This support from Alexander Campbell's literary establishment continued throughout her long career as her chosen vocation was to continue her father's work by furthering Campbell's mission and helping shape his church. So for over 40 years Jessie Brown wrote fiction, as well as poetry, lyrics and essays, for a series of Disciples' publications. Most notable in the early years was her contribution to the two leading publications of her denomination, *The Christian Century* and *The Christian Evangelist*.

What transformed Jessie Brown from a volunteer poet into a writer capable of establishing a following and earning her living by her pen in the early 1880s? After she dropped out of Hiram College, Jessie Brown was invited to join Isaac Errett, family friend and editor of the prestigious *Christian Standard,* in Cincinnati where she worked for several years as an assistant editor. This publication, at the time called "the most influential religious paper in all the world" (Wilcox 45), was the western region's most widely circulated Disciples of Christ paper. Until his death in 1888, Errett's was a "voice of moderation" within the Disciples of Christ church; he also provided the channel through which Jessie Brown's work began to reach a broad readership. Isaac Errett served as her mentor in the Disciples' literary and publishing world, editing her work for publication, encouraging her liberal interests, and promoting her career.

As a consequence, Jessie Brown's Cincinnati editorial job helped to professionalize her writing and transform her from a neophyte into a recognized author with a wide, regional audience. She continued to publish short fiction in other journals, like *The Disciple of Christ,* and as early as 1886 published her first book—a novella and three stories in *A Woman's Doing and Other Stories*; three years later Jessie Brown published another anthology, *Runaway and Other Stories.* Overall, between 1885 and 1918, she published more than 80 stories and sketches. Novels also appeared: *Norman Macdonald* (1884), *Roderick Wayne* (1888), and *The Ironclad Pledge* (1890). After her 1896 marriage to the minister John Pounds there were three more: *The Popular Idol* (1901), *The Young Man from Middlefield* (1901), and *Rachael Sylvestre* (1904). Her *oeuvre* was completed posthumously with a retrospective collection, *Jessie Brown Pounds, Memorial Selections* (1921).

By 1896 when she married at 35, the frail, independent and spirited Jessie Brown Pounds had earned a respected name in the region as a Disciples of Christ editor, poet, and prose writer. She remained committed to her family; her father Holland Brown died in 1885, and her mother, after living with her married daughter for 21 years, died in 1906. Marriage changed Jessie Brown Pounds in a number of ways; it led to a new independence in terms of traveling to support her husband's pastoral tasks, which led them away from Cleveland to Indianapolis, then back to Cleveland until his retirement from ministerial work in 1906. They retired to the village of Hiram where three years later John Pounds was appointed pastor of the local Disciples of Christ church, the same congregation Jessie Brown's father had once served as an itinerant preacher.

When she "retired" with her husband in 1906 to Portage County's Hiram township, Jessie and John Pounds built and moved into a home on Wakefield Road, which they occupied until her sudden death in 1921. Their household included two adopted daughters and provided a haven for countless Hiram students who considered this to be their ideal "house by the roadside." Jessie Brown Pounds' marriage of 24 years was happy; John Pounds was desolate after her sudden death and rapidly declined, dying in 1924.

Pounds' fiction after her 1896 marriage reveals what the new role of minister's wife may have revealed to her about the social dynamics of religious institutions. No longer a minister's daughter, the role of working as minister's wife put tremendous demands upon her. Jessie Brown Pounds needed to entertain, lead such groups as the Ladies Aid Society, and help her husband in the parsonage. She evidently reveled in this role, which led to three insightful novels written at the beginning of the twentieth century, two in 1901, *The Popular Idol* and *The Young Man from Middlefield,* and her historically-based final novel three years later in 1904, *Rachael Sylvestre.* After ten years of marriage and moving to Hiram in 1906, Jessie Brown Pounds ceased writing novels and concentrated upon shorter forms, especially poems, essays, sketches and stories. At this time she produced some of her best fiction which was retrospective and nostalgic about the culture of the Western Reserve.

During the last phase of her remarkably circular life, after her return to Hiram, Jessie Brown Pounds began writing for the liberal *Christian Evangelist* (1910-1911), edited by James H. Garrison. In *The Christian Evangelist,* Pounds edited a department called "Woman's Realm" which included both fiction and nonfiction prose, ranging from brief didactic essays to articles on contemporary and historical subjects—for instance, the anti-war poem " It Is Quiet Tonight in Flanders" and the religious story "In the Palace of Herod." Here she also published "Hillsbury Folks," five vivid village sketches of the school ma'ams, doctor, parsons, drunkard, and scalawag included in this anthology.

In 1917, four years before her death in 1921, Pounds was named contributing editor to *The Christian Century,* an influential nondenominational publication read throughout the United States. *The Christian Century* affiliation connected her to what has been called the "foremost organ of liberal Christianity in America" (Harrell 853). Joining the editorial staff of this prestigious University of Chicago-based publication was a milestone in Jessie Brown Pounds' professional career spanning 40 years and a self-identity defined, as she reported to the 1900 census, by working at the occupation of "editor." Its distinguished editor Charles Clayton Morrison, a prominent advocate of "Social Christianity" who encouraged her thoughtful essays upon current affairs and political issues, supervised her work at *The Christian Century.*

Nonetheless, it is this Western Reserve woman's reputation as an author that should retain significance today. Growing from narratives that typically focus upon regional culture and illustrate Victorian literary conventions, especially women's writing for young people, Pounds created early protagonists, like Myrtle Mowbray, Roderick Wayne, Norman Macdonald, and Phil Darrington, who do not compel modern readers' credibility; these novels are sentimental and domestic, featuring stock plots, characters and themes. However, Pounds' mature novels written at the beginning of the twentieth century are more original and probe contemporary social issues; for instance, *The Young Man from Middlefield* (1901) and *The Popular Idol* (1901) shrewdly analyze the psychology and sociology of Cleveland and its suburbs. Her last extended narrative, *Rachael Sylvestre* (1904), is Pounds' most interesting novel; it presents a first-person narrator who nostalgically spins an autobiographical tale about struggling pioneers of Blue Brook, the role played by enterprise, atheism, and family values, as well as the nascent Disciples of Christ representatives on the Western Reserve frontier. This novel is a tribute to Jessie Brown's father's generation and its role in founding the early pioneer church.

Jessie Brown Pounds' only historical novel traces the consequences of the birth in 1800 of a man named Stephen Aarondale whose life is recorded by his aged brother in 1882. The background of the region shaped this protagonist's life: after the Revolutionary War, the Land Ordinance of 1785 led surveyors to draw up six-mile townships in the Territory Northwest of the Ohio River. In 1786 Connecticut transferred title of its western claims to the national government while reserving a section to be granted to war veterans. The Northwest Ordinance of 1787 provided government, and New Englanders, like Pounds' ancestors, began to settle the Western Reserve after 1796. Col. Daniel Tilden of Lebanon, Connecticut, purchased the fifth township in the seventh range of the Western Reserve and named it "Hiram" after the Biblical carpenter Hiram Abif of Jerusalem who built Solomon's temple. By 1820 the center road from east to west was completed, and Thomas and Alexander Campbell who were promoting a new religious movement in the region visited Hiram. Alexander Campbell was born in Ireland, taught at the University of Glasgow in Scotland and then emigrated to the United States; in 1809 he was joined by his father, Thomas. The two men believed sectarianism was wrong. They sought nondenominational Christian unity, a new slant on authority emphasizing the Bible: "Where the Scriptures speak, we speak; where they are silent, we are silent."

By 1811 the Campbells were, nonetheless, proclaiming a new Christian Association, which led first to "Campbellism" and finally to the new denomination called the Disciples of Christ. By 1827 a Campbellite congregation was meeting in Mantua with Sidney Rigdon preaching; the following year, Hiram village founder Symonds Rider heard Thomas Campbell's simple doctrine at Mantua and was baptized, and in 1829 the Hiram congregation founded its own church. By 1830 the Campbellites are believed to have converted over 12,000 people. In 1835 the new Disciples church in Hiram had thirteen members, and fourteen years later its numbers had grown to 121. Campbell and James A.

Garfield became famous as religious debaters who vanquished doubting foes. This is the relevant historical outline that informs the plot of *Rachael Sylvestre*.

The characters in Jessie Brown Pounds' novel live in a fictional village called Blue Brook, Portage County. Two families are juxtaposed: the Aarondales and the Sylvestres; the first family has a Baptist mother and Christian father; the second family consists of an infidel patriarch who substitutes *The Age of Reason* for the Bible and suppresses his Presbyterian wife. The children in the provincial village, including two boys from the Aarondale clan and two girls from the Sylvestres, are familiars. Early in the novel, the elder Aarondale son, Stephen, hears a sermon by Campbellite Walter Scott and becomes a convert to the Disciples of Christ. Stephen may be modeled on James A. Garfield, as both were self-instructed ministers and noteworthy debaters in the early Reserve. Stephen Aarondale's challenge is converting the region's dubious Unitarians, Universalists, Baptists, and Presbyterians. Among his converts are his parents, Martha Sylvestre, and his younger brother, Joseph. Eventually the older Aarondale daughter after whom the novel is titled, Rachael (who later becomes a Sylvestre by marriage), is converted, too. The novel includes a melodramatic plot that centers on Joseph's ambiguous attachment to the Aarondale sisters and the parental tyranny that drives the younger Sylvestre girl, Martha, from home and into the destructive arms of an outsider who is a bigamist.

Pounds develops the role of a male narrator in this novel, her sole experiment with first-person point of view. Joseph recalls the charismatic Alexander Campbell's visits to the bucolic Western Reserve. He also describes the religious quandary of the strong heroine whose intellectual conversion and marriage grow, not from romantic love, but from a sense of ethical obligation. Thus Rachael Sylvestre's mental and spiritual strength remain uncompromised. Joseph, her respectful brother-in-law, like his Biblical namesake, is effectively impotent; however, he becomes the empathetic father figure to her children, while her virile husband Stephen travels on church business. Joseph is thus an unusual character in his own right; he is androgynous, a district school teacher who remains close to his mother, homebound, provincial, and domestic. In old age, he says, "my long life has been encompassed with mercies, . . . I am glad I have lived."

Pounds' adaptation of Ohio's history was supplemented by her familiarity with the work of contemporary women writers. Among her predecessors were originators of the village sketch and domestic novel, such as England's Mary Russell Mitford, and New England's Maria Sedgewick, Charlotte A. Fillebrown Jerauld, and Emily Chubbock

Judson. Western writers included Julia Dumont (1794-1857) the first outstanding Ohio woman regionalist who was praised by W. H. Venable in his *Literary Culture in the Ohio Valley* (1891) as the first woman to deserve a literary reputation. Preserving early Ohio's pioneer customs, Dumont's "The Picture: A Western Sketch" (1836) ironically mocks the era's paradigm for regional fiction: "Romantic it certainly must be, and pathetic, and chivalrous, and tender, and glowing, and imaginative; and above all, it must be *Western.*"

By mid-century, Ohio's next generation of women writers was less chauvinistic; Alice Cary was the most famous woman to develop regional realism in skillful short stories. Escaping both romantic refinement and frontier crudity, Cary's contribution was a new, dark realism. She repeatedly describes deprivation in the western frontier town of Mount Healthy, Hamilton County where she spent her first 30 years. Alice Cary's *Clovernook* (1852) is the first of several anthologies of stories that are noteworthy for their characteristic grimness (Fetterly xx).

Ohio's other mid-century regionalist to influence later Ohio writers was Harriet Beecher Stowe, who lived in Cincinnati for 18 years. Before publishing her polemical *Uncle Tom's Cabin* in 1852, she only wrote New England regional sketches, enthusiastic depictions of women's lives in volumes like *The May Flower* (1843) which celebrate women's strength and independence.

The post-bellum era's writers might be called third-generation regionalists. Earlier writers taught observation, but the Civil War experience led to self-conscious promotion of regional writing as an antidote to cold-blooded sectionalism. By the 1880s when Jessie Brown Pounds' career was underway, Ohio, once the West, had transmuted into the Middle West, and love of the region led to artistic issues—like the need to preserve the rural past, and ethical issues, such as how to confront problems raised by social dislocation and amoral wealth. As Robert E. Spiller points out, regionalism emphasized "old faces, manners, customs, recipes, styles, attitudes, and prejudices [which] were undergoing rapid change or total extirpation" (861).

Pounds shared many concerns with her female contemporaries, growing from her beginning career publishing fiction in the late 1880s in *The Disciple* and *The Christian Standard* to her work in the *Christian Evangelist* before World War I. Assured an audience, Pounds consistently demonstrated her knowledge of women's regional style. On April 30, 1889, for example, her story "The Little School Mis" appeared, which is remarkable for its effective use of German dialect and description of a frontier schooling dilemma—a 13-year-old, Abbie Ellsworth, is challenged as she teaches 37 reluctant, immigrant farm children. The story may remind a reader of Alice Cary's "The Schoolmistress," printed 37 years earlier in *Clovernook; or, Recollections of Our Neighborhood in the West* in 1852. But whereas Cary uses the representative orphan teacher named Caty as an opportunity to show her frightened courtship and removal from the school setting, Pounds' story affirms the abilities of the teacher and exhibits the belated appreciation of an ex-student who seeks another Yankee teacher for the country school house. In essence, Pounds follows Cary's literary guideline stated at the beginning of her first *Clovernook* collection: "there is surely as much in the simple manners, and the little histories of every day revealed, to interest us in humanity." At the end of her second *Clovernook* volume, Cary, the quintessential regional author, adds that a writer must limit herself "to that domain to which I was born."

Pounds' early regional writing anticipates her later work in both form and content; it emphasizes justice and becomes increasingly realistic. For example, the sketches in "Hillsbury Folks" demonstrate the moral qualities of half a dozen denizens of a vanished Western Reserve village near Cleveland, perhaps near Wadsworth or Brooklyn, which is resurrected from a graveyard to its earlier glory—two stores, a post office, three churches, and a brick grade school. These sketches are not purely autobiographical, but Pounds does draw upon rural Western Reserve traditions to recreate colorful characters who are clearly rooted in her narrator's personal and communal knowledge. They preserve a disappearing rural heritage and chronicle local issues which center on the power base of church life in the Western Reserve.

After 1911, Pounds' fiction in *The Christian Evangelist* reveals how her narrative style has matured. For instance, the Hillsbury folks' sketches build upon earlier narrative themes like the greed and selfishness represented by Bijah Morrison in "The Ten Acre Lot" (1889). And her two Craydock Corners stories, "Trouble at Craydocks Corners" and "An Orthodox Heretic," left unpublished at her death, offer keen perspectives on village life in the Western Reserve. The story included in this anthology, "An Orthodox Heretic" (1921), for example, modifies the early theme of "Children's Day at Slocum's Corners" (*The Christian Standard*, 1889) and transcends the awkwardness of its narrator. Such well-crafted regional stories served Pounds as a means for recreating the past and continuing her narrative role in fiction as life's observer. Her undated Craydocks Corners stories are Pounds' supreme achievements, witty narratives that only became available when Samuel Clayton Morrison included them in *Memorial Selections*.

Pounds always signed her work, except when she adopted the pseudonym Auris Leigh for the "Hillsbury" sketches. By writing under her own name, Pounds signals her seriousness as a writer. She, moreover, could be said to sign her fiction through titles, like "Rachel Hartwick's Sacrifice" or "Mrs. Ormsby's Thanksgiving" which invoke the specific and particular, the individual, rather than the generic. Unlike earlier writers like Catharine Sedgewick, whose allegorical "A New England Tale" (1822) generalizes region, Jessie Brown Pounds tends toward the concrete and specific; she would not have written "An Ohio Tale." In fact, Pounds' titles reflect the fact that her interest lies in individuals as is often shown in the use of names—"Janice," "Betty," and "Margery" are titles that illustrate how women on the western frontier may provide a focal point, serve as protagonists, and represent the human condition. Places also symbolize the merit of local, such as "Broadcourt," "Slocum's Corners," "Ingleside," "Bethesda," "Mount Victory," and so forth. The strength of her best fiction resides in this insistence on the specific and her resistance to sentimentality; her gift is for humble, domestic realism.

In fiction, unlike her conventional poetry and lyrics, Jessie Brown Pounds became a writer with a unique subject, the early Western Reserve, which provided her with settings as a kind of spiritual metaphor. Characters, events, places, and issues appear and reappear, each providing some new angle or information to reconstruct the worlds that young Jessie Brown discovered when she was growing up in northeast Ohio, Connecticut's old Western Reserve. Unlike other regional writers, such as Alice Cary who moved to New York City in 1850, Jessie Brown Pounds stayed in Ohio. And unlike Cary's passionately involved narrators, Pounds' narration is either omniscient or, if first person, remains more distanced from events. An example of the characteristic tone achieved by a Western Reserve story teller in Pounds' tales is the nameless woman in "An Orthodox Heretic" who comments at the story's opening: "He was seventy-four years old. . . . the most charming of old men, until he began to obtrude his orthodoxy. After this, one might perhaps weary in his society."

In her writing, as in that of her contemporary Ohio regional writers, like Mary Hartwell Catherwood and Constance Fenimore Woolson, women's isolation and limitations are defining elements of human experience, but though Pounds writes about such topics as loneliness and bad parenting, her women are never totally without power. Like her predecessor Harriet Beecher Stowe, who immortalized Little Eva in *Uncle Tom's Cabin* (1852), Pounds also demonstrates the ethical significance of family life, emphasizing women and children. Her fiction unmasks self-centeredness and highlights virtuous children. For instance, in her 1889 story "Children's Day at Slocum's Corners," youthful Melury Haines recounts in dialect how her Grandpa learned to forgive a man who sold him a "balky" horse.

Many of Jessie Brown Pounds' female storytellers avoid dialect, which the characters use, a technique devised by Harriet Beecher Stowe in her trail-blazing regional sketches. And Pounds' narrative consciousness is similarly based within an understanding and acceptance of community mores, a bemused and affirmative tone that avoids the rigor of Stowe's portraitures or Cary's emphasis upon female thralldom. Thus, Pounds' stories locate midwestern regional consciousness within realistic dialect which is local, plain, egalitarian, informal and exhibits how humans' interior reality is a product of environment and group interaction. Readers may see this consciousness, for example, in a series of patriarchs—Bijah Morrison yearns for land and earns an impecunious grave; Colonel Bristow charms and avoids ministers; and the exuberant Deacon Briarly intemperately proposes temperance. What is unique is Jessie Brown Pounds' use of wit and wisdom. For instance, Deacon Briarly uses "extravagant expression" to oppose the opening of a local whiskey shop. He pontificates about the "ungodly scamps acrost the road" from the church who take "some o' the fire from t' other world down yender bottled up." Briarly demonstrates the evil of whiskey:

take all the snakes and the lizards an' the creepin' things of the airth; all. . . . the hyenys and the wild beasts of Ashey an' Atriky, an' bile 'em down, and et the strongest concentrated meanness that could be made out on the hull on 'em, ye wouldn't hev anything one hundred billionth part ez mean ez the man thet brings the trail of this whisky sarpent's foot into the blessed Eden of home. . . .

Stories like "Dean Briarly's Repentance" which use irony and a comic mode to present Western Reserve life demonstrate what George Stewart in "The Regional Approach to Literature" means by saying that regionalism cultivates "an intelligent provincialism" (47). Jessie Brown Pounds dedicated her life to promoting this theme in dozens of regional stories that illustrate her fascination with this subject matter—growing from the pithy wisdom of "The Ten Acre Lot," "The Little School—Mis," and "Children's Day at Slocum's Corners" in 1889, to "Ingleside Missionary Collection" and "Deacon Briarly's Repentance" in 1891, to her superb and unique village sketches in "Hillsbury Folks." Her regional skill is also evident in her novels; the most interesting today is *Rachael Sylvestre,* which descriptively chronicles such Western Reserve events as a camp meeting, a barn dance, and a debate, all celebrating her father Holland Brown's ante-bellum era half a century earlier.

Like most nineteenth-century American women writers, Jessie Brown Pounds did little theorizing about her writing. She was personally reticent, on the one hand a women's literary convention, as was her shyness about saving correspondence and manuscripts. On the other, it is in the essays she wrote at the end of her career for the *Christian Century* that Pounds finally outlined her views. Like her mentor, Charles Dickens, she believed fiction ought to provide "amusement" by tickling the "fancy." Her imagined reader is described as the "child within" to whom authors ought to sing, not preach. "Rubbing in the Moral," as she called it, could only alienate readers. Her domestic realism is designed to move readers toward the beautiful and heroic, as well as to repudiate the comic reprobate, because "Falstaff sits in front of the corner grocery," she said. Thus, Pounds' late work includes thoughtful essays that celebrate the "romance of isolated Americanism," one that valued the world before the homogenizing influences of the centralized school, railroad, rural mail delivery, telephone, and flivver. She supports human contact and cooperation, an unself-conscious "provincialism" Jessie Brown Pounds calls "small-town stuff." But her regional stories reveal affection for village life that is based on recognition of the dangers inherent in provinciality. She does not naively idealize the Western Reserve but adapts its subject matter as a way to purge "bigotry and self-complacency' ("The Passing of Provincialism"). Pounds similarly rejects much twentieth-century fiction for being decadent or sordid and traditionally argues for heroes and heroines who conquer "environment through sheer goodness and courage" and the "romance of isolated Americanism" ("Books of Yesteryear").

Following in the steps of such distinguished Ohio foremothers as Alice Cary and Harriet Beecher Stowe and combining purpose and theme with contemporaries like Mary Hartwell Catherwood and Constance Fenimore Woolson, Jessie Brown Pounds deserves to be acknowledged as a significant regional author. She shares their commitment to a special style that exhibits local types, witnesses regional events, and exposes universals within the local. Such regional stories do not idealize; they are startlingly realistic and evocative by revealing the continuity of human nature and the precarious values of provincial life that may nourish or chill the human spirit. Jessie Brown Pounds wanted writers to insist upon the significance of little people because, in her words, "the cure for littleness is to see big things."

Bibliography

Bailey, Fred. A. "Disciples Images of Victorian Womanhood." *Discipliana* 40.1 (Spring 1980): 7-12.

Bernikow, Louise. *The World Split Open.* New York: Vintage, 1974.

Dumont, Julia. "The Picture: A Western Sketch." *Western Literary Journal and Monthly Review* 1.5 (1836): 3, 290-309.

Erdrich, Louise. "Where I Ought to Be: A Writer's Sense of Place." *New York Times Book Review* 28 July 1985: 22-24.

Fetterly, Judith, and Marjorie Pryse, eds. *American Women Regionalists, 1850-1910.* New York: Norton, 1992.

Fuller, Margaret. *Papers on Literature and Art.* New York: Wiley, 1846.

Gallagher, William D. "A Periodical Literature for the West." *Western Literary Journal and Monthly Review* 1.1 (Nov 1844): 1-9.

Garland, Hamlin. "Local Color as the Vital Element of American Fiction." *Proceedings of the American Academy of Arts and Letters and the National Institute of Arts and Letters.* New York: American Academy of Arts and Letters, 1951-1976. 41-45.

Hale, Sara Josepha. "The Frontier House." *The Legendary* 1. Ed. E.N.P. Willis. Boston: Goodrich, 1828. 269-89.

Harrell, David Edwin, Jr. "Restorationism and the Stone-Campbell Tradition." *Encyclopedia of American Religious Experience* II. Ed. Charles H. Lippy and Peter W. Williams. New York: Scribners, 1988. 845-58.

Kingsley, Ruth Reynard. "A Great Little Lady." *Western Reserve Magazine* 10.2 (Jan.-Feb.1983): 7-8.

Martineau, Harriet. *Society in America.* Garden City: Anchor, 1962.

Morrison, Charles Clayton. "Jessie Brown Pounds, An Appreciation." *Jessie Brown Pounds: Memorial Selections.* Ed. John E. Pounds. Chicago: Disciples Publication Society, 1921. 5-11.

Parker, Sandra. *Home Material: Ohio's Nineteenth Century Regional Women's Fiction.* Bowling Green, OH: Bowling Green State University Popular Press, 1998.

——. "A Yankee with Crust: Ohio Writer Jessie Brown Pounds." *Ohioana Quarterly* 33.1 (Spring 1990): 2-7.

Pounds, Jessie Brown. "Children's Day at Slocum's Corners." *Christian Standard* 1 June 1889: 354.

——. "Concerning Hymns." *Memorial Selections.* Ed. Samuel Clayton Morrison. Chicago: Disciples Publication Society, 1921. 84-90.

——. Deacon Briarly's Repentence." *Christian Standard* 6 June 1891: 476.

——. "The Doctor." *Christian Evangelist* 28 July 1911: 958-59.

——. "The Drunkard." *Christian Evangelist* 27 July 1911: 1066-67.

——. "Ingleside Missionary Collection. *Christian Standard* 1 Mar. 1890: 136.

——. "The Little School—Mis." *Christian Standard* 30 Apr. 1889: 230.

——. "The Parsons." *Christian Evangelist* 19 Oct. 1911: 1456-57.

——. "The Passing of Provincialism." *Christian Century* 27 Jan. 1921: 7-8.

——. "Rubbing in the Moral." *Christian Century* 5 Aug. 1920: 6. Rpt. in *Memorial Selections.* 139-41.

——. "The Scalawag." *Christian Evangelist* 7 Sept. 1911: 251-56. Rpt. in *Memorial Selections*: 251-56.

——. "The School Ma'ams." *Christian Evangelist* 14 June 1911: 837-39.

——. "The Ten Acre Lot." *Christian Standard* 2 Feb. 1889: 70.

Spiller, Robert E. *Literary History of the United States.* New York: Macmillan, 1948.

Stewart, George. "The Regional Approach to Literature." *Western Writing.* Ed. Gerald Haslam. Albuquerque: U of New Mexico P, 1948. 40-48.

Wilcox, Alanson. *History of the Disciples of Christ in Ohio.* Cincinnati, OH: Standard, 1918.

THE TEN ACRE LOT

"I orto hev it," said Bijah Morrison emphatically. "Thet ten acres o' pastur notches right out o' my farm, an' it'll jest squar my line with Jonas Riggs, when I git it. Jonas, he's hed his eye out, but he won't git it—not while my name is Bijah Morrison."

Bijah looked across at his wife, sure that she would approve his words. He was a great, powerful man, who had never known a day's illness, and she was a little, nervous woman who was subject to "poor spells"; but on the subject which was known between them as that of "'gittin'" they were a unit.

"You boys must stir yourselves lively, if I lay out to buy thet lot," said Bijah, turning to his two sons, who sat on a wooden bench behind the stove. "No more foolin', an' huntin' an' fishin', till it's paid for. They's as much pleasure in gittin' an' savin' as they is in spendin', if you only think so. An' remember, it's all yours when I'm done with it."

A glitter, like that in the eyes of a cat which has spied a bird, showed itself in the greenish-gray eyes of Matt Morrison, Bijah's eldest-born; but Sammy, the handsome, fun-loving younger son, looked impatient.

"Botheration, father! he said. "What do you want more land for? I think it would be a great deal better to paint the house and barn, and buy mother a sewing machine."

"See here, young man, you're gittin' a great deal too smart. I don't want to hear any more o' that," and Bijah glowered fiercely upon his son.

Sammy was not in the least disconcerted by his father's glance, but shuffled his feet about restlessly, and softly whistled "Dan Tucker."

It was not an attractive place—this farmhouse kitchen in which the mistress of the house toiled all day, and in which her husband and sons were expected to spend their evenings. To be sure, it was clean enough for comfort, for though Mrs. Morrison was "saving" in every other respect, she was prodigal in the expenditure of her own strength, and delighted in scrubbing and scouring. But even the cleanliness of her kitchen had something dismal and unwholesome about it. The floor had been mopped, the last thing before supper, and was still wet in the corners farthest from the fire. Half a dozen wooden chairs had been recently washed and turned down to dry. A tin boiler stood upside down, upon the

17

cracked old cookstove. A line filled with stockings and aprons—the last end of today's washing was stretched across the room. One sickly looking tallow candle stood, in an iron candlestick, on the bare kitchen table. Sammy looked upon the familiar surroundings, and turned up his shapely nose.

"I'm going over to see Si Riggs," he said, catching up his cap.

"No, you ain't!" asserted his father, sternly. "You git off to bed, both on ye. We've got thet plowin' on hand tomorrow, and we've got to be stirrin' arly."

Sammy sprung to his feet with surprising alacrity, and led the way up the dark staircase to the unplastered chamber under the eaves, which the two boys occupied together. Then he sat down upon an inverted nailkeg which stood in a corner of the room, and waited.

"Why don't you crawl in?" demanded Matt, presently, from under the bedclothes.

"Cause I've got other intentions," was the nonchalant reply.

Sammy listened to the tramp of heavy boots in the room below, as his father locked the door and wound the clock. At length, all was still.

Matt's first snores were interrupted by a sound at the window.

"Hi! what's that?" he demanded.

"Hist!' whispered Sammy, as he swung himself out of the window, to the roof of the woodhouse, "I'm going to Si's. Don't you dare squeal!"

"I'll tell father, in the morning," threatened Matt, sleepily.

"Tell him, then, if you want to" was the reckless response, as Sammy disappeared.

A fire was burning in the "best room" of the Riggs farmhouse, dispelling the chill and damp of the April night. A company of rough, jolly boys was gathered about the table, in the midst of a merry game of cards. Sammy, who was a favorite among them, was warmly welcomed, and it was past midnight when he made his way back to the little chamber under the eaves.

The days went by, rapidly lengthening into years, and transforming Matt and Sammy into young men. The result deemed so desirable by Bijah Morrison—the purchase of the ten acre lot had not yet been attained; but some other results, not generally deemed so desirable, had been reached. Matt Morrison was a twenty-two-year-old miser. Sammy Morrison was a twenty-year-old drunkard. Mrs. Morrison was a sickly, hysterical woman, old before her time. Sammy had been her darling; and though her motherlove had not conquered her love of gain, now that he was hopelessly lost she was filled with remorse at the thought that she had not tried to save him.

At length, Sammy was stricken down with what the doctor merci- fully called brain fever. It was said that, in his ravings, he constantly accused his parents of having driven him into evil ways. "If I'd had a decent home, I might have stayed in it, and let cards and whisky alone," was his oft-repeated cry.

At last the agony was over, and the body of the bright, winsome boy, who had once been loved by the whole village, was carried to a drunkard's grave.

From this time, his mother was never herself again. Her mind seemed to have been unhinged by her troubles, and though her habits of industry clung to her, she could no longer work intelligently, even in the treadmill of her familiar household duties. Two things she did over and over again—cleaning and mending. The kitchen floor was mopped a dozen times a day, and Matt's new Sunday coat was covered with patches of every shape and variety. There was something singularly pathetic in the sight of this nervous activity, in one whose mind had lost all power to direct the body. Bijah Morrison grumbled and fretted and talked about "expense."

"We can't afford to keep a girl," he told his son. "Girls is awful slack an' wasteful. Matt, you must look around for a wife."

Matt obediently looked around, and found a wife in the person of Melia Riggs—a sharp-tongued woman, several years older than himself. Her coming crushed out the little life that was left in Mrs. Morrison. On the very day of Matt's wedding, she took to her bed, and, a fortnight later, she died. The last of the money which had been hoarded for the purchase of the ten acre lot, went to pay the expense of her funeral.

"Ef you want Melia 'n' me to stay here an' take care o' you," Matt said to his father, "you must deed me the farm. Ef you won't do thet, we'll go some 'ere's else."

"It'll all be yours when I'm done with it," said the old man feebly. "Pity ef I can't hold on to it while I live, after workin' the best part o' my days to get it."

But Matt again raised the threat that, if the farm were not deeded to him, he and Melia would go elsewhere; and, in the father's utter help- lessness, the son carried the day. Then began a veritable reign of terror. "Bejah Morrison is gittin' his pay in this life, for the way he's brought up his children," said the village gossips, when they heard how the old man was driven to smoke his pipe on the back porch, on chilly nights, and sent to sleep in the same little unplastered chamber under the eaves which his sons had once occupied.

"I'll git that ten acre lot, yit," said Matt Morrison to himself, the glitter of covetousness shining in his green-gray eyes. "An' then, when old man Riggs dies, Melia'll git the even half o' his farm, an' my land'll run clear through to the creek—pretty nigh a clean two hundred acres!" And Matt smacked his lips in greedy anticipation.

But he did not get the ten acre lot. Complaint was made that the village burial ground was becoming crowded, and the trustees decided to purchase land for another, a little way out of town. So, much to the chagrin of the Morrisons and Riggses, the ten acre lot was bought for this purpose.

One dreary November day, when the sky was covered with lead-colored clouds, and the wind dismally rattled the few dead leaves which still clung to the branches, the new burial ground received its first occupant. With a few witnesses, and with scanty ceremony, the body of Bijah Morrison was laid to rest in the ten acre lot.

THE LITTLE SCHOOL MIS'

One cheerless November day, five and fifty years ago, Abbie Ellsworth sat before a blazing logfire, in the living room of her new Ohio home, putting marvelously small stitches into the shirt she was making for her father.

A very demure-looking little maiden was this thirteen-year-old Abbie, in her neat blue calico gown, and her glossy dark hair parted in an unwavering line and combed smoothly back behind her small, shell-like ears. A very pretty maiden, she had been pronounced once by an indiscreet visitor, who noted how the color deepened and paled in her softly rounded cheeks, and how mirth and tenderness contended for possession of her great brown eyes. Abbie had overheard this incautious remark, but like the good child that she was, she had striven to forget it, and to reflect more than ever on the homely aphorisms which judicious parents had early instilled into her mindsuch as "Pretty is that pretty does," and "Beauty is only skin deep."

A low moan from one of the recesses adjoining the living room brought the little seamstress to her feet, and she hastened to the bed where a fair, delicately formed girl of seventeen lay, with the flush of fever on her wasted cheeks.

"Did you have a good sleep, Cynthia? Is there anything I can do for you?"

"No, thank you, Abbie. Hasn't mother come home yet?" questioned the sick girl, in a thin, sweet voice. "Sit down here by me. I want to talk to you."

Abbie obeyed, covering one of her sister's thin hands with both of her own firm, plump ones.

"Abbie, do father and mother ever talk as if my sickness was a great burden and expense to them?"

"No, no, indeed they do not! They only wish you could have more comforts and better care."

Cynthia sighed. "But I am a burden," she said. "And I meant to be a help. When we were in the old home in 'York State, and father began to talk about coming out here to the Western Reserve, I said to myself, 'In a new country I can teach school, and so help father and mother.' And now, when we have been here only three months, I am helpless." And the poor girl sighed again.

"But you may be better soon. Mother says the long ride across the country was too much for you. I liked it," added Abbie, remembering with a thrill of delight the happy days she had spent in the covered wagon, looking out on the changing sky and the long stretches of forest.

"I am glad you are stronger than I, little Abbie. You must do your best to help father and mother. You will, won't you?"

Abbie hastily promised, as the door opened and Mr. and Mrs. Ellsworth entered. The mother busied herself about her household tasks, the father unfolded an ancient newspaper which he had borrowed at the post office and began to read. Abbie again sat down before the fire, and took up her work, but her thoughts were no longer fixed upon her even rows of stitching. If she might do something very brave and helpful! If she might make her parents feel that, even though poor Cynthia lay ill and helpless, they still had a daughter upon whom they could depend!

There was a clatter of horse's hoofs on the frozen ground, a rustling of dead leaves as the rider dismounted, then a rap at the door. In response to Mr. Ellsworth's "Come in!" a short, stubby man entered, with a whip in his hand and a fur cap on his head. He was recognized and introduced by Mr. Ellsworth as Mr. Peter Hartmann. Abbie remembered to have heard that he was the thriftiest member of a colony of thrifty Germans who had settled in the south part of the township some years before.

Evidently Mr. Hartmann had an errand. After greetings had been exchanged, he looked into the fire for some time, as if searching for words in which to proclaim his mission. Then he suddenly turned and said to Mr. Ellsworth:

"You got gal dot can deach goot school?"

Mr. Ellsworth's face clouded. "Yes," he said, "I think my daughter Cynthia is well qualified to teach. But she is now sick, and she may not be able to do anything for a long time."

"So!" Surprise, sympathy and an appreciation of the circumstances of the case, all seemed to be expressed in this monosyllable. "You got no more gals?"

"Only this little one." And Mr. Ellsworth nodded toward Abbie.

"O father!" cried Abbie, breathlessly. "why couldn't I teach?"

And then, amazed at her own boldness, the little maiden rose, and stood at her father's knee waiting for her answer. Mr. Peter Hartmann regarded her curiously. "Haf she got goot larnin'?" he asked.

"Yes," answered Mr. Ellsworth, "Abbie is almost as far advanced as her sister. I think she could teach very well if she should undertake it. How large is the school in your district, Mr. Hartmann?"

"Dere vas tirty last summer, but dis winter I dinks dere vill pe more. Der pig poys always come in de winter. Ve haf shust puilt a new school-house, and ve bays goot vages—oten shilling a week."

"A dollar and a quarter a week!" exclaimed Abbie, to whom this sum seemed like vast wealth. "O, father, please let me go!"

"Do you think she would do?" her father asked of Mr. Hartmann.

The visitor measured Abbie with his small, keen eyes, and, for the first time, his gravity relaxed. "I dink," he said, smiling broadly, "dot she would make a pooty goot little schoolmis!"

"Then," said Mr. Ellsworth, "it shall be as her mother says." Abbie went over and stood beside her mother. "I can earn the money to buy medicine for Cynthia," she said. And she could not have chosen a more effective argument. In the mother heart, anxiety for the child who was sick conquered anxiety for the child who was well, and Mrs. Ellsworth consented to let Abbie take the winter school in the Hartmann district.

It was, of course, necessary that Abbie should obtain a certificate from the school examiners; but these gentlemen, hearing she intended to teach, saved her much inconvenience by calling at her home in a body, a few days later, and volunteering to conduct the examination then and there.

There were three of the examiners—old Dr. Moseby, the Rev. Mr. Edson, and Mr. Perkins, who had himself been a teacher in his younger days. Abbie was much awed by the presence of these dignitaries, and felt her heart beat fast and hard as Dr. Moseby said, in his majestic way.

"Shall we proceed to question the young lady?"

"I think we may as well," answered the Rev. Mr. Edson. "Will you, Doctor, propound a few questions in arithmetic."

Whereupon Dr. Moseby drew himself up, adjusted his spectacles, and looked severely at Abbie as he solemnly said:

"What is arithmetic?"

"The science of numbers," answered Abbie, beginning to breathe more freely.

"What are the ground rules of arithmetic?" demanded the Doctor, still more solemnly.

"Numeration, addition, subtraction, multiplication and division." was the prompt reply.

Thus the examination went on. When it was completed the examiners retired to a corner, consulted gravely, and announced that the applicant had demonstrated her right to a certificate for one year. And Dr. Moseby added, as he bowed himself out of the room, "You have acquitted yourself with credit, Miss Ellsworth, and we wish you success."

Miss Ellsworth! Had she come to be that? Abbie glanced down at her blue calico gown, from which she had that morning taken the tucks. Actually, it reached almost to her ankles! She was not such a child, after all.

But when the time came to say goodby to her parents and Cynthia, Abbie found it very hard to be "grown up," and to keep back the tears that were trying to find their way to her brown eyes. Cynthia kissed her, and said, "Brave little Abbie! you are doing your best to help." And Mrs. Ellsworth smoothed the dark hair of her youngest born, as she whispered, "Dear child! it seems hard that these young shoulders must bear so much."

Abbie choked down the lump that had been in her throat, and went to the door, where Mr. Peter Hartmann was waiting for her. He was mounted on a mild-looking sorrel horse, and he indicated to Abbie that he expected her to occupy a seat behind him. She had never ridden on horseback, and she made several ineffectual springs before she succeeded in gaining a seat. At last, however, she found herself perched behind Mr. Hartmann, with one hand grasping his coat and the other clinging to the saddle. She turned to say a last goodby to her mother, but at this moment the sorrel started off at a brisk gait, and Abbie found she must give her undivided energies to the task of retaining her position.

The new schoolhouse proved to be a log structure of the most primitive kind, set in the very heart of the forest. On its slab benches sat the scholars—thirty-seven of them. They ranged in age from five to twenty-three, and Abbie trembled as she thought of ministering to the needs of such a variety of minds.

But, after all, their demands were not exacting. Abbie was relieved from the necessity of teaching geography and English grammar, by the fact that there was not, in the entire district, a textbook treating upon either of these branches; and as the highest class in arithmetic had but just begun to wrestle with compound numbers, her knowledge of this science was found to be more than sufficient.

Sometimes she wearied of making quill pens, and of setting copies for the more ambitious of the young scribes, who importuned her to "cut them some capitals." Sometimes she wearied of hearing little Jake Lowhiser stumble over long words in the dogeared "American Preceptor," which was handed to him every day, after his three older brothers were through with it. But, on the whole, Abbie liked her new work.

"The little school mis'" was regarded, by most of her scholars, with unmixed reverence. These American-born children of German parents were singularly simple hearted and sincere. They were full of superstition, and delighted in narrating long accounts of "spooks," and other supernatural appearances. Partly, perhaps, because of their delight in whatever was marvelous and unusual, they loved and yet stood in awe of the little maiden who ruled them so gently and yet so firmly that her power seemed to them something more than human.

But there was one boy who did not fall in with the general admiration of the new teacher. August Baughman was by no means the oldest scholar in school, but he was much the tallest, and he decided that he was much too tall to submit to the authority of a damsel who measured four-feet-ten. And one day, at the morning recess, August disappeared. "He said he was goin' off where the schoolmis' wouldn't get aholt of him again," piped little Jake Lowhiser. "Said he was too big to be comin' to school to a gal."

Abbie's heart grew heavy. The Baughmans were people of much influence, and this influence would, she feared, be turned against her. How could she hope to convince the directors that August was a dull, ignorant boy, who had not yet "cyphered through" long division? Doubtless they would be led to believe her incapable of either instructing or governing her scholars, and perhaps they would send her home to her parents in disgrace.

But a sudden emergency diverted her mind from this anxiety. Just after the school had "taken up" for the afternoon, a black cloud settled over the sky and a fierce wind came up. It swept over the forest with appalling power, and great trees were uprooted and fell crashing upon the dead leaves. Abbie did her best to avert panic in the schoolroom, but the teeth of the younger children chattered with fear, as they tried, by the failing light to spell out the words in the fineprint copies of the New Testament which served many of them as textbooks. "Schoolmis'," whimpered Jake Lowhiser, "do you think it's the day o'judgment?"

"No," said Abbie, with decision, "I don't think it is. And if it were, we should want to have good lessons, just the same. It is too dark to read, but we can spell down. Tilla Hartmann and Mose Swartz, you may choose sides."

A spelling match was a panacea for all ills. In the excitement of a close contest, the scholars failed to notice that the wind had abated its fury, and that the snow was falling, silently and steadily. The interest in the match was at its height, when three loud raps were heard.

"Open the door, Jake, please," said Abbie.

Jake hesitated. "I'm afeart it's a spook," he said, tremulously.

Jake started to obey, but at this moment the door was thrown open with a resounding whang, and two tall snow-covered figures strode into the room. Little Jake screamed with terror. To his excited fancy, it seemed that these were "spooks," and no mistake.

Abbie was scarcely less frightened. She had recognized the new comers as August Baughman and his father, and she feared they had come to upbraid her for being so small and young.

But she was reassured when she saw that Mr. Baughman, Sr., held his son's arm in a vise-like grip, for she augured from this fact that possibly parental authority had arrayed itself on her side. "Go to your seat," commanded the elder Baughman of the younger, as he released him. Then the irate father turned to Abbie. "You make dot poy stay by dis school an' stoody his pook. An' if he no want to stoody, shust you lick him to it!"

The incongruity involved in the suggestion that this young giant should be "licked" to his duty by a mere child, was evidently not noticed by the scholars; but Abbie was obliged to suppress a smile, as she bade her visitor a respectful adieu.

"You may remain in during recess," said Abbie to August, when order had been restored and the spelling match concluded, "I want to have a little talk with you."

"Schoolmis' is goin' to lick August!" shouted little Jake Lowhiser, gleefully, as the scholars bounded out into the snow. "She ain' afeart of him—she ain't."

Nothing less tempting than the first snowstorm of the season would have kept these curious boys and girls away from the windows of the schoolroom, during the fifteen minutes that followed. If their love of sport had not conquered their curiosity they would have been eyewitnesses to the fact that the birch rod which hung above the fireplace was not taken down. But, as their eyes were elsewhere at the time, they continued for some weeks to believe that Abbie had, on this occasion, administered to the culprit a thorough and well-deserved "licking." What really transpired was this:

Abbie crossed the schoolroom and sat down beside August, whose gaze was fixed on the puncheon floor.

"August," she said, "I want to tell you why I came here to teach."

She told, in her simple, childish fashion, of her parents' poverty, of her sister's sickness, and of her own desire to provide for herself and to help those at home.

"Cynthia may die for want of medicine, if I can not earn the money to buy it for her. And it all depends on you. I am only a little girl, and you are large and strong. Which will you do—make trouble for me, or help me to save my sister's life."

August hitched about uneasily, and crossed one foot over the other. "I ain't got nothin' much against ye," he said, sheepishly, at last.

*   *   *

Twenty-five years had passed. On the porch in front of the village parsonage, in a little town a dozen miles from the Hartmann district, sat a pretty woman of eight and thirty, her dark eyes bent upon the muslin ruffling she was hemming with dainty care. A stubby, gray-haired man rode up to the gate, dismounted, and came up the path. The lady rose, a puzzled look showing itself on her face.

"Yes, sir, I am Mrs. Lyons." And she courteously offered her visitor a chair.

He sat down, and began to study her face with embarrassing closeness. "You Mr. Ellsworth's gal?"

"Yes, I was Mr. Ellsworth's second daughter. My sister, Cynthia, married Judge Foster. Your face is familiar, yet I can't remember where I have known you."

"Hartmann, my name vas—Peter Hartmann.

"Why, surely!" And Mrs. Lyons held out her hand in unfeigned pleasure at the sight of her old friend.

But Mr. Hartmann's visit was not made for pleasure merely. He listened gravely, as Mrs. Lyons told how often she thought of him and his neighbors; then he said, "You got some gals?"

"Yes, indeed! I have three good girls. Edith!"

In response to this call, a slender, handsome girl of sixteen came through the open door, and was introduced to "mamma's old friend." Mr. Hartmann regarded Edith critically for a moment, then turned back to her mother. "Haf you got a gal dot can deach a goot school?"

Mrs. Lyons smiled. "I'm afraid not," she said. "Edith is the oldest, and she will not be through school for two years."

"So!" This time, the monosyllable expressed disappointment and acquiescence. Mr. Hartmann meditated for a moment, then he said: "I dink maype you might haf a gal like you. Our last deacher vas a man, an' der poys locked him up in der woodgloset. August Baughman's poy vas der vers the was crate for kricks. Put his dad says to him, 'If you haf der leedle schoolmis' I haf once, you nefer vant to lock her in der voodgloset.' Dot vas you." And Mr. Hartmann chuckled merrily.

"I am very glad he remembers me so kindly," said Mrs. Abbie, a mist gathering in her eyes. "And when my Edith is ready to teach, I hope she can begin her work where I began mine—in the Hartmann district."

Then Peter Hartmann mounted his horse and jogged away, muttering to himself, "Dot gal looks pooty goot, put she ton't coom up to her mutter. I dink it vas hart to peat der leele schoolmis'!"

CHILDREN'S DAY AT SLOCUM'S CORNERS

"Goin' to keep Children's Day at Slocum's Corner?" repeats Miss Melury Haines, with a ring of pride in her cheery old voice, as she sews the lace on a white wrapper for Mrs. Barr's city boarder. "Yes we be. An' you won't wonder at it, when I tell you what happened here on last Children's Day.

"It was all Libbie Barnum's notion, our havin' Children's Day. Libbie is a great girl for notions. She's the best little creature that ever lived. Seems as if she must have been born with a natural hankerin' atter Sunday-school, an' prayer-meetin's, an' the like. 'They keep Children's Day in other places,' says Libbie, 'an' why can't we keep it here. The children orto be taught to give their pennies to the poor heathin,' says she, 'instead of spendin' 'em all for chewin' gum. They orto be taught how ignorant an' needy the poor heathin be. Why, Miss Haines,' says Libbie, her big black eyes gettin' bigger an' blacker. 'over in Chiny the children are taught to worship their pay-rents an' grandpay-rents! Think o' that, says she.'

"'Land!' says I—I like to poke fun at Libbie, once in a while, jest to see the color flash out on her cheeks—'I don't see but what Chiny's a step ahead of Ameriky, then, for here all the pay-rents an' grand-pay-rents worship the children!'

"Well, Libbie went around to all the elders to see if we couldn't keep Children's Day. Old Father Lukens said he wasn't in favor of givin' up Sunday morning to the children. 'The Scripter tells us not to forsake the assemblin' of ourselves together,' said he, a-lookin' solemn. 'But it don't say anything aginst your bringin' your children along with you, does it?' says Libbie, not a bit scared out by his way. With that he looked solemner than ever, an' said he thought we orto come together for mutual edification; but at last he give in.

"Now," says Libbie, "As long as his name stands among the elders of this church, he orto be consulted." An' off she went.

"We all felt bad about Uncle Sile. He'd been an elder in the church for nigh twenty years, an' we loved him 'most as if he was a father to us. I remember the day I joined the church—eighteen years ago last February—an' the brethren and sisters all marched around, a'givin' me the right hand of fellowship, an' when it come Uncle Sile's turn, there was tears in his eyes, an' 'God Bless you, Melury,' says he—'God bless you, lass.' Dretful tender-hearted man in such things, Uncle Sile always was.

"If only he could have been jest a morsel tenderer-hearted to Zack Minor. Not that I apologized for Zack—not one bit. No, he done wrong, an' everybody in the church knew he done wrong. But nobody expected much of Zack Minor, an' we all expected a great deal of Uncle Sile.

"You never heard anything about the trouble between the two? No? Well, you would have heerd a great deal, if you'd been visitin' at Slocum's Corners a year ago.

"You see, Zack had always been a rough fellow, not over honest, gettin' his livin' by tradin' and jockeyin', an' not much thought of, nohow. But a year ago last winter, when the Blue Fork preacher was here holdin' a protracted meetin' for us, Zack up and joined the church. We was all tickled to death, Uncle Sile most of all. 'We're havin' showers of blessin',' says he, an' he went around singin'

"Amazin' grace, how sweet the sound."

When it came towards spring, Uncle Sile wanted to buy a horse; an' what did he do but go right straight off an' get a balky old animal of Zack Minor's! Of course, Uncle Sile didn't know the horse was balky, an' Zack didn't tell him. When Uncle Sile found out, he was awful upset, an' said a feller that dishonest enough for such a trick ought to be put right out of the church. Zack said he hadn't lied about the horse—that Uncle Sile hadn't asked whether he was balky, an' he wasn't bound to tell all he knew, without bein' asked. Of course it was just as good as lyin', an' we all knew it, but the other elders was for takin' time, an' considerin', before puttin' Zack out of the church. With that, Uncle Sile got up, his lips as white as tombstones, an' marched out of the meetin'; an' he hadn't been into the meetin'-house since.

"As I was sayin', everybody felt bad about it. Nobody could bear to think that his name was left standin' among the elders, an' no one ever tetched to sat in the chair he had set in so long.

"He didn't seem to want anything to say about the business. The other elders went an' tried to labor with him, but he wouldn't be labored with. Libbie Barnum—she was his sister's child, and his niece in the flesh as we all was in feelin'—tried to tell him how we missed him, but he only said, 'There, child, we won't say anything about that.' So I wondered how she dared to go to him about Children's Day.

"She said afterward that he only looked at her for a minute, in a curious kind of way, an' then said, 'Do what you please, child. I've got nothin' to say about it!'

"The week before Children's Day, I was to Uncle Sile's, sewin' for Elviry—that's his married daughter. She's kep' house for him ever sense his wife died, an' he sets everything by her, an' her two children, Bess an' Carl. They are mighty knowin' children, an' it's no wonder Uncle Sile is proud of 'em.

"All that week, them two children was talkin' about Children's Day an' practicin' their songs over an' tellin' about the pieces they was goin' to speak.

"'Me an' another feller's goin' to have a di'logue,' says little Carl, 'me an'

"His ma looked at him kind of sharp, an' he stopped, but pretty quick he begun again.

"'Grandpa, you'll go to Children's Day, won't you? say, won't you, grandpa?'

"His ma an' I looked at each other kind of anxious but Uncle Sile didn't say ay, yes, or no. He jest went on eatin' his strawberry short cake, as if he'd rather tend to that than to Children's Day.

"Sunday mornin' came. I had stayed to Uncle Sile's overnight, so's to be handy to church for I knew ther'd be an uncommon crowd. Elviry an' I was hurryin' around to get the children ready, when Carl bethought him to ask his grandpa again if he was goin' to Children's Day.

"'No,' says Uncle Sile, kind of gruff an' short, 'I ain't a goin'.'"

"With that Carl set up a howl. 'I can't go without grandpa,' says he, 'I can't say my piece, not unless he goes.'

"Well, he cried an' cried. I would have give him a good switchin', and I told Elviry so, but she said he wasn't stubborn, only grieved. An', while we was wonderin' what to do, Uncle Sile come out, with his best broadcloth clothes on. 'Well, Carl, I s'pose grandpa has got to mind you, as usual,' says he, an' the two trudged on ahead together.

"Well, all together, Slocum's Corners has never seen such another time as that Children's Day. The walls of the meetin'-house was covered with flowers an' evergreens an' birdcages; an' the people there was there!— it was jest a mortal, livin', breathin' wonder where they all come from.

"It was jest amazin' to see them little midgets speak off their pieces —jest as serious and important as grown up-folks. I never see the beat of it. An' when Carl and Zack Minor's little Johnny walked out on the plat- form hand in hand, an' spoke their di'logue about 'Two Little Workers for Jesus,' there wasn't a woman in the crowd but wanted to grab the little chaps right up in her arms, an' hug 'em tight.

"I was settin' right where I could watch Uncle Sile. At first he looked awful put out, seein' Carl with Zack Minor's boy. But when the two little fellers spoke up, so cute an' pretty, it was more than the old man could stand, an' the tears begun to creep out of his eyes. I knew then that he was glad he come.

"After the children was through speaking, Libbie got up an' told how the little folks had been savin' up their pennies for ever so long, so's they might have a part in the good work of sendin' the gospel to the heathin. An' she asked the grown folks if they didn't want to help the children, and get a share of the blessin'.

"Carl an' Johnny went around with the basket; an' the way the nickels, and dimes an' quarters, was rained in was sonethin' astonishin'. But when little Johnny came around to Uncle Sile, the old man didn't stop to feel among his loose change, but just drew out his long wallet, and threw a five dollar bill into the basket.

"After the Children's Day meetin' was dismissed, everybody looked to Uncle Sile, to see whether he would go out while the Lord's table was bein' spread. But he didn't stir from the place where he'd been settin'— in the little, low seat by the door.

"Libbie went back an' set by him, slippin' her hand into his.

"'Child,' says he, 'I've been a fool, an' worse than a fool. Promise me that you'll pray for your Uncle Sile.'

"An' of course, Libbie promised. Jest then, Father Lukens come up. 'Brother Nesmyth,' says he, 'will you take a seat at the communion table?'

"Uncle Sile shook his head. 'No, no,' says he, 'not there! But I've got a word to say, if the brethren'll hear me.'

"Father Lukens nodded, an' Uncle Sile got up. 'Brethren,' says he, in a trembly voice, 'I have done wrong. I ask my Father in heaven to forgive me. I ask you to forgive me—even as God, for Christ's sake, hath forgiven you.'

"Zack Minor dropped his head. I believe, upon my word, he'd never been really ashamed of himself until that minute.

"Everything was still as the grave for a few seconds; then Father Lukens says, 'Brethren, as many of you as feel like forgivin' Brother Nesmyth, stand up.'

"We all stood up, an' then Father Lukens made a prayer—a real good, feelin' prayer, for him, he bein' generally given to mentionin' folks's failins to the Lord, pretty freely.

"An' when we sang,

'Blest be the tie that binds.'

I guess there wasn't one of us but felt that Slocum's Corners was a little nearer to heaven than it had ever been before.

"No, Zack Minor wasn't turned out of the church. He offered to take back the balky horse, an' pay back Uncle Sile's money, an' I hain't heard of his playin' a dishonest trick from that day to this.

"There goes Libbie Barnum! Look out of the front window an' you'll see her. She's goin' to the church, to hear Carl an' Johhny speak over the di'logue they're learnin' for Children's Day. 'Goin' to keep Children's Day at Slocum's Corners this year?' Of course we be!"

THE INGLESIDE MISSIONARY COLLECTION

There had never been one taken up before. That is why I have called it the Ingleside Missionary Collection. Several of the former pastors of Ingleside's only church had proposed the taking of missionary collections, but the elders had always said that there were enough people at home who needed salvation quite as much as the heathen could possibly need it. For instance, there was Colonel Bristow.

It was wonderful how all the benevolent intentions of the Ingleside Church seemed to have Colonel Bristow for their object. When an evangelist came to Ingleside to hold a meeting, he was given to understand that his labors would be considered well nigh in vain, if he should fail to "get hold of Colonel Bristow." When the meeting was over, sighs were exchanged, and the old elders observed, sadly, "Too bad!—only a few Sunday school children baptized! We must have a different kind of preaching, if we expect to move Colonel Bristow." When a new pastor took charge of the church—which was, generally, on the first Sunday in each January—he was warmly exhorted to "get on the right side of Colonel Bristow." And when December having come around, the pastor prepared to take his departure, the elders lamented the necessity which demanded a change, but said they noticed the outsiders—Colonel Bristow, for instance—no longer came to church regularly, and they felt that every church had a duty to perform, in the conversion of the world.

The present occupant of the Ingleside pulpit had been called to his position on the recommendation of a prominent evangelist, who said that Mr. Cornwall had utterly broken down in health while in charge of a large city church, and that he desired to spend a year in some such quiet village as Ingleside.

"To spend a year!" That was suggestive, to say the least. And, to show their disapproval of such suggestiveness, the elders declared they would not invite Mr. Cornwall to settle with the church, unless he would consent to an indefinite engagement.

He consented, and came. A mere shadow of a man, he looked, and the elders almost repented of having called him. But his ringing sermons dispelled their anxiety. No one, not even Colonel Bristow, could fail to be pleased with such a winsome presentation of forcible arguments.

Mr. Cornwall's family was all that a minister's family should be. His home was a model, and its doors always stood hospitably open. His daily walk and conversation were such as must bring honor, not reproach, upon the church. He had as cheery a heart as ever beat in a painracked body, and he never shrank from other peoples' burdens. In fact, he had no grievous fault, save that he did not fully realize the duty of the church to the unconverted—that is, to Colonel Bristow.

"Who is that handsome, soldierly-looking old gentleman?" he had asked, on the first Sunday after his arrival in Ingleside.

"That," said 'Squire Morrison, the senior elder, impressively, "is Colonel Bristow. Most influential man in the place, Bro. Cornwall. He is quite friendly to the church—been attending, off and on, for twenty years. His wife is a member."

"The little, tired-looking woman who was with him this morning?"

"Yes. I tell you what it is, Bro. Cornwall, we ought to bring Colonel Bristow into the church. I hope you will make it convenient to call on him soon. His influence would do wonders for us. I think the preaching we've had hasn't been of just the right kind to reach the Colonel. I really hope, Bro. Cornwall, that you can get hold of him."

Mr. Cornwall had, soon after this, called upon Colonel Bristow. Colonel Bristow had returned the call, and had invited the minister and his wife to dinner. But Mr. Cornwall had also called upon Colonel Bristow's washer-woman, and he and his wife had dined also with the family of the church janitor. So it could scarcely be said that the new pastor showed any especial interest in Ingleside's "friendly outsider."

On the first Sunday in February, Mr. Cornwall announced that, four weeks later, the March collection for Foreign Missions would be taken up.

The elders, when they had recovered from the shock of their surprise, looked at each other in dignified disapproval of the new minister's course. A most unwise proceeding this was, truly! Bro. Cornwall must be labored with, at the earliest opportunity.

But what was this, that he was saying? "I am going to make a suggestion to you, dear friends; I'm going to suggest that, between this and March 1st, each of you lay by one day's wages, or an equivalent proportion of your yearly income, for this collection. This is a small offering to make for so grand a cause, and, no doubt, some of you will feel like doing more. But I suggest this, that we may have a general preparation for and participation in this contribution, and that we may all, whether rich or poor, taste together the sweet blessedness of giving."

"One day's wages, or an equivalent proportion of your yearly income!" Sunday though it was, and in church though he was, 'Squire Morrison found himself performing several sums, by means of mental arithmetic. There was his stock in the Commercial Bank of Danbridge.

There were his government bonds. There were several notes, all well secured, and drawing eight per cent interest. There was the block, in Danbridge, which he had leased to responsible parties for a term of years. Three hundred, in four thousand five hundred, yes! The 'Squire had been trying to forget the lease on the River Farm, and the rent of five pretty cottages here in Ingleside. But these items, too, obtrusively presented themselves to his mind again and again. Of course, he did not intend that any missionary collection should be taken. There were heathen enough at home. Brother Cornwall must be labored with. But the old 'Squire had a fancy for figures, and, now that he was at it, he wanted to find out how much, in his case, that "equivalent proportion of the yearly income" would be. "Twenty-one dollars?" Impossible! His calculations must be wrong somewhere.

He went over them again, so carefully that I fear Mr. Cornwall's strong sermon on "The Sin of Covetousness," was all but lost upon him. Yet I am not sure but his calculations supplied him with a few forcible illustrations of the point which he had missed.

The elders did "labor with Brother Cornwall."

"We are not in favor of foreign missions," the 'Squire said, with a shake of his fine old head. "Where there are people right here at our doors, who are not yet converted."

"Yes," put in Dr. Mumford, the junior elder, "I see work enough to be done, right here at home. When there are men like Colonel Bristow, standing, as it were, under the droppings of the sanctuary."

"Brethren," said Mr. Cornwall, gravely, "if Christ had said, 'Go ye therefore and teach Colonel Bristow,' I would try to obey the command. But I can not, I dare not, give such a narrow interpretation to the marching orders of our King. You say that Colonel Bristow has been a more or less regular attendant upon the services of this church for twenty years. I suppose that, in the labors of pastors and evangelists, not less than two thousand sermons have been preached, each aimed, more or less directly, at Colonel Bristow. Thousands of dollars have been expended in the effort to bring him to Christ. I find no fault with this. We can scarcely overestimate the value of a soul, or labor too zealously for its redemption. I shall continue to work and pray for Colonel Bristow's salvation— though I fear that the love of money and the pride of leadership have so taken control of his heart that the love of Christ and the humility of discipleship will never get in. But what I wish you to think about especially, is this: that, while Colonel Bristow has had two thousand opportunities of accepting Christ, more than half of the human race have never had one—have never so much as heard that Christ came into the world to save sinners. This church has wealth sufficient, not only to support a pastor here at home, but also to support half a dozen missionaries in foreign lands, or in destitute parts of our own land. And I think the Master of us all would say, 'This ought ye to have done, and not to have left the other undone.'"

The elders went away stunned, but not convinced. "Half a dozen missionaries!" Brother Cornwall was wild! Perhaps his poor health had given him a fanatical turn of mind. Why, the church was always in arrears to its pastor at the end of each year! And there was a heavy coalbill still outstanding. "Half a dozen missionaries," indeed! But 'Squire Morrison's mind kept reverting, with singular persistence, to the "calculations" of the day before. Twenty-one dollars! that would be his share for the collection, and that he, 'Squire Morrison, should feel like contributing. And that was but one day's income. His yearly income was more than seven thousand dollars. He had never before realized that it was quite so much. Suppose he gave a tenth to the Lord—that would be over seven hundred dollars.

"But we are under the Christian dispensation, not under the Jewish," he told himself, nodding the fine old head in emphasis of this undeniably orthodox statement.

But the fine old head was already entertaining another puzzling question: Shall the Christian, whom God makes a steward of his bounty, render back less than that which the Israelite was required to render? Does the sacrifice of Christ make our obligation less, or greater, than his?

"I wonder how much I am giving now. H'm!" And the 'Squire began a fresh calculation. "Fifty dollars for the support of the church; h'm!—five dollars to the Temperance Society—I'm not sure I would have given that, if they hadn't elected me Chairman; h'm!—five dollars to the Relief Society—that's sixty—well, say seventy-five."

"Dr. Mumford," this time the 'Squire spoke aloud, "I think I'll just step in and settle that coal bill. It reflects on the honor of the church to neglect such matters so long."

"I've been thinking of the same thing," responded Dr. Mumford. "Twenty-six dollars, the bill is, isn't it? Just count on me for half of that."

Mr. Cornwall did not withdraw his call for the March collection. On the following Sunday his subject was, "The Gospel for All the World," and, at the close of the service, he said, "I shall be glad to have all who will contribute at least one day's income to the March collection, give me their names after service today."

And 'Squire Morrison, whom the sermon had so touched that he became, for the hour, almost forgetful of pressing needs at home, said to himself, "I'll do it—I'll give a day's income. And I believe I'll make it up to twenty-five dollars, for good measure. I've been prospered, and I'm afraid I haven't been as liberal as I should have been. Any how, I'm going to quit hiding behind Colonel Bristow's back—may be I can cheat the heathen in that way, but it's a poor way to cheat the Lord."

The March collection was taken. It was so large that every person in the church, save Mr. Cornwall, was startled. Was the aggregate daily income of the members, then, so great? If so, then Brother Cornwall was not so "wild," after all, in saying that the Ingleside Church might well support half a dozen missionaries.

Another collection for foreign missions will be taken up in the Ingleside Church this year. And Mr. Cornwall, who, though his health is quite restored, still remains in Ingleside, has asked the members to give double what they gave last year. But Colonel Bristow has not yet been brought into the church.

Perhaps he would not have been, even if the March collection had not been taken up.

DEACON BRIARLY'S REPENTANCE

For months, the righteous souls of Dexter Center church-goers had been vexed within them at the sight of a low groggery, which flaunted its sign opposite the little white "meeting-house" where the various denominations represented in the village were wont to worship in turn; and now it was rumored that another whisky-shop was to be started under the very eves of the sanctuary. This was more than these quiet-loving men and women could endure. Less in response to the formal call, than in response to a common impulse, they came together in the little church, to hold a council of war. Arthur Allan, the young minister who preached at the Center church once a month, opened the meeting, and briefly stated its object. Others followed, speaking in unstudied language, yet with that unconscious eloquence in which intense feeling often expresses itself. By and by Deacon Briarly, the village oracle, arose, and placing his hands on the back of the pew before him, began to speak, projecting the words from the mouth as if he were sending shell into the ranks of the enemy.

"Ef somebody was to come among ye tonight, dealin' out bottled-up fire to your children," he said, "I guess you wouldn't set in your seats quite so comfortable. But these ungodly scamps acrost the road hev got some o' the fire from t' other world down yender bottled up, and they're sellin' it to your boys, to burn 'em, body and soul! I tell ye what I'd tell them ef they was here—which I needn't say they ain't—that if ye was to take all the snakes and the lizards an' the creepin' things of the airth; all," he paused for breath and for a fresh comparison, found both, and went on: "All the hyenys and the wild beasts of Ashey an' Atriky, an' bile 'em down, and git the strongest concentrated meanness that could be made out on the hull on 'em, ye wouldn't hev anything one hundred billionth part ez mean ez the man thet brings the trail of this whisky sarpent's foot into the blessed Eden of home, to break the hearts of trustin' wives, to darken the lives of innercent little children, and bring the gray hairs of old fathers and mothers down in sorrer to the grave."

The Deacon sat down, overcome by his feelings. There were no more speeches that night. All felt that the climax had been reached, and after passing some spirited resolutions, the meeting adjourned. One heart was exceedingly heavy. Arthur Allan, strolling through the moonlight with pretty Eva Briarly leaning on his arm, was not so happy as young men are supposed to be under such circumstances. "Deacon Briarly is altogether too zealous," he was saying to himself. "His extravagant speeches injure the very causes he most desires to aid. I feel it to be my duty as his pastor to greatly exhort him to greater caution."

Inspired by this laudable purpose, at the breakfast table the next morning the young minister almost ignored the fairhaired Eva and her hospitable mamma, in his anxiety to pave the way for the coming exhortation.

"Did you sleep well, Deacon?" he asked, with an admirable affection of interest, when grace had been said, and the coffee poured.

"No, Elder," said the Deacon, as he heaped the minister's plate with sausage and potatoes, "I didn't shet my eyes to sleep the hull night through! The fact on it was, thet when I come home I was thet excited I couldn't go to bed, an' so I set here by the fireplace, thinkin' over the meetin'. I kep' a-sayin' over to myself what an opportunity I'd hed to say suthin' on this pesky whisky business, an' then to think thet when I got up there I couldn't say a word! I'd jet got ez eloquent a speech as ever you heerd, planned out, thet I might hev made, ef only I'd thought on it in time, when thet nasty little whiffet of Mis' Perkins' commenced to bark! I set an' bore it for two mortal hours, an' then I went out to the woodpile an' went to throwin' at the everlastin' nuisance. An' there I kep' at it, till I'd throwed more 'n thirty cord o' wood at thet dog, an' never hit him once!"

"That is a great deal of wood," said the young dominie, mildly, thinking this an opportunity for driving an entering wedge.

"I guess it is," assented Deacon Briarly cheerfully, "an' I tell ye, ye jest begin to get a realizin' sense of how much 't is when ye have to throw it out, a stick to a time, at a dratted little dog! An', by the time I got to bed, I was thet used up, I couldn't no more hev gone to sleep than I could hev flew off to the moon."

Mr. Allan felt that the present was hardly the time to administer the contemplated exhortation, yet the necessity for it was clearer to him than ever before. So intent was he on finding some "short and easy method" of carrying out his purpose, that all the morning he seemed a trifle absentminded, and Miss Eva decided that she had been mistaken in pronouncing him the most agreeable young gentleman she had ever met. But at dinnertime an idea dawned upon his mind, and he immediately became so suave and genial that the young lady returned to her first opinion of him.

"Deacon," he said, gently, "I have decided to have a Bible reading tonight, in place of the regular prayer meeting—that is, if you are willing."

"Yes, I be," said Deacon Briarly, emphatically, "I kin git more edification out of a passage of Scripter any day, than I kin from hearin' old Dan'el Mayfield tell that seventeen year ago the ninth o' last March, the Lord saved his soul. Ef I hed ez small a soul ez he's got, I wouldn't do such a powerful sight of talkin' about it."

"I have selected 'speech' as the topic for our instruction this evening," continued the minister, wisely ignoring the subject of Mr. Mayfield's soul. "I shall ask you to read the thirty-seventh verse of the fifth chapter of Matthew, and to comment on it."

"Wal, I'll read the Scripter, an' mebbe I may feel like sayin' a few words, but I seem to be losin' all my gift for public speakin'. I'll see though—I'll see."

That night, when Deacon Briarly entered the little church, his daughter and the minister having preceded him, Mr. Allan was surprised to find that the old gentleman's face, instead of the subdued expression he had expected to see there, wore a look of unwonted exhilaration. When his passage was called for, he rose, and read, in clear, emphatic tones: "'But let your communication be yea, yea; nay, nay; for whatsoever is more than these cometh of evil.' Brethren," he continued, emphasizing each word, in his sharp, crisp way, "I take it that the Master of us all meant this for a solemn rebuke to them that refuse to stand out on any question, either for or against it. I tell ye this everlastin' quibblin' an' guess-so-in' an' mebbe-so-in', can't come from nothin' but evil, an' the prince of all evil at thet! Why, when I read this passage over today, I felt mean clear way down to the soles of my boots, to think I didn't come out on this whisky question last night, in a way thet ye might all on ye understand me. Brethren"—the dear old man's voice trembled—"we're all on us selfish, an' we don't realize danger thet don't come nowheres near us, but we want to remember thet there ain't a home in Dexter Center but thet is threatened by this hydry-headed monster. You hev sons—bright lively boys, that'll be men afore long, an' ye look to 'em to be the stay o' your old age. But jest ez bright boys ez yours hev filled drunkards' graves. I hev a daughter—she's a good, dutiful girl, thank God—an' I'd gladly give the little thet's left of this worn-out life of mine to make her happy. But jest as good girls ez mine hev married drinkin' men, an' hed their young lives wrecked, an' gone down to airly graves thet mebbe they was only too glad to fill." The Deacon was in tears, and his were not the only moist eyes. "Brethren," he went on, with a sudden burst of holy wrath, "when I think on these things, I want to see these grog dealers sent down to the lowest depths of perdition, an' I want to foller 'em down"—people held their breaths, wondering what would come next—"an' cram brimstone down their throats with a redhot poker!" concluded the Deacon, as he took his seat, and mopped up his tears and perspiration with a red bandana handkerchief.

By this time, all had forgotten that they were convened for a Bible reading. One after another spoke, each pledging his time and property to the wiping out of the disgrace that had fallen on Dexter Center. Need I say that their efforts were successful—that the flame of enthusiasm, kindled by Deacon Briarly's torch, spread, until the little village became altogether too warm for the comfort of the saloon-keepers?

So far as I know, no other attempt has ever been made to "reform" the Deacon. If his pastor is sometimes tried in spirit by some unusually extravagant expression, he is careful to refrain from remark. For Mr. Arthur Allan, who has been, for many years, the good old man's son-in-law, long ago came to share in the opinion held by all of us who know him best; that if, among the crowns of heaven, there are some of transcendent glory, one of these will surely belong to Deacon Briarly.

AN ORTHODOX HERETIC

He was seventy-four years old, and looked older. He had come to Craydock's Corners when on the site of the great city forty miles away there had been only a cluster of log cabins, and he had cleared the farm on which he lived. Of those old times, and his part in their toils and victories, he talked modestly and delightfully. Altogether he was the most charming of old men, until he began to obtrude his orthodoxy. After this, one might perhaps weary in his society.

When Paul Reid came to preach at Craydock's Corners, Father Winniston was too feeble to come to church often; but he was still a ruling elder in the strictest sense of the term, and governed with a hand of iron in a glove of velvet.

It was early in the first year of Mr. Reid's pastorate that, one sunshiny Sunday, the old man ventured out. He sat in a chair close to the pulpit, and held his ear-trumpet poised carefully during the entire service. Reid thought him the most beautiful old man he had ever seen, and wondered a little—this was before the preacher had come to love his people with the whole-hearted devotion he gave them afterward—how patriarchal a personality could possibly belong to Craydock's Corners.

How he listened! Poor Reid, starved for appreciative hearing, felt such an inspiration as he had not felt for months. His preparation had been unusually meager, but he was so gratified by Father Winniston's attention that he hit upon the happy expedient of grafting upon what he had expected to say a large part of his trial sermon, and was greatly pleased with the result. The subject of the trial sermon had been, "The Ten Plagues of Modern Life," and the preacher felt that his ingenious adaptation of the ancient history to our own time was by far the cleverest piece of work he had ever done. Ten popular sins were identified with the ten plagues, and the Pharaoh of selfishness, indirectly responsible for all, was done to the life.

It was a trifle embarrassing to repeat the sermon to an audience that had heard it so lately, but it had been a great hit on its first delivery, and, besides, he felt sure that every member of the congregation would desire him to do his best for Father Winniston at any cost. The old man had himself been given to edification in his time, and was venerated by his brethren as a miracle of information on points of doctrine. Naturally, the young minister was quite determined upon producing an impression.

And it seemed that he succeeded. The old man took his hand after the service and invited him to his house, and the young preacher's heart was warmed as he thought of the hearty sympathy and fatherly counsel which undoubtedly awaited him.

The next day he went to call. Father Winniston's home was the most comfortable he had found at the Corners, not even excepting that of 'Squire Seakin where there were lace curtains at the front windows and a tapestry carpet on the parlor floor. In the Winniston farmhouse there was neither lace nor tapestry; but a certain hospitable largeness of the house and garden and orchard and barns gave a pleasant suggestion of welcome which the preacher had not found elsewhere.

The door was opened by Father Winniston's granddaughter, Sabrina. Sabrina was a tall, slim, broadbrowed girl, and was exceedingly pretty. Paul Reid was not married at this time, but he had gone far enough down the road of Romance to have decided preference for very small women. He thought Sabrina too tall, but very well in other respects.

It was the first time he had ever exchanged half a dozen words with her. He had fancied that she stood a little aloof from the young people of the Corners. In truth, she was regarded by them with some suspicion, as having "been away to school," and being dangerously indifferent on the subject of quiltings and surprise parties.

He face lighted so quickly when Paul inquired for her grandfather that he at once decided she was quite pretty as Maretta Lummis, popular opinion to the contrary, notwithstanding.

"He is taking his nap," she said brightly. "He always lies down just after dinner. I will call him."

Paul insisted that she should not—he could was as well not, he said. So they sat down on the porch together, and noting her quiet, self-contained manner and her soft, mirthful laughter, he wished that Lucy knew her. For Lucy would surely like her very much.

Yes, she had been at school in Darkwood the past year. She would go back there in the fall, if Grandpa could spare her. She was very anxious about Grandpa when away from him, but he wished her to stay in school another year if possible. It was very kind of him to spare her, and she hoped it wasn't wrong for her to be away from him.

There was a gentle eagerness in her tone, when she mentioned her grandfather that was almost touching. Paul, having taken her to be a girl of high spirit and independent ideas, was somewhat surprised. He had seen little of the world and he had not yet learned that there is no surrender so complete as the joyful and willing dependence of the naturally independent.

Presently her grandfather awakened and called her, and she hurried away. Paul remembered the long story which loquacious Mrs. Lummis had told him—how Sabrina's father, the old man's only son, had married against the father's wishes, a handsome, "shiftless" girl, who had wasted his substance and broken his spirit and driven him into an early grave. The old man had avowed that he would never receive his daughter-in-law, and had kept his word. But he had nursed his son in his sickness, and after the funeral had taken the child into his heart. The widow disappeared and it was said that she had married again, but neither Sabrina nor her grandfather spoke. The child had grown up under the old man's eye, and she obeyed him because she loved him. If she had inherited some of his own high spirit, she seemed to have no occasion to show it.

When he came in, his beautiful white hair had been freshly brushed, and the touches of dainty ministering hands still seemed to be upon him. Sabrina followed, and listened with pride and love in her eyes while he talked.

"My dear young brother," the old man said, in the gentle tones and with his black eyes beaming a benediction, "I was grieved at many things in your sermon last Lord's day morning. I would warn you that it is dangerous to speritualize on the Scripturs. We ortn't to be wise about what is written."

"I didn't know I was doing that," said Paul, who was dreadfully hurt, but who was the best-natured of men, and felt that so old and so noble-looking a critic must not be abruptly contradicted. "There are some lessons, I think, which belong to one age as much as to another."

Father Winniston had not heard him. He seldom used his ear trumpet in private conversation, and he preferred to do the talking himself. So he went on with his discourse.

"In interpretin' the Bible, we must always consider, Who speaks? Who is spoken to? and, Under what dispensation? We ortn't to jedge the lord, or affirm thet He would do this or thet under Christian dispensation because we are told thet He did it under the Jewish of the patriarchal. Now the Law of Moses—"

It was quite a disappointment, to find that such a distinguished auditor could be so tiresome. Paul soon grew weary of listening, and was, indeed, too little interested to take the situation very seriously. Yet he was ashamed of himself for his lack of interest. For Father Winniston, with his finely shaped head and intelligence of expression, could not be altogether common-place, into whatever trite forms of expression he might have fallen.

And indeed it did appear presently that the old man's conversation was not drifting, but was thoroughly well directed.

"I hev heerd preachers," he said, "a-quotin' from the Psalms of David, jest as if David hedn't been under the law thet was nailed to the Cross. Now them that argies from David for the use of instrumental music in the churches are workmen thet orto be ashamed, for they hev never learned to rightly divide the Word of Truth. The Lord never ordained thet orgin should be played in the worship of sanctooary, but the devil ordained it, an' the devil allays knows a passage of Scripter to suit his purpose. So he set the preachers to quotin' the Psalms of David."

Paul had no opinion to express on the organ question, and, as he could not have made himself heard in any case, he was content with a slight movement of the head which might have meant anything or nothing. Father Winniston took heart, and warmed to his subject. His bright black eyes glowed, and his lips and hands were tremulous.

"This curse of the devil, the orgin," he proclaimed, "is tearing' down the churches an' definin' the worship of Zion. I am an old man, but I am not too old to lift up my voice against it. As long as I breathe the breath of life I will cry aloud an' spare not."

He was so excited that the younger man became alarmed, and presently slipped away. But he continued to call now and then, and to receive instruction meekly and philosophically.

In the following May, Paul Reid was married, and brought his wife to Craydock's Corners. They fitted up a modest home, and in July, eager to display his house and his bride, Reid asked his favorite college friend to come and spend a Sunday with him. Ross Littleton was a bright, independent and thoroughly sincere young fellow, who had studied for the ministry from perfectly worthy motives, but had lost no whit of faith in himself during the process. He expected to do good and save souls, but he also expected to electrify the world. For preachers, though undoubtedly better than other men, are still of like passions.

Mr. Littleton preached for his friend on Sunday morning. He was a far better preacher than Reid, although, to do him justice, he was too loyal a friend to be conscious of it. He thought his style more popular than Reid's, but not nearly so profound. When it came to points of doctrine, he felt comparatively helpless.

At the dinner table, the young man commented upon Craydock's Corners and his inhabitants with a freedom which rather shocked little Lucy Reid. The preacher's wife was rather sensitive that morning, for she had worn a hat of which the Corners disapproved, and had been made to feel the disapproval.

"That man with the tuning-fork amuses me," averred Littleton. "He could hardly wait for me to finish my sermon,—he was so eager to get the doxology poised correctly. Imagine the angel choirs waiting for a piece of cutlery to give them the correct pitch!"

"I don't know what it mightn't as well be a tuning-fork as a harp, if you are only just used to it," protested Lucy, gravely. "A thing always looks queer when it is new to you. Mrs. Squire Seakin wants to have a organ in the church, but I don't know as it would be so much better."

"Why in the name of sense don't you have an organ, if Mrs. Seakin wants it? I supposed from what I had seen around here that you always had exactly what Mrs. Seakin wanted." He had indeed read the situation of affairs at the Corners with surprising accuracy. "By the way, who is the beautiful girl who was at church this morning?"

Reid had been married but a few weeks, and I am ashamed to say that his glance strayed to his wife's face. He was surprised that any other face in the congregation at the Corners should be described by so big and bold a word as "beautiful."

"Could he mean Maretta Lummis?" he asked feebly of his wife.

"No, of course he means Sabrina Winniston," she said, confidently. "She is the most beautiful girl I ever saw, I think. Anyhow, there is no one at the Corners to compare with her."

Littleton looked pleased and grateful. He had never before realized that his friend's wife was so discerning. "She is the one, I am sure," he said, with enthusiasm.

"It's Sabrina's grandfather who opposes the organ," Paul explained.

"Her grandfather! So she really does belong to this primitive neighborhood. I had taken her to be a disguised princess. What a cruel fate, that put a married man—or as good as married—into the pulpit at Craydock's Corners!"

That was the beginning. Perhaps it would be too much to say of an ardent youth like Littleton that he thought of Sabrina Winniston constantly until he saw her again. But at least he did not forget her—which is something to be able to say.

It was more than a year afterward that he came to the Corners to assist his friend in a protracted meeting. The other denominations represented in the community held "revivals." The worshippers at the Corners scorned this term, and conducted a "protracted meeting" in October of each year, beginning "in the light of the moon" and when the "going" was still good. Brother Thornberry, over at Blue Point, rather delighted in bad weather, muddy roads, and a sectarian prejudice; but Brother Thornberry was a veteran and had debated with the Adventist.

Sabrina was at home now, and she and Lucy Reid had become great friends. The good sisters of the church were wont to argue afterward that Lucy might have foreseen the danger. But Lucy was very innocent, and, like many innocent persons, had a vein of romance within herself which she had never supposed to be dangerous. So she invited Sabrina to tea, and sang her praises to Littleton, and was, I fear, rather exultant than otherwise over the young man's preference.

The meetings attracted such crowds as had been unknown at Craydock's Corners before, except of funeral occasions. Littleton had a handsome face, and a confidence not altogether attributable to the sublime audacity of youth. He had, moreover, an amazing vocabulary, and a happy gift of illustration. Nothing was talked of but the meetings, even among the loafers who sat on the cracker boxes at the village store—those traditional seats of the scornful.

"They'll git a lot of jiners yit," Sam Dustin told Hank Adkins. "The sinners are kinder hitchin' forrard, an' thet youngster'll hev 'em on the front seat 'fore they know it."

Sabrina Winniston was always at the meetings, earnest, anxious, and more and more beautiful as the repressed soul within her shone more and more clearly through her eyes. She did not confess to herself that she was at all interested in the preacher, aside from his office. She conscientiously repeated his sermons in the ear trumpet to her grandfather, and tried to be as just in her criticisms as in her praise. But she was young and unused to the world, and Ross Littleton was, in his way, a charming fellow. So the end was what any wiseacre might have reasonably expected.

Mrs. Squire Seakin was in her element. She went in and out among the sinners and backsliders, reproving and rebuking, with very little long suffering and a great deal of doctrine. As the meeting progressed, a new idea took possession of this good woman. There must be an organ, and her Lury May, who had taken three terms of music lessons and could do the "Royal Banner Quickstep" in a truly amazing fashion, must play it. With the keen eye of a genius for manipulation, she saw in Littleton a natural ally, and went to him at once with her plan.

"We can take our orgin over for the present," she said, diplomatically. "I'll have Jason hitch up the spring wagon after supper, so there won't be no talk. An' Sunday morning we can set it in the wood room while the morning meeting is going on. I don't want to do nothing to hurt old Father Winniston's conscience, but I do say he's prejudiced, an' I don't believe in hendering the gospel from running an' being glorified."

"I wish we had an organ," said Littleton, with ready acquiescence. "I don't know who would play it, though. Mrs. Bassett can play, but the singing would hitch badly without her."

"My Lury May can manage all right, if you'll just pick out the pieces the day before an' let her practice 'em over. She's young, an she ain't got the confidence I'd like to see, but she'll manage—I'll see to that. I've spent my money on her music lessons for this very thing, for I see the time was coming, an' I didn't mean to be took unawares."

Littleton was sorry that he had committed himself so rashly, but, being young, he never revised an opinion after it was once expressed. He did explain the situation to Raid and his wife, and was somewhat conscience-smitten when he saw their anxiety.

"Oh, I hope she won't do it!" Lucy cried, tremulously. "Sabrina will be so hurt! She loves her grandfather so much that I think she even loves all his queer notions and prejudices. I wouldn't like to say anything harsh to Mrs. Seakin—I can never forget how good she was to us when we needed help so much—but I really think we ought to tell her that it isn't right."

Littleton, feeling himself included in the blame, began to argue Mrs. Seakin's side. "I think it very absurd to go on humoring an old man who belongs to a past generation," he said. "Sabrina is too sensible to misunderstand such a thing. Indeed, I doubt if she would ever speak of it to her grandfather."

Lucy knew better, and made up her mind to have a talk with Mrs. Seakin at the first opportunity. The preacher's wife was the pet of Craydock's Corners, and a privileged character everywhere.

But she had reckoned on having ample time for such an effort. To her surprise, and to the secret consternation of Ross Littleton, the organ was already in its place at the time for the evening service.

No outward demonstration was evoked, unless the triumphant nod of the feather on Mrs. Seakin's bonnet could be characterize as such. Lury May blushingly assured the preacher that she could play "Happy Day" and "There Is a Fountain," but she lost her blushes and grew pale at the suggestion of a selection in three sharps. Mrs. Lon Bassett looked scornful when the little organist forgot to count time, and the sinners on the cross sets by the stove viewed the situation with unconcealed interest.

Before the evening was over another excitement almost drove the episode of the organ from the mind of the preacher. Lowizy Benslow, who had been publicly "turned out" of the church a few months before, came down the aisle, leading a distressed looking two-year-old boy by the hand, to make confession and be restored to fellowship. Lowizy was under general condemnation as being "shiftless"; but the Corners loved a sensation, and she was received back as heartily as she had been voted out. Paul Reid's eyes filled with tears as he welcomed her, and he unconsciously laid his hand on the head of the little boy. His own child slept in the graveyard, and Lowizy Benslow's face recalled the dark night of his bereavement.

After the meeting Littleton did the conventional handshaking, and then went to look for Sabrina. She was near the door, and did not look up until he spoke.

"You are not well!" he said, in genuine alarm. "What is it Sabrina?"

She bent her queenly head in the direction of the organ. "Do you think it is kind?" she asked. "It will break my grandfather's heart."

And without so much as a goodbye she moved swiftly out into the night.

Mrs. Seakin's carry-all stood before the little white cottage occupied by the preacher and his wife. This would have been a significant fact at any time, but in the present unsettled state of society it was positively portentous. It was understood that when Father Winniston should be apprized of the advent of the organ his quiet and supposedly holy wrath would be unbounded. It was impossible that the present visit from the chief regulator of public affairs should not in some way pertain to the situation.

And it did. Mrs. Seakin looked with but poorly concealed interest at the blossom on Lucy Reid's monthly rose, and utterly refused to respond to Mr. Littleton's inspiring allusions to the fine fall weather. She folded her broche shawl by severely correct lines, untied her bonnet strings with the air of one seeking spiritual liberty, and opened her mind, apparently with a similar impulse.

"I've heard something about Father Winniston," she said, solemnly. "I've heard a thing I could never have believed of it hadn't come straight. Brother Reid, I am told that Father Winniston has departed from the faith and denied the gospel that he once declared."

"I don't know what you mean," Mr. Reid said, quite mystified, and wondering if Mrs. Seakin had suddenly taken leave of her ponderous wits. "I'm sure that if any man seems to stand for the faith in a painfully square manner, it's Father Winniston."

"That's what I've always thought," asserted Mrs. Seakin. "You could have knocked me down with a feather when I found out. There ain't a man at the Corners that can quote Scripture with Father Winniston. They say he knows the whole Book of Acts, and most all of Romans, by heart. But it's been told around for a good while that he had his own notions on the Book of Revelations; and now I've got it straight from Brother Thornberry, over to Blue Point, that he told him he believed sinners would burn all to once, in the lake of fire, instead of burning everlasting."

There was a hint of triumph in Mrs. Seakin's tone. To do her justice, this was not wholly due to her opposition to Father Winniston. The true Heresy hunter is instinctively proud of a discovery.

"Perhaps Brother Thornberry has misunderstood him," Reid said, cautiously. "With the old man's deafness it is very difficult to carry on a conversation with him."

"Brother Thornberry ain't one that likely to misunderstand. He ain't debated with the Adventists all these years without learning the Scriptures. No, Brother Reid, Father Winniston is straining at a gnat and swallowing a camel. He's strict enough about the organ, but he's straightly said, against the plain teaching of the Scripture, that he don't believe the burning of sinners will be everlasting."

Ross Littleton, who had been sitting by the window in a dejected attitude, suddenly roused himself. "I'll go and have a talk with him about it," he said.

Reid looked at him in surprise, for he was sure that Sabrina had not spoken to the young preacher since the first evening on which the organ had been used. Being a man, and not especially imaginative, he supposed his friend would wish to keep out of her way under such circumstances. But Lucy's face immediately brightened.

"By all means, go and talk it over with him," she pleaded. "It will do him good to know that you understand."

Mrs. Seakin looked surprised, and a trifle hurt. She had expected to have all the sympathy on her side. But while she was for the most part firmly established in the conviction that Lucy Reid could do no wrong, she sometimes conceded that she was "a soft-hearted little piece."

Sabrina met the young man coldly. He tried to scorn her for scorning him, but he could not. Indeed, he was almost ready to admire her loyalty to the old man who had been all that she had known of love and protection.

To his surprise, Father Winniston seemed to be in ignorance concerning the matter of the organ, and received him as if nothing had happened. The two got on amazingly well. Evidently Sabrina had not yet told the story. An allusion to Brother Thornberry's recent visit brought up the subject of the old man's heresy, and he became very communicative. Ross was certainly guilty of no intentional insincerity, but what with his desire to seem as kindly disposed as he felt, and what with the old man's deafness, the younger man managed to convey the impression that he was quite in sympathy with his elder's opinion concerning the duration of future punishment.

"All God's punishments are merciful, are they not?" the young man asked. He felt a strange sense of reverence in the presence of this gently stern old man. The feeling was good for him, though he did not know it.

Father Winniston did not hear him, but he took the mild tone and interested expression to mean acquiescence. "It satisfies justice, so fur as

I can see," he went on. "Brother Thornberry says it's as bad as soul-sleepin', but I say it ain't." He unconsciously grew dogmatical as he went on to argue his point. "There's them that say it ain't reasonable to suppose we'll reign a thousand years an' then come out an' be crowned. But thet's Scripcher, an' I stand for Scripcher. Brother Thornberry says it's just as plain that the punishment of them that die in their sins will go on forever, but I say it ain't."

Littleton saw the situation at once. The old man loved an argument, and would never lose an opportunity for one. On the other hand, having taken a position for the sake of argument, he would never admit that he had been worsted. In this case he had been especially rash in arraying himself against the doughty Thornberry, but having once entrenched himself of doubtful ground there would be no chance whatever of persuading him to leave it. The hope was that the controversy would die and be forgotten before Mrs. Seakin had made too much capital out of it.

Littleton went away encouraged. Evidently Sabrina had not yet told her grandfather the incident of the organ, or, at least, she had failed to connect his name with it. He was heartily ashamed of his part in the affair, and hoped to make some humble apology which would set him right in the eyes of Sabrina.

In vain. This was on Saturday. Sunday was a great day at Craydock's Corners. It has been told far and wide that the "joiners" who had been received during the protracted meeting would be given "the right of congratulation" and added to this was the interest in the episode of the organ, from which a sensation might be developed at any time. So the buggies were lined up as at funerals, and the cross seats by the stoves, the possession from time immemorial of the "outsides," were filled before ten o'clock.

Those who expected a sensation were not disappointed. Just before the time for service Father Winniston appeared. Sabrina herself drove the old white horse, and helped him from his carriage with the greatest possible care. Mrs. Seakin, in the flush of her triumph, had purposely omitted to have the organ removed to the wood room, and poor Lury May, driven to the verge of hysteria, narrowly escaped starting up the "Royal Banner Quickstep" instead of "Cannan's Happy Land."

A chill seemed to fall upon the meeting. There was a noble scorn in the curve of the old man's lips, and the hint of swift retribution in his eyes. Never before had Ross Littleton felt himself at such a tremendous disadvantage. Genuinely kind of heart, the thought that he had given this honest old man pain was most humiliating to him. His usual happy confidence deserted him altogether. He went to his task without hope or inspiration, and he preached a little worse, perhaps, than ever before.

Father Winniston listened with his usual benignity of expression, but Littleton knew that the time of reckoning had come.

After the sermon the congregation sang "How Firm a Foundation," and the members of the church gave the hand of congratulation. It was an imposing sight. Lowizy Benslow had a new hat for the occasion—a gorgeous affair, with a big purple bow on the very top. Poor Lowizy! It was the first new thing she had since her wedding day, and she felt painfully conscious and happy.

The women marched around first, and when they had shaken hands with the new converts, the elders and the preachers, they sat down in the seats vacated by the brethren, who had by this time joined the procession. It was the only occasion on which they sat on the men's side, and they felt that the eyes of the world were upon them.

Father Winniston occupied a seat at the communion table, opposite 'Squire Seakin. It was the first time in months that he had officiated, and the trembling of his hands as he passed the bread and wine told how fast the helplessness of old age was coming upon him.

"He will never be here again," Lucy Reid said to herself. "O, why need they break his heart at the very last?"

The communion service over, the old man arose, leaned heavily upon his cane, and began:

"Brethren, I've served the Lord in my weak way sence before most of you was born. Before the first of you that are alive now went down into the waters of baptism I helped cut the logs for this meetin' house that stood on this ground before this one was built. I ask to-day whether or not I hev' a right to speak."

He had a right, and the ring of his voice told that he knew it. "In my weakness you hev done what you would not hev dared to do in my strength," he went on. "You hev brought that invention of the evil one into this holy place, and desecrated the altars of the sanctooary. You thet have done it hev disturbed the peace of Zion, and I charge you with it. An' him thet's come among you, claimin' to be an under shepherd, an' yit a-countenancin' this thing, I charge him with bein' a wolf in sheep's clothin', an I warn the flock thet if they foller him they will be utterly destroyed."

Poor Sabrina! Her beautiful head drooped lower and lower, and a bright spot of red burned on either cheek. Littleton would have risen to speak, but his head reeled and he could not command himself. Paul, with unusual tact and quickness, was on his feet before him. "Let us pray," he gently said.

Crushed and humbled, Ross went to his first pastorate, a little church in a small mining town, fifty miles away. He had not dreamed that it was in him to care for any one as he cared for Sabrina Winniston. He wrote two sermons on "Illusions," for the sake of persuading himself that his little romance was a thing of the past. And then he tore them up, and confessed to himself that every day he lived intensified his torture.

He had been in his new position but two or three months when he received a note from Lucy Reid. "I am going to tell you something you will feel very sorry about," she wrote. "They have put Father Winniston out of the eldership. You will wonder how they could scarcely know how it was done. Paul tried his best to keep them from it but he couldn't. They said it wasn't safe to have him when he held such wrong views. I thought it didn't make so much difference when he never bothers any one with his views, and is so old and deaf any way, but Mrs. Seakin says right is right. Sabrina is so very unhappy—it makes my heart ache just to look at her. Can't you come and see us, and talk it over with her?"

"Good little Lucy!" murmured Littleton. "There ought to be one star added to your crown for that letter. Come and see you? Yes, I'll do that fast enough. But to talk it over with Sabrina—I fear that must be forever impossible."

The very next week, moved by a restlessness which he could not shake off, Littleton resolved to act upon Lucy Reid's invitation and pay a visit to Craydock's Corners.

It was almost dark when he left the train at Blue Point, and started his four-miles' walk to the preacher's home. Night was settling when he came in sight of the Winniston farm. There was a light burning in the front room. As he approached the gate, old Dr. Caskey climbed into his buggy and drove away. Littleton hurried on to call after him, and then stopped. He had not the heart to ask a question.

The light in the front room seemed to him like a signal of distress. It must be that Father Winniston was ill. With the thought that Sabrina was in sorrow and that she perhaps needed him there came forgetfulness of all her coldness. He loved her and there was a chance that he might serve her. That was enough.

Sabrina herself came to the door, and stood with her hand above her eyes as she peered out into the darkness. Then recognition and gratitude conquered grief and anxiety in the beautiful face. The alienation of these two seemed to have been forgotten. He was her friend, and he had come when her need was greatest.

"He is going to die," she whispered, as she led the way across the hall.

The old man lay in the front room, and though Littleton had never seen death, he felt sure at the first glance that its shadow was fast falling.

Paul and Lucy Reid were sitting beside the bed. They rose and shook hands without a word. Lucy, at least, was not surprised to see him there.

Presently the old man raised his head feebly from the pillow. Sabrina laid her hand in his. "I am here, darling," she said, the passion of a woman's devotion in her voice. He was not an ideal saint, perhaps, but she had given him the love of nature made for loving. "Do you need me, grandpa? I am here."

He drew away his hand quickly, peering curiously into her face the while. "I know who you are," he said. "You are Ellen Winters, and you want to marry my son."

There was something terrible in the severity of the soft, quivering voice.

Tears filled the girl's eyes. "He thinks it is my mother," she said. Her sorrow had made her unconscious of what would at another time have seemed to her like humiliation.

"I will never consent to it in the world," the old man went on, with dreadful earnestness. "The Winterses are shif'less. Their father before 'em was shif'less. I won't hev my son marry amongst 'em. I've brought him up different, an' I won't—hev—it."

Littleton's love for Sabrina on the one side, and on the other the associations and impressions of a life-time, gave balance to his judgment and enabled him to see this old man as he really was, honest, narrow, loving and intolerant, with the habit of giving the name of convictions to his prejudices, and of preserving in them to his own and others' hurt. After all, no nature is all together simple, and if we could look into the hearts of the commonplace men and women round about us we might find them stirred by motives and feelings as complex.

He caught sight of Littleton, and, strangely enough, he seemed to connect his presence at once with his former visit, when the young man listened so patiently and considerably to his heresy.

"They say it ain't Scripcheral? A thousand years are but a day. How do thet the burnin' will be everlasting'? How do we know, I say? Hey?"

"We know that God will do right," said Littleton, gently. His heart was hushed and solemnized as it had never been before. He was no hero, but it is only fair to him to say there was in his heart no shadow of resentment against the old patriarch who was so near another world.

There was a bustle outside the door, and Mrs. Seakin entered. It was well that she came. Every tradition of Craydock's Corners demanded her presence on such an occasion as this. She went to the bedside, looked with a professional interest upon the beautiful old face, and shook her head. "He won't last till morning," she decided. "Has he said anything in particular?"

Sabrina was dumb. She looked imploringly toward Lucy Reid, who said, interrogatively, "Anything in particular? I don't know what you mean Mrs. Seakin."

"About dying. I hope he's been told that he ain't long for this world?"

"Father Winniston has certainly known for some time that he could not stay with us many years," Paul Reid said, remembering Mrs. Seakin's genius for spiritual irritation.

"I thought maybe he'd want Sabrina's ma sent for. He's been dreadful set against her, and he's never been one that gives up easy."

She planted herself firmly beside the bed, and through the whole night she stayed there, patiently waiting for a revelation of some sort from the parched lips of the dying man. Craydock's Corners delighted in the picturesque, and a deathbed ecstasy was never forgotten.

It was nearly dawn when a change came over the face on the pillow. The eyes unclosed, and the fire of youth seemed to come back to them.

"Tens of thousands, and thousands upon thousands!" the old man cried out, rapturously. "From every people and kindred and tribe and tongue . . . From east and the west . . . to sit down with Abraham an Issac and Jacob. . . . Bless the Lord, O my soul!"

They gathered about him, but he did not see them. Sabrina's lips were pressed to his brow, but he did not feel their touch.

"Every gate a pearl . . . and the wall of precious stones, first jasper, and the second sapphire, the third a chalcedony, and the fourth . . . the fourth—"

Memory, so active for a moment, wavered, and then took up the thread again. "No sun or moon to shine in it, for the Lamb is the light thereof. Nothing that worketh abomination or maketh a lie. . . . And the leaves of the tree are for the healing of the nations!"

There was silence for several moments. It seemed to Littleton that he had never before stood face to face with God. And yet he could find no words of prayer.

"Music! Music!" the old man murmured, presently. "The harp . . . the psaltery . . . the instrument of ten strings! Hark!"

Alas, they could not hear. For the first time, Sabrina sobbed aloud. The ticking of the clock appalled her. The precious moments were going fast, and the end was close at hand.

"Tens of thousands, and thousands . . . thousands upon thousands," he began again. "With palms in their hands. . . . With a harp, and the voice of . . . the voice of a psalm . . . the harp—"

Mrs. Seakin had risen, and stood with uplifted hands. "The Lord is in it," she said. "The Lord is certainly in it! He's taking back all he has said against instrument music in the Lord's house!"

With the harp . . . the harp . . . and the voice—"

The murmur ceased. The old man was dead. The book had been closed and passed to the great Adjuster of Accounts, who adds infinite love and mercy with the poor sum of every human life.

A month later a fine new organ with varnish and adorned with two rows of stops, was placed in the meeting-house at Craydock's Corners. Mrs. Seakin still rehearses the marvelous story of how Father Winniston, in his last moments, repented of his opposition to instrumental music in the churches. In her view, as I believe, Sabrina Littleton fully shares. If she had not so held, she could scarcely have brought herself to forget the past and marry the man of her choice. As for Littleton himself, he has his doubts on the subject of Father Winniston's change of heart—doubts which he mentions to no one, least of all to the wife whose judgment, save at this one point, he has never had an occasion to call in question.

HILLSBURY FOLKS I

THE SCHOOL MA'AMS

Auris Leigh

It will be quite useless for you to try to find Hillsbury, for in our day it no longer exists. Forty years ago, at the time of which I write, it was a dull little village, the type of thousands of such villages scattered throughout the Middle West. The Great City was indeed within driving distance, but it had no influence upon the life of the village, except as it furnished a market for the produce of the gardens and the surrounding farms. By the thought and the social customs of the city we were never touched. Our mothers would no more have thought of having dinner at six o'clock than they would have thought of tying their bonnet strings in the back. A six o'clock dinner hour belonged to the city, and we were of Hillsbury.

But, as I said, that was forty years ago. Irving tells a legend of a convent which, with all its inmates, was engulfed so completely that only the tip of its spire remained above the earth. Hillsbury has vanished as completely. Only the little old graveyard, with its slanting tombstones and their quaint inscriptions, is left of the old village of our childhood. Commerce claims the hills over which we hunted wintergreens and chestnuts. Factories pour forth their smoke from the common where we used to play "pull-away" and "sailor boys." The Great City has swallowed Hillsbury.

Perhaps you will not be sufficiently interested in our Hillsbury folks to even care whether or not our village still exists. No doubt they will seem to you sadly antiquated. Certainly they were wholly, and, one might almost say, needlessly, provincial. They were quite satisfied with Hillsbury. Naturally, a Hillsbury man would have preferred being village postmaster to being a United States Senator, just as he would have preferred owning a Hillsbury garden patch and cottage to owning a castle in Spain.

There were two stores in Hillsbury. One represented Republicanism, and Righteousness, the other, Democracy and Depravity, according to one party; according to the other, these neat characterizations could be reversed and used with equal appropriateness. Joe Wetzel, a nery little ex-soldier, "kept" the Republican store; George Bemis, a cool, sarcastic, witty Yankee, presided over the Democratic headquarters.

Between these two the war for the control of the post office went on daily and continuously. The possession of this office was the great political issue, according to Hillsbury patriots. There were no scratched tickets in those days. If there was any voter in the village whose voting habit was not known to every man, woman, and child in the township, you might be assured that he had been a citizen of HIllsbury for less than twenty-four hours.

There were three churches—and they did not love one another. The Methodists, having the largest number of members and the best financial support, was thought by the Congregationalists and the Disciples to carry things with a rather high hand. The Congregationalists, being kept humble, did not call the Disciples "Campbellites," and often invited the latter to their ice cream socials. Adversity is a great leveler, as has often been remarked.

But the great pride of Hillsbury was the "graded school." The school building was of brick, and by far the finest structure in town. There were three grades, and presiding over these were our three school ma'ams.

I shall not say much about "Miss Fanny," she of the "primary." We "intermediates" thought her a very absurd person, with but a slight stock of brains—bright enough to teach babies (we had never heard of "kiddies"), but quite unworthy the serious attention of boys and girls of our size. She had been to the city high school—which no doubt accounted for her inferiority. A Hillsbury young lady would never have been so silly. She wore a monstrous "waterfall," used a tone that we thought highly affected, and, when she came in to give us our singing lesson, was always bothering us to sound our final "g's." We disposed of Miss Fanny satisfactorily, according to our youthful sense of justice, by dubbing her "Miss Stuck-Up."

But what shall I say of our "Miss Emily?" I have known all along that language was to fail me here. I have even tried to get some help from the magazine stories and novels—whose descriptions of the charms of their heroines I would shamelessly appropriate if they would serve me—but they are tame and colorless compared with Miss Emily as she appeared to our childish eyes. She was tall—how I hoped I would grow, and grow, and grow! She was fair—how I wished I were! Her hair curled in soft ringlets about her face—I rolled mine up on "rags" over night! She had a straight nose—I tried the effect of pinching mine with a hairpin! But over and above all, she was Miss Emily—every day told me more clearly the utter failure and fruitlessness of life, since another Miss Emily there could never, never be!

Miss Emily was an ardent Methodist. This was, in all my eyes, her only weakness. When I lay in my little bed at night, dreaming of my adored teacher's smile, and thinking of what I would do to please her, I always drew the line just here—I would never join the Methodists, never, never! But I wished the ladies of my mother's church could pray as Miss Emily could, and that they could speak in her beautiful, direct, unembarrassed way, on the subject of religion.

Much as I loved her, however, I watched her constantly, lest she should promulgate dangerous doctrines in the school room. Once we were talking of miracles—imagine a discussion of such a subject in a modern fourth grade! Miss Emily spoke with great reverence of God's miracle-working power as manifested in the olden time, then added, "And he seems to work miracles still. How often we see the conversion of some one who has seemed utterly beyond the hope of redemption!"

Horrors! were such teachings, even when given from the sweetest lips in the world, to go unrebuked? Up went my hand on the instant.

"What is it?" inquired Miss Emily.

"Please," I urged, "when God converts people now, he uses means!"

A kind of spasm passed over Miss Emily's face. "You are a funny little thing," was all she said. But she came down to my seat and patted my rag-made curls with a kindliness that took the hurt of her mirth away. She was adorable—was our Miss Emily.

Mrs. Caroline More was "principal of the grammar," and in her was vested the final authority in matters of discipline. She always appeared to me as the visible embodiment of Law. I thought she looked like the Old Testament in female form, and with a black stuff dress on. She was a Calvinist of the deepest dye, and remained aloof from the Congregational Church of Hillsbury because she regarded it as too liberal. Undoubtedly she was an excellent woman, according to her lights, but she believed us youngsters to be thoroughly saturated with original sin, and felt that her position had been bestowed upon her that she might remove the old Adam from each evil little heart.

The great effort of our lives was to keep from deeds so terrible that the story of them must go to Mrs. More's ears. Miss Emily was herself a firm, though a gentle disciplinarian, and I do not remember ever to have seen her authority openly defied. We felt that she would stand between us and Mrs. More's long black ruler as long as she could do so with justice and fairness, but that, if she should find it really necessary to resign us to the untender mercies of the "principal," we should be lost, indeed.

It was Conrad Wetzel who invited the lightnings. Conrad, whom we all—except the teachers—called "Cooney," was a burly, stubborn, dull boy of twelve, who resented the fact that his dullness kept him in the grade with children of nine and ten. He ran away from school, and was sent back by his fiery little German-soldier father. Miss Emily, who seldom reprimanded a pupil publicly, had a long talk with him after school. How did we know she did? Because we waited and watched outside the schoolhouse, of course. If there was a whipping involved in Cooney's evil-doing, we wanted to know all about it.

There was no whipping that time. Cooney seemed more subdued for a few days, and gave some little attention to his books. But I suppose that study must have been torture to him, for in a week he ran away again.

We saw that his seat was vacant, and suggested to each other, by means of sign language, that the mischief would certainly be to pay this time. But the morning passed and nothing happened. Between the first and second afternoon bells, some boys brought the exciting information that Cooney was hiding back of Bailey Barton's tan-bark shed.

"He's gettin' pretty hungry," they reported, "so he'll have to be goin' home 'fore long. Then he'll ketch it!"

Early in the afternoon there came up an awful thunder shower. Never have I felt such an agony of fear as was mine that day, though in later years I have tried to repeat the mental experience simply for the horrible thrill of it. Indeed, I have never since been able to name fear as such—so faint was it by comparison with the tortures of that hour. A heavy darkness settled down upon us, so deep that all attempt to work was abandoned, though Miss Emily tried to control our minds by having us sing the multiplication table, and the little songs whose words we knew. All in vain. Our teeth chattered so that we could not sing. Here and there a child cried aloud. All of us shrieked each time the red glare of the lightning came, with its simultaneous burst of thunder. Miss Emily had enough to do in keeping our terrified little souls from uncontrollable panic.

In the midst of it all there was a heavy knock at the door. Miss Emily started toward it, carrying sobbing little Hattie Bemis in her arms.

"O teacher!" cried Fritzy Schaeffer, "don't you dast go to the door! Maybe it's the end of the world already!"

Miss Emily had no need to go to the door. It was thrown open, and Cooney was projected into the room by his father. Some sense of propriety kept Joe Wetzel from swearing before school children in English, no doubt, for he burst into a storm of German invective. Whether he was raging against his son or against Miss Emily, none of us ever knew. His wrath seemed soon to spend itself, however, and he went as abruptly as he had come. I believe it is said that one cannot be the victim of two great passions at the same time. The storm without was henceforth unheard. Our fears were forgotten. Our minds were entirely concentrated upon the subject of what was going to happen to Cooney.

We were not left long in doubt. Who summoned Mrs. More I do not know, but she was there, almost as soon as Joe Wetzel had taken his departure. And her long black ruler was with her.

"Are you willing to say you are sorry?" she asked of Cooney, bending her gaunt form over him and turning her deep-set, burning eyes upon his face.

"No!" grunted Cooney, sulkily.

"Then I must administer discipline. It gives me great pain, but you have been willfully disobedient, and this is not your first offense. Take of your coat!"

Cooney took off his coat, and for two mortal hours the black ruler fell upon his back and shoulders. I say for two hours, but there were intervals in which Mrs. More paused to ask him if he was willing to say he was sorry for what he had done. He shook his head each time, and the dreary process of discipline was resumed.

Miss Emily had whispered at the beginning something which we guessed to be a request that she might take the rest of the school into the assembly room during the punishment. But Mrs. More had shaken her head decidedly, "I wish every one of them to see the penalty of disobedience," she said.

It was long after the usual time for dismissal that Cooney, so limp that he drooped across the seat in front of him, growled out a word which we took to be "Sorry!" Mrs. More smiled grimly.

"He says he is sorry," she said. "He desires to be forgiven. I forgive him freely. Miss Emily, do you?"

"Yes," came in a choked voice from a far corner. And then we saw that Miss Emily was crying. That wicked woman had actually made our darling teacher cry! As for us, we girls had not once stopped wailing all the afternoon, and the boys had their times of sniveling, in shame-faced, boyish fashion.

We realized that the storm had spent itself, without as well as within. A streak of sunshine came through the west window. Mrs. More went to the platform. "Boys and girls," she said, I hope you have profited by what you have witnessed. I trust no one will ever be guilty of disobedience. I desire to say that I shall remember Conrad in my prayers tonight."

I am afraid to tell you what our childish thoughts were. I know we all felt that the most dreadful thing that could happen to us would be to get mentioned in Mrs. More's prayers.

As I have said, that was forty years ago, and Hillsbury exists no longer. I have not seen Miss Emily since those childhood days. They say she is a grandmother now. Certainly she must be a gracious and lovely one. I would that heaven might return to her children's children some share of the blessing she brought to me!

Cooney Wetzel has made half a million in the manufacture of glue. I believe he is the only Hillsbury man who has become wealthy. In his case we have another of the many examples that the pursuit of wealth is one of the callings for which a liberal education is not necessary, perhaps not even desirable.

Mrs. More has long time since left the world. So, too, we may be glad to believe, have her discipline and her theology. But—I wonder! For Mrs. More's own daughters, trained under the black ruler and law, are among the sweetest and rarest-natured women I know. Their own children have never known a black ruler. I wonder if they will be as sweet.

Evermore, the noblest and best are those who come up through tribulation. But what of those who perish in bitterness and rebellion by the way?

HILLSBURY FOLKS II

THE DOCTOR

Auris Leigh

Dr. Meecham, the Hillsbury physician, was very young, and looked even younger. He had married and had cultivated whiskers, in the hope of achieving age and wisdom, or at least the appearance thereof, but quite in vain.

Dr. Meecham had "read medicine" with his predecessor, "the Old Doctor," and had married into the latter's practice. The Old Doctor had retired to enjoyment of his little market farm with the strict understanding that he should never be called unless there was a leg to be cut off. The Old Doctor had been an army surgeon, and an amputation was his delight.

The Young Doctor, as he continued to be called, was as devout and as excellent a young man as lived upon the earth. He carried tracts along with his pill-boxes, alternated his doses of calomel with doses of pious counsel, and offered religious counsel when his professional offices failed. To his sincerity and his single mindedness, both as regarded his medical and his religious profession, the worst enemy he had would have cheerfully borne witness. But in both religion and medicine his range of knowledge was sadly limited.

He lived in dread lest he should miss some terrible disease by a too-easy diagnosis. Therefore he struck the worst possibilities first, and came down gradually to slighter ailments. If a child had feverish flushes there was a probability of scarlet fever; if not that, of measles; at least, indigestion. He guessed consumption first, then bronchitis, then a cold. He began with a horrible suggestion of cancer of the stomach, and ended with the confident opinion that the patient had eaten too many green apples. Traversing so much ground, it would seem that he could have missed no ailment, but he did usually miss the right one. Some men seem to be born unlucky.

Though he belonged to a later age than the Old Doctor, he had inherited all the former's joy in calomel. His other favorite remedies were cod liver oil for a cough, iron for the blood, and whiskey as a medicine he seemed to have a faith which was matched only by his aversion to it as a beverage. He would give it unflinchingly to the worst toper in town, accompanying the dose by an incisive temperance lecture, and by a strong expression of his opinion that no drunkard can inherit the kingdom.

There were two things that the Young Doctor hated with a perfect hatred. These two were cold water and fresh air. I can recall as if it were yesterday the pleadings of fever-stricken patients for a draught that might cool their parched tongues, and it was denied them as if they had asked for poison.

Like all persons of his time, the Young Doctor regarded "night air" as a breeder of pestilence. To sleep beside an open window was to breathe in malaria. To walk beneath the stars was to walk toward disease and death. "Drafts" were more to be shunned than contagion. We had never heard of screening our doors and windows against flies and mosquitoes, but we knew how to cork them against the air.

I remember a terrible case of pneumonia which came near being the Young Doctor's Waterloo. A brave little German housewife, after having fought against the disease for days when she should have been in bed, staggered to the lounge at last in terrible pain. Dr. Meecham was hurriedly summoned. For once his first and worst diagnosis proved to be correct. He carried his patient to the bed, and ordered that none of her clothing, save her shoes, be removed. The tidy little woman, horrified at this desecration of her immaculate bed-linen, protested between painful gasps for breath, but in vain. She was destined to lie for eight days without having even her stockings changed. Meanwhile the Young Doctor had taken a vigorous hand in the management of the household. Strips of clothe were pasted about the windows and the closed doors. Entrance to the house was to be had only by way of the woodshed, whence the constant stream of callers were led to the kitchen and made to warm their clothes thoroughly. From thence, through the sitting-room warmed by an air-tight stove, they passed to the bed and steal oxygen from the sick woman, who was alternately muttering in delirium and crying out for the two boons denied her—water and air. Yet she recovered. I wonder how.

Perhaps the doctor, ignorant though he must seem in the light of a later-day science, was as near to his patients in intelligence as is the modern practitioner, for we were all companions in ignorance. However, not all were so far behind the dictionary as was our next-door neighbor, a middle-aged woman whose old mother lay at the point of death. I was sent to inquire concerning the sufferer, and was told that she was going fast, that she had had a collapse, which had been followed by more than forty spavins!

It goes without saying that our Young Doctor, who was neatness itself in his personal habits, knew nothing of the scientific cleanliness upon which modern hygiene insists. He would have fallen into a paroxysm if he had been told that one hair of his head was on the wrong side of the part. But it was his pleasant habit in vaccinating us school children to puncture the skin with an old jack-knife which he had carried in his pocket for years and which he used for every conceivable purpose. When little Carrie Skelton developed an ugly ulcer on the face, Dr. Meecham removed the scab by means of this same jack-knife, comforting the wailing child during the operation with the assurance that the spot would look a lot nicer when it healed over again!

It is no wonder that diseases spread, when we did not even know that we should guard against infection. When little Jimmy Morey died of diphtheria there was a great church funeral, for which the schools were dismissed, six of his playmates acted as pall-bearers, and we all cried over the casket and laid our flowers about the dear, freckled, so familiar and yet so strange face of our little chum. One careful mother did indeed suggest a closed casket—for diphtheria was the black specter of the cradle in that day—but the rest of the village laughed at her. How could you catch a disease from a dead person?

A doctor's experiences in that day were varied. There was no dentist in Hillsbury, and when there was a tooth to be pulled the patient went to Dr. Meecham.

Once, when Joe Wetzel had walked the house all night with a raging toothache, swearing in English and German alternately, he walked into Dr. Meecham's office in the early morning, almost screaming, "Bull him! bull him! Bull te consarnit ting!"

The doctor pulled and Joe howled. There was silence for a moment as Joe realized that the pain had ceased. Then he began to swear more lustily than ever.

"You fool Yankee sawbones!" he cried. "I'll haf te low on you— fool! fool! You haf bull te wrong tooth!"

"Hush," said Dr. Meecham, sternly. "I do not allow blasphemy in my office. And since I have accidentally extracted the wrong tooth, I will not charge a cent for it—not a single cent!"

Whereupon Joe went away comforted, reflecting upon the extraordinary luck through which he had cured of a toothache without the expenditure of a penny.

Once old Eben Adams, who was considered the stingiest man in the county, went into the doctor's office.

"Doc," he said, "I've got an old snag of a tooth here that's botherin' me consid'ble. Do you s'pose you could yank it out?"

"Certainly." The doctor took out his forceps and quickly executed the task.

"How much do you tax?" the old man queried.

"Fifty cents is the regular fee for extracting."

Old Eben handed the doctor a ten-cent "shinplaster" and three pennies.

"What do you mean?" the doctor demanded. "You have given me only thirteen cents."

"Sartain," was the response. "I cal'late I've give you enough. You say you charge fifty cents for extractin' a hull tooth, an' I leave it to you to say whether this was any more than a quarter one!" And he put away his pocketbook with the air of one who has met all the requirements of virtue.

The end of the Young Doctor's career in Hillsbury followed one of those tragedies which have been known in the lives of far abler men in his profession. The incautious use of an anesthetic in the case of a patient with incipient heart disease brought death, and the censure of the public was more than the conscientious young man could endure. He sold his practice, moved to a distant state and died only a few years later.

The doctor's weaknesses and mistakes were largely those common in his time. There were great physicians and great surgeons in his day, but they were men of large mind, with native judgement and a sense of initiative—men who were bigger than the fragmentary science of their age. That age was hard on men like the Young Doctor. They would be safer now, when the science they profess is comparatively complete, and when other minds have done the reasoning which they were incapable of doing for themselves.

If the age was hard on the Young Doctor, it was also hard on his patients. Living when he did, knowing nothing of germs or disinfectants, having no fear of mosquitoes or flies, sleeping and studying in air-tight and infected rooms, I wonder that the Hillsbury children ever did grow up.

HILLSBURY FOLKS III
THE PARSONS

Auris Leigh

There were in Hillsbury two churches—the Methodist and the Congregational—and a "Disciple" mission. The name "Christian Church" was entirely unknown in our neck of the woods, and that of "Campbellites" had only a vague significance. When the superintendent of the Methodist Sunday-school, in the midst of that painful performance called "the general review," asked, "What did the new ruler of Egypt do?" little Jimmy Sparks called out, triumphantly, "He put all the Campbellites into bondage!" He must have known that we were a peculiar people.

The "Disciples" owned no church building and held services only intermittently. They were short on finances, but long on debate, and came out strong whenever erroneous doctrines were promulgated in union revival meetings. We children lisped in controversy and contended for the faith of our fathers and mothers while we were still at the knickerbocker and pinafore age. I remember what a sensation was created when Dolly Mason and I stood up in a hysterical "children's meeting" and quoted texts designed to chill the fervor of the occasion. I believe Dolly's text was Romans 10:17, and mine, Acts 2:34. The Congregational pastor looked horrified and the Methodist organist giggled until she came near falling from the organ stool. But we infants were bursting with spiritual pride and saw neither the horror nor the humor of the situation.

We children—"Disciples" and all—went both to the Methodist and the Congregational Sunday-schools. Lest the youth of that time be supposed on this account to have been extraordinarily pious, I hasten to add that our purpose was to have access to both Sunday-school libraries. The books were not much as books, but they were all the printed matter at hand, and so were eagerly sought after. Usually they were strictly religious. I remember one story whose heroine was "hopefully converted" at the age of six and a half. She "testified" in revival meetings and prayed with "seekers" at the altar for a period of a year and a half, and died gloriously just before reaching her eighth birthday. I do not know why such books did not make infidels of us, but good angels must keep children from the harm that pious idiocy would otherwise do them.

All the books were not of this sort. I remember one which introduced in the first chapter an eager youth, a sentimental maiden incarcerated by hard-hearted parents, and a rope ladder devised for the purpose of bringing these two fond hearts together. I do not know how the story came out, for a good mother, more watchful than were the authorities of the Sunday-school, swept down upon us and bore the book away when only the first chapter had been read.

The best part of Sunday-school was the singing, especially that of the Methodist school, where noise rather than harmony was the object. How we used to roar out "The Evergreen Shore," and "There is a Happy Land," and "O golden Hereafter! thine every bright rafter Shall shake with the thunders of sanctified song!"

It was years before I had ceased to think of heaven as a big Dutch bank barn, with gilded beams. There was one song which began, "Never be late to your Sunday-school class, Children, remember the warning! Try to be there, always be there. Promptly at nine in the morning." To this song the more virtuous among us objected strenuously, on the ground that our Sunday-school did not begin until a quarter past nine, and that the words therefore implied an untruth. We were too young to have learned the important lesson that when truth and poetry come into collision, poetry is always given the precedence.

The two churches were so different in their services and spirit that you could almost tell from a person's looks to which he belonged. You could have guessed at a glance, for instance, that Deacon Sayres, the Congregational patriarch, could not have shouted "Glory!" or that Brother Tomkins, the Methodist class leader, could not have passed a contribution box with such impressive dignity as to rebuke miserliness by the very act.

At the Methodist Church there was a choir made up of giddy young people, who sang new and popular religious songs, and passed glances and notes to each other between whiles. At the Congregational church the members of the choir were nearly all gray-headed and nothing livelier was ever sung than

"Plunged in a gulf of deep despair."

I can still recall the shock I received when a visiting clergyman announced, "By cool Siloams's shady rill." In that solemn place it sounded almost sacrilegious.

The young people of the village attended the Methodist church, especially on Sunday night. After the service the boys "lined up" in the long vestibule, and each grasped firmly the arm of the young lady whom he had elected to escort to her home. Sometimes the girl seemed to be surprised, but we all considered this the merest affectation.

No young man ever went to the Congregational church, so far as I knew, unless he became hopelessly engaged to a Congregational girl. After that there was no escape for him.

Brother Baxter, the Methodist pastor, was a loosely built, homely man, whose customary speech was singularly simple and direct, but who spoke with a mighty "roar-ah!" and a terrible "drawl-ah!" when he was in the pulpit. He had a fringe of hair about his head and a fringe of whisker beneath his chin, and great false teeth which closed with a snap. His smile came readily and he always remembered to shake hands with the children. I used to think it strange that such an even-natured man should have times of desiring to shout—it seemed to me he should shout every day or else have left off altogether. The chief charm for me in a revival meeting was the transformation in Brother Baxter from the genial friend of the children to the frenzied petitioner at the "altar." Sometimes on such occasions he came down the aisle to where we children were sitting, and exhorted us to "flee from wrath before the evil days." We did not know what he was talking about, but were of the general opinion that a revival meeting worked some strange spell on our good friend.

Brother Baxter was a man of simple faith. When he tried to be theological I fancy he was rather absurd, for his mind was not built for the solution of abstract questions. But he knew and loved God and there were times when he could say so with telling power.

He had unbounded faith in men, and never was there a sinner so low but Brother Baxter was able to entertain hopes of his salvation.

One year the annual revival meeting went on for a month without apparent results. Usually Tony Byers and his wife, the town paupers, could be counted upon to seek the way of repentance each year when the thermometer touched zero. But even they had failed—Tony's rheumatism having kept him from the means of grace and at the same time acted disadvantageously on his none too amiable disposition. So the revival languished and Brother Baxter was disconsolate.

One morning "Bully" Heading walked into the pastor's study. Brother Baxter, with his ever present belief in the possibility of the apparently impossible, felt sure that the scalawag, so long impervious to his exhortations, had at last felt the stirrings of conscience. So he clasped Bully's hand and pressed him into the easiest chair.

"What can I do for you, Mr. Hedding?" he inquired, sympathetically.

"Wa'al," began Bully, leaning back comfortably and speaking at his usual leisurely gait, "'twas me that kind of counted on mebbe doin' something for you. I guess you're a leetle mite discouraged, ain't you? Sinners are kind of onconsarned about theirselves, I take it—kind of slow about startin' on the road of salvation, so to speak?"

"They do seem sadly indifferent," Brother Baxter confessed.

"Do you suppose some decoy ducks would do any good?" inquired Bully, with the appearance of great solicitude. "Me and my wife and children don' want to go into religion permanent. If 'twould help to start the sinners we wouldn't mind goin' down to the alter just once. I thought mebbe a good starter would do the business. You see, I reason like this: Sheep and sinners is some similar. Get the sheep kinder started through the gap, and all's as good as done. But if you wouldn't care to try it—"

Brother Baxter was a man of great good sense. He did not pause to urge salvation upon the audacious scalawag. Instead, he promptly dropped his big manner and good-naturedly showed Bully out of the study. "You ought to be ashamed of yourself, my friend," he said. You ought to be ashamed of yourself, and I believe you are!"

Dear, faithful, narrow-minded, big-hearted Brother Baxter!—type of the heroic men through whom Methodism stamped itself upon the life of an earlier day! He went to his reward long ago, but even in this world his works and those of his kind still live.

The Reverend James Burdick, the Congregational minister, was very young, had side-whiskers, and read his sermons. Ever since his day I have felt that side-whiskers and written sermons ought to go together.

He was an extremely conscientious young man, and persons who dozed over his preaching were ready to praise his godly life. It was said that he had contemplated work in the foreign mission field, but had been hindered by ill health from carrying out his plans. He knew little of the world's wickedness, and still less of how to fight it in the lives about him, but he knew how to deal justly and love mercy, and walk humbly before his God.

Mr. Burdick had come to Hillsbury unmarried. Naturally his appearance there caused something of a ripple among the pious young women of the town. The four Bingham sisters, all of whom sang in the Congregational choir, looked upon him with timidly admiring eyes, noted his extreme youth, and knew he was not for them. For Miss Fronia, the youngest, was thirty-eight. But there were younger maidens—modest and retiring, as the Congregational maidens always were— who secretly hoped.

It scarcely need be said that the conduct of Mr. Burdick was above reproach. Never was he known to walk home from choir practice with a young lady, not even to make a pretext of giving the organist a list of the hymns for the Sunday following. At church quiltings, where he was usually the only man present, he talked to the eldest and the most decrepit females oftener than to the youngest and most blooming. Not once was it said that he called oftener at the homes where maidens dwelt than at those where there were none.

With such discretion added to his goodness and his reputation for scholarship it may be seen easily that the Reverend James Burdick had a strong hold on the hearts of his people. It seemed strange that this hold should after all have been loosened by a woman, yet this was the case.

One day a dreadful whisper crept through the village. An unbelievable thing had happened. The Congregational pastor was married to Mary Corwin, the giggling organist of the Methodist church! The gray-haired deacons shook their heads and the good women of the Congregational church shed tears.

A month later Mr. Burdick resigned. There was really nothing else to do. It was said that the pretty Mary cried bitterly over having injured his prospects, but that the young minister himself showed an independent spirit, which surprised even his best friends. His wife, he said, was a woman in a thousand. The price of such was above rubies. He was fortunate beyond his dreams in having won the heart of such a woman. If the people of the Hillsbury Congregational Church could not appreciate her, he would fare forth and find people who would.

And he did it. In a Western mission field they have had a long and happy term of service, though Mary is now the stauncher Congregationalist of the two. Their oldest son is a professor in the theological seminary. I believe he is suspected of higher criticism, having expressed some very modern views concerning the authorship of the Book of Lamentations.

Our parsons had their limitations, but what would Hillsbury have been without them?

HILLSBURY FOLKS IV

THE DRUNKARD

Auris Leigh

In speaking of this notable in the singular, I am aware that I lay claim to a state of mortality for Hillsbury which our village certainly did not possess. We had several drunkards, but only one was picturesque. For obvious reasons, I have chosen to write of the picturesque one.

We had two saloons in the village, and one a mile away, on the road to the Great City. When I hear the Christian pessimists of our day grieving over the victories of the liquor traffic, I wish I might transport them back to Hillsbury. I believe I do not overstate when I say that half the young men of the village spent their spare hours in these saloons, and even after the lapse of forty years I sicken at the thought of how many of these youths were carried to drunkards' graves in the little cemetery.

One of the village saloons was kept by Old Leech, a pitiful relic, who had once been a man of means and standing. Now, he asked nothing of life save whiskey enough to keep him in a state of forgetfulness.

The other saloon was kept by Jake Schaeffer, a rosy, smiling little German. He was not in the least ashamed of his business. Indeed, I think he looked at himself in the light of a public benefactor. When, a few years later on, the Woman's Temperance Crusade broke forth and overspread the land, a band of Christian women went to pray with old Jake. He met them smilingly, and knelt with them on the floor of the saloon. When Mrs. Caroline More, principal of the Grammar, had finished a long prayer, Jake interrupted to say, "by Chimminy—she can pray as long as she can whip!" And when the ladies rose from their knees and tearfully begged him to pour his whisky into the street, he took their breath away by delivering an eloquent temperance lecture, in which he set forth the moral beauties of a decent saloon, kept by a devout Lutheran, who read his Bible every day and never allowed a man to drink more than he could stand up under.

Both saloons were chary of Old Bill Higley. Old Bill lived in a tiny shanty at the edge of Skelton's woods. He claimed to be a shoe-maker, and at times he worked for a few days at a time, to supplement the meager allowance doled out to him by the township trustees. After each spasm of industry Old Bill allowed himself a glorious carouse. It was during these carouses that he became picturesque.

For Bill, who was as quiet as a cowed animal when he was sober, and who never stepped inside of a church on ordinary occasions, became spectacularly religious the moment that whisky had begun to fire his veins. He talked every moment, and with weird and impressive eloquence.

"Why do you talk so blame pious?" George Bemis once asked him? "You old idiot, don't you know you're drunk?"

"Certainly, George, m'dear frien'—certainly!" Old Bill responded! "F' I wasn't drunk I couldn't talk, y' unnerstan', George, 'f there's one drop o' grace in my heart, a good drink o' whisky allays brings it out!"

His only companion was Fan, his clever little Scotch terrier. Fan never failed him. If Old Bill slept in the gutter, the patient little animal kept watch beside him. He had taught her a variety of tricks, and when he was sober he took a kind of dumb pleasure in seeing her perform for the benefit of us children. But when he was drunk he seemed to fear Fan's presence as if she had been an accuser. If we saw old Bill coming down the street, with Fan beside him, the dog carrying a basket, which was to be filled from the returns of Bill's township "order," we knew everything was right, and that we might venture forth with safety. But if Bill was swearing at the dog and trying to skulk away from her, we ran to the schoolhouse for protection. Old Bill was drunk.

Just after Brother Baxter moved into the Methodist parsonage, Old Bill, whom he had never seen before, appeared at the door. The good dominie looked upon the strange figure in amazement. Bill, who looked like a whipped cur when he was sober, had the appearance of a wilderness prophet when in the first stages of drunkenness. He was tall, gaunt, bent, with shaggy hair, beard and brows, and with a light in his eyes which seemed to be from heaven until you learned that it was from the other place.

"Brother Baxter?" he said, interrogatively.

"Yes. Welcome, brother. I fear I do not know your name—"

"Never mind." The strange visitant swept the implied question away with the air of one to whom mere mortal names have no meaning. "I came to enjoy the hour of family worship with you. Brother Baxter, I want to sit with you, as under the shadow of a great rock in a weary land."

Brother Baxter was not superstitious, but he was intensely and emotionally pious, with a sense of the literalness of spiritual manifestations which is denied to this generation. His morning prayer had been for every direct demonstration of power from above. What was he to think but that it had been granted to him in the presence of this unworldly guest?

"Come in!" he begged. "We have had our hour of family devotions, but it will be a precious privilege to kneel with you. Come into my study, brother, and let us have a season of worship together."

They went, and Old Bill prayed as only Old Bill when he was at this stage of drunkenness could pray. Brother Baxter wept. Why had he not known that Hillsbury held this mysterious saint? Or did he belong to Hillsbury at all? Had he not been sent from afar on his errand of blessing?

They rose from their knees. "Come again," begged Brother Baxter. "I need you, my friend. Come often."

"Ah, my brother," Bill exclaimed, with emotion, "you are indeed one of the friends of the Lord! I love you, brother, I love you! Come with me," he leaned over and whispered affectionately in Brother Baxter's ear—"come and take a drink!"

It says much for Brother Baxter's simple faith in providential manifestations, to affirm that it was quite unshaken by this experience.

The great man of Hillsbury just at this time was Sam Slatterlee, a big, pompous, overbearing fellow, who had married the daughter of a well-to-do stock dealer, settled himself comfortably in his father-in-law's home, and proceeded to patronize the entire village.

One day Sam was in the post office—which was just then in George Bemis' store—indulging in what the village loafers called "big talk." There was a rather larger crowd than usual, and Sam was enjoying his audience. His disquisitions were interrupted by Old Bill, who entered, with Fan at his heels.

Old Bill was drunk, and one glance told the practiced eye that he was drunk enough to be tipsily fluent. He steadied himself against a pork barrel and listened as well as he could for a moment while Sam continued to brag. Then he broke in suddenly!

"Dust and ashes, brethren—all dust and ashes! Wealth crummle— crummle all pieces—vanity, vanity, vanity—go, too, weep'n—howl— weep'n howl—all dust 'n' ashes 'n' vanity! Sam'll be poor beggar 'n' nex' wor'—poor beggar 'thout a drop o' water t'cool his tongue! Dust 'n' ashes 'n' vanity—dust 'n' ashes 'n' vanity!"

The crowd laughed and Sam's face reddened. "See here, o'd man," he said, "don't you know you're drunk?" You ought to be ashamed of yourself."

"Awful shamed myself—awful!" Bill began to cry softly. He staggered through the crowd and put his arm affectionately about Sam's neck. "I'm poor critter, Sam—desprit poor critter. Lost critter, that's what I am, jes' los' critter. Poor los' drunken critter. I don' ask nothin' for myself, Sam, but one thing I pray for—I pray to see poor, los', undone, hell-doomed Sam Slatterlee throw himself down at the foot 'o the cross an' plead for divine mercy! Won't ye, Sam—won't you, poor los' soul?"

They said Sam swore frightfully. But there were men in that crowd who felt a strange power in the drunkard's incoherent pleading.

Old Bill grew too feeble to go out, and his condition from this time on must have been pitiable. A basket of groceries was sent to him every week by the town authorities, but they refused him whisky, and it was said that his pleadings for it were terrible to hear. For a time he succeeded in deceiving the officers by asking them to send him alcohol for his shoemaker's lamp, but when they found that he did no cobbling, but drank the vile stuff thus provided, they refused to give him any more. So he lived his last days in enforced sobriety, the tortures of an unnatural thirst added to the sufferings of a mortal disease.

One day the Skeltons, who had given him his tiny cabin rent free for twenty years, noticed that there was no smoke coming from his chimney. They hurried over, and found him in bed and near his end, with poor little Fan keeping faithful watch beside him. He wanted the Methodist minister called, and Brother Baxter, always eager for an errand of evangelism, hastened to obey the summons.

The story the dying man told was one which might have made a prophet out of a smaller man than Brother Baxter. As he told it, we Hillsbury children never forgot it, and after the lapse of forty years I can live the tragedy over again.

Old Bill had been a regularly ordained minister of the Methodist Church, and an evangelist of wide influence. Brother Baxter said his eyes kindled even when he was dying, as he remembered the days when his eloquence had called scores and even hundreds of persons to the altar. But he learned by way of New England hard cider to love the taste of intoxicants, and in time he was the helpless creature of his appetite. The discovery of his habit brought shame and havoc to the churches among which he labored, and he slipped away from the familiar scenes, hoping to hide himself among strangers. His wife stayed by him while she lived, but she had now been dead for many years, done to death by the memory of the past and the struggle of the present.

Brother Baxter told us that the remorse of those last hours was beyond the telling. In burning words Old Bill pictured what he might have been and what he might have done if he had been strong enough. For the future he seemed to be quite without hope. "I suppose heaven can't be made such a beautiful place but I would leave it for a drink of whisky," he said.

He died at midnight, and the day following he was buried in the potter's field. Poor Fan was the only mourner. She died a week later. Old Bill was a poor wretch, but I am glad he had Fan.

HILLSBURY FOLKS V

THE SCALAWAG

Jessie Brown Pounds[1]

It is strange, when one really comes to think of it, the directions that local pride will sometimes take. I know of more than one village whose vanity centers in its cemetery vault.

We Hillsbury folks had two objects of pride—our Graded School and our Scalawag. We regarded these as, respectively, the best and the worst of their kinds.

The name of our Scalawag was Bolingbroke Hedding, but he was generally known at "Bully." I believe he had himself adopted this name, probably for advertising purposes.

"Bully" Hedding had seen the world. He had scoured the deck of a man of war, he had fished off the coasts of Newfoundland, he had mined in Colorado, he had hunted in Maine, he had marched in the war with the Army of the Potomac. At least, he said he had done all these things. To this day I do not know whether he was an experienced traveler or merely a born novelist.

To the Hillsbury mind, Bully represented irresistible humor blended with accomplished villainy. He was more than an ordinary village clown. He was a clown whose antics had a sustained purpose. It was for this reason that the small boys admired him and that the preachers held him up as an awful example.

Bully had many trades, none of which seemed to interfere with his daily occupation. This was to sit on a pork-barrel at Wetzel's executing lies of all sorts with great originality of construction and freedom of expression, or else entertaining his present audience with accounts of the tremendous effect produced by his romancing on former audiences. It was thus delicately that he flattered a Hillsbury crowd with the belief that they were less gullible than other people.

That Bully and his family did not starve was due to this habit of mental inventiveness and the trustfulness of the public upon which he preyed. His wife, when judged by Hillsbury standards, was a perfectly incomprehensible person. The story of their marriage was still current.

On one of Bully's periodical visits to his old home in New England he had chanced at a neighborhood picnic, to fall in with a quiet little woman who was a "preceptress" in the village academy. By what arts of the tongue he had worked upon her sympathy it would be impossible to say; perhaps the poor creature had never been wooed before, and for this reason the woman within her was unable to resist. At any rate, he prevailed upon her to marry him within a month from the time of their first meeting, and to come with him to his miserable little cabin on the outskirts of Hillsbury. If she repented of her bargain she certainly made no sign. We of Hillsbury felt a certain awe-stricken pride in her learning, which we considered prodigious, and a few boys who were ambitious for a college education employed her to tutor them in higher mathematics. This was almost her only means of contact with her neighbors. What her lonely life was like, and whether or not she really admired her Scalawag, none of us ever knew.

Bully drew a pension. Seated on his favorite pork-barrel and expectorating tobacco juice with wonderful precision of aim, he told how this remarkable piece of luck had come to him:

"It's certainly true," he began, "in these days of criticism and suspicion, when a feller can't mix in enough bad eggs with the good ones to make sure of a decent profit, that a stiddy income from Uncle Sam is a mighty pleasant sort of incident. I usedter kinder hanker after a pension, for it did seem to me that a feller who had served his country for ninety days, and helped to end a bloody and turrible war, deserved some sorter financial recognition at the hands of his country. There was old Cap Farnsworth, now—he ain't got his pension all right. Sure, he had four years' service an' permanent disability, but I maintain the country owes more to me than it does to him. 'Cause why? 'Cause that old fire-eater hain't got one mite of objection to war. He'd have gone on fightin' till the crack o' doom, an' liked it. But I didn't. I was down on the fightin' front the first smell o' powder, an' you see I brought things to a double-quick stand-still. So I thought something was due me, but I didn't know how to get my hand on it, till the Old Doctor put a notion in my head. Says he, one day, when I'd been spinning a little yarn about the way I done old Shailey Roberts out of his gray horse, 'Bully,' says Old Doc, 'you're crazy as a loon,' says he. He meant this for a kind of compliment to my gift of talk, you understand.

"'Doc,' says I, 'would you have any objection to makin' affidavit to that?'

"'What for?' says he.

"'To git me a pension,' says I. 'I was in a tent once when a shell went whizzin' by, takin' a piece right out of the canvas. I b'lieve it made me be loony, an' I want a pension,' says I. The Old Doc was game, an' he stood by me. He was an old soldier himself, and not the feller to desert an old comrade. So he signed my papers an' I got my pension. It ain't much, but to a feller of simple tastes an' the soul of a philosopher I owe it comes in handy."

If Bully had been asked to name his calling, he probably would have said that he was in the butter and egg business. He was wont to declare that earlier in his career he had found this business profitable and interesting. But of late he was meeting difficulties.

"The human mind seems to delight in harborin' mean suspicions of its feller human minds," he was accustomed to say, "which makes the pursoot of your livin' by means of your wits more complicated every year. Now, time was when my business was easy an' pleasant. I could pick up all the stale butter an' eggs for forty miles round, an' be sure of findin' grateful and appreciative buyers. But times is sadly changed. For years it has been my cheerful custom to buy up the soap-grease butter of our friend Wetzel, here."

The storekeeper pretended to occupy himself with folding a bolt of calico, but Bully would not let him escape: "Sho, Joe, don't blush, the butter smelt to heaven, an' you know it. But I couldn't refuse the stuff, at ten cents a pound, for I calc'lated there was a way to combine rancid butter with genius in such a way as to make it sell. I packed it in tidy little crocks, with a skinny layer of Mother Bauder's best home-churnin' on top—twenty-five cents a pound I had to pay the old lady for it, but it brought the returns, all right. Then I put on my oldest clothes—which is sayin' a good deal—splashed a little extry mud on 'em, harnessed Dobbin to the green spring wagon, an' drove into the city. There I hitched my horse before the most elect houses on the bullyvard, rung the front doorbell, an' insisted in seein' the lady of the house. Sometimes I struck a man in buttons, an' got an exodustin. But if 'twas a girl that opened the door I al'ays stuck to it till I got her to call her missus. Then I told my story, about my leetle farm, an' my cows that was treated as members of the family, an' my nice old woman, and the spring house where we kept our milk, jest like the one her grandmother must have kept her milk in. Then I begged her to git a spoon an' taste the real country article. She'd do it, an' of course she'd buy, for nobody could resist Mother Bauder's best. She'd pay me an extry price for it, too, smilin' while she counted out the change, to show she wasn't above an ignorant old farmer an' callin' after me to come to the back door next time. But there wasn't no next time, that was the one drawback. I had to spot that house an' give it a polite margin in the future. But wors'n that has come. Last week two of them mean-heartin', suspicionin' females jabbed their spoons right down through the layer of Mother Bauder, an' brought up a taste of Wetzel's soap grease! One of 'em even threatened to have the police after me. I'm afraid there's nothin' ahead of me but ruined fortunes an' a seat on this pork-barrel for the rest of my life.

This was indeed our Scalawag's fate. As he grew old, he became less inventive and more garrulous. Where the boys of one generation had admired and imitated him, those of the next played jokes upon him. In his old age he was indeed a sorry figure. Even Wetzel grew tired of him, and the Scalawag bid in vain for an audience to whom he could tell his old stories over. He drank more and more heavily and the wit upon which he had prided himself was stolen, long before he died, by the enemy he had put into his mouth.

His son, as dishonest as his father and less shrewd, went to the penitentiary for stealing horses. His daughter ran away with a circus rider. His wife died—of grief, no doubt, though no one ever really knew, for her long reserve was unbroken.

And so, deserted and unmourned, Bully himself died, to be speedily forgotten. I should not have remembered him now, save for two items which I read in today's paper. One was a paragraph concerning the inspection of dairy products under the pure food law of the state. The other was an account of the effort being made by a group of women's clubs to abolish the loafers' seats from village stores.

The world does move!

Note

1. The Editors of the *Christian Evangelist* on Sept. 7, 1911 (1270) explain the transition from Auris Leigh to Jessie Brown Pounds: "If you have any delight in real folks, you must not miss those of Hillsbury, as they are presented from time to time in our story pages. We have had the schoolma'ams, the doctor and the drunkard. Now comes the scalawag. The fresh country air blows through each chapter. The goodness of bad people comes out redeeming and the badness of good people is honestly apparent. Somehow they seem not only like acquaintances of ours, but 'most like kinfolks. Mrs. Pounds has concealed until now her identity as the writer of these delightful sketches under the pen name of Auris Leigh. When we made the discovery she consented to have all our readers share the secret. So we have promptly put her own honored name at the head of the story."

RACHAEL SYLVESTRE, A STORY OF THE PIONEERS

A WORD BEFOREHAND

It is the year of our Lord, Eighteen Hundred and Eighty-two, and I, Joseph Arrondale, am seventy-six years old.

As the years come, I feel the garrulity of old age creeping upon me. At first it manifested itself in my tongue, and threatened to make me a nuisance to my neighbors, who had before this regarded me as an inoffensive and rather slow-spoken old man, not at all given to reminiscences. But, fortunately for them, it may be, my increasing deafness has shut me off more and more from the society of my fellows; so I have taken to my pen, which is certainly, in my case, a comparatively harmless instrument.

Fifty years ago, when I was a country schoolteacher, my goose-quill was my companion through many a night, spent before the roaring hearth-fire. I could sharpen it a bit, too, for the sake of a sly thrust at some adversary in our little debating school. But now for many years I have been little accustomed to use the pen, and as I take it up I find it speaks no language but that of memory. It is in the past that an old man lives. It is of the past that I wish to write.

There are few left who will care for my memories. At seventy-six every man is in a sense an exile—at the best, a wayfarer, who lies down to sleep in a tent by the roadside, and dreams of reunions that are to be.

But I am not yet quite alone. Some of those whose blood is akin to mine are still spared to me. And there is a certain four-year-old boy, by name Sylvestre Arrondale the Third, for whose eyes I pen these pages. Those eyes are dark and soft, like a pair I once knew; and this is one of the many reasons why I love the child.

Long before Sylvestre Arrondale the Third shall be old enough to understand what I shall try to write, all those who carry these memories in their hearts will have passed away. And so I set them down, in my clumsy fashion, not only because the story itself may give him passing pleasure, but because it is the story of those from whose blood the fountains of his own life are filled. To know their history may help him to understand his own nature and to guide his course aright.

I shall have as little as possible to say of myself, beyond what is necessary to set forth the lives of others better, and better worth knowing, than I. The boy who reads these pages may guess some things concerning the lonely old man who writes them, which are nowhere set down in so many words. There is much, indeed, which I have sought neigher to reveal nor to conceal, that belongs of right, if he shall choose to read it, to the boy whose eyes have the Past written in them.

Since I must in any case soon leave this world, I wish to stand to record here that I leave it with no bitter feeling toward any, dead or living. If I tell the faults of some who have long been dust, it is only that other lives may be understood and rightly judged.

And I desire to bear witness, at the close of a long life, not free from heavy sorrows, that God has been good, that my seventy-six years have been meted out in mercy, and that when the call shall come to go to him and to those he is keeping for me, I shall be glad that I have lived and glad to die.

CHAPTER I

THE ARRONDALES

There were two of us, Stephen and Joseph Arrondale, with a gap of six years between us. We were alike, except that in everything Stephen was stronger than I. I never came within four inches of his stature, although I am by no means a short man. He was fleeter of foot than I, and surer of aim, and had more endurance in the woods or the harvest-field.

When it came to books, we were more nearly matched. He used indeed to say that I went ahead of him here, but this was not true. Perhaps I was a little quicker with my pen or with figures, but he was patient and clearheaded and he loved to know; so, in the end, I think he was beyond me.

We had grown up in the woods of northeastern Ohio, but with advantages a little beyond those of our neighbors. My father was a Connecticut man, with a quick wit and a knack at making money by honest dealing. I have often thought that he must have been born with a knowledge of the world, but it seemed that so much of it could not have been acquired in one short lifetime.

He made many good bargains; the best one he made when he married my mother. I have heard him say that when he, the enterprising Yankee farmboy, asked her, the bonny little Yankee schoolma'am, to marry him and go with him to the wilds of Ohio, she said, "Why, Samuel! you didn't suppose I'd let you go alone, did you?"

My mother always laughed at this story, and said father would make a good novel-writer—he was so good at inventing. But we boys knew very well that she loved my father with a beautiful, self-forgetful love, and that her pride and faith in him had made him a far better man than he could ever have been without her.

How shall I describe my mother? I shall tell you of more beautiful women by and by, but her face had a light upon it such as I have never seen on any other. She did not often say "God bless you!" to us boys, but she looked it every time she spoke. I have never known any other woman, past her early girlhood, who laughed so much. I know now that she must have laughed sometimes when her heart was heavy, but I did not guess it then. I only thought how the light ripple of laughter was like the sound of the brook in the meadow, as it flowed over the pebbles and went to join the larger stream just beyond the mill. I suppose this is why, even now when I am an old man, the sight of a clear stream flowing over white pebbles always makes me think of mother.

She was the daughter of a minister, who had ventured beyond the customs of the time and taught her Latin and algebra. Those of our neighbors who were a little jealous on account of her accomplishments called her strongminded. But most of them liked her, and merely said that she was "smart."

The death of her father and mother had early thrown her upon her own resources, but she had found it easy to gather together a little school from among the children of her friends. She had not needed her Latin and algebra, but she kept both stored away in her memory, and they came into use when she had two book-loving boys of her own to teach.

She was a deeply pious woman, a Christian by instinct, a Baptist by inheritance, and a Calvinist by logic. Given wrong premises, and there was never a more logical system than Calvinism. I heard my bright-witted mother argue it all over with my father a hundred times, as I lay in my trundle bed and watched the snapping pineknot fire, and I wondered each time at the neatness with which she fitted foreordination into predestination, and predestination into sovereignty, and all the rest. But even then I wondered if she didn't mentally quarrel with her false premises, and reason all the harder to keep down the questionings of her loving heart.

Father was not religious, and this was that dear heart's heaviest burden. He listened pleasantly enough to my mother, but in the end he would always say: "Well, Abigail, I don't see but what the Lord has settled the question; so there is nothing for you and me to do. I'd like to bear you company in the next world, but as long as I'm not called in that direction I see nothing for it but to go with you as far as I can, and say goodby to you when I must."

This hurt her a little, for I suppose she thought it was said to tease her. Besides, she loved my father so much that I am sure she was terrified at the thought of spending the future apart from him. So she usually stopped talking for that time. But it would not be long until the question came up again, to be dropped again in the same way.

The Western Reserve was later settled than other portions of Ohio, so that my father and mother were pioneers.

My father cleared his patch of ground and built his one-room cabin, and there Stephen was born. The clearing was a large one when I came into the world, but I was ten years old before the first log cabin was superseded by another and larger one.

Our neighbors were for the most part Connecticut people, like my parents, as poor as they were, and no poorer. This is as much as to say that there was no poverty at all among us, for where there is equality there is no burden.

Stephen and I went to school in winter barefooted, or with homemade sandals of bark strapped upon our feet, but we did not suffer, either in our feet or in our pride. There were other barefooted boys at school, and our blood was young and warm.

I think I was about eight years old when father came in one day and said:

"We are to have new neighbors, Abigail. That man from the East, who has been looking around here for a week or two, has bought out Richard Sandborn. He seems to have plenty of moneys they say."

And, not being a prophet at eight years old, I little dreamed what the coming of the Sylvestres would mean to Stephen's life and mine.

CHAPTER II

THE SYLVESTRES

It is about our neighbors, rather than about ourselves, that I shall try to write. If, in spite of this promise, I have a good deal to say about the Arrondales, you will understand it is because the Arrondales get in the way of my story, and have to be got out.

The first time I ever saw the Sylvestres was, as I have already hinted, when I was about eight years old. We were to have a three months' school that summer, and Stephen was to go, though he was fourteen years old, and other boys of his age were kept at home for the sake of the farm work. Mother always insisted that we must have such a chance to study as we could get, and father always gave in to her about it. I think he liked to give in to mother.

Serena Bly was to teach the school. Mother thought highly of Serena, because she had "government." From the toes of her ample shoes to the top of her big horn comb she seemed to represent correct discipline; and we all respected the representation. It was said that she had quelled three schools from which the male teachers had been forcibly ejected by mutinous pupils.

The Blue Brook school was a comparatively easy one, and I suppose that Serena took it after many trying experiences in the line of discipline, just as she might have picked up her knittingwork after doing a large washing. It was mere play to her. But none of us who knew her fame ever dreamed that it would be play for her pupils.

Serena could parse, too, and had, far and wide, the distinction of being "a good grammarian." It was said that she had parsed every sentence in "Paradise Lost," merely for recreation; and that she knew every grammatical pitfall in Young's "Night Thoughts." I never had occasion to test her knowledge as far as this, and so I can not vouch for the truth of the statement. But I can see her sharp, greengray eyes, even now, watching my early struggles with the mysterious science of language, and can recall the catlike little springs she used to make at my failures, as she cried out, "What case did you say?"

It was not easy to secure a teacher who even professed a knowledge of grammar; so the district took a natural pride in Serena.

The morning that school "took up," Stephen and I started out early, in the hope that some of the other boys would be early also, and that we might have a play before going to our task. When houses are half a mile apart, boys are naturally scarce articles, and we seldom had playmates except at school.

We had gone as far as Blue Brook—the little stream from which the schoolhouse got its name—and were in sight of the schoolhouse, when we saw two little girls trudging on ahead of us. They had on blue calico dresses and pink sunbonnets, and I remember that the larger one had pushed back her bonnet so that it hung by the strings about her neck. The most remarkable thing about them, to my eye, was the fact that they both wore shoes. I had never before seen a child wearing shoes in mild weather and on a weekday.

"They are the new people," Stephen said. "They are from the East. That's why they're dressed up so."

We had grown up with the idea, which I suppose our mother must have given us unconsciously, that all Eastern people were elegant and polished. I looked at the little girls with a new curiosity.

When we overtook them we found them in difficulty. Some one had taken away the bridge of logs that usually spanned Blue Brook, and there was no way to cross except by wading.

"We'll spoil our shoes, Rachel," the little one was saying. "And we'll get all wet—you know we will." She seemed just ready to cry.

I think it was as easy for Stephen to be kind to people as it was to breathe. "Never mind, girls," he said. "I'll carry you over. I have no shoes to spoil, you see."

The little sister looked out shyly from under her pink bonnet. I can see the great brown eyes and the sweep of their long curling lashes, even now. I have loved and watched the beauty of childhood all my life, but I still think hers was the most beautiful childface I have ever seen. I wish I had a picture of it, to put beside that of little Sylvestre Arrondale.

The older girl looked first anxious and then determined. Her face was as striking as that of her sister, but her eyes were sharper, and the lines less delicate. "I'm too big to be carried," she said. (She was, as I learned afterwards exactly eight years old—four months younger than I.) "Besides, I don't know you." She sat down on the bank and began to take off her shoes.

"Mayn't he carry me?" begged the little sister.

Stephen did not wait for Rachel's answer. He picked up the little creature, carried her across, and held her by the hand until Rachel came over, holding her shoes and stockings tightly grasped in one small brown hand.

I did not like Rachel, for I thought she had snubbed us. But Stephen was fourteen, and I suppose no girl of eight could put him out of countenance.

He actually got down on the ground and dried Rachel's feet with his clean slatecloth. I hated her for accepting this act of condescension from one so far her superior, and especially for her scanty acknowledgment of it. I was not used to seeing people slight Stephen, and if I had not liked little Martha so well I should have set her sister down as a contemptible little aristocrat, worthy of no further thought.

But Stephen was magnanimous by nature, and as we parted at the schoolhouse door he patted Martha's hand and said, "I'll carry you over every morning, if you want me to. And your sister, too, if she'll let me."

The schoolhouse was of logs, with slab benches and puncheon floors. We boys dug our bare toes down between the logs of the floor and into the chinking of the walls, as we sat at the plank desk which ran around the outside of the room and wrestled with our pothooks. I was just learning to use the quill, which afterward brought me so much happiness; but Stephen was already quite an artist with his, and Serena had written at the top of his sheet of foolscap, in bold script, the copy,

> "Many men of many minds;
> Many birds of many kinds."

We were in the very midst of these exercises when a chorus of screams arose on the girls' side of the house. In a moment half the girls in the room were standing on the slab benches, and many of them were crying noisily.

It did not take me long to discover the cause of the disturbance. A common striped snake had crawled up through a crevice in the floor, and was calmly surveying the situation. This was a frequent enough occurrence, but snakes are something that women folks never seem to get used to.

The two Sylvestre girls were quite near me. Martha had climbed upon a bench, and was hiding her face in her sister's dress. I dare say that Rachel was frightened, but she patted Martha's hand and whispered to her not to be afraid.

In a moment Stephen had seized the shovel, which chanced to lie near, and had made an end of the reptile. In another moment Serena Bly, who had been busy in another part of the room, was upon us, and saw what had happened.

"For shame, girls!" she said. "Afraid of a harmless reptile! If you make such a disturbance again, you will be punished severely—every one of you. As for you, Stephen Arrondale, you have been very unnecessarily officious. If you kill any more snakes without permission, you will feel the cut of the birch afterward."

I thought little Martha was rather more terrified by this harsh speech than she had been by the snake. Rachel's nostrils quivered, and I thought she was on the verge of "answering back" to Serena Bly. It was well for her that she controlled herself.

As for the rest of us, we cared little for Serena's threats, not because we doubted their sincerity, but because threat and punishment were both so familiar to us that we took them as a matter of course. Children were far less considered in those days than they are now, and we accepted life as we found it.

I noticed that, at the noon hour, while the rest of us laughed and chatted over the contents of our dinner pails, the Sylvestre girls sat by themselves and ate in silence. I think they were too proud to make overtures to the other girls, and the other girls were too bashful to approach them. As I have said before, we were not used, in Blue Brook school, to children with shoes on.

It was a great surprise to Stephen and me, when school was over, to find Rachel and Martha waiting for us.

You are a good boy," said Rachel, looking straight into Stephen's eyes. "It was brave of you to kill the snake. If that woman had tried to hurt you, I would have made her stop."

I was about to explain the difficulty of this proceeding, but Stephen gave me no chance. "What are boys for, except to kill snakes?" he asked, smiling.

"And carry girls over the river," put in Martha, shyly.

"That isn't a very big river," Stephen told her. (We were back at Blue Brook by this time.) "But there is no need to carry you over now. We boys came out and put the logs back where they belong. Take hold of my hand, and you will find it a fine way to cross."

As I have said before, I was only eight years old, but I considered myself a very long way from babyhood. So my dignity received a severe shock when Rachel, stepping on the log first, turned and said to me, carelessly, "You can take hold of my hand, if you want to, little boy." But I took her hand, and knew that I was honored.

After that, for many years, it was our habit to walk home with the Sylvestre girls. In time, I grew used to Rachel's fine airs, and grew rather to admire them. As for Martha, she had no fine airs, and was everybody's darling.

I remember that my feelings received quite a shock when I learned what accomplished persons our new acquaintances were. I could read in the spellingbook as far over as "baker," and considered myself quite advanced. But little Martha, who was only six years old, was assigned to read with me; and I found that, in spite of a most bewitching lisp, she read quite as well as I did. As for Rachel, she, when asked to show her readingbook, walked up to the teacher with a neat calico-covered copy of "The American Preceptor," and read, as I told Stephen afterwards, "like talking." It was the first time I had taken hold of the idea that reading and talking had anything in common.

The proficiency of the two little girls was quite a spur to me. I told my mother about the "American Preceptor," and I think the matter touched her pride a little, for heretofore her boys had been considered rather in advance of the other children of the neighborhood. So she got out for me Stephen's discarded book. (He read now in the "English Reader," and knew pages of its selections from Addison and Johnson by heart.) When my chores were done at night I used to sit on the doorstep, with the last rays of daylight on my page, spelling out the words; and now and then my mother would come to look over my shoulder, to help me with a hard word, and to say, "Keep right at it, my boy, and you'll be up with Rachel Sylvestre, sometime,"

My hour of triumph did indeed come. Before the term was over, one morning, when I had won special favor in Miss Serena's eyes, she advanced to face the entire school, and announced, in the tone of one conferring a title:

"Hereafter, Joseph Arrondale will read with Rachel Sylvestre."

There, now! I wonder if I am not saying more about the Arrondales than about the Sylvestres!

CHAPTER III

THE HARVEST DANCE

There have been times in my life when it seemed to me a pity that we did not always stay children.

Talk about "achievement" and "possession"! Who is the richest landed proprietor in the world, if it is not the little child? He owns all of the earth that he can see, its wooded hills, its daisy-starred meadows, its fertile valleys. He owns acres and acres of the blue sky above him, and would scorn to part with even a small strip of his possessions. He is inclined to think that a corner of the moon, and one or two of the stars, belong to his portion, and that he will go up and survey them as soon as street car connections shall have been established.

It is a temptation to me, now that the old man's love of what is remote is upon me, to write of those days when life was new, and when the voices of the world had not drowned the songs of birds or the whispers of angels.

But I know my weakness, and realize that these pages will never be filled out if I permit myself to dally by the way.

In our way we grew up, Stephen and I. It was not the worst way. Stephen was, as I said at the beginning, a tall, fine fellow, a little shy and quiet, but open and manly, clean and honest, with a skillful hand and a tender heart. As I have also said before, I seemed on the surface somewhat like him, but I was in every way less a man. In all ways there was more than the difference of our years between us. We both had a bit of temper. Mine was lasted, but his was conquered early, poor lad!

It was the summer after my seventeenth birthday. Stephen and I were working through haying at Colonel Sylvestre's, not for money, but for neighborliness. Most of the young men of the community were there, for in those days of the slow scythe and cradle the operation of haying and harvesting was a serious one.

Yet, on the whole, it was more of a frolic than a task. We dared one another to daily competition in our work, and made merry over it with song and story. Stephen was a fine singer, and his companions called on him every day for the few songs he knew.

We were royally feasted, for Mrs. Sylvestre and Rachel were famous cooks, and they served us with their best. My own folks were frugal livers, and the table set for us at the Sylvestres' seemed to me like splendid luxury. I remember to have been surprised at the quantity of crockery set forth, and to have wondered how my mother managed to get along with such a slender stock as she possessed.

Colonel Sylvestrehe had been in the war of 1812 was the most imposing man, both in looks and manner, that I had ever seen. He was six-feet-four, portly but not heavy, and with a soldier like carriage which seemed to make his slightest movements important. His hair was prematurely white, and he wore it long, even for the fashion. His talk was entirely unlike that of any other man I knew. He had read a great deal, and his sentences had a stately, highstepping style that contrasted oddly with the Yankee-Ohio dialect of the backwoods.

Mrs. Sylvestre was a dark, angular woman, with an intellectual face and sad, brown eyes. Rachel had her cut of features, but without her angularity or sadness of expression.

People were beginning to call Rachel a beautiful girl. She was as slim and graceful as a willow-tree, and her great eyes flashed and glowed and cooled like the embers on the hearth. I remember to have wondered one day, as she flitted here and there and cut slices of her own snowy bread and poured out fragrant coffee for the hungry men, whether any sorrow or change would sharpen her face into a spiritual likeness to her mother.

What made Mrs. Sylvestre a sad woman I could not guess. Judged by the narrow standards which my experience afforded me, her lot was most fortunate. Her husband had more land and honors than any other man in the neighborhood, and her daughters were envied by every girl for miles around. Perhaps the look of sadness was, after all, only an expression she wore through habit, as she wore the neat white cap over glossy locks which certainly no one could care to conceal.

Rachel was her father's pride, and Martha was his pet. I fancy girls were older at seventeen and fifteen then than they are now. At any rate, the young girls I see about me nowadays seem to me much less staid and womanly than these seemed then. Rachel kept her father's accounts with exquisite neatness, and Martha's needlework was the pride of the neighborhood. Their accomplishments were those of a bygone time, no doubt, but they were womanly and daughterly, and at the time they were thought of highly.

Rachel sang well, though she had never had what they call now "voice culture." She seemed to dislike anything like parade of her talent, but her father was very proud of it, and often asked her to sing for us in the evening.

"My eldest daughter has a melodious voice, albeit not strong," the colonel used to say. I think Rachel's voice was fairly strong, but it was not considered proper for a man to give his children unqualified praise.

One night Stephen asked Rachel to sing, "Come, Ye Disconsolate." He did not care for the religious sentiment of the hymn, perhaps, but its associations meant much to him, for it was a favorite with our mother. Beyond this, the noble air, no doubt, appealed to his ear.

Rachel frowned slightly, and looked at her father. He shook his head. "I think Rachel is not in the habit of singing the piece you mention," he said, with grand politeness.

Martha slipped her hand into her father's. "I think it is a beautiful piece," she said, with her winsome smile.

Her father smiled back at her indulgently, but Rachel sang no more that night.

The incident would have made no impression upon me, had it not called up the statement I had often heard that Colonel Sylvestre was a bitter infidel, and that he kept "The Age of Reason" on his table instead of the Bible. I had never heard him say anything about his opinions, but no doubt they had influenced Rachel, who was the constant companion of her father.

We boys slept on the hay in the big barn. I have slept on few better beds since, judging from the soundness of my slumbers.

One night some one proposed an impromptu dance on the floor of this same barn. Colonel Sylvestre sanctioned the idea very heartily, but cautioned us about using lights, as there was still a quantity of old hay in the loft, and a straw stack just outside.

"The amusement of the young people is a very desirable object," he said, in his fine way, "but scarcely to be purchased at the cost of my buildings and stock."

"The moonlight is good enough for us," said Ross Turner, who was keen for the frolic. "We can see enough by it to have a power of fun."

The colonel compromised by allowing torches for the fiddlers, and, our day's work being done, Stephen and I started off in a big wagon to gather up the girls in the neighborhood. Thus informal was society, even among the upper ten, in that far-agone time of which I write.

I tell things as they were. The farmer who did not set forth good whisky for his hands in harvest was accounted mean and miserly. Colonel Sylvestre's whisky was good and plentiful, and some of those who had partaken of it freely in the harvest field that day partook still more freely at the dance. The whisky was a better article than the vile stuff which bears that name today, but it was whisky.

Ross Turner, long before the evening was over, became even more silly than nature had made him. Arabel Holcomb needed nothing to improve upon nature. He made foolish jokes, and she giggled at them until he thought they were good. Between drink and vanity, he was in a pitiable state.

Rachel danced but a few times. I suspect that she cared little for our rude amusements, though she made pretense that her duties as hostess kept her busy.

About ten o'clock, Ross Turner sauntered up to Rachel and said, in a familiar way, "Come and have a turn, Rachel."

Talk about seeing things in people's faces! I wonder if any other face ever showed as much as Rachel's did that night, when she turned to Ross, her nostrils dilating and her eyes flashing, and said, in the terribly quiet voice I learned to know well afterward, "If I dance, I shall dance with *a man*!"

Ross slunk away, and I saw him no more that night. In a moment Stephen came us, and said, "Are you not going to dance with me just once, Rachel?"

She did not turn her head toward him, but she answered, pleasantly enough:

"Not just now. Ask again in half an hour, and I will tell you."

He must have asked her again, for in half an hour they were moving over the floor, and everybody was looking after them. They were both tall. He was nobly built, and she was exquisitely graceful. Both had a certain high-born manner, which I do not know how to describe, but which seemed in a way to set them apart from the other young people of the neighborhood. Perhaps it was family pride that put the idea into my head, but it seemed to me that the young women were envying Rachel almost as much as the young men envied Stephen.

Once, as they came near me, I heard Stephen say, "Oh, but this is pleasure!"

And in the light of the torches I thought I saw a frown on Rachel's face, as she answered:

"It has always seemed to me a rather childish pleasure."

I was not at all displeased with this, as I was young enough to think it rather charming for a pretty girl to be perverse.

When Rachel came by again, she asked me to go to the house and look for Martha, who was mysteriously vanished.

As I entered the unlighted kitchen, I heard Martha saying:

"But you do not think it wicked to dance, do you, mother? I will never do it any more, if I make you unhappy."

"No, no, child do not mind me at all. I do not think it is wicked. I wish you to please your father in all things, as you know. I was brought up differently, and I can not enter into your pleasures, but I have no desire to deprive you of them. Go back and enjoy yourself, my child."

I would have slipped out without being seen, but the jar of the door betrayed me. Martha was kneeling on the floor, with her hands in her mother's lap. I could see only outlines in the moonlight, but I guessed there were tears in the girl's eyes. She sprang to her feet.

"It is I Joseph," I said. "Rachel has sent me to say she needs you," I said awkwardly. But Mrs. Sylvestre spoke at once:

"Go back to your company, daughter. You have been away from them too long already."

I thought Martha was trembling as we went back to the barn. She was a loving, sensitive creature, and could never bear to have any one near her unhappy.

"Mother's parents were very strict Presbyterians," she said; "they thought dancing and all such amusements were wrong. She agrees with father about all such things now, only she can't get used to them. I'm so sorry!"

It was two o'clock in the morning when the gaiety was over. The girls were to be Rachel's guests for the rest of the night. As for us boys, we tumbled down upon the hay in our loft with scanty ceremony.

I was not tired. I was only a boy, but I, too, had danced that night with Rachel Sylvestre.

CHAPTER IV

THE CAMP-MEETING

It was only a month or so later that we heard there was a camp-meeting going on in Fullman's woods only six miles away. Excitements were scarce in those days, and we never thought of missing anything that came in our way, whether it was a dance or a camp-meeting.

We had worked hard ever since spring opened, and felt that we deserved whatever amusement we could find. I am ashamed to say that we included camp-meetings in our list of amusements, but such was the case.

I was not in the least inclined to be religious. I admired my mother's beautiful piety, and should have missed it if it had gone from her as I should have missed the light from her dear eyes. But I do not think I had realized, at this time, that it was her piety that made her the dear mother she was. I thought of it as one of her many adornments,—that was all.

Unconsciously, I had fallen into our father's careless way of speaking about religious matters. I went to all kinds of religious meetings or to none, as the fit took me, and got about equal pleasure out of the fervent exhortations of the Methodist circuit-rider and the severely logical disquisitions of the Hardshell Baptist preacher who appeared once in two or three months at Bluebrook schoolhouse. To each in turn I listened with some curiosity. So far as I remember, none awakened within me in a sense of personal responsibility or even a desire for larger knowledge. I am not at all proud to tell this, but it was the fact.

To-night the chief attraction was not the camp-meeting, but the fact that seven or eight of the young people were to take the ride together in a big wagon. For some reason, I can not now understand why, the Sylvestre girls were to be of this number. I say I can not understand why, because Rachel and Martha seldom joined in the rough frolics of the neighborhood, and were thought to be rather exclusive. I suppose their mother's ideas of propriety must have been more strict than those that generally obtained in our primitive society. But for some reason the girls were with us to-night, and entered into the spirit of the occasion with more than their usual animation.

Ross Turner was in the company, and kept close to Rachel. It was said that he had followed her like a mastered dog, ever since she had snubbed him so at the harvest dance. Stephen thought the lazy fellow wanted a strip of Colonel Sylvestre's land. I thought and still think that he was paying tribute to his conqueror.

The ride through the August twilight was beautiful enough to set one's pulses beating to the voiceless music which was in the air. I was ever a lover of the out of doors, and I confess that for me there was more pleasure in the dream the outer world awakened in the inner, than in the light talk of the boys and girls who rode with me.

For the most part we were passing through dense woods, with the faint gray light coming through the opening cut for a road. Now and then we came to a clearing and to the stubblefields from which nature had gathered her harvests, and where she seemed to walk content with the year's work done.

"Joe's in love!" said Ross Turner, at last. I do not know what he or his companions had been saying before, but his coarse words recalled me to myself.

"What do you mean?" I asked rather hotly. "I have always been of quick blood, and then I was but a boy."

"I mean I've spoken to you twice, and have got no answer," said Ross, with his ill-natured grin. "Your wits are wool-gathering. It is plain that you are in love."

I was ready to give him an ugly answer, for I took fire at every foolish provocation. It would be pleasanter when we are old to remember none but pleasant things of ourselves, but I tell the story as it was.

"If Joe is in love, it is with one of his story-book girls," Stephen said. "It is of Rebecca or Rowena that he dreams, not of the pretty girls hereabouts.

"I hope it is of Rebecca, and not Rowena," said Rachel, with a flash of her dark eyes.

"Why not of Rowena?" I asked, laughingly, though I thought I knew what she would say.

"Because Rebecca was worth dreaming about, not a bundle of millinery for men to lose their senses over."

"But is not Rowena the most womanly character?" I asked; not because I thought so, but because I wanted to hear her answer.

"Is it not womanly to be brave and true? Was Rebecca more or less than that? The old and the sick and the little children have a right to be helpless and dependent, but a woman's place need not be with these classes, need it?"

"It not only need not be, but it is not," said Stephen, speaking with a great deal of firmness. "I admire Rebecca, but I admire Rowena, too. A woman may be brave and true, and still keep to the ordinary path of a woman's life. Extraordinary heroism is seldom demanded of any one, either man or woman."

Ross Turner had not read Sir Walter Scott's novels, which we had borrowed of Colonel Sylvestre the previous winter, and had devoured with the avidity of book-hungry boys. He was annoyed by talk in which he had no part, and began to tell what he had heard of the camp-meeting which we were to attend.

"They're getting a big crowd of mourners," he said. "Jack Dasher and the Bailey girls went up night before last. I'll go you what you please that Jack don't hold out six months. I see him yesterday, and I says, "hulloa, Jack, got any religion to spare? I'm pretty nigh strapped myself." 'No,' he says, real serious-like, 'I'm aseekin', but I ain't through yet.' Just wait till chopping-time comes, and we'll catch him swearing in fine style."

"Seeking!" said Rachel, with a curve of her lip and the tilt to her nose that always seemed to give her a scornful expression. "I wonder what they think they are seeking. What nonsense it all is, anyway!"

I can not tell you how this speech startled me. It seemed as if some one had given me a sharp, sudden blow. As I have said, I was not religious, but through my mother's devotion I had learned to look upon piety as a necessary grace of womanhood. I think I must have considered that religion is in some sense natural to women, and that it is easier for them to care for such things than it is for men. I am sure now that I was wrong, and I set down this boyish opinion here merely to show why Rachel's opinion surprised and wellnigh shocked me.

"Foolishness, for sure," said Ross, quite pleased to hear such an expression from Rachel. "Religion is all right for old folks, but we ain't ready to die and go to heaven yet—eh, Rachel?"

"I don't see what being old has got to do with it," she said, her upper lip still curving. "A thing that isn't true, isn't true. A fable is no more truth to a dying man than it is to you or me, although he may be more ready to believe it. A drowning man will catch at straws or at doctrines."

Stephen's firm voice broke in again. "Do you mean that you think the whole thing a delusion?" he asked.

"How can it be anything else? It is a beautiful dream, but beauty without truth is a dream with an awakening."

Martha had not heard our talk. She was sitting on the back seat beside Arabel Holcomb, and the two girls were chattering gaily, now and then breaking out in a fragment of some popular song. In those days Martha seemed lighter of heart and more companionable than her sister. Rachel was often gay, and always quick of tongue, but she seemed at times to be burdened, as if with thinking thoughts beyond her age. It may be that her father's opinions had something to do with this.

As we approached the camp-ground, a burst of song greeted us. The scene was picturesque enough—the crowd of worshipers in the shadow of the great trees and of the gathering night, their faces showing first dark and then light in the uncertain flame of the pine knots burning here and there.

Three or four itinerant preachers, whom I knew by sight, walked up and down in front of the congregation, clapping their hands and keeping time to the music with ecstatic shouts. A local preacher of the neighborhood lined out the hymn. It chanced to be that fine composition of Lady Huntington's which I afterward learned to love:

> "When Thou, my righteous Judge, shall come
> To take Thy ransomed people home,
> Shall I among them stand?"

Careless as I was, the words arrested my attention, even then. Perhaps what I had just heard Rachel say had something to do with it. I know I thought that, if the religion my mother and many other good people believed in were true, I should be but poorly prepared to stand at the judgment seat.

You may be sure our company did not join the circle of worshipers. We threw ourselves down on some logs, just within sound of the preachers' voices, and I fear we were, for the most part, very poor listeners. Other young people began to straggle in, some coming in wagonloads and some on horseback. They were mostly, like ourselves, bent on fun, and we were acquainted with them all, for in those times we knew our neighbors in the next township better than you of today know your neighbors in the next block. So we exchanged jokes and gossip in undertones, and almost forgot that we were attending a religious meeting.

It was only when the "seekers" were called to the mourners' bench that we became really interested. Little Livonia Bailey was one of the first to go. She cried much and seemed much distressed because of her sins; but when the local preacher, in adjuring her to forsake "worldly vanities," pointed to the string of gold beads about her white throat, she sat suddenly upright, and would kneel in prayer no more.

Jack Dasher, on the contrary, was humble and persistent. I liked the determined look of his face, though I could not make out what he was determined upon. He prayed noisily, but in monosyllables; and at last he sprang to his feet, shouting, "I got it! I got it! I got it!" and leaped to and fro in the excess of joy. Whereupon the believers broke into a chorus of "Amen!"

Within the prayer circle was Wesley Wyatt, son of the local preachers who lined the hymns. He had been a schoolmate of Stephen's and mine, and we did not like him. So far as I now remember, there was nothing wrong about him, except that his piety, though no doubt sincere, was of the unctuous and ostentatious sort.

As he walked up and down, encouraging the mourners to continue seeking, Wesley caught sight of us. He made his way through the circle and came at once to where we were sitting.

Martha chanced to claim his attention first. "Child, have you found free grace?" he asked.

"No," she answered, timidly, and shrank closer to Rachel.

Wesley evidently did not think the older sister a favorable subject for his attentions. He turned to Stephen.

"Will you not flee from the wrath to come?" he demanded.

"What about your fleeing from what's already here?" asked Stephen.

Wesley walked quickly back to the circle he had just quitted, and, in the next lull, his voice was raised in what he evidently considered a prayer.

"O Lord," he said, in a voice of seven thunders, "I desire to ask of thee the soul of Stephen Arrondale. Thou knowest what his heart is. Thou knowest that he seeks the company of the godless and scorns the counsels of the righteous. And thou knowest that at this very moment, while he laughs at the danger that threatens and mocks the voice that calls to repentance, that he is hair-hung and breeze-shaken over the gulf of everlasting perdition!"

I hate to write it of the best man I have known in this world, but I believe that if Wesley Wyatt had been within reach at that moment, Stephen would have thrashed him.

CHAPTER V

MARTHA

I will say for myself that I never once thought of blaming religion or even Methodism on account of Wesley Wyatts' very pointed prayer. I thought it due to his conceit and his mistaken estimate of his own virtues, and mentally decided to tell him my opinion when we should next meet.

He had scarcely ended his prayer when a good woman from our own neighborhood arose, and began to relate a marvelous experience. She had seen a bright light shining in the heavens at midnight, so she said, and had heard a voice calling, though she had not been able to make out the words. It was so much like the call of Saul of Tarsus that she had known immediately it was meant for her, and had begun at once to shout for joy.

I had heard the sister's story a good many times, and was not deeply interested in it. So I was rather relieved when an excited brother broke into the pious hymn, beginning

"The devil hates the Methodists."

"I agree with the devil," said Ross Turner at my elbow. Young men who try to be smart can make themselves disagreeable in any age.

I heard a little sob behind me, and saw that little Martha was crying.

Rachel had evidently seen it, too, for she was watching Martha with a peculiar expression on her face. It might have been indignation or pity, or the two combined. Rachel saw that I must have noticed, for she leaned over and said to me in a quick, anxious way:

"Martha must get home. She is quite worn out. She is not used to going about at night. Help me to get her home at once."

"Let's get the horses, Steve," I said, jumping up. "Rachel is tired of this," which I knew was the truth.

By the time we got to the wagon Martha was quiet. I do not know what Rachel had said to her, but I suppose she must have spoken with much firmness and authority to effect such a speedy change. She herself sat on the back seat beside Martha, and the chattering Arabel and I sat on the middle one.

I have ever disliked loquacious women, and I think perhaps Arabel may have given me a prejudice against the whole class. This seems unreasonable, for she was not a really silly girl. Now and then she had something sensible to say; but, unfortunately, she did not defer speech until those rare occasions. Moreover, she had a habit of giggling between every two sentences, and the less humor there was in her tongue the more inevitable became the giggle.

Tonight she was at her worst. She mimicked the exhorters whom we had just heard, and so badly that I was only less ashamed of the badness of the performance than of the irreverence of the performer. She shrieked with merriment over the idea that Jack Dasher had "got religion," and made out a long, imaginary story about how Jack would come to the next dance without a cravat, and line out a hymn for the edification of his old comrades.

"And did you see Martha?" she suddenly broke out. "I thought she was going to 'get it,' sure. Wouldn't it have been great fun to see Martha shouting and carrying on down there at the mourner's bench, and to hear Wes Wyatt praying out loud about her sins?"

Rachel flashed a warning look at Arabel, who had turned about to face the two girls. But before her sister could speak, little Martha was sitting bolt upright. Her eyelids were red from weeping, but the eyes beneath were strangely bright.

"How can you make fun of people when they are so in earnest?" she asked. "There is something terrible in their earnestness. It makes me want to be good."

"Hush!" said Rachel, almost sternly. "Don't talk about that now, Martha. It is all new to you, and you have had your nerves played upon. Tomorrow you will see the folly of it all. Makes you want to be good, indeed! You talk as if you had committed murder or highway robbery."

"I am good," broke out Martha, impetuously. "Those people who talk about 'forgiveness' and 'free grace' speak a language that I don't understand. It is something beyond me."

Rachel's face seemed to grow older and harder. "You are talking the merest foolishness," she said. "What reason is there in such wild rantings as we have heard tonight? No wonder you say those people speak a language you can not understand. No rational being could understand them. Their appeal is not to the mind, but to the nerves. They excite weak natures, and to what end? Wesley Wyatt is a fine example. They make them the victims of wild delusions for awhile, and then leave them weaker and more miserable than they found them."

Stephen swung around from the high seat in front. "Don't lay anything up against Wesley," he said; "I'll have a quiet settlement with him."

"But he meant it for Stephen's good, didn't he?" Martha asked, trembling with eagerness. "Why should he pray, only for Stephen's good?"

"For his own pleasure, may be," said Stephen, rather grimly. I was surprised to see how keenly he had been cut.

Martha said no more, but Rachel roused herself to talk in a spirited way about other things.

Stephen asked her if she would not attend the meetings of our debating school, which would reopen in September. He and I had taken great interest in the debates of the previous winter, and looked forward with eagerness to a renewal of these intellectual tournaments.

"I shall not be here," Rachel told him.

"Not be here?" Stephen and Ross Turner spike together.

"I am going East to school. I have wanted to go for a long time, and at last mother feels that she can spare me. I shall be near her relatives, and spend my vacations with them."

"And how long will you be gone?" asked Stephen.

"Two years."

"Two years!" This repeat of Rachel's words came from all of us.

"The East" was along, weary stage journey away, and two years seemed to our impatient young hearts like two eternities.

"How I wish I was going with you," broke in the voluble Arabel. "I suppose you will have a lot of new frocks. And you will never come home, you know, because you'll pick up a nice beau back East and get married."

I had thought of the same thing. And even if Rachel did not marry some polished man while in the East, how would we backwoodsmen look to her upon her return? For the first time there came to me the longing with which I grew very familiar, to go out and try what I, too, might learn in the great world.

"I shall come back," said Rachel. "Martha must have her turn."

It seemed unnatural to think of Martha as going away to acquire accomplishments, and I did not think she would ever take her turn.

"I suppose you'll learn a whole lot of things," Arabel ventured" drawing and French and all. Good land! How I'd like to get away from here and see something of the world. Betsy Putnam had seven offers while she was in Albany last winter."

Rachel's nose tilted. "I'm not going for the sake of getting offers,' she said. "I want to know something and do something."

"I think you know a good deal already," put in Martha. "And you can do a lot of things."

CHAPTER VI

THE FIRST SORROW

It was nearly three years after this that I saw Rachel Sylvestre again. I chanced to be away working in the woods at some distance from my home when she left for New York State, and she did not return to Ohio for her vacations. I heard of her occasionally through Martha, but postage was expensive and mails uncertain, and an absence from home meant a more complete separation then than it does now.

About twice each year Rachel wrote to Stephen, and her letters, which were read aloud in the family, I regarded as marvels of literary skill. Sometimes Maude Arrondale, mother of Sylvestre Arrondale the Third, writes me a note in angular characters and abounding in adjectives, and I smile to think what the lively Maude would have thought of the Addisonian composition of this maiden of the olden time. Yet, though I may be partial to my own generation, I do not believe Rachel's letters would suffer in the comparison. She was ignorant of much that is taught in the schools today, but she was what people in my time called "serious-minded," and was not altogether devoid of reasoning power.

I have searched much among Stephen's papers for these letters, and have found only one. I think it was the last he received during her absence. I will copy it down here, that the Rachels and Marthas of to-day may know what a schoolgirl's letter was like in my time. It may be I should say that Rachel's conversation was ever far more lively than her letters. These showed more of the precise habits to which she was trained than they did of the quality of her own mind.

I omit a few passages relating to the events of school life and to characters with which this history has nothing to do:

ESTEEMED FRIEND:

Some months have been allowed to elapse since your letter came to hand. During this time I have continued to pursue my studies, though my *diligence* has not, I feel sure, been all that my teachers could desire. Now that my school life is drawing to a close, I could wish that I had profited more fully by the instructions I have received, and that I had *retained* much that I find has been forgotten.

* * *

I trust the good health of your family continues. My own is excellent. I hear people speak of being *"thankful for good health."* I have never learned this pious formula, but I am not sure but I could use it with some truth. I am, I trust, thankful for the *inheritance* of a sound constitution, although it is a debt to *my ancestors* and can not well be paid. Perhaps this is as *good* a kind of thankfulness as the other.

* * *

As the day for my return draws near, I begin to reflect much concerning the future. I fear that, with the stimulus of *daily instruction* removed, I shall soon cease from the habit of study, and become that which I most abhor, an *idle-minded* woman. I say I abhor such a woman, and indeed I do. In my own home I saw a life for my sex *circumscribed* indeed, but with certain *intentions* and *impulses* which saved it from the petty *monotony* which obtains in older communities. Pioneer women, like your mother and mine, must of necessity be spinners and weavers, must brew yeast and boil soap and perform other homely duties day by day. Yet in a certain sense they share with their husbands in the work of making homes in the wilderness, and felt the power of purpose in life not unworthy of them. But I confess that, since I came East; I have often been disgusted by the *gossip* and *tittle-tattle* with which the women here fill up their lives. The more I see the more I am convinced that the so-called "education" of women is *artificial* and *unsatisfactory*. The mind is not trained to cope with real problems and difficulties of life. I can not see why the education of women should not be *essentially the same* as that of men, in order that they may be trained to *reason* correctly and *inform* themselves concerning the great questions and events of the day.

My aunt, with whom I have been living, is a woman of much more than ordinary intelligence, and we have frequently discussed this matter, without, however, arriving at any *satisfactory conclusion*. I trust that, when I return home, my sister can come here and study with more profit that I have done.

*   *   *

Please give my respects to your parents and to all *enquiring friends*. I hope to see them all soon.

With apologies for so *hasty* and *poorly composed* a letter, I remain,

Your friend to command,
Rachel Sylvestre.

Rachel's return to her home was hastened by a sad event—one which proved to have a lasting effect upon us all. Her mother died of pneumonia, after an illness of only a few days. It was a bitterly cold spring and there was much sickness. My father, like many others, was afflicted with a hard cold and severe pains in his chest. Our good mother, always easily alarmed when any one of us was ailing, wanted to call a doctor, but my father objected, as old Doctor Ware lived six miles away, and was none too well pleased when called to take this long ride without good reason.

But that very afternoon Dr. Ware came riding by, and Stephen called him to come in.

"On my way back," he answered, and we knew from the way he drove down the hill that he was anxious. He did call on his way back, and then it was that we learned of Mrs. Sylvestre's illness. The doctor had been called the night before, just at midnight, and had ridden through the dark and cold in response to the urgent summons. He had found her in great pain and much distressed for breath.

"Bad case," he said; and we knew from the way he sighed that he had little hope.

My mother waited only long enough to be told that father's condition was not serious, and then she had Stephen bring out the horses and take her to Squire Sylvestre's. She did not return that night, but that did not surprise us. Mother was the favorite nurse of all the families for miles around, and turned out cheerfully at all hours of the day or night to render service. In this day of the trained nurse there is comparatively little need of such homely ministries. No doubt the new order is better, but the world misses knowing what heroic sacrifice women of my mother's type are capable of. She had left Stephen and me many charges concerning father, who, now the doctor had treated his case so lightly, was determined to be at his work as usual. It was only when all the morning chores were done, therefore, that I ventured to leave him and go to inquire concerning Mrs. Sylvestre.

I knocked at the door of the great kitchen, and Martha let me in. Her eyes were red with weeping, and I felt more sorry for her than I had ever before felt for any one.

"Is she so bad?" I whispered, sitting down beside Martha on the wide settee. The girl nodded. "I heard her talking to father a little while ago," she said. "She could speak only a few words at a time, but she said there were some things she must tell him. Your mother and I were both in the room, so there was no secret about it. She wanted him to give her love to Rachel, and tell her to be a good daughter and sister, and try to fill her mother's place. Then she said the strangest thing.

She said she knew now she had not been as brave as a woman should be. 'You will not blame me for saying so now, father,' she said. 'I have tried to be a good wife, and you will not blame me for saying this now, when I am going to die.' Father tried to quiet her, and told her she was not going to die. 'Yes, I am,' she said; 'and the future is dark. I have tried to be a good wife, and I have let go of everything else. I haven't been a brave woman. But I want you to do one thing, father. I want you to send for a Presbyterian minister, and let me be buried as my mother was.' He told her she was getting excited and mustn't talk any more, and indeed she was so tired that she had to rest. Father sat by the bed a long time, looking oh! so strange and frightened, like a man who has been found out in something. You know my mother was brought up to pray and go to church, but father persuaded her to give it up. And now I am sure she is sorry. Oh, Joseph, don't you believe there is a God, and a heaven where good people go? My mother says if there is a heaven, it is only for the elect, but I am sure that those who try to be good must go there. Don't you think so, Joseph?"

As I think I have said before, I was not what is called a religious boy; but when Martha appealed to me in this way I could think of nothing but my own dear mother's beautiful life, and the feeling I had that the God she loved must be a real person, who would keep her and take care of her. Boys of twenty are seldom infidels—especially boys with mothers like mine. So I answered quickly: "Yes, indeed I do."

Mother came out and asked how father was, and when I told her that he seemed better, she said she would stay on through the day with Mrs. Sylvestre. Then she bade me be sure that the milkpans were kept clean and that father did not expose himself, and hurried back to the sickroom.

At midnight Mrs. Sylvestre died. My mother, who was still with her, said she was unconscious for several hours before the end came, but opened her eyes in one bright look of recognition just at the last.

My first thought when the news came was for Rachel. In this day of the railroad and telegraph, the terrors of death are somewhat softened. Its chamber becomes a place of reunion for those who love each other and who find themselves dawn nearer together than ever before by the bond of a common grief. Each carries away a perfect memory of the dead, to be kept perfect through all the after years. Our memories of the living face become in time confused and interchanged, but our memory of the features in death remain, in its strange beauty and dignity and mystery, until the end.

But at the time of which I write separations were inexorable. Distance had no bridge, save that of a hopeless longing, that but made it seem the greater.

I did not know whether or not Colonel Sylvestre would have respected his wife's wishes had they been known only to himself. As my mother and Martha had heard what she said, there was really no way for him to avoid sending for the minister without showing himself to them as quite heartless; and Squire Sylvestre was not an altogether heartless man. So Stephen drove over to Cordingville, twelve miles away, and brought Parson Ellsworth to preach the funeral. I judge, looking back now upon the occasion, that the sermon was a rather tedious theological dissertation, containing little either of comfort or of instruction in duty for the living. But I was glad the poor woman, who had so seldom had her wish in life, had been allowed to have it in death.

As soon as the slow-going message could reach her, and she could respond to it, Rachel was back in the old home. She was very sad, but she was one of the women whom sadness becomes. In her lively moods I confess I did not altogether like her; for no young fellow of twenty altogether likes a girl whose tongue is nimbler than his own. But now, with her beauty and the accomplishments she had gained in these last years chastened by her sorrow, I was drawn to her as never before.

But, though she was brilliant and more accomplished, she was neither so beautiful nor so winsome as Martha. All who knew the two agreed in this.

CHAPTER VII

THE "CAMPBELLITES"

The years which had made an accomplished and dignified young woman out of Rachel had been busy with our Stephen as well. You young people of today no doubt look upon us old fellows as an illiterate lot, but for his day Stephen was a well-educated man. Indeed, I would be inclined to say that he was an educated man for any day, in whatever goes to make the real value of education.

He worked in the fields and in the woods with a skill beyond any of his fellows, developing such muscles as would have made him a hero in what they nowadays call "athletics." At the same time, he studied all the books he could lay his hands upon, and studied them to good purpose. Many a night I have wakened from sleep to find my brother sitting by the window of our little bedroom, picking out Latin or history by the light of the moon; and what he got in his hard way stayed with him. We were all proud when Sylvestre Arrondale the Second carried off the first honors at one of the great Eastern universities, but I think Stephen had a grip on the fundamentals of an education quite beyond that of our honor man. But this is merely my opinion, and it may be shaded by my partiality. This much I will say, though, that Sylvestre Arrondale the Second, with his mother and sisters to applaud him and his father to write checks for him, never worked for his education as Stephen Arrondale worked for him. (I want to say right her, though, that Sylvestre Arrondale is the finest fellow of his generation, and that he married the sweetest woman who has been born into the world since the women of whom I am writing now!)

I was myself a gangling youth, with great feet and an ever-present tendency to fall over them. The presence of women was, until much later than the time of which I write, a source of great embarrassment to me. But Stephen had a natural courtliness, due, I think, to the fact that he thought little about himself, and was ever solicitous for the comfort of those about him. He had none of the obtrusive gallantry which was affected by the would-be beaux of the neighborhood; but women, old and young, naturally turned to him for help, and he gave it freely.

After Rachel's return, we fell into the habit of spending many of our evenings together at the Sylvestre home. Rachel was able to help us younger ones with our studies, and she and Stephen read or studied together. After our more serious work was done, we ended each evening with an hour of pleasure, spent over the works of Shakespeare or Scott. I never hear the steady patter of rain on the roof but it brings back that rainy week in November when we read "The Merchant of Venice" together; and my Portia is always slender and graceful and looks like Rachel Sylvestre.

These happy times had gone on, I think, for nearly a year, when one day Stephen surprised and grieved us by the announcement that he was going to leave home for an absence of several months.

"I have never been away, you know," he told me. "Home is the best place in the world, but there are some lessons that can't be learned there. I will go for a little while, and then come back and give you a turn at it."

It seemed strange to me that he should be in such a hurry to go, when he had never even mentioned the matter before, and I could not help connecting his plan with Rachel. This I was still more inclined to do when he went away without going over to the Sylvestres to say goodby. I remembered that, on the Sunday night before he announced his intention, he had been there without me; and I easily argued that Rachel might have said something to wound him. She had seemed more gentle since her mother's death than in the old days, yet I was never quite able to shake off my childish notion that she felt above us.

Stephen went to the little town of Rocksford, twenty miles away, where an old neighbor of ours had bought a mill. Mr. Osburn knew Stephen's skill and faithfulness, and readily promised him employment. I shall never forget the morning he went away. My mother looked in his saddlebags again and again, to make sure that he had plenty of linen; and as often as she looked the tears started into her eyes, for Stephen's going made the first break in our happy home life. Even father was dispirited, and it needed Stephen's constant effort at cheerfulness to keep us up.

"Why, mother," he said, "one would suppose I was going to Indiana or Missouri, by the way you take it. It is only a little ride to Rocksford, and I will be coming home often."

I remember this remark of Stephen's, because the words "Indiana" and "Missouri" gave me such a chill. I thought how terrible it would be if he should really go so far away. Sylvestre Arrondale the Second, who runs across Europe every summer for a vacation trip, will laugh at our idea of distances; but that was before man's invention annihilated space.

I can see Stephen at this minute, as he rode down the lane on his roan mare Kitty. I turned away from the open door and put my arm about my mother, and she gave a little sob as she said, "You must be my big son now, Joseph." And I think I really stepped into manhood all at once, as I answered:

"I'll try it, mother."

For awhile I was shy of the Sylvestres, resenting any possible ill-treatment which Stephen might have had at their hands. As I think I have said before, the Sylvestre girls seldom attended the small merrymakings of the neighborhood, and it was some time before I was thrown with them again. I think it was my innate stubbornness that finally led me to resume the old relations.

It happened thus: A Universalist preacher, a man of some natural ability and of quite wide reading for his day, was preaching at the center of the next township, and one Sunday afternoon I took a notion to ride over and hear him. The name "Universalist" meant nothing to me, but I was always anxious to see and hear any one who came from the great outside world of which I dreamed.

It is not of the sermon I heard that I started out to tell; yet it may be worth while to say that it impressed me far more than I had been impressed by any preaching I had heard up to that time. Mr. Vincent, the preacher, was Eastern bred, quoted poetry at great length, and was not without skill in reasoning. The reasoning was directed, I must say, more against the doctrines of others than in proof of his own. Perhaps I liked it the better for this, for I was still enough of a boy to love a debate. At any rate, it pleased me to hear the arguments against a "limited atonement" put into such graceful forms. I had been accustomed from childhood to hearing these arguments stated less elegantly, in the discussions between my father and my mother, and had been half unconsciously convinced by them. In truth, the Universalism of that day was not so much a formal system as it was a protest against the Calvinism of the time, and as such it naturally found many sympathizers.

What I started to say about the service that day was, that I was greatly surprised to see Colonel Sylvestre and Rachel there. Their presence was explained when, after the service, they greeted me cordially and introduced me to their guest, the Reverend Cady Vincent, of Albany.

I learned afterward that Rachel and Mr. Vincent had met during one of her school vacations, at the home of her aunt, and had discovered that their fathers had been friends in boyhood. On such a foundation a friendship was easily established, especially as the two young people had many tastes in common. They met several times afterward, and had exchanged occasional letters since Rachel's return. It struck me as singular that Rachel had never mentioned to me so close a friendship; I was almost certain that Stephen knew nothing about it, unless he had learned it on that last Sunday night. I began to wonder if this girl, whom I had always accused, in my own mind, of being coldhearted, was in love with the elegant young clergyman.

This suspicion aroused me. I would not admit that the Arrondales could be so easily set aside for flowery English and fine broadcloth. To my own surprise, I accepted the Colonel's invitation to ride home with him. I determined to forget my big feet, and to be master of the occasion. And I rather think I succeeded.

Rachel and Mr. Vincent rode on before us. Rachel was mounted on a spirited black horse, and I had never seen her slender figure show to better advantage. She was an accomplished horsewoman, and, when she put her animal on his mettle, Mr. Vincent, who rode a soberer nag, had enough to do to keep up with her. I fancy that her wit outrode his as well at times, for sometimes he looked vexed at her quick replies, and seemed to have no words ready.

I stopped with the party at the Sylvestre home, and partook gratefully of the good things set forth by Martha's willing hands.

Perhaps I might have withdrawn after a short stay, but to my disgust Ross Turner came driving up, and proceeded to make himself at home before the big open fire. He addressed himself more particularly to Martha, while Mr. Vincent continued to monopolize Rachel. Once more I decided that the Arrondales should not be put aside so easily, and settled myself down to spend the evening.

Ross had lost none of his offensiveness since the old days. He and the loquacious Arabel Holcomb were supposed to be lovers; yet ever after one of their frequent quarrels he returned to his old admiration for Rachel, who snubbed him as systematically as if she had been paid a regular salary for the service.

Evidently he found Martha more kind. They had chatted together for some time, when Ross suddenly leaned over and addressed Mr. Vincent.

"Say, I didn't tell you I saw Steve, did I?"

"No; where did you see him?"

"Over to Rocksford. Getting me a buggy made over there. Going to have the best turnout around here when it's done. Yes, took dinner at Osburn's, and had a good visit with Steve. Know he's joined the Campbellites?"

"The *what*?" I demanded.

"The Campbellites. New kind of religion. Got lots of it around Rocksford. Locked 'em out of the churches, and they went to the schoolhouse. Locked 'em out of the schoolhouse, and they took to preaching in the woods. Queer lot, and all the folks around there are down on 'em. Funny, Steve should take up with them, ain't it?"

There was no need that I should answer, for Colonel Sylvestre was ready with a word of cutting comment.

"One would suppose," he said, "that the old forms of religious insanity were quite enough. But it seems necessary that new forms should be developed year by year."

Perhaps the Reverend Cady Vincent did not relish having his own beliefs characterized as "insanity." But evidently he did not care to enter into a controversy with his host, and thought it wiser to vent his annoyance on an absent adversary.

"These Campbellites have a very pernicious influence, I am told," he said. "I have never met any of them, but I have been told a great many strange things concerning their teaching. In many cases they have broken up churches, and even swept preachers and church officers into the current of their belief."

"In short," said Colonel Sylvestre, with a rather unpleasant smile, "they are doing exactly what you are yourself trying to do."

Mr. Vincent laughed good naturedly. "Well," he said, "I admit that we Universalists are still considered too heretical to be respected as heresy-hunters. But the other fellow's heterodoxy is always dangerous, is it not, Miss Sylvestre?"

Rachel turned, and, as she did so, I caught her look of scorn, and saw how utterly Stephen had abased himself in her eyes.

CHAPTER VIII
A LETTER FROM STEPHEN

The next day, Stephen's letter came. It is a document which has had an important bearing upon many lives, and which has been kept carefully for more than fifty years. I am glad I can copy it here, for I feel that it will enable you to know Stephen better than you could possibly know him through any description of mine.

ROCKSFORD, OHIO, May 14, 183–.

MY BELOVED PARENTS:—I have delayed writing, hoping that I might have an opportunity to go home and have a long talk with you concerning the things that are on my heart. But Mr. Osburn can not well spare me just now, and certainly it would be a poor return for all his kindness if I should leave him at the time when my services are most needed.

It may surprise you somewhat to learn that I have recently made a profession of faith in Jesus Christ as the Son of God, and have been immersed upon that profession. I have been led to this step first by the Christian example of you, my ever dear mother, and more immediately by the teachings of the people known as Christians, or disciples of Christ.

Concerning these people you may be still uninformed, as I was until a few weeks ago. Undoubtedly you have heard that they are baptizing thousands of persons in this part of the country; but if you have learned of them hitherto only through their enemies, you may be glad to know the little I can tell you concerning their real spirit and purposes.

The movement which they represent is simply an effort to return to the faith and the practice of New Testament Christianity. It originated with Thomas Campbell, a very devout Scotch Presbyterian minister, who came to this country in 1807. He was greatly distressed in mind over the divided condition of Protestantism, and the consequent confusion of the people concerning the claims of Christ upon the soul. A little later he was joined in his work by his son Alexander, who, during his separation from his father, had been pursuing a train of thought remarkably similar to that followed by the elder Campbell. They joined heart and mind in their studies, avowing their determination to accept no doctrine as authoritative save such as are taught in the New Testament itself. They further declared that whatever teaching they found in the New Testament they would follow whithersoever it might lead them.

I do not know how it may look to you; but to me one of the most wonderful things I have ever known is the thought of these two brave men starting out alone to blaze their way through the forest of mystery and superstition, that they might come to a plain knowledge of God's word. They were bound to the past by many tender ties, but they were willing to relinquish all in order to learn and do the will of the Lord more perfectly. In our simple frontier life examples of remarkable physical courage are not wanting; but in my limited experience I have found the courage of conviction much more uncommon; and there is no trait that I so greatly admire and respect.

Their investigations led them much further than they anticipated from the teachings of their past. As you, dear mother, can readily see, they found that the baptism of infants was without warrant in the Scriptures, and must be relinquished. It then became necessary for them to seek Scriptural baptism, which they found could be nothing else than immersion. Thus they went on, step by step, until they found themselves very far indeed from the teaching of their fathers, but rejoicing with joy unspeakable as they discovered the exceeding simplicity and reasonableness of God's requirements. They had been joined from time to time by other and likeminded students of God's word; and as their position became known it was evident that many persons in different parts of the country, having grown weary of the burdens put upon them by the religious systems of the day, were eager for a plain statement of God's will for them.

And now, my dear parents, I must go back and tell you my own story. I suppose you know but little of it, for Joseph has ever accused me of being over-close-mouthed where my private affairs are concerned.

The Bible has been to me from childhood a source of much pleasure. I remember well, my mother, how Joseph and I sat at your knee on Sunday afternoon, and heard you read the wonderful stories of the Old Testament and the beautiful lessons of the New. When you gave us passages to commit to memory, I learned to delight in the words, even though I scarcely comprehended anything of the thoughts contained therein. As I grew to manhood, I began to be concerned for the salvation of my soul. I knew that I was not fit to live or ready to die. I listened to the religious teachers who came into my way, but it was not long until I became hopelessly bewildered. I could not reconcile this teaching with my idea of God, as drawn from the Bible itself. There he is represented as infinitely loving, longing for the salvation of his human creatures, and sending his Son into the world to make that salvation possible. It seemed to me preposterous that men should think it necessary to implore and importune him to save them. I do not know how it was that I came to have such faith in my own knowledge, but I grew more and more settled in my conviction that the teachers of the day misunderstood and misinterpreted the word of God.

I confess that, as I grew older, doubts often obtruded themselves. I asked myself why, if the Bible really were divine, it could be so easily misinterpreted. At times the great truths of the incarnation and resurrection staggered me. Because they were too much for my intelligence, I thought they were too much for my faith. I remember that one June night, after a hard day in the hayfield, I walked out and threw myself down on the new-cut grass. In a moment I was asleep, and when I awoke it was late and the stars were out. The thought came to me that our world was only one in a universe of worlds. Were those others, like our own world, written over with the record of human struggle and passion? Were they reddened with crime and bloodshed? Had their inhabitants grieved a just God by their wayward acts? Then suddenly I sat up, thinking how small I was and how great God is. I said to myself that the Maker of this universe could not be mindful of me, a tiny atom of one of his far-off worlds. And I groaned aloud at the thought. Yet almost immediately came the thought, "He does care. He has said so. He would not have created me, to leave without the assurance of himself. God cares. I know he cares."

By degrees, however, I became quite hopeless about ever finding a solution for my difficulties. I attended revival meetings, and heard the converts tell of the wonderful experiences through which they had found the assurance that God had accepted them. But it was not emotional experiences for which I looked. These did indeed come to me, as on the night of which I have told you; but I knew they were the expressions of certain moods to which I have always been subject, and that they would soon pass away. Perhaps I could have told as good a story at the anxious seat as many another, but my reason and my knowledge of God's word both told me that this was not the assurance that was needed. What I wanted was to know, not merely to feel something which I might cease to feel upon the morrow.

Joseph will remember a camp-meeting which we attended with a party of gay young folks three or four years ago. At that meeting Wesley Wyatt, in a spasm of what he supposed to be religious zeal, prayed for me by name. Of course, I was annoyed and for a time afterward I was inclined to stay away from religious meetings altogether. But at length I fell back into my old habits.

I had ceased to hope for any immediate answer to the question that oppressed my soul. But, little by little, I settled down to this conviction, that God, in the New Testament, had made plain to men the way of approach to him through his Son; and that, if I ever found any church or religious people teaching what he teaches there, I should at once identify my life with such a movement. By this determination I have tried to live. I had heard of the teaching of the Campbells and their coadjutors only in the most general way, and not once did it occur to me that their leading was toward that New Testament way for which I sought. Four weeks ago it was announced that Walter Scott would preach in the Baptist Church at Rocksford. Mr. Osburn informed me that this man was the close companion of Alexander Campbell, and a man of masterly powers. He had preached at the schoolhouse on the occasion of a former visit, and had been pressed to remain; but a previous appointment at the next town made this possible. Now, by special invitation of Mr. Osburn—whose influence among his Baptist brethren you well know—he was to speak at the church.

Of course, I wished to hear this remarkable man, and for this purpose I went to the church long before the time appointed. The doors were closed, but a crowd had already gathered. Mr. Osburn came up presently, and, standing on the church steps, informed the people that the officers of the church had decided that Mr. Scott could not have the use of the meeting-house.

"But I have driven Mr. Scott to the schoolhouse," he said, "and I trust every one of you will go there to hear him. If any of my brethren ask of me a justification of my own course in this matter, I have only to cite to them the words of one of the olden time: "If this counsel or this work be of men, it will come to naught; but if it be of God, ye can not overthrow it, lest haply ye be found to fight against God.""

At the moment I was somewhat surprised at the independence of Mr. Osburn's action; now it seems the most natural thing in the world.

The preaching of Walter Scott was a revelation to me. He is the first truly great man whom I have ever known, and his is far more than mere intellect greatness. It is intellectual greatness moved by overmastering convictions. He is a man of marked appearance, and speaks with a rich Scotch accent. So much I noted in the beginning. But when he began to preach, the message drove from my mind all consciousness of the man who brought it.

His theme was "The Messiahship of Christ," and, as he spoke, Jesus of Nazareth lived again, first as he lived in the minds of patriarch and prophet, and then as he lived among men in the fulfillment of promise and prophecy. The Bible became to me a new Book. It was no longer a bundle of fragments. With Christ as the center, I could clearly see how the several parts had a vital relation to one another.

In closing his sermon, the speaker made an appeal that seemed to be intended expressly for me. He spoke of the many who were waiting for a clearer knowledge of the way of salvation, and ready and anxious to follow it when it should be known.

"Men and brethren," he said, "Jesus the Christ is of supreme authority on earth and in heaven. No man, living or dead, has the right to bind that which he has left free. Who will accept the terms of salvation which he has laid down? Who of you will cast aside human creeds and confessions, and build upon the foundation of the apostles and prophets, Jesus Christ himself being the chief cornerstone?"

It seemed to me that my whole life passed in review before my mind in the next five minutes. Here, beyond doubt, was the conception of the New Testament church, with Christ in his place of supreme authority. Here were the people with whom I had promised to identify myself. My heart bounded at the thought. My dream had indeed come true. I scarcely knew which feeling had the better of me—my unworthiness or my great joy.

My first impulse was to respond at once to the preacher's invitation. But you know you have always named me your cautious son. I had been many times disappointed, and my happiness seemed too good to accept without question. I heard the preacher bidding those present to give him their hands and God their hearts; I saw a dozen persons press forward in answer to the invitation, and yet I held back, still questioning my happiness.

We went at once to the river, and when I saw those who had just confessed Christ go forward in baptism, I could no longer wait, but made my way to the water's edge, gave my confession, and was immediately baptized.

There you have my story. It is a long one, and I fear you must have wearied in the reading. Mr. Scott remained for nearly two weeks. About forty persons were baptized, and a score more came out from among the denominations to take their stand upon the Bible alone. Among these last were my kind friends, Mr. and Mrs. Osburn. The schoolhouse has been closed against us, but we met regularly every week in the Osburn home for the breaking of bread and prayers.

I expect to pay you a visit in the near future, and to explain all these things more fully. Until such time as I can see you, I remain

Your obedient son,   STEPHEN ARRONDALE.

Father read this letter aloud, and, long before he was done, my mother was in tears. "It's a good letter," she said. "But I wish Stephen were a Baptist."

Father said nothing. I remember thinking afterward how strange it was that he did not even tease mother.

CHAPTER IX

AT THE RIVERBANK

Mr. Cady Vincent had gone from Colonel Sylvestre's when next I went there. Rachel said nothing about his visit, but the Colonel spoke of him as a cultured gentleman, whose friendship he highly valued.

"As for his religious belief," he said, with something like a sneer, "there is not enough of that to harm anybody."

Rachel seemed annoyed at having the subject brought up, and quickly changed it. "Did you know that Martha is leaving us?" she asked. The sisters were sitting side by side, and as she spoke the elder smoothed the hand of the other affectionately. Rachel was at times a trifle sharp-spoken with others, but she was ever most tender and gentle with Martha.

"I am going to school at Rocksford," Martha explained. "Rachel was for having me go East, but that would take me too far away from her and father. There is a very good select school at Rocksford so Mrs. Osburn has written to Rachel and I can be spared to go there for a few months."

I started to say that at Rocksford she would be near Stephen—a prospect which naturally presented me as the most inviting in the world—but I remembered that Stephen was now a "Campbellite," and held my peace, for I had a strong impression that, as a "Campbellite," Stephen would have less favor in Rachel's eyes than he had had hitherto.

"Rachel is so much wiser than I am that I am greatly ashamed of myself," Martha went on, with her arch little smile. She seldom laughed aloud, but this smile was a beautiful thing to see. "And when I try to take lessons of her, she becomes so strict that I am terribly afraid."

"Martha has never been away from home," said Rachel, patting the small, white hand again. Rachel's own hands were long and slim, and had in their every movement a strange sort of eloquence which I know not how to describe. "There is not much of the world to be known in Rocksford, but she will at least learn how people live outside of Blue Brook Township. Mrs. Osburn has kindly offered to receive her into her home, and to have a care over her."

I wondered if Rachel knew that Stephen lived at the Osburns'. Probably she did not, for, so far as I could judge, there was no interchange of letters between her and my brother.

The next week Martha went away. The Saturday night following, I distinctly remember, we looked for Stephen to come home for his long-promised visit. My mother, usually calm and sensible under all conditions, was fairly nervous with anxiety. She baked the pound cake of which Stephen was particularly fond, put the house in perfect order, and then walked down the lane again and again to look for him. Even father manifested some slight restlessness, and came into the kitchen again and again to look at the clock.

But darkness settled down, and Stephen did not come. We sat up later than usual, and when father rose to wind the clock, I saw there was a look of real distress on his face.

It is strange how plainly I remember these details, and I think it goes to show how keen was the disappointment which has stayed with me so long. One little incident stands out more clearly than all the rest. We were an undemonstrative family, and Stephen and I, since we had grown to manhood, kissed our mother only when we were leaving home, or on our return. But tonight her wishful, worried face gave me an impulse which I could not have explained, and I crossed the room, after I had taken my bedroom candle, passed my free arm about her, and kissed her tenderly.

"I am so afraid something has happened to Stephen," she said.

"Nothing can have happened to Stephen," I said. But in spite of myself I was a little uneasy.

"He sent word that he would be here," she said. "You know how careful he always is to keep a promise."

"Something has happened at the last moment to hinder him," I told her.

"I don't know how I can bear the suspense until I hear from him," she said, speaking low, so that father would not hear.

"I'll tell you what I'll do, mother; I'll ride over to Rocksford in the morning and see Stephen."

"Tomorrow is Sunday," she reminded me.

"What of that? Could I make any better use of the day than to see my brother and allay your anxiety? I will start early, and, if you say so, I will go to church in Rocksford."

"I am not sure that it would be right." And my mother looked perplexed enough, for her Puritan conscience was pulling in one direction and her anxiety for her boy in the other.

But her anxiety conquered, and the next morning I set off before daybreak. It was early November, and the woods were turning brown. Winter still seemed a long way off, however, for the air was warm for the season. I did not like to contemplate the prospect of a winter with Stephen away. It was our first separation, and it went very hard with me. Not only would I miss his company at home, but with him and Martha away, the pleasant times in the Sylvestre home would be of the past. I confessed to myself that I would enjoy an occasional tilt of wits with Rachel, but I did not care to risk an encounter in which I was pretty sure to come out second.

The road to Rocksford was a familiar one, for I had often gone there with my father to purchase articles which could not be obtained at our village store. My thoughts were good companions that morning, and, as the clear air and the calm judgment of the morning hour had practically taken away my anxiety, I greatly enjoyed the ride. I felt confident that I should find Stephen safe and well; and I was conscious of a little curiosity as to whether or not I should get a glimpse of Martha.

In my enjoyment I had forgotten to hasten my journey, and the morning was well advanced when I found myself nearing my destination. According to my recollection, there was a small stream to be crossed just before Mr. Osburn's mill and dwelling were reached. A sudden turn in the road brought me to this stream. And there I saw a sight which lives in my memory as if I had seen it yesterday.

On the bank around a gentle curve in the stream were assembled forty or fifty persons, all of them with earnest, serious faces; and midway of the stream, standing waist-deep in it, were two persons. One was a young man of about my own age, whom I had never seen before. The other, who stood with one arm about the youth and the other upraised to heaven, was Stephen.

In a moment, I knew what was transpiring. Frequently I had gone with my mother to see persons baptized in Blue Brook, near our home. Indeed, the sacred ceremony had always had a peculiar fascination for me chiefly, I think, because it appealed to my boyish sense of poetry. But to see it administered by my own brother, at a time and place like this, gave me a feeling that none but unexpected events could evermore come to pass in this world.

I could not hear the solemn words of dedication, but I clearly caught the familiar song which burst from the little company on the bank:

> "O, happy are they
> Who their Savior obey,
> And have laid up their treasures above;
> Tongue cannot express
> The sweet comfort and peace
> Of a soul in its earliest love."

The young man who had just been baptized was received by the persons on the bank with hearty handclasps. Stephen raised his hand again for a moment, as if in prayer, and then the little company broke up.

My first impulse was to slip away unnoticed, and appear at Mr. Osburn's house later. I can not account for this impulse even now. I think it was a kind of feeling that I did not want to be responsible in any way for Stephen's being a "Campbellite."

But I had already been seen. Martha came toward me, and shyly held out her hand. I slipped from my horse and returned the greeting.

"Is anything wrong at home?" she asked. "I was just a little frightened, when I saw you."

"No, all at home are well. I came because we expected Stephen last night and mother was distressed because he did not come."

"He was so sorry! But just as he was ready to start Mr. Osburn came home, and told him that a young man was coming from the next town this morning to be baptized. Stephen had never baptized any one before, but he speaks and prays in the meetings every week, and the people love to hear him. So he could not refuse to do this, though he was very sorry to make his mother anxious."

"I should think the young man could have waited until a regular minister came around," I said.

Martha's cheeks reddened. "It is not a thing which can safely be allowed to wait," she said, "though I have waited and am waiting." She paused a moment, and smoothed my horse's mane with her little white hand. Then she turned her clear eyes up to mine. "If I could be baptized this morning," she said, "I should be the happiest woman in all the world."

My mind caught at the word "woman." Was little Martha really a woman? I had always thought of her as a little girl.

"Why are you not baptized, then, if you care so much about it?" I asked.

She turned her eyes away, but not soon enough to hide their look of pain. "I have always been taught to obey my father," she said. "Sometimes I think I will not wait, and then again I think I must gain his consent, if possible."

Stephen came up in a moment, eager and anxious. I explained to him how I chanced to be there, and then I went with him and Martha to Mr. Osburn's home.

But all day long there was a constraint upon us three; for I felt that the others had thoughts into which I could not enter.

The thing which I noticed most was the change in Martha. She had been away from home less than two weeks, yet already she was greatly altered. It was not merely that she seemed more womanly. There was about her a sense of harmony with her surroundings, such as I had never known in her before. The religious atmosphere of the Osburn home seemed to suit her perfectly. The conversation on Bible themes was an evident delight to her. She had suddenly become a radiant creature, whose pulses seemed to be bounding with life and joy.

I have since learned, through half a century's observation of human character, that there are in the world a few persons of what might be termed religious genius. The contemplation of religious subjects is to them what the contemplation of a sunset is to an artist, or the study of harmony to a musician. Their spiritual convictions come to them not by the slow processes of logic, but by impressions and intuitions that can not be analyzed.

To this class Martha belonged. I remember thinking in those days that her impressibility was due to the excess of femininity within her. Now I know it was due to the preponderance of the spiritual.

The next day after my return from Rocksford, I came upon Rachel in our kitchen. She had come over to consult my mother in some of her housewifely perplexities.

"I saw Martha over at Rocksford," I said.

"So your mother tells me," she answered. "I hope that Campbellite brother of yours won't undertake to convert our little one." She laughed, as if what she had suggested were the most unlikely thing in the world.

What could I say? I laughed feebly, and went on about my work.

After our visitor had gone away my mother said, "Rachel Sylvester is certainly the most capable girl I have ever known. Such an excellent housekeeper, and with such a head for books! It is a terrible pity that she is an unbeliever."

CHAPTER X

AT THE SCHOOLHOUSE

In January Stephen came home with the intention of remaining at least for several months. He had been with us for a few hours on Thanksgiving Day, which was, in our home, a much greater festival than Christmas. The one thing that I recall distinctly about this hurried visit was that father requested Stephen to "ask a blessing" before we partook of our Thanksgiving dinner. This struck me as a kind of formal recognition of my brother's new position; and I fancied that my mother was much gratified that father had thought of such a thing.

My mother had not the nature of which sectarians are made, and she could not, under any circumstances, have had a sectarian feeling toward her boy. Martha was at home again, and had given us great accounts of the favor with which Stephen's public exhortations had been received in Rocksford. So it was not many days before mother said to him:

"Stephen, I wish I could hear you speak in public. There are many about us who need instruction, and you ought not to hide your light under a bushel."

"I am going to speak at the schoolhouse next Sunday," Stephen answered. "I have already posted the notice."

So it came about that Stephen preached the first sermon ever preached in Blue Brook Township by the so-called "Campbellites."

There was no limit to the excitement when it was known that young Steve Arrondale had turned "Campbellite," and that he had come back to preach in the log schoolhouse. Everybody was talking about it; and, as I was judged a harmless sort of fellow, the talk went on in my presence without interruption.

Over at Skinner's store, everybody had a word to say.

"That boy come to set his elders right, eh?" asked old Zephaniah Leech, scraping out his pipe. "Wa'al, now, Steve's a good one at harvestin'; but I guess he's better leave preachin' alone till his beard's growed."

"It's a sin an' a shame that as likely a boy as Stephen ever got took in with the Campbellites," says Deacon Meacham. "It'll be the ruination of him, an' I knowed that boy when he wasn't higher than a chair." Then the deacon gave a deep sigh, put his bundle of store sugar in his saddlebags, and rode away with his head down, thinking, I suppose, of our Stephen's wasted life.

To tell the truth, I was thinking of the same thing. I had a boy's share of ambitions for myself, but I had far more than the ordinary brother's share of ambition for Stephen. I knew very well that I had no special gift for winning my way among men, but what I could not do by any sort of effort, I well knew that Stephen did without any effort at all. For him to lead others was as natural as for him to breathe. He was made that way. And, ignorant boy though I was, my own limitations taught me that such a gift brought great possibilities. In our little world, Stephen might, I knew, be a great man. It seemed to me that he had thrown away his chances.

As far as his new notions of religion were concerned, they seemed to me to be of the wildest. I had for myself no idea of doctrines, but I had a strong idea of respectability, and my general impression was that, to be a "Campbellite," or, as Steve said, to be a disciple, was not exactly respectable. I have learned since that no new teaching is considered altogether respectable. Peter and Paul discovered the same thing.

The general feeling against Stephen's course did not hinder people from going out to hear him. Not more than half of those who came could be crowded inside the little schoolhouse. The rest stood outside the open windows and listened.

I wonder what a modern audience would think of that scene—the roughly chinked walls, the slab benches, the puncheon floors, and the few sputtering "dips," scarcely giving light enough to make the darkness visible. I can see it all as if it were yesterday. Yes, more, I can see half a dozen of the faces I saw that night far more clearly than, with these dull old eyes, I see the dear young faces that are round about me as I write.

I had been of a dozen different minds about going to the schoolhouse that night. I did not want to hear Stephen preach the strange notions he had accepted. My mother had been nervous and anxious for days, and once she slipped her plump little hand into mine as she said, "I tremble for Stephen, Joseph. What if he should hesitate and stumble before all those people?"

But, somehow, I did not tremble for Stephen. I had never known him to undertake anything that he could not carry through. But I did not want to hear him. It seemed to me that it made me more conscious than ever of the change in his life, and of what had come between us.

But curiosity got the better of me, and I went. Rachel too, was there, drawn in spite of herself, I think, as I had been. I can see the hard look about her mouth and the proud set of her head. Little Martha sat beside her, very quiet, but, I thought, with an eager, hungry look in her eyes. The look went to my heart, though I little thought, that night, that those eyes held the secret of the future.

Steve's hand trembled a little, I thought, as he drew out his pocket Testament, but he did not show embarrassment in any other way. Indeed,

I do not think he was embarrassed. People who are really in earnest get beyond that.

"Friends," he said, "this is a new way I have found since I left you. I am persuaded that it is the old way of the apostles and the early disciples. I know it is a way everywhere spoken against, but it is my purpose to walk in it. Who will go with me? Who is there, of these old friends and comrades, who will come forward here to give me his hand and God his heart, and walk in the good old way?"

I felt a queer tugging at my heart, and a longing to go forward and give my hand to my brother. In a moment, I was ashamed of this feeling, and told myself that it was no real desire, but a mere impulse, born of brotherly sympathy and the emotion of the moment. I had no idea that any one would respond to the invitation, and I was surprised at Stephen's look and tone of expectancy. The new doctrine might do in Valleyville, but it would never do among the shrewd Yankee folk of Blue Brook.

Then I noticed a little rustle in the crowd a little ahead of me. After the fashion of time, the men sat on one side of the schoolhouse and the women on the other. I was on the back seat, not so much because I fancied the company of the rough boys who sat there, as because it seemed easier and less embarrassing to listen from that distance.

When I saw the stir, I was anxious for the moment, lest some one should be seeking to make a disturbance. Then I saw what had happened. My father had crowded into the aisle and was walking to the front.

Looking back upon it now, I know that moment marked a change in all of our lives. I think Stephen knew it then. As he came up the aisle to meet father, he had the look of a man whom God had blessed beyond his hopes.

Both were strong, self-contained men, but there were tears on the cheeks of both as they grasped each other's hands. As they reached the front, father turned and faced the people. Stephen motioned them to be seated.

"Friends and neighbors," said father (I had never known before how much he and Stephen were alike. Their voices, even, had the same firm tone), "I have lived among you all these years as a man who had no fear of God before his eyes. It has been my fault that you thought of me in this way, but it is not quite the truth. All my life long, and especially since I have had with me the example of my good wife, I have wanted to serve God. But there were many things in the creeds of those about me that I could not understand, and many more which I could no accept. I tried, I will tell you frankly, to be content as an unbeliever, but I could not be. I could not be rid of my feeling of accountability to a good God, who had created me and before whose judgement seat I must a last appear. I knew that, if there were a God at all, he must be a God of reason and justice. He would not demand one thing of one person, and another of another. He would not ask all to follow him, and then close the way against any. But when I inquired of human guides, all was confusion and darkness. Neighbors, I wish to stand before you tonight for what I am. I can truly say,

> "This is the way I long have sought
> And mourned because I found it not."

"Neighbors, I take no man for my guide, but I am willing to take the Scriptures for my teacher, and to follow where they lead. I have come into the vineyard late, and for this I am sorry; but though it is at the eleventh hour, I bear you witness that I have come at the first call that I could feel sure was meant for me. Pray for me, that I may prove faithful."

All the time that father was talking, Stephen stood shaking with sobs, yet with happiness like that of an angel's upon his face. It seemed almost as if his joy were greater than he could bear.

When father had finished, Stephen said, "I am going to ask who else is ready to go with my dear and honored father."

I caught sight of poor little Martha. She had taken Rachel by the hand, and seemed begging her for something. It was not hard to guess what, for Rachel shook her head again and again, and the hard look seemed to set itself more firmly about the corners of her mouth.

So busy had I been watching Rachel and Martha, that I had not noticed my mother. She had gone quietly forward, slipped one hand into my father's and given the other to Stephen.

My dear mother! An odd thing about her was, that when she was very happy, a look of girlishness came over her face, so that she looked many years younger than she was. So marked was it at this moment that one could scarcely have believed the tall preacher was her son.

Everybody respected my father, but in all the country round about, no other woman was loved as mother was. Her great great-grand-children can tell today stories that they have heard of her neighborly kindness and sympathy. Every woman in the house was in tears—every one, that is, except Rachel, whose face was as cold and stern as ever.

But after the service Stephen sought her out and spoke to her. It seemed that, in the joy and overflowing gratitude of his heart, he instinctively demanded the sympathy of his old friend.

"Will you not welcome me home, Rachel?" he asked.

"No," she answered, coldly. "I do not welcome you to such work as you are doing now. I expected better things of *you.*"

CHAPTER XI
A WOMAN'S HAND

I suppose it would be quite out of the question to make persons of the present time understand what a stir was created on account of what my father and mother had done. It seems a simple enough matter now, but at that day it meant tearing at the roots of old prejudices and associations. These new people, who called themselves disciples, were deemed heretics of the first order, and that such staid and respectable people as my parents should consent to be allied with them, could not but cause the bitterest criticism. Wherever I went, I was met with questions concerning the new faith, most of which, I confess, I was quite unable to answer.

To tell the truth, I felt very sore over the affair. It seemed to me that my good parents had done a strange thing, and one quite out of keeping with their past lives. I thought that, if father had wished to make a profession of religion, it would have been much more seemly in him to join the Baptist Church with my mother than to take a course calculated to excite so much unfavorable comment. Of the doctrinal difficulties of which he had spoken I understood very little. Doctrines in those days meant next to nothing to me.

Stephen was with us all the time now, and I was bound to confess that our home was far happier than it had ever been before. Father read the New Testament as eagerly as Stephen and I had read Scott's novels the year before, and he and mother, instead of debating on Calvinism, as they had done in the old time, talked of the good new time that had come, and of the way of salvation that now seemed so plain to both of them. Mother fully believed that all the world would see it as clearly as she did, and that all sectarianism would seem to be a thing of the past. But father was not so hopeful. "Human nature is human nature, Abbie," he used to say. "And some people have got it, as well as some mules. Stephen thinks the millennium is just a short piece before us, but there are a lot of sinners like me to be converted before we get there, and, what's more discouraging yet, a log of saints to be persuaded that the millennium will come in God's way and not in theirs."

Every day I was more surprised in my father. His knowledge of the Bible was far greater than I had supposed, and I saw that, in spite of his shrewdness and his love of a good bargain, he had tried to be guided by its teachings and by the example of my godly mother. Thus had he established his reputation for honesty and veracity. It seemed to me hard then, and it seems to me harder now, in this day of liberty and Christian charity, that such a man should be kept from Christian fellowship during the active years of his life, merely because he lacked the emotional temperament necessary to what was called "a religious experience."

Stephen and I shared the same room, as we had done from babyhood. I knew he had something on his mind, and I guessed that it related to Rachel; but we were not on our old confidential terms, and I could ask him nothing. Our hearts were as tender toward each other as ever, but he knew that I did not sympathize with him in his religious life, and this knowledge put a barrier between us.

But one night he came upstairs late, with a look on his face that went to my heart. There was no light in the room, but the moonlight showed me his secret.

"Steve," I said, "has Rachel Sylvestre been hurting you again?"

"Again?" he said. And then he came and sat down beside me. "I didn't suppose you knew she ever had hurt me."

"I'm not so blind as that. She has treated you cruelly, since you joined these new people. I can read the pain in your face, but, more plainly still, I can read the cruelty in hers. Don't worry about it, Steve, she isn't worth it."

Ah, how his eyes flashed in the moonlight! There is such a thing as a noble resentment, and Stephen was capable of it.

"You must not judge Rachel in that way," he said. "Her training has been very different from ours. Her father has taught her that all religion is irrational, mere superstition, unworthy of intelligent men and women. Her mind has been developed at the expense of her heart, that is all."

I wondered even than how Stephen could be so just and patient where his heart was concerned so deeply. It was his way, and I knew it was a better way than mine.

"Martha has heart enough," I said, to keep myself from saying anything more about Rachel.

"Martha is a child." he answered carelessly. But in this I thought he was mistaken.

He sat in silence a little while, then by and by he spoke of what was giving him pain.

"I didn't mean to tell any one," he said, "but is may be best that you should know. You will understand then why my life must lie away from here. And we have been so happy here, in these last days. O God, we have been so happy."

These last words were at once a prayer of Thanksgiving and the cry of a broken heart. I reached out and grasped my brother's hand.

"She has always had my heart, I think," he said, after awhile, speaking very quietly. "It was for her sake that I struggled to get a little education, and to know something about the great world outside. I don't know that, in those boyish days, I really hoped to win her, but I could not bear to put her to shame by my ignorance. Then, when she came home from school, I knew my destiny. She must be first in my life whether either of us wanted it to be so or not. I *had* to care what she liked, to know how she would feel about whatever I did. Don't think, Joseph, that she has ever, by so much as one look, encouraged me to believe that she cared for me. There has never lived on earth a woman with a nobler scorn of pretense and coquetry. Her face is an open book, and in it I have read friendship, companionship, interest, but affection, never. This, though, did not discourage me. I knew it would take years to win her, but she was worth it. I knew that a man of her own world, one with gifts to match her own, might come at any time to claim her, but I couldn't help feeling that our boy and girl friendship made a kind of tie between us; and if waiting and working were what was needed, I knew I could do both. Jacob served fourteen years for a Rachel whom I knew must have been less fair than mine.

"When I heard the sermon that showed me my duty and my future, my first thought was of Rachel. I knew her first feeling would be against the new religion. But I knew she had known the gospel of Christ only as it was covered over with error and human doctrines, and it seemed that the truth must win even her. At any rate, in this one matter, her wish could not influence my choice. Perhaps you do not fully understand me, Joseph; but God grant the day may come when you will realize that one must follow the truth when it sees it to be true.

"When I began, in a stumbling way, to take part in religious meetings, the thought of speaking to the people on the first day of the week had never come into mind. But the brethren put me forward, and, before I knew it, I was telling sinners what they must do to be saved. I knew only the little I could learn from my New Testament from day to day, but the people, long fed on the husks of meaningless doctrines, were hungry for the Word, and took the meager meal I had to give them. Many of them, hearing, believed and were baptized; and I was too happy to have any anxious thought about the future.

"You know the story of my first sermon after my return, but you will never know the joy I had in seeing father obey Christ, and in seeing him and mother united in the faith. You heard what Rachel said when we came out of the schoolhouse that night—but I must not speak of that.

She was greatly agitated, for Martha had been moved by the preaching, and Rachel somehow blamed me for this.

"To-night I have been there for the first time since my return. Perhaps I was foolish to go, but I could not help it. I wanted to see her, and I hoped she would let me tell her something about my new life and my happiness in it. I think there is always in us a feverish impatience to know the worst—to have any anticipated agony over and done with. That is the way I felt. I told her everything—everything!—how much she is to me, and how much more yet my faith is to me. And now everything is over. I am not quite a coward, I hope, but I want to get away—to be where I can get used to the thought of living without her. I ought to tell you, though, that I think my belief has nothing at all to do with the matter. Without that barrier, I might perhaps have remained her friend and comrade, but that would never have been enough. Such a friendship might even become a source of agony to me, when the time came to give her up. Some one will woo and win her, and it is better that I should be away."

He was silent for some time. When he spoke again, the excitement was past, and he began, in a very quiet tone, to tell me his plans.

He had received several letters lately, urging him to preach the gospel in an adjoining county. There were several infant churches there which had been organized and left with no one to care for them. The church at Rocksford also desired his services whenever he could give them. Here was his work, and he would go to it as soon as might be.

"And who will support you?" I asked. I had heard of wild-goose chases, and it seemed to me that this was one of them.

"I have supported myself since I was twenty-one. There is plowing in the spring and fall, and haying and harvesting in the summer, and chopping in the winter. The kind of work that I can do is plenty everywhere."

"But when will you study your sermons?"

Stephen laughed, and then grew sober. "I shall study the book as I can—in the saddle, at noon in the field, at night by the fireside. But I fear the sermons will get studied very little. I shall tell the Story as well as I can—that is all I know how to do."

CHAPTER XII

CAST ADRIFT

It became known in the neighborhood that Stephen was going away, and that he would speak only once more in the schoolhouse. He was a favorite among the young folks, as he had always been, and they all came out to hear him. Not half of those who came could be seated on the benches. The rest stood up and leaned against the log walls.

Father had grumbled a good deal when he found that Stephen was to leave him again, and in the busy time of the year, but we all knew about how seriously to take father's grumbling. He was proud of Stephen, and he believed the new doctrine with all his heart. So he was really pleased to know that his boy was going to a larger life than he had known among us.

To-night he and mother sat near the front, and would not look at each other or at Stephen. In those days parents were much afraid of spoiling their children by showing pride in them.

Martha came to the meeting late, and seemed to be alone. I thought she looked very pale and anxious. But oh, how beautiful she was! I heard a shrewd person say only yesterday of Maude Arrondale (the young aunt of Sylvestre Arrondale the Fourth) that she cheapened the looks of every other woman when she entered a parlor. But the Maude Arrondale of to-day would be as moonlight to midday beside the Martha Sylvestre who sat opposite me on that evening long ago.

I am ashamed to say I can not remember what Stephen preached about that night. I know he was in earnest, and that he swayed the people as he would. I remember I thought what a strange thing it was that he, who had always been so sensible and staid, could be so taken up with mere doctrines as to be quite lifted out of himself. For the rest, I was thinking of other things than the sermon—of Rachel, especially, and her unkind treatment of Stephen.

Martha never once took her eyes from Stephen's face. Her chin was set hard, and for almost the first time I saw that she could be like Rachel. When the invitation was given for those who wanted to stand for the New Testament order of things to come forward, Martha started at once and walked to the front seat. She looked quiet and determined then, but in a moment she gave way and fell into a passion of sobs.

Stephen's quiet voice seemed to soothe her, and she stood up bravely before all the people, and said she believed that Jesus Christ is the Son of God. I have heard that confession thousands of times since, but it has never stirred my heart as it did that night. I was a careless lad, and a moment before the great truths of revelation had had little meaning for me; but just then I seemed to realize what is meant by a surrender to the authority of the divine Savior.

After the meeting the women gathered about Martha and kissed and coddled her, as good women love to coddle a sweet, motherless young creature. The rude torches were brought out, and we hastily fell into line for a march to the baptismal water. It was a weird sight—the long, wavering line of men and women, a face here and there lighted by the flicker of a torch.

Some one broke into a song, and in a moment many voices took up the refrain:

"How happy are they
Who their Savior obey."

I was near the end of the procession when we stopped at Blue Brook, lining up along the banks and on the bridge. Oddly enough, as it seemed to me, the spot chosen for the baptism was just below that where, when we were all children, Stephen and I first saw the Sylvestre girls. I smiled now at the memory of that day, remembering how Rachel had insisted on wading, while Martha had allowed Stephen to carry her across.

Stephen and Martha were already standing in the water when I came up. The light of a torch fell upon them, and I thought then, as I think now, that I had never seen two nobler faces.

"I baptize thee in the Name" never had the sacred words seemed to mean as much.

After the baptism, the people crowded up to shake hands with Stephen, expressing regret at his leaving us, and wishes for his happiness elsewhere. I think the heartiness of their manner surprised him, for he was ever inclined to think poorly of himself.

"I shall come back soon," he told me, as we walked home together. "A little church might soon be gathered together here from among those who are tired of party creeds and names. Here, as everywhere, people are hungry for the gospel. The desire salvation, but they know not how to seek it."

"I wonder what Colonel Sylvestre will say to Martha?" I remarked.

"Poor little girl!" said Stephen, in a tone of compassion. "I fear she has a sorry time ahead of her. But I know her nature, and I feel sure she will not shrink."

We had much to say and do that night, for Stephen was to leave us in the early morning. It was past eleven o'clock when we retired, and we were but just in bed when we heard a frightened voice calling:

"Mrs. Arrondale! Oh, Mrs. Arrondale!"

I heard my mother rise quickly and open the door. She was in such demand as a nurse that I doubted not it was some sudden illness in the neighborhood which called for her presence. But for some time I heard low voices in the kitchen; then mother came to the door and spoke very softly to Stephen and me.

"Colonel Sylvestre has turned Martha out of doors," she said, "and she has sought a refuge here. I thought it best to tell you, so you need not seem surprised when you see her in the morning. Do not answer me—it will be better for her not to hear us talking. Only"—even in a whisper mother's voice betrayed her excitement—"slip away very quietly in the morning, Stephen. The Colonel threatens to horsewhip you if he gets a chance."

Mother slipped downstairs again, but for a long time Stephen and I talked under our breath of the dreadful thing that had happened. It seemed incredible that a father who was as indulgent as Colonel Sylvestre usually showed himself to be, should be so utterly cruel in dealing with his daughter's religious feelings, especially a daughter as obedient and gentle as Martha had always been.

"If it had been Rachel," I began. But Stephen loyally reminded me that Rachel, too, was a most dutiful daughter.

"But why did Rachel let her father cast Martha off?" I demanded.

"You will find that Rachel knows nothing about it," he insisted. "She is not always gentle, but she always tries to be just. And her influence over her father is very great."

Next day, after we had said goodby to Stephen, my mother told me the whole story. Martha had again and again asked her father for permission to be baptized, and had always received a peremptory refusal.

"Religion is simply childishness," he told her once. "The race had its childhood. It began with gods that were close at hand, and by degrees it has put them farther and farther away, until now even the credulous believe only in a remote Being, to be turned to merely in the extremities of life. The really intellectual have no use whatever for such a being. You, my daughter, should have come out of the childishness of credulity long before this."

Martha persevered in her request, but to no purpose. She begged Rachel to plead with her father, but this the elder sister refused to do.

"You will think differently about these things when you are older," said Rachel. "These persons play upon your feelings and lead you to imagine all kinds of painful things. Try to forget it all, my little one."

I do not think it ever occurred either to Rachel or her father that Martha might finally act in opposition to the wishes of her family. They were so accustomed to her gentle obedience that they anticipated nothing else. They little dreamed of what such natures are capable. The fires of martyrdom have been lighted for women of Martha's type.

Rachel had left home on the previous day for a visit with a friend who lived five or six miles distant. Martha fancied that she chose this time purposely, not wishing to show sufficient interest in the meeting to attend it, and scarcely daring to absent herself without an excuse. This seemed highly probable to me, knowing what had passed between her and Stephen.

When Martha returned from the meeting, in company with some of the good women who had assisted at her baptism, she was surprised to find her father still up. She learned afterward that Ross Turner, bent on mischief, as usual, had stopped and told the story of her disobedience.

Martha said good-night to her friends, slipped into the house, and went straight to her father.

"I have come to tell you what I have done, father."

He felt her damp hair for confirmation of what he had heard. Then he pushed her from him.

"I have heard," he said. "You have disobeyed your father. When a child of mine disobeys, she ceases to belong to me. Go back to your ranting, hymn-singing crew. Go back and ask them if they put disobedience to parents among the cardinal virtues. Go back to them—your place is no longer here."

I am sure than, in his coarse rage, he said other things which both her daughterly loyalty and her maidenly reserve forbade her telling. I am sure that, in some rude way, he accused her of a liking for either Stephen or myself. This I judge from what I saw afterwards.

"You do not mean that you are sending me away from home?" asked Martha, in amazement.

"Have I not made it plain? You shall not sleep another night under this roof. I tell you, I am done with you—do you hear me?"

There was not a house but ours within her reach, where Martha felt that she would be understood and welcomed. Thus it was that she came, with wet hair and tear-stained cheeks, to the door of the Arrondales that night.

CHAPTER XIII

THE PIONEER PREACHER

Martha remained with us a little more than a week. She seemed shy, and pitifully afraid of giving trouble; and I fancy there were times when the thought of her father's cruel treatment made her very sad. But when she sat with my mother, and engaged in conversation, I noted in her that same freedom and delight which I had first seen in the Osburn home at Rocksford. To be in religious society and speak of the subjects nearest her heart gave her intense happiness.

A day or two after she came to us, the voluble Arabel Holcomb appeared. She said she had come to get the rule for my mother's pound cake, but I knew this was a mere excuse. She had heard that Martha had been sent from home, no doubt, and desired full particulars. Persons like Arabel are not really malicious, but they must talk, and the fresher their gossip the readier the market they find for it.

My mother was ever of the quickest wit, and when she saw Arabel riding up the lane she sent Martha away to her room.

"I'll attend to Arabel, my dear," she said. "Joseph shall stay with me, and between us we will protect you."

As Arabel entered, her eyes took in every detail of the room, from the big fireplace, which Martha had just filled with fresh green boughs, to the big-flowered curtains of the "recess" which served my mother as a bedroom.

"Why, where is Martha?" she asked. "Ross Turner said he was sure he saw her here this morning. I was over at her house last night, and her father said she was away. That's every word I could get out of him. I suppose he sent her away for getting baptized. Ross thought he would, though he didn't say a word when Ross told him. The Sylvestres are queer people, aren't they? They never seem to have anything to say about their own affairs. Do you suppose the Colonel will cut Martha out of his property? Ross says it would be just like him."

Mother broke in at about this point to say that Martha was indeed spending a short time with us, but was very weary, and had been persuaded to rest for a time in her room.

"Oh, indeed!" exclaimed My Lady Arabel, quite undaunted, "I'll go in and see her for a little before I go away. I know she would be disappointed if she did not see me."

I was casting about for some means of averting this dreadful catastrophe, when there came a gentle knock, and Rachel Sylvestre entered at the open door.

The Sphinx herself could not wear a more inscrutable face than belonged to this young woman as she advanced in greeting. She kissed my mother, which surprised me a little, for, except with Martha, Rachel's manner had ever seemed more dignified and self-contained than is common with girls of her age.

I think she guessed before she came that she would find Arabel at our house. At any rate, she betrayed no surprise.

"How is Martha today?" she asked my mother. "Rather tired and nervous, I fear."

"She is tired," my mother answered, "but most admirably self-contained."

"Indeed! I will not bother her about trifles today, but I have some gowns to make for her, and must see after the fitting by to-morrow. I suppose you know, Arabel, that Martha is going back to her school in Rocksford soon?"

"La! is she, though?" asked Arabel, quite taken aback by this piece of information. "Why, I thought she came home to stay!"

"Martha is far too young and unsophisticated to leave school for good. She was very happy at Rocksford, and was making good progress there. She did indeed feel that she was needed at home, and ought to come back, but father and I both think it is best that she should go on with her studies for some time yet."

"And will she board with the Osburns again?" asked my mother, with a little eagerness.

Rachel's eyes flashed and then cooled. "No," she said, carelessly, "she will be in the home of the school principal."

She looked up at the clock. "I have many things to do and must hurry back," she said. "Perhaps Martha is sleeping, and I will not disturb her. Give her my love, and tell her to accumulate a stock of patience, so she will be ready for the gowns. Come, Arabel, you can walk your horse past our house, can you not?" And she actually carried the light-headed girl away with her.

The indignation in our little community, when it became generally known that Colonel Sylvestre had turned his daughter out of doors, was almost unbounded. He was not a popular man, although his imposing airs kept people in a certain awe of him. Rachel, too, was feared rather than loved. With all of her goodbreeding, there was about her an air of pride and conscious superiority which was generally resented. But little Martha (it seemed natural to say "little Martha," although she was really a tall and stately looking girl) was everybody's favorite. None feared or stood aloof from her. Girls like Arabel copied Rachel's style, but they borrowed Martha's patterns.

"It's a burnin' shame," said old Zephaniah Leech, to his audience at the village store. "It's a burnin' shame for old man Sylvestre to come down so hard on that pooty little gal o' his'n. Religion? What's the harm in religion? Women air bound to hev it, an' I hold that is does 'em good —makes 'em kinder peaceable, an' easy satisfied. Now, ef that oldest Sylvestre hed some, it might 'a' took the highan'mightiness out o' *her*."

"I wonder," said Ross Turner, thoughtfully, as he carefully carved his initials into a pine stick, "whether old man Sylvestre will cut Martha out of his property."

"I guess probably not," was old Zephaniah's conjecture. "I guess not, or he wouldn't be payin' for her schoolin'."

But the public little knew how the matter of her "schoolin'" had been achieved.

I learned afterward that Rachel, on returning from her visit, had found her father in a storm of rage over what he called Martha's ingratitude. He declared that he would never again receive the girl into his home, that she had made her bed, and might lie in it.

Rachel was very quiet during this outbreak. She was always quiet when she was angry, and I think that she was angry now both at her father and at Martha.

But after a little she began to talk to him about the unpleasant comment there would be, if Martha should continue to live in the neighborhood and outside of her own home. She was not prepared to earn her own living, and it would be a disgrace to her father to let her religious friends support her. How much better, then, to send her back to school, until such time as her longing for her home should bring her humbly back to seek it!

No one else could have conquered the Colonel, but Rachel did. She knew his weak point, and toward it she aimed the arrows of her woman's wit. Before she was done with him, she made him promise that Martha should be sent to school again.

To my surprise, Martha did not altogether like the plan. "I want to go and work," she said. "It must be there is something I can do. I am not as ignorant as Rachel thinks. It is only because she herself knows so much, that I seem to her so helpless. I can sew, and I know that in some large town I might find families who would give me employment as seamstress. I have thought it all over, and I would rather have it that way."

I knew how she felt—that it would be painful to receive support from a parent who refused to recognize her as his child. It was love, not money, that Martha craved. But my parents advised her to fall in with Rachel's plan, since to refuse would be but to harden her father's heart the more resolutely against her.

So Martha went back to Rocksford, where she found a warm welcome from the Osburns and other members of the little church. I heard nothing from her directly for many months, and I have little record of the time that followed her departure. It must have been without incident, or I would recall more concerning it. Among my old papers I have been able to find nothing save this letter from Stephen. I give it in full, for, though some parts of it relate to matters outside of this family history, it tells the life of the gospel pioneer of those heroic days:

ROCKSFORD, OHIO, JULY 10, 18.

MY DEAR JOSEPH:—

As Mr. Osburn goes to Blue Brook to-morrow, I make haste to pen a few lines to be sent by him. I have been here for a week now, helping him and his men in the harvest field by day, and by night speaking to the brethren and others as I have opportunity. It surprises me that the people will come together at night after their hard day's work, but I tell you, Joseph, souls are hungry for the bread of the gospel. They have been fed upon the husks of theology too long. almost every night we go from the place of meeting to the waters of baptism, and often, as we go down into the water, persons press forward to make the good confession.

Before returning to this place, I spent two weeks in M—, where much interest was manifested. I went out one day to a schoolhouse, seven miles from town, at the urgent request of a good sister who desired that her husband might know the way of the Lord more perfectly. The man, at the conclusion of the discourse, came forward to be baptized, and with him five others. I had not thought to take a change of clothing with me, but I was kindly provided for by the candidate, and baptism was administered in the same hour.

Traveling about at my own expense has depleted my purse, and my wardrobe is none the better for some months of horseback riding. So I am glad of an opportunity to earn a little of the means with which to replenish. The brethren give me free welcome to their homes, and I have a good bed and good food wherever I go. But of cash they themselves have little, and my horse and my clothing I must find for myself.

Martha is a great blessing to the little company of believers here. Really, there is in this gentle young girl a strength of purpose and a power of persuasion which I could never have believed to exist. Night after night she leads her young friends forward to the front seat, her beautiful face shining as with the joy of heaven. She makes me think of the vestal virgins of the olden time, set apart sacredly to the service of the temple.

Write a line and send it back by Mr. Osburn, if it is convenient for you to do so. Tell me particularly concerning the health of father and mother. I desire greatly to see you all, and trust I may do so soon.

Do you ever see Rachel? Please do not be afraid to write concerning her. I have sometimes thought you avoided the subject, through fear of giving me pain. A thought has come to me concerning her of late which I am bound to mention. Is your heart enlisted there? If it is, do not be afraid to say so. I could not but grieve to see your life linked with that one who has no faith; but so far as I am concerned there is no reason why you should fear. Rachel Sylvestre and I are as far apart as if we had never looked into each other's faces.

With great affection,

Faithfully yours,

STEPHEN ARRONDALE.

CHAPTER XIV

THE CHALLENGE

One evening in September I went over to the Sylvestres on an errand for father. I had not seen Rachel in weeks, and it struck me that she had changed greatly. Her face was thinner and sharper than before, and her eyes had a worried look which was quite new to them. I remembered when I saw her to have heard someone remark that her father was growing peevish and quarrelsome, and that it was very difficult for any one to please him.

I did my errand and was going away, when Rachel said, "Wait just a moment, Joseph—I must speak to you. Does Stephen mention Martha in his letters?"

The look of eagerness in her face went to my heart. I told her the little I knew—Martha was well, and busy with her studies.

"Father does not wish us to correspond," Rachel said, as if in explanation of her question. "It seems like a hard requirement, but Martha and I are agreed that it is wise and right to obey. You will send her my love, will you not, Joseph?"

She looked into my eyes as I promised, and a sudden feeling came to me that I was near to her and understood her heart. "Rachel," I said, "if you believed as Martha does, you would do exactly as she has done."

"I could not believe as Martha does," she said, turning away and trying to speak coldly. "But"—her eyes turned back to mine"—I do not blame Martha."

"Why, then, do you blame Stephen?" I was tempted to ask; but prudence came to my aid and stopped my tongue.

I hoped that we might be better friends after this, and that I might help her to keep informed about Martha. But when next we met there was the old reserve and formality.

Stephen made us two or three visits, and each time he left a message from Martha, but he did not go to the Sylvestre home. On the last two of the visits, however, he saw Rachel.

The incidents of these visits stand out in my mind more clearly than does most of this history, for they were of a character quite new to our community. Excitement of any kind was scarce, and whatever transpired was long remembered.

Stephen was to spend Sunday with us, and through the instrumentality of some of our more influential neighbors, he was asked to speak in the new Town Hall. This building had just been completed and was an object of some pride in our primitive community.

The hall was filled. A few extremely partisan members of the two churches had remained away, but they were all. The rest of the town was there.

"Makes me think of a funeral," said old Zephaniah Leech as he came shuffling in. He did not mean that there was anything at all funereal about the character of the services, but that the occasion had called out a general attendance of all classes. In these days people are so much occupied that they can not take time for the funeral of an acquaintance unless they are bound by the obligations of some lodge or drafts union; but then it was very different.

As I looked about the room, I was surprised, almost startled, to see Colonel Sylvestre on the back seat. To this day, I do not know why he came. I suppose he thought he had an idea that there might come some opportunity to revenge himself upon Stephen, whom he undoubtedly hated with a deep and dreadful hatred. But he may have come simply with the thought of entertaining his guest, for beside the Colonel, and between him and Rachel, sat Cady Vincent, the young Universalist preacher.

If I was surprised to see the Colonel there, I was scarcely less surprised at the sight of Rachel. I am sure that she herself could not have told why she came. For one brief moment I had felt that I understood her. Now she seemed further from my comprehension than ever before.

The situation was as difficult for Stephen as could well be imagined. Here was the woman who had rejected him, his apparently favored rival, and the enemy who had threatened to have vengeance upon him. And before all these he must preach.

I may say right here that I had never feared that Colonel Sylvestre would carry out his threat of horse whipping Stephen. He had too much dignity, and cared too much for the respect of his neighbors, to seek revenge in such a primitive fashion. The threat had been made in a moment of bitter anger, and no doubt it had caused poor Martha much anxiety. But I knew perfectly well that it would never be executed. The Colonel's retaliation would be of a more polished sort.

Perhaps it was because of the peculiar circumstances and the intensity of my sympathy; but I know that Stephen's preaching took hold upon me that day as it never had taken hold of me before. Looking back upon that time, I am led to believe that the character of his preaching had changed very greatly. He was no longer a boy, repeating what he had learned from the lips of others. He was a man, with a man's message, straight from the Book itself. Stephen could not have been an ordinary man, in any event, for he was a born leader and would have influenced other lives anywhere; but he never could have been as great elsewhere as he was in the work which called out the deepest convictions and made the expression of them a part of his very life.

Up to this time I had conceived of religion as largely a matter of sentiment and emotion. While I was never what is called an irreligious boy, I had never been given to studying the Bible for myself, as Stephen had been, and the preaching I had heard had made no direct appeal to my reason. But today, the thought of my personal relation to God took sudden hold upon me.

Perhaps there had come to me, in these last months, an unconscious desire to be one with those I loved, in the holiest of all bonds. If so, that desire really made itself known to me to-day for the first time.

In the little Bible which I bought soon afterward is marked, in ink now so faded that I can but just see the lines, the text from which Stephen preached that day:

"For I delivered unto you first of all that which I also received, how that Christ died for our sins according to the scriptures: and that he was buried, and that he rose again the third day according to the scriptures."

If I should tell you what he said, my sweet Maud Arrondale would be sure to cry out, "Why, Grandpa Joseph, that just what my pastor said last Sunday! I don't think there is anything very wonderful about *that*!"

Yes, my dear, but please remember that Stephen preached his sermon first! The truth is, that the pioneers made the great sermons we hear to-day. Your modern preachers merely put on the ornamentation.

The argument from prophecy was clearly laid down; prophecy was verified by history. Before I was aware how I was being carried along by the message, I seemed to stand before the conquering Son of God, the one victorious over death and hell, the one who is alive forevermore.

"The tremendous fact of the resurrection of Jesus Christ," said Stephen, "stands as a challenge to the world. The evidence is complete. It can not be disproved. Many persons of today would be glad, like those of the olden time, to give large sums of money to do away with this fact and the responsibility it brings, but they can not. There remains to confront them, not the stolen body of a Galilean peasant, but the presence of the living Son of God, growing every year more powerful, marching, as the centuries pass, to greater conquests; the Messiah of the Old Testament, the Savior of the New."

"I accept the challenge!"

The words cut through the stillness of the room like the snap of a whiplash. Colonel Sylvestre had risen, and stood with his finger pointed at the speaker. Stephen paused, and waited respectfully for the Colonel to go on.

"I accept the challenge," he repeated. "The young gentleman speaks with the extreme confidence of ignorance. He will be wiser after some years of investigation. He says that the fact of the resurrection stands as a challenge. I accept the challenge. If he is willing to stand by his guns, well and good. I will, within a week, bring here a man who will prove that the resurrection of Jesus is a myth, that the so-called miracles had their origin in the folklore of a credulous people, that the teachings of Jesus were borrowed, that he was himself a misled enthusiast. What do you say, sir?"

"I say bring on your man!" Stephen's voice rang out like the call of a trumpet. Perhaps the Colonel had not anticipated such a prompt response. At any rate, he sat down without more ado.

After this interruption it was difficult to bring the meeting to an orderly close. There was a little buzz of comment through the room. I continued during the hymn, and was scarcely hushed for the concluding prayer. After this, the people gathered together in little knots to discuss the situation.

If Stephen had represented some other religious organization, public sympathy would have been most decidedly with him. Colonel Sylvestre was not popular, and the manner of his challenge was considered discourteous. But as Stephen was one of the so-called "Campbellites," it was natural that there should be a difference of opinion.

"The only way to get Campbellism out of this town is to stomp it out," said Deacon Meacham. "I've heard how it is in Rocksford, and it'll be the same here. Give 'em an inch and they'll take an ell. They ort to be stomped out, no matter who does it."

"I guess Old Man Sylvestre ain't going to let go of Steve Arrondale any too easy," Ross Turner said. "I heard he threatened to horsewhip him for baptizing Martha."

"He's gettin' pretty old for that kind o' business," said Zephaniah Leech. "But we never get too old for tonguelashing—not in this world."

Years afterward I head of other comments which were passed that afternoon. Colonel Sylvestre, Rachel and the Reverend Cady Vincent rode home together in the fine, new carriage which the Colonel had just bought. Rachel was silent and the Colonel seemed weary and unnerved. The burden of conversation, therefore, fell upon the guest.

"You flung down the gauntlet quite fearlessly to-day, Colonel," said Mr. Vincent, in his deferential fashion. "I only wish a Universalist might have the honor of accepting your challenge."

"I fear I made a mistake," said the Colonel, in his grand fashion. "The temptation to have the boy's ridiculous arguments exposed was too much for me at the time, but I presume it is foolish to notice such ignorance so far as a challenge its statements. No doubt I merely catered to the fellow's self-esteem, instead of correcting it."

"I judge from all I can hear," said Mr. Vincent, "that these Campbellites are in general a very ignorant people. Men like the Campbells themselves, and other leaders among them, are college-bred, but their preachers are for the most part illiterate men, who have taken up their calling on a week's notice, and are poorly prepared to be leaders for the people."

"Stephen Arrondale is not an illiterate man!" cried Rachel, flashing up as she used to sometimes when we were children. "You heard him to-day, and you know he is not. I met no man in the East who was his superior in real education. You and father both know that it is unjust to call him ignorant."

Mr. Vincent was at that stage of his love-making when one is inclined to take everything playfully. "Aha, Miss Sylvestre," he said, "so you like his preaching better than mine! I am really inclined to jealousy. Let us sees he not a brother of the young Arrondale whom I met at your house last year? He was evidently a most humble worshiper at your shrine. Perhaps it is for his sake that you champion this very unconventional young preacher."

"The Arrondales are the best friends we ever had, Mr. Vincent," Rachel said, speaking, I doubt not, in the dignified tone that we all feared. "Stephen and Joseph were the playmates and protectors of my sister and me in childhood. Their mother closed the eyes of mine in death. It would ill become us to withhold from them now the respect and friendship which are their due."

Mr. Vincent and Rachel were sitting together on the backseat. Colonel Sylvestre, form his position in front, had been listening closely to the conversation. Now he turned around, and said in a loud voice:

"Rachel, you need never speak to any of the Arrondales again or mention them in my presence."

No doubt Mr. Vincent was delighted, but he need not have been. There are some women who can safely be commanded, but we Arrondales knew very well that Rachel Sylvestre was not one of them.

CHAPTER XV

THE DEBATE

Next day Colonel Sylvestre rode away. As he passed our house, Stephen told us that he was undoubtedly going after a well-known infidel lecturer by the name of Horatio Lemmerman.

That night I overheard father and mother "talking it over." They always talked everything over. I have known but one other household where there was the same reasonableness in the discussion of family affairs. Sometimes they thought differently, and neither was by any means a person of weak will. Yet in the end they agreed, and there was no "last word." Each modified the other, and in action, when the time came for it, there was a beautiful unity. Their religious discussions had seemed to be the only ones which did not end in this way; but now that they had ended I could see in them, too, there had been the same desire for a common meeting-ground.

About the proposed debate they held very different opinions. Mother thought that Stephen, in his youth and inexperience, ran a great risk in debating with a man accomplished in all the arts of intellectual juggling.

"You know it is not for Stephen that I am concerned. It is for the great cause of religion in this community. Much is at stake. Don't you think it would be better to send for some experienced debater, who will know about what this infidel is likely to say, and be able to meet him?"

"No," said father, "I can't look at it in that way. Colonel Sylvestre wants to crush Stephen and ruin his influence. He hoped, by that challenge, to stop Stephen's mouth, or, at least, to put him at a disadvantage before the audience. But Stephen stood by his guns and won the day. If he should send for somebody else now, the Colonel would use it to his harm. I own it's a risk, and I feel anxious; but the boy has always known what he was about, and I guess he does now."

The debate was to begin on Thursday morning of the following week. In the meantime Stephen rode over to Rocksford to consult some books owned by one of his friends. Books!—how scarce they were and how we craved them. The little library of Colonel Sylvestre was the only collection owned in our community, and in it there was not a book which had been bought within the past twenty years. Stephen had not more than fifteen volumes in the world, and only two or three of these bore upon Christian evidences.

"I have only one thing in the way of preparation," he told me. "In times past I have been so put to it for books that I have read all that the Colonel has in his library. They did not hurt me then, and they may be useful to me now. At least, I know what the infidels were saying twenty-five years ago. They may have a new set of arguments by this time, but I have no means of knowing what they are."

Considering how sparsely settled the country was, and how slight were our means of communication, it was surprising that the news of Colonel Sylvestre's challenge and Stephen's acceptance traveled as it did. When the day for the debate came, vehicles of all kinds came from all directions, bringing those who desired to hear the discussion. It was twenty miles to Rocksford, yet nearly every member of the little church there was present. The interest of the people there was very keen, not only, as I learned afterward, because of their loyalty to their faith, but also because of their personal love for Stephen and Martha. Naturally, they judged Colonel Sylvestre to be a tyrant; for Martha was so gentle and affectionate that none but a hard parent, whatever his belief, could have dealt severely with her.

It chanced that I did not see Mr. Lemmerman until the morning on which the discussion began. He was a large, rather loosely built man, with a flowing gray beard and bright but not keen dark eyes. He and Colonel Sylvestre came in arm in arm, with the air of conquerors marching to victory. Following them came the Reverend Cady Vincent and Rachel Sylvestre.

I did not, of course, know that Rachel had been forbidden to speak to Stephen and me, but Mr. Vincent did, and I fear her conduct did not give him a high opinion of her daughterly obedience. For, as she passed near Stephen on her way to a seat, she bowed and smiled gravely. Her father's eyes were upon her, but he took no notice of her action, then or afterward. Probably he would have excused his own laxity by saying that she had not spoken and that he had not forbidden her the privilege of bowing to the Arrondales.

I am quite aware that the different things I write down concerning Rachel Sylvestre often must seem inconsistent. But since that time, and even down to the present, I have known many beautiful and high-spirited women whose actions had the outward appearance of inconsistency.

The moderator of the debate was old Judge Oliphant, who was considered the ablest lawyer in the county. He was a rotund, jolly old gentleman, who took snuff frequently and laughed immoderately at every sally of wit.

I wish I had notes of the discussion, but perhaps if I had, there would be little in them to interest the present generation. That day was long ago—farther away from us in religious thought than in actual years. I have but to close my eyes to live over again that past of which I once was a part, but only the pen of genius can make the past live again for those who have never shared it. And I am no genius, but a trembling old man seeking to set down a few plain facts as they come back to him.

If I remember correctly, the points of discussion were about as follows:

Is the Bible the inspired word of God?
Was Jesus of Nazareth the divine Son of God?
Are we justified in believing in a future life?

On the first point, Mr. Lemmerman had the opening speech. In denying the inspiration of the Scriptures, he indulged in many jests which I could not but think in poor taste. He laughed at the plagues of Egypt and at the idea of Joshua's stopping the sun in the heavens. He complained of the destruction of the Canaanites and the smiting of the firstborn. That was all. He brought forward no arguments beyond the general inference that a just God could not express himself in acts like these.

Yet the impression upon the audience had been surprisingly strong. The speaker's big, assertive manner, his coarse humor, even his apparent satisfaction with his own effort, told for much. I was surprised that it was so, but the evidence was there in scores of admiring faces. Colonel Sylvestre looked triumphant. Rachel studied the tips of her pretty boots while the Reverend Cady Vincent whispered something in her ear.

Stephen began very quietly, reminding the audience that his opponent had not spoken to the question of the inspiration of the Bible, but merely concerning the justice of certain acts there recorded. He then gave a rapid outline of the Bible, in its general divisions, and some rules of interpretation. He urged his hearers to distinguish carefully between the different epochs of God's dealing with men and his messages to each. He said that God's word to the race in its childhood was a word to a child, spoken sometimes in the plain language of physical rewards and punishments. Then he began to speak of the testimony of the Bible to itself, the unity of its parts one with another, the whole an expression of God's effort for the race as finally consummated in the gift of his Son.

It is old ground now, but in those days people had less conception of the logical arrangement of the Scriptures. A Bible verse was a Bible verse, whether found in Deuteronomy or in John's Gospel.

It was difficult to judge of the effect of Stephen's speech, so lacking was it in the play of wit which pleases a popular audience. In the afternoon Mr. Lemmerman wasted half an hour in an attempt to reply to it, but I noticed that his humor was rather less merry than it had been in the morning.

Rachel was absent from the afternoon session, but the Reverend Cady Vincent was there, keeping close to the Colonel. Stephen made the opening speech on the second question. I need not go into it at length. It laid stress upon the acknowledged existence and genuineness of the prophecies concerning Christ, of the unrefuted testimonies concerning his life, the proofs of his resurrection, the witness of those who gave up their lives for him, and, above all, the impossibility of his life and character having been the creation of human intelligence. If his life were an ideal, why did other human ideals fall so immeasurably below it? Why had men for eighteen hundred years, in all poetry and art and philosophy, borrowed from this ideal, instead of improving upon it?

It was at this point that Stephen suddenly changed and became a man of fire. It seemed to me that I had never known him before. Heretofore he had been quiet, cautious, feeling his way, careful never to force his conclusions. But now his theme took possession of him. He became suddenly assertive, with the divine assertiveness of him who sees the chariots of heaven and the horsemen thereof.

"Parallel, if you can, the sayings of the Man of Nazareth," he cried out. "They are divine, and can not be paralleled in human speech. Do you say they are put in to his mouth by another? By whom? By Paul? Then it is Paul whom I worship. By Peter? Then it is Peter at whose feet I sit. But leave us the utterances of Jesus, and we still have the utterances of the Son of God."

In his reply, Mr. Lemmerman showed himself a man of much smaller caliber than I had supposed him. He was no debater, in the proper sense of the word, but was merely a retailer of the stock of objections and the coarse jests of a certain class of infidels of his day. He called up some so-called discrepancies in the records of the four evangelists, then left the direct line of discussion altogether to ridicule the idea that the world could be saved from sin through the shedding of innocent blood.

It was well on toward night when he finished, and the busy farmers who had been listening to the discussion all day should have been about their "chores" by this time; but when the moderator said it should be left to the people whether or not they would listen to the closing speech on the second point before adjourning, they were all for going on.

I realized by this time that the sympathy of the audience was with Stephen, and I gloried in it, though in my heart it was a subject of mortification to me that he had not a foeman more nearly worthy of his steel. I did not know then, nor do I know now, whether Horatio Lemmerman was a representative champion of the infidelity of his day. I only know that he was the one furnished for it. But I might have known even then, if I had paused to reason upon it that truth will always have stronger advocates than error.

In replying to Mr. Lemmerman's last speech, Stephen had opportunity (thanks to his opponent's digressions) to bring in review the sacrifice of Christ for a ruined race. In those days there was much mysterious and confusing teaching concerning the Atonement, and I dare say Stephen was glad to set forth the plain teaching of the Scriptures. He cared little for a mere victory of words; but, like Paul, he was ever watchful of an opportunity to preach the gospel to some who might not otherwise hear it.

Many were moved by his argument that day, as I well know, for many told me afterward that they dated a change in their lives from that day. For myself, I no longer saw upon the cross a helpless victim, needlessly crushed beneath the weight of human sin, but a divine will, voluntarily bowing itself to human limitations, that once and for all the human and divine might meet.

"It was the only way," said Stephen, solemnly, in closing; and my own heart answered, "It was the only way."

In leaving the building, I came upon Rachel. How or when she had come I did not know. I was about to speak to her, when she was joined by the Reverend Cady Vincent.

"At last!" she exclaimed lightly. "I thought this was to be a debate, but it turns out to be a revival meeting."

My heart had been full of good thoughts a moment before, but they seemed to take sudden flight. I was a very foolish and hot-headed boy, and at that moment I almost hated Rachel Sylvestre.

CHAPTER XVI

THE SEQUEL

The next morning the Town Hall was filled at an early hour, for all wished to hear the concluding speeches of the debate. Rachel was again present. She did not sit with her father, but with the other ladies, quite to the other side of the house. She did not notice Stephen or me in any way, but I saw that she bowed to my mother, and presently exchanged a few words with her. I do not know whether or not the Colonel would have considered my gentle mother "an Arrondale."

I had wondered that Mr. Lemmerman, after claiming to set aside the authenticity of the Scriptures and the authority of Christ, should have cared to discuss the question of a future life. Stephen had taken it, as I learned afterward, that he would discuss merely such evidences of the continuance of life as exist in nature and in the human reason, and had prepared himself quite carefully on these points.

But what Mr. Lemmerman had desired was merely a new point for his attack on Christianity. He began as he had begun the day before, with coarse ridicule and sarcasm. A good God these Christians must have, indeed, to create immortal souls, and then damn them for his own glory! A beneficent law, indeed, which condemned the innocent and the guilty to suffer together for the vindication of a righteous God!

His attack was, of course, quite foreign to the question as it had been stated; but it dealt with matters which, though seldom touched upon in these days, were of vital interest then. Stephen was on the alert in a moment. My father's keen old eyes twinkled. Indeed, I had often, in days gone by, heard him argue these questions with far more fairness and intelligence than Horatio Lemmerman was capable of showing.

It was a great day. From nine in the morning until four in the afternoon the battle was on. Yesterday Stephen had had all Christian believers with him. Today the large proportion of them stood aloof, shocked at the coarse atheism of Stephen's opponent, indeed, but scarcely less shocked at the audacity of the bold-fronted young "Campbellite" who dared to condemn as unscriptural and misleading many doctrines which they had venerated from childhood—aye, that had come to them as part of the inheritance for which their forefathers had died.

"You say," he told his antagonist, "that Christianity stands for the sovereignty of a tyrant. I tell you that the Holy Scriptures stand for the sovereignty of a loving Father, who has, in a beneficence which he will not revoke, bestowed upon each of his children the right of free and intelligent choice. In him is no caprice, no injustice. He lays hold upon none against their will, either for approval or condemnation. He has made known his will for us through his Son, in whom is eternal life. On each of us he lays the burden of choice. All doctrines concerning the whys and wherefores of God's gift of eternal life are mere speculations, and we have no right to bind them on any man. But it is our right and duty to set before every one life and death, blessing and cursing, that he may have the opportunity for choice. And by that choice God himself will abide."

By the will of the audience and the permission of the moderator, each speaker was allowed three speeches, two each on the question of the day and one each for a general summary. Most of the people had brought lunch with them, and, during the recess, I noticed that they gathered together in little groups. The Baptists were by themselves and so were the Presbyterians, and so were the Methodists. The few outspoken infidels gathered about Horatio Lemmerman and Colonel Sylvestre. The Reverend Cady Vincent had said a word to Rachel, and then left the building. I saw him walk across the fields and into the woods beyond, and wondered why he had so suddenly come to prefer solitude.

At the conclusion of the debate Judge Oliphant made a long speech, in which he complimented both speakers, the Bible, atheism, the audience, and every other person and thing which he could call to mind. When he could think of nothing else, he said, "I believe our very profitable session is now at an end."

"Not quite. With your permission, Mr. Moderator, and that of the gentlemen who have engaged in this discussion, I wish to say a very few words."

I recognized the thin, clear voice at once. The Reverend Cady Vincent, with a strange look of agitation upon his face, was making his way to the front.

"He is going to challenge Stephen to a debate on the question of eternal punishment," I said to myself. Probably the moderator thought the same thing for he nodded with apparent comprehension as he said, "I am sure we are all willing to accord the reverend gentleman the privilege for which he asks."

The look of agitation on Mr. Vincent's face deepened. "I wish to ask Mr. Arrondale a few questions," he said.

Stephen nodded, as if to intimate that he was ready to answer. I suspected that there was a trap, and that Colonel Sylvestre had baited it.

"You are identified, I am told, with a people who call themselves Christians, or disciples of Christ, but are sometimes called 'Campbellites' by their enemies?"

"I am."

"Is it true, as I have heard, that the people with whom you stand take the Holy Scriptures as their only rule of faith and practice?"

"It is."

"Mr. Arrondale, I am known to this community as a Universalist preacher. Knowing me as such, would you receive me to baptism on such a simple confession of my faith as I have indicated?"

"I most certainly should, and thank God for the opportunity."

"Then this audience is entitled to an explanation, which I shall try to make as brief as possible. For six years I have been preaching Universalism. I realize now that my teaching has been not constructive but destructive. It has been directed against doctrines which, as I believed,

and still believe, rob God of some of his attributes as a loving and beneficent Father. But I now see that I have merely sought to overthrow the
speculations of others with speculations of my own. I am not sure that,
in all minor matters, I agree with the people known as disciples of
Christ, but I am willing to recognize my obligation to examine all theo-
ries in the light of this one great central truth of the divinity of our Lord
Jesus Christ, to speak where the Scriptures speak and to remain silent
where they are silent. Mr. Arrondale, yesterday I was here to listen, to
question, perhaps to criticize. To-day I am here to require baptism at
your hands."

I had not liked Cady Vincent very well hitherto, but now my heart
went out to him in a sudden gush of admiration. It seemed to me then,
and it seems to me now, that his act was one of the bravest acts that I
have ever known. No one could see him in the presence of Rachel
Sylvestre and doubt his love for her. He had left ease and cultured associations in his Eastern home to be near her. Her father had given him
every evidence of favor. Yet for conscience' sake he had put all this
aside—had arrayed himself with an unpopular people and against the
woman he loved.

Colonel Sylvestre was on his feet now, his face purple with anger.
"Mr. Moderator," he cried, "I regard this as an insult to Mr. Lemmerman
and to this audience. This is no place for theatrical conversions. I move
the adjournment of this meeting."

"Mr. Moderator," said Stephen, in a ringing voice, "there has
always been, since the days of the apostles, a fitting place for such noble
scenes as this, and that is at the waters of baptism. We will repair there
immediately, and to this end I second Colonel Sylvestre's motion for an
adjournment."

An adjournment it was indeed, for I believe that all, with the excep-
tion of Colonel Sylvestre and Horatio Lemmerman, went to the stream
with Stephen and Mr. Vincent.

As my brother stepped down into the water I followed him, and
slipped my hand into his. "I want to go first, Stephen," I said.

He had been under a great strain for several days, and his mind was,
naturally, much engrossed. For a moment he looked as if he did not com-
prehend my meaning. Then a great gladness broke over his face.

"Dear old Joe!" he whispered; and again our lives were united and
again our dreams were one.

There, standing in the stream, he took my confession—the confession of my honest but hot and wayward boyish heart. My eyes fill at that
memory, and I can scarcely see the page on which I try to write. I have
often, in hasty speech and action, dishonored the Lord I confessed that

day, but I can say, after all these years, that the central purpose of my life has been true, even as it was true that day.

After he had baptized me, Stephen led Mr. Vincent down into the water and baptized him, and we three walked home together, while the audience dispersed, and the three of us sang together, softly:

> "How happy are they
> Who their Savior obey."

"I hope you will make our home yours while you stay in this neighborhood," said my mother, hospitably. "I suppose you will scarcely feel at home with the Sylvestres after this."

"Scarcely," said Cady Vincent, smiling. He thanked my mother warmly for her kindness, but said no more about the Sylvestres. One little incident I myself might have told. As we stood near the water, just before the baptisms, Rachel had come and held out her hand to Mr. Vincent.

"Do you want to say good-by?" she asked. You can not be father's friend after this, you know."

"But can I not be yours, Rachel?" he asked. The two were close beside me, and I could not but hear the words. "You are too just a woman to refuse friendship to a man because he follows his conscience."

Rachel lowered her eyes, then raised them again. "You are a brave man," she said. "I admire your courage, but I do not like your cause."

She turned away, and I looked after her in pity. My heart was full of gentleness to-day, and my resentment against Rachel was gone.

CHAPTER XVII

THE FIRE

"Bro. Cady," as we learned to call him, remained in our home over the next day, and he and Stephen talked over plans for the future. I gathered that the young minister whose sudden change of faith had so surprised us, was in easy circumstances, and in no way dependent upon his pulpit labors for a support. This was well; for those who preached the "ancient gospel," as they used to call it, did it without money and without price. They must, therefore, either be of independent means, or be compelled to labor with their hands for each day's bread.

I wish to say, however, in justice to Bro. Cady, that if the latter alternative had presented itself to him, he would have accepted it without a moment's hesitation. Worldly considerations weigh little when put into the scale with a great conviction.

I saw at once that Stephen had conceived a great admiration for this man. There were many reasons for this. He had taught him the new faith, and it is evermore the way of the teacher to love the one to whom he has imparted the great lesson of his life. Especially is this true when in most things the pupil is wiser and more experienced than his teacher. Bro. Cady was not a learned man, but he was what is nowadays called "cultured." If he were a young minister of our day, he would be in demand to read "papers" at all the literary clubs that our Maude Arrondale is so fond of attending. He always had an appropriate verse of poetry at his tongue's end, and could quote it with such feeling that you seemed to get a new meaning out of it, however familiar it might be. His accomplishments were of just the kind of charm Stephen, who felt so keenly that he belonged to the backwoods, and had missed the elegances of life.

Another thing that appealed to Stephen strongly was that Cady had given up his chance of winning Rachel for the sake of the gospel. Stephen had done the same thing, it is true, but not so openly and certainly. Besides, he chose to believe that his chance had been of the slightest, and that Cady's had amounted almost to a certainty.

"She must have learned in time to care for him," he told me once, long afterward. "He is of her world—the world she knew, and to which she naturally belonged."

But the affection between Cady and Stephen was not one-sided. The man of the world gave to the man of the woods the full tribute of gratitude and admiration. Stephen's was the stronger nature, and none knew it better than his new friend.

They would go together and preach as they had opportunity. This was the outcome of all their planning. Stephen was to introduce Cady to the little circle of churches to which he had been accustomed to minister, and assure them of his worthiness.

"The way will open," said Stephen, confidently. In this happy hope they rode away, their saddlebags containing plenty of simple food from my mother's larder, and the single change of raiment apiece with which the preachers of that day thought it necessary to be prepared in case of a wayside baptism. Their Bibles they carried in their pockets or their hats, that they might bring with them out and study as they rode. Father had business in Rocksford, and he decided to ride that far with the young preachers. I suspect that he wished to hear what Mr. Osburn and other of his own friends would say about the debate.

It was seldom that my mother and I were left in the house alone over night, and perhaps that is why I remember so distinctly all the incidents of that evening. The wind was high, and had a threatening sound. I know that mother drew the curtains over the windows, took the green bough out of the fireplace, and lighted a fire on the hearth of the front room. I was surprised at this, for usually we sat in the kitchen when there was no company.

"Are you cold?" I asked, fearing that she might be falling ill.

"Oh, no," she said, "but the wind sounds dreary, as if the fall were here. I believe I am always a little nervous when your father is away."

Dear mother! she was homesick for her grayhaired lover, and I both laughed at her and kissed her as I told her so.

We had a long, long talk that night. She told me how she thanked God that her prayers for me had been answered, and that I had followed Stephen into the kingdom.

"But I am not Stephen, nor shall I ever be," I said. "You must never expect me to be."

No matter what she said. It is only God and mothers whose faith in human nature is complete.

"Perhaps in a year or two you will be preaching the gospel, too," she said, with a great longing in her voice.

"No, mother," I told her, "I must be a humble scholar, not a teacher. I have not the aptitude for that, as Stephen has. Some one must stay here and help father, and I, who have no great gifts of any sort, am just the one for that."

She did not argue the point, but smoothed my hair as if she were satisfied. By and by she said:

"Mothers never get quite to the place where they have no anxiety about their children. Now I think of the time when my boys will marry, and of the women who will help to make or spoil their futures. Of course, you are still too young to consider such matters." (I did not at all agree with my mother in this), "but Stephen must soon think of marrying. Sometimes I wonder if he has not already thought too much about Rachel for his own peace of mind."

I could not betray Stephen's secret, even to my mother; so I only said:

"Stephen does not meet many girls who are Rachel's equal in point of intelligence."

Mother looked at me with quick alarm. "I hope she has not spoiled *your* peace of mind," she said. "She is a smart, capable girl, and I love her in spite of her faults. But I can't help feeling that a godless woman will ruin any man's life. Bro. Cady escaped from her influence none too soon. Now he will make a useful man; and perhaps some good woman will make him a happy one."

(I ought to say that my mother had no conception of a happy life apart from marriage. Without a wife, though with the consolations of religion, a man might be submissive, even cheerful, but not, in the full sense, happy. This belief was one of the compliments she paid to her own married life.)

We talked so earnestly that we forgot all about the passage of time; and when the old clock in the kitchen struck twelve, we both sprang to our feet in surprise. It was long since my mother had kept such unseemly hours.

"We have had a good talk, anyway," she said. "Haven't we?"

For answer, I kissed her again, and as I did so I noted that look of girlishness which came over her face when she was very happy. Ah, what a mother Stephen and I had!

I went upstairs but had only just begun to get ready for bed when I heard My mother calling:

"Oh, quick, quick, Joseph! Colonel Sylvestre's house is on fire!"

I did not stop even to look in the direction of the fire. In a moment I was in the stable, loosening the halter of Queenie, my faithful little brown mare. I did not wait for a saddle, but flung myself on Queenie's back and rode as for the lives of those in the house on the hill. As I passed the house, I saw my mother standing, with strained eyes, in the door.

But I saw at once that the danger was less terrible than she had supposed. The fire was not in the house, but in the stable. The wind blew away from the house, but toward the great barn where the harvests of the year were stored. I remembered, as I rode, how Colonel Sylvestre had warned us against a fire in this barn when we danced there years before.

As I approached the place, one wild, hoarse cry after another fell upon my ears. Could it be possible that there was some one in the burning stable?

"Rachel! Rachel! Come out, Rachel! You will be killed—oh, Rachel! Rachel!"

Colonel Sylvestre stood helplessly before the burning building, his arms outstretched toward it. He had dressed hurriedly, his feet and head were bare, and his long white hair was blown back by the wind. Before or since, I have never seen such a picture of hopelessness.

Catching sight of me, he ran and pulled at me, as if to hasten my actions. "Save her! save her! She is inside! Great God, man! Rachel is in that barn!"

Was he really calling upon the merciful God whom he had so long blasphemed? I suppose not, for in his madness he did not know what he said. I flung myself from Queenie's back, and ran toward the stable.

The smoke choked and blinded me, but just inside the door I felt myself firmly grasped. My heart cried out in thankfulness as I drew Rachel out into the air. It was some moments before she could speak, but she kept pointing back toward the stable.

"Is there some one in there still?" I kept asking. She shook her head, but still pointed to the stable.

"The poor horses!" she gasped at last. "I thought I could save them, but they would not come out!"

Then I knew what had happened. She had unfastened the horses, thinking they would find their own way out; but the poor creatures, in their terror, had only plunged into the smoke, to perish miserably.

"I could not have breathed in there another minute," she added; "I was groping my way to where I thought the door ought to be, when I found you."

It seemed entirely useless to enter the building again, but the look of horror in Rachel's eyes, when at last she opened them wide, drove me to the attempt. She was ever a lover of animals, and the horses were her especial pride. If they had still been fastened in their stalls, I might possibly have been able to lead them out one by one; but poor Rachel's bravery seemed to have made their rescue quite out of the question.

I took a long breath and plunged in, trying to keep my bearings and to follow the pitiful neighs of the horses. Again and again I thought I must turn back, but at last I found one of the animals, wound my hands into his mane, and tried to speak. I was sure from the height that it must be Dolly, Rachel's spirited little saddlehorse, and I thought she might know my voice. I do not know to this day how I got out of that building, much less how I got Dolly out with me. Rachel came flying to meet me.

"I thought I had sent you to your death," she cried. "Didn't you hear me calling? It seemed as if you would never come."

A strange weakness had come over me, and for a moment it seemed that I could not rally myself for further exertion. Just then my mother came riding up the lane on one of the farm horses. I realized at once what she had done. The women of those days were equal to emergencies; and my mother had been out to rouse the neighbors and tell them of the fire.

There were not many neighbors, but those who came were soon at work, and, my faintness past, I found myself able to work with them.

There was little to be done. The house was not in any real danger, for it was at a considerable distance from the stable, and, as I have said, the wind was blowing the sparks in the opposite direction. But the great barn was threatened every moment, and we had no means of fighting fire. We half-dozen men did what we could with buckets and wet blankets, but I felt from the beginning that it was hopeless. Now that Rachel was safe, the Colonel had regained his composure, and directed our work, in his old tone of authority. Once, when I was near him, however, I noticed that he was shaking from head to foot, whether from cold or excitement I could not judge.

I proposed that the wagons and farming implements, which were stored in the great barn, be removed. While we were busy with this work, a cry from the women on the steps caused us to look out at the straw stacks. They were on fire, and in a moment the fire had spread to the barn.

The work of destruction was swift. Already the stable was in ruins, and the big barn, containing the harvests of the year, seemed to blaze up in a dozen places at once. There was nothing more to be done. I joined the women on the porch, and waited for the flames to do their work.

"Have you any idea how the fire started?" I asked of Rachel.

"I can only guess," she said. "Father smokes a great deal in the stable, when he is about his chores. He would never let his hired men do this, but lately he has grown careless. Last night, I remember, he had his pipe when he went to the barn, and it seemed to me afterward that he came in without it."

She was quiet and controlled, although her lips were white. In truth, Rachel usually seemed to me too controlled and self-possessed for a woman. I had liked her better a little while before, when she had come to meet me with a cry of gladness at my escape. Moments like that one were what kept me in the faith that, under all, Rachel had a human heart.

Presently she slipped away, and she and my mother busied themselves inside the house. We saw the rafters of the big barn crash in, and the huge timbers quiver and fall. Then there was nothing left upon which the fire could feed itself, and it slowly died down, until there was left only a smoking heap of ruins.

Then Rachel came and called us in. The table was spread out, and laden with good things. "You are all going home tired," she said, almost merrily, "but you must not go home hungry. I insist that you eat an early breakfast with us before you leave."

I hesitated, for in those days I had a stubborn pride, and Bro. Cady had told Stephen and me how Colonel Sylvestre had forbidden Rachel to speak to the Arrondales. I felt that I could not partake of his hospitality under the circumstances.

Rachel came to the door again. "Why don't you come in, Joseph?" she asked.

I was a hot-headed youngster, and I told her what I had heard.

"You are a very foolish fellow," she said. "You will risk your life for us, but you will not eat in our house! Your brother would have better sense."

That was true. Stephen would say I was behaving very foolishly. For his sake I went in and ate my breakfast.

CHAPTER XVIII

A NEW ARRIVAL

The next I heard from the Sylvestres, the Colonel was very ill. Ross Turner drove up in his fine new buggy and imparted this information. The old man had taken cold from exposure on the night of the fire, and on the following day had gone to bed. Rachel had been caring for him night and day.

It seemed strange that five days should have been allowed to pass, since the fire, without any effort on our part to learn of the welfare of our neighbors, especially just after such a calamity had befallen them. But my father was a driving farmer, and he had come home from Rocksford full of enterprise. The fences must be mended and the sheds put into good condition for the winter. So I had little time at my own disposal.

I will admit, however, that there was another reason. My boyish pride was still at work, and I thought that after all that had happened, the advances should come from the Sylvestres.

Turner leaned over the dashboard and looked confidential. "If the old man should die now, I suppose Rachel would get it all." I suppressed a desire to cut him across the mouth with his own buggywhip, and merely said:

"I'm sure I don't know anything about it."

"It ain't likely he'd do anything for Martha, after the way she has acted. Now, I wouldn't so much mind Martha. A little too pious, maybe, but that ain't the worst thing in the world, 'specially in a woman. But Rachel! She'd lead a man a life of it, now, wouldn't she, Joe? She'd just set her little foot down on a fellow's neck, and keep it there for a lifetime. Have you any idea how much there is, Joe?"

"How much is there of what?" I asked sulkily.

"How much the old man is worth?"

"Not the least idea in the world."

"That's very strange, when you've lived by him so long. But Rachel is a queer one. A fellow don't like her, and yet he can't keep away from here. I don't like her, and I've always liked Arabel. There's a girl one can have a little fun with, and not be everlastingly put down and domineered over. But old man Sylvestre has got a pretty pile of money—there ain't no denyin' that."

I was glad when the selfish scamp drove away. I walked over to the Sylvestres, and found Rachel looking more worried than I had ever seen her. I condemned myself mercilessly when I saw the cares which had settled down upon her. There was no man about the place, and though there was no stock to care for, yet there was wood and water to be brought and many errands to be done. Her father was in bed and seemed almost helpless.

I busied myself about the place for a little while, and then went in to ask if I could be service to the sick man.

Rachel shook her head. I more than suspected that her father was a difficult invalid.

"I can manage very well," she said. "There is no immediate danger, but the shock has been great and he needs a long rest. But there is something that you can do for me, Joseph. It is a great deal to ask, but there is no one else of whom I *can* ask it. Can you get the word to Martha, and ask her to come home?"

I suppose my surprise showed itself in my face. At any rate, Rachel knew very well what was in my mind.

"Father has consented," she said quickly. "He imagines himself dying, and I told him that Martha must come."

I had learned long before that this slim young woman was a mistress of diplomacy. How she had managed the old man no one ever knew; but I suppose she had allowed his fears of death to run riot until he resentment weakened and his natural parental affection asserted itself.

"I will go to Rocksford to-day, and bring Martha home with me," I said, with boyish eagerness.

Rachel's manner at once became chilly, and I realized that I had made a mistake. "There is no such need of haste," she said, in her most formal tone. "Mr. and Mrs. Osburn would bring her home, if they knew she was needed. Perhaps Ross Turner would go, if I should ask him."

If she should ask him! She should not ask anything of that mercenary scoundrel. I hastened to put on my most humble manner, and to assure my lady that I would ride over to Rocksford, see Mr. and Mrs. Osburn, and ask them to bring Martha home as soon as convenient.

Then I departed, feeling much like a worm of the dust. It was thus that I usually felt after an interview with Rachel Sylvestre.

Queenie and I had a fine ride together. The woods were in their autumn glory, and the air had that frosty nip which is better than a tonic. Her and there I reined up beside the fence to talk to some farmer who was at work in the clearing. Ah! those great fires of log and brush, in which so much of the glorious timber of this country was consumed! They were a part of the price of civilization and civilization always comes high.

I was almost within sight of Rocksford when I was joined by another rider, a lightly built young man—I guessed him at twenty-eight, though he might have been much more—well dressed, and with the suggestion of conscious superiority about him.

We passed the time of day, after the manner of travelers in that time, and we rode on together. His name, he said, was Charles Easton. He had come to Rocksford recently from New York, and was thinking of investing in land and settling in the vicinity.

"The people hereabouts have made a mistake in beginning life in such a narrow way," he said. "They have allowed the land to be cut up into small farms, instead of keeping it in tracts large enough to be farmed with real profit. I have been managing several thousand acres, so these clearings look rather small to me."

"We poor folks have to farm what we can get," I said. "Besides, with no markets within reach, there would be no special profit in large farming."

We argued the matter for some moments. He was not convinced, nor was I, and perhaps that was one reason why we never liked each other. Possibly I have confused later impressions with those of that first meeting, but it seems to me in the recollection that I always disliked Charles Easton, always listened with distrust to his assertions concerning himself.

Yet I can not tell why. His face had not the strength of Stephen's nor the refinement of Bro. Cady's, but certainly it was not unmistakably coarse. He was boastful, but not offensively so, not more so, indeed, than many well-intentioned men I knew. It is hard for me to tell why I disliked him. Perhaps it was because I saw that he had set me down as a backwoods gawky. That would have been a convincing reason.

He asked me where I came from, and when I told him what neighborhood it was, he at once inquired about Colonel Sylvestre.

"I know some of his friends in New York State," he said. "I must pay my respects to him, and ask his advice in placing my investments."

I opened my mouth to tell him of the Colonel's misfortune and illness, and of my errand to Rocksford; than caution interposed and I kept still. He was no acquaintance of the Sylvestres, and was entitled to no confidence concerning them.

We were at the Osburns by this time, and my new acquaintance and I parted company. Mr. Osburn was away from home, but his wife received me hospitably, and was both pleased and anxious when I told her my story.

"Martha must go home at once," she said. "We can not risk the chance that the old man may change his mind. The poor girl suffers greatly through feeling herself shut out from her home. I doubt if she will be any happier there than here, but we could never forgive ourselves if the chance for a reconciliation were lost. Besides, there is another reason." The good woman looked worried. "A man named Easton has been staying about these parts lately, and has done everything possible to engage Martha's interest. He even attends our little meetings, though I hear he sneers at the teaching when he is with the worldly. So far as I can learn, Martha has accepted no attention from him, but he visits much at the school and seems determined to see as much of her as possible. I shall feel better when she is back among her own people. She is too young and too beautiful to be alone."

I was alarmed at once. There could be nothing in common between Martha and this man, yet no one can guess where the heart of an innocent, trusting girl will fasten itself. I began to wish, with Mrs. Osburn, that she was back with her own people—that is to say, with Rachel.

Mrs. Osburn insisted that I remain over night. In the morning she would drive Martha home, under my escort. I did not see how even the fastidious Rachel could object to this; and so I stayed. After supper I went over to the house of Martha's teacher, with whom she lived. Martha herself met me at the door. I think my coming aroused her anxiety, for she at once inquired after her father and Rachel.

"And I am to go—to go *home*?" she asked, with a pitiful emphasis upon the word. I realized at that moment how bitterly she had felt her exile.

"Mrs. Osburn will go with you tomorrow," I told her. "Do not feel anxious about your father. Rachel assured me that there is no cause for anxiety. They both need you and want you—that is all."

"Rachel wrote me about the fire," she said. "It was so good of you to save dear old Dolly."

"Oh, that was nothing at all," I said. "Your sister's risk was far greater than mine." Still, it was pleasant to be praised by Martha.

I had hoped a little to find Stephen in Rocksford, but he and Bro. Cady had stopped but for a night, and then had hastened on to the county seat of the next county, where they were to hold what was called, in the speech of the brethren, "a meeting of days."

The next day we started for home as soon as it was light. I had just helped Martha, in my awkward fashion, to mount her horse, when Mr. Charles Easton came up.

"Miss Sylvestre!" he exclaimed. "How near I came to letting you get away without a parting word! I am distressed indeed to learn of your father's illness. And how unfortunate that you should be called from your studies just at this time!"

"I am very glad indeed to go home to my father and sister," said Martha, in her sweet, serious way. "I am sure my sister needs me, although she would never say so. I have been away for a long time, and she has had a heavy burden."

I watched her narrowly as she told Charles Easton goodby. If he was in reality her lover, she seemed entirely unconscious of it. She held out her hand, and he bent over it with what I considered (being myself a backwoods boy) an entirely unnecessary display of gallantry. But Martha, I fancy, would have thought it unwomanly to judge any man her suitor until he had avowed himself such.

"I shall come to see your father as soon as he is sufficiently recovered to receive visitors," he told her. "May I not trust you to let me know when that time comes?"

"You can ask Mrs. Osburn," Martha said, looking into his face with frank simplicity. "She is sure to keep informed of father's condition."

Mr. Easton's jaunty manner seemed to be a trifle subdued by this innocent speech, but he said goodby with proper grace. Then we rode away, Martha and I to breathe in together the intoxication of nature and the spirit of youth.

Martha Sylvestre was a creature fashioned for happiness. Birds and sunshine belonged within her soul. But her affections dominated her, and failure and loss there meant quick misery. To be loved and to serve those she loved meant not only happiness, but freedom—the power to be herself and to express herself naturally. To-day she was herself, for she was going home.

Good Mrs. Osburn, too, was happy. The thought of Mr. Easton's attentions to Martha had distressed her, and she was glad to turn the girl over to Rachel. For, whatever Rachel's failings might be, she was certainly an irreproachable guardian.

So we made a merry party, and I think even the frisky squirrels may have hastened their steps to listen to our laughter that morning.

Rachel came down the lane to meet us, and Martha slipped from her saddle and threw herself into her sister's arms. I believe I have said somewhere that I am not what is called emotional, but at that moment I felt like a woman, and a hysterical woman at that.

Rachel kissed Martha and smoothed her hair for a moment; then she loosened the girl's arms, and came to where I stood. I remember that I was foolishly playing with the bridle of my horse, and trying to choke back the big lump in my throat.

"Thank you, Joseph," she said. There was the old comradeship of our school days in her voice, the old friendliness in her eyes. I wondered how matters would fare in the future between the Sylvestres and the Arrondales.

CHAPTER XIX
AN UNWILLING SACRIFICE

For several days I went to the Sylvestres daily, and did such little services as come in my way. Then the Colonel began to creep about again, and I thought it prudent to remain away.

However, mother went frequently, and brought home tidings. The Colonel was not his old self. He seemed almost fiercely anxious to be well, and to resume his old duties, but he wearied easily, and was irritated when any one seemed to notice his weakness. Mentally, too, he had failed. Often he lost himself, and was obliged to leave the most casual remark unfinished. He seemed to realize this and to be especially annoyed by it; for he had been particularly proud of his conversational powers.

Mother reported that he seemed to treat Martha as if nothing unpleasant had occurred; but it soon became evident that he meant to deny her all religious privileges. She never came to any of the meetings of the brethren and sisters, though it was plain enough from her eager inquiries that she had lost none of her interest. I knew that she could not have counted upon this deprivation when she had returned to her home so gladly, and that she must feel it sorely.

Once, the only time she and I were alone together that winter, she told me how glad she was that I had "obeyed the gospel." (I have loved this quaint Scripture phrase from that day. Martha's speech on everyday subjects was unusually simple and childlike, but she fell easily into the language of the sanctuary when she talked on religion.)

"I am so glad," she repeated, with sweet earnestness. "It is a step you will never regret. I can not tell you what the precious promises are to me. So long as I have my Bible, there is cheer and comfort, whatever comes." Then she blushed a little, as if she had been surprised into speaking of herself too freely.

"I'm glad, too, Martha," I said. "I believe the Bible, and I want to stand for what it teaches. But I'm not a very good sort of fellow. I'm hot-blooded and impatient, and frequently I have feelings that are not at all like a Christian. As often as once a week, for instance, I want to thrash Ross Turner."

Martha's merry little laugh rang out. "You will never again care to thrash Ross Turner," she said. "He is going to be married."

"Going to be married! To whom?"

"To Arabel Holcomb, of course. Who else would marry *him*?"

"Not Rachel, certainly," I ventured. I had never before known that Martha's delicate little nose could be tilted exactly like her sister's. But the present experiment in that direction was a perfect success.

Martha was right. Within a week, Ross and Arabel drove to Rocksford together in the new buggy, and returned a wedded pair. It was a satisfaction to know that the vacillations of this foolish fellow were at last ended. I may as well say right here that Martha's prophecy proved true, and that I never again had the slightest temptation to thrash Ross Turner. He was entirely safe with Arabel, and there I was content to leave him.

As I have intimated, I saw Martha alone but once, in the winter that followed her return. I merely caught a glimpse of her now and then, when I went to the house on an errand; for their father's semi-invalidism kept both of the girls closely confined at home. In the early spring, my mother told me it was generally believed that Martha was preparing to be married to Charles Easton.

"Martha!" I exclaimed. "Why, Martha is only" I stopped short. I had started to say that Martha was only a child. But in that moment I realized that she was a woman and had the right to choose.

But had she not, too, the right to know? My old, instinctive dislike of Easton overswept me again. It was horrible that this pure creature should give herself to a man of whose past she knew nothing. I was only a boy myself, and a boy of singularly limited experience; yet I had distrusted the man. Why had not Martha been warned by a similar intuition?

Strangely enough, the only person to whom I thought of going with my burden of soul was my old enemy. Rachel was Martha's care-taker and second mother. Rachel could always bring things about. I would go to Rachel.

That very evening, I saw Martha drive by with Easton. I walked over at once, and found Rachel alone. She received me kindly, but seemed, I thought, extremely sad.

I had hoped to lead up to my errand gently, but no opportunity offered itself. So I was obliged to begin boldly and bluntly.

"Rachel," I said, "we were children together, and I have no sisters. Do you remember how you enraged me once by calling me your little brother, when I was half a head taller than you? I want to be your little brother again for half an hour—your naughty, meddlesome little brother. I have always let you scold me—you may scold me as much as you please when I am done. I want you to talk to me about Martha and Charles Easton."

She raised her beautiful eyes and searched my face. "What do you know about them?" she asked.

"I know nothing. I hear they are going to be married."

"Why do you ask questions?"

"I promised to let you scold me after I am done. But tell me first what I want to know."

"What do you want to know?"

"Whether your father or any of his friends have had previous knowledge of Mr. Easton—whether you know him to be the kind of man who will make Martha happy."

Rachel shrugged her shoulders. "Happiness is an uncertain quantity," she said. "How can we tell what kind of man will make any woman happy?"

"Don't bandy words, Rachel. If you know Mr. Easton to be a man of character and responsibility, I have nothing to say. I told you in the beginning that I had come to be meddlesome."

Again she looked into my face searchingly. "Have you heard anything against him?" she asked.

"Not one thing. I will tell you the whole truth, and then your sense of justice will at once be up in rebellion. It is simply that I do not fancy Mr. Easton—that I feel he is not worthy of Martha."

The mask lifted from her face, and her anxiety and doubt looked out upon me. "I feel so too," she said. "But I have not a particle of reason. And we must be just, Joseph—we must not misjudge this man."

Somewhat reluctantly I agreed with her. I was not, to tell the truth, so much concerned about doing justice to Charles Easton as I was about Martha's chances for happiness. I wanted to say, "Does she love him?" but such a question would be meddling indeed, and Rachel would probably be prompt to resent it.

"Father is greatly set upon this matter," Rachel went on. "I never saw him so set upon anything. You know he has never felt quite at home in this country, and he likes every one who brings the air of the East with him."

"Yes, he intended to marry you to Bro. Cady," I said, with my customary bluntness.

Rachel reddened and ignored the interruption.

"Mr. Easton brought excellent letters of introduction from prominent persons in Albany—persons of whom my father knows, though he is not personally acquainted with any of them. Martha met Mr. Easton first in Rocksford, and he seemed to be received without any question there. I suppose he was attracted to Martha, even then." He came here soon after she returned, and almost immediately made his wishes known to my father. Father did not tell me at once, but when I knew—"

She stopped short, but the compression of her lips and the swelling of the veins upon her forehead told me with what strength she had opposed her father's will. But for once her opposition had been in vain.

"And Martha?" I asked, feeling that her confidence gave me an opportunity to speak. "How does she feel about it all?"

Rachel looked troubled. I knew that her longing for some one to share her anxiety was battling with her life-long habit of reserve. It was agony to speak the secrets of her sister's heart, and yet she spoke.

"I do not think Martha wishes for the marriage. She is timid by nature, and she is frightened at the thought of giving her life to one who is almost a stranger. But she is tractable and yielding by instinct—not at all like me." And Rachel laughed a sad little laugh. "She says that when she—when she was baptized, she had decided that was the one thing a child might do against the wishes of a parent. And, even in that, she suffered more than any of us knew."

I nodded, remembering the look of exile in Martha's eyes when I saw her at Rocksford.

"She says she can not disobey again. She has begged father to let her wait, but he has grown strangely impatient. Mr. Easton urges haste, and father tells Martha that, if she refuses to obey him, he will send her away and never take her back again."

Then something happened that I never expected to see. Rachel bowed her head upon her hands and burst into tears.

"Don't be alarmed, Joe," she said—again came the sad little smile—"I don't do this more than once a year."

"Oh, don't mind that," I begged, and added, with quite unnecessary candor, "I am so relieved to think you do it at all!"

She did not mind. "I must not do this man an injustice," she said again. "I know absolutely nothing of him that is discreditable."

"Is there nothing discreditable in the fact that he wishes to hurry an inexperienced girl into a marriage that would be distasteful to her?" I demanded hotly. "If he were half a man, he would not want to cheap a victory. He would have her heart or nothing at all."

Rachel looked at me in some surprise, as if she would say, "Whence this sudden acquisition of wisdom? Who taught *you* where real victory lies?" But she said nothing and I rose to go.

"Is there nothing to be done?" I asked, "nothing to prevent this sacrifice?"

"I know of nothing. You may be interested in knowing"—now for the first time, it was the scornful, bitter Rachel who spoke—"you *will* be interested in knowing that Mr. Easton has promised Martha perfect freedom in the exercise of her religious convictions."

I made a wry face. "I shall be interested in knowing," I said, speaking bitterly in my turn, "that he keeps any of the promises he makes to her."

Then I went away, for Rachel's nervousness warned me that Easton and Martha were liable to return at any moment.

I wrote to Stephen, urging him to make careful inquiry in Rocksford concerning Easton, and to let me know at once what he learned. He did so, and came home to bring the result of his investigations.

They were very meager. Easton had brought letters of introduction, had used money freely, had done nothing especially reprehensible while he stayed in Rocksford. Yet substantial men, like Mr. Osburn, thoroughly distrusted him. There was much that we could feel and guess, but nothing that we could carry to Colonel Sylvestre with any hope of influencing him.

Stephen took the news of the approaching marriage to heart deeply. "It is too terrible to think of," he said—"far more terrible, to my mind, than death. A sanctified soul and an unsanctified marriage—what could be worse than that? And the worst of all is that the poor child will do this unholy thing in the name of conscience—will believe that in obeying her father, she is honoring her God. I must see her—I must warn her. It can not be too late."

I had never seen Stephen so aroused. He paced the floor excitedly for an hour, trying to think how he could get speech with Martha. To go to her home was quite out of the question. Neither the Colonel nor Rachel could be trusted to give him welcome.

Quite unexpectedly, the coveted opportunity presented itself. At the announcement that Stephen was at home came the demand that he should preach that night in the schoolhouse, and Martha came to the service. My mother was greatly encouraged to see her there, but my own heart sank, for I judged her presence there to be an earnest of her anticipated liberty.

Stephen walked home with her, and I sat up to wait his return. He came up to the little chamber which we still shared whenever he was at home, and I read disappointment in his face.

"It was quite useless," he said, dropping down wearily upon the bed. "But what a ghastly sacrifice! I tried to tell her, but I could not make it plain enough. The child has fixed in her mind the idea that in a matter of religion alone one has the right to refuse obedience to parents. I tried to explain to her that marriage is a matter of religion, that marriage without love is a sin against the God who gave us the gift of life. She shed some bitter tears, but at the last she would only say that her word was given and she must keep it. She has never known what love is. That is one comfort; she is not sinning against a knowledge of what love really means."

I looked at him closely.

"Are you sure," I asked—I would try to save her at any cost—"that Martha does not love *you*."

"Me!" he cried; and then he groaned aloud. "Oh, no, no, no! You can not mean it. God grant that it may not be so!"

CHAPTER XX

THE WEDDING FEAST

In April, Charles Easton and Martha were married. At the command of the Colonel there was a great wedding, and even the despised Arrondales were honored with an invitation.

As an amazing concession made in honor of her crowning act of daughterly obedience, Martha was allowed to choose the minister who should officiate on this occasion. Some instinct must have told her that Stephen would refuse, for she did not ask him, glad as she would no doubt have been to make the reconciliation between the two families thus public. But she chose Bro. Cady, and thus that true gentleman was once more brought beneath the same roof with the woman whom he had once wooed so ardently. "How do you like being a Campbellite?" Rachel asked him as she held out her hand.

He smiled upon her with brave, kind eyes that had in them not a hint of resentment. "So well," he said, "that I would that thou were both almost and altogether such as I am."

She was not vexed; and I fell to wondering whether this fact argued that she did or that she did not care for Bro. Cady.

Rachel was the life of the company, and only I, of all the number, guessed what a heavy heart she bore.

The bride was as lovely as a bride could be, and if she seemed more shrinking and quiet than usual, it seemed but natural in one so young, forced into the central position on an occasion of great ceremony.

I must say that Charles Easton acquitted himself well. His manner was triumphant, as might have been expected, but his cordiality was without the slightest appearance of condescension, and most of those who had been doubtful of him went away with a sincere admiration for him. Even Bro. Cady said that he had underrated the man, and that he now thought Martha might be very happy with him.

As for Stephen, Rachel and I, we kept our thoughts to ourselves.

Mr. Easton told us that he had intended to make heavy purchases of land this spring, but that Colonel Sylvestre had prevailed upon him and Martha to remain in the old home for at least a year. He did not seem especially pleased over the prospect; indeed, he said it was a disappointment to him not to be able to carry his bride at once to a home of their own.

But the Colonel was more than gratified at the idea of having his son-in-law with him, and waxed eloquent over it, quite in the old, pompous fashion.

"My son-in-law has submitted himself to my advice in the matter," he said, "albeit, perhaps, to his own disadvantage. But having no son to direct my affairs, it is most convenient to lean upon Charles, until my health shall be somewhat more fully restored."

I noticed that Martha did not say "Charles," as her father did. She called her husband "Mr. Easton," as if she were addressing a distinguished stranger. On the other hand, he said, "My love" to her, as if he were in a novel. We simple Blue Brook people thought this very questionable taste—being used to a kind of love that is chary of possessive pronouns.

Easton kept his promise to Martha, so far as allowing her to attend religious meetings was concerned. She came quite regularly to our little gatherings, and, on those rare occasions when we had a speaker from abroad, her husband usually came with her.

"Perhaps she will bring him in," said my mother, who was always looking for a Pentecost.

Perhaps she would; but it struck me that Martha herself did not expect it.

There came that year a kind of readjustment in our religious community. There had once been a small Baptist church, not far from my home. To this my mother had belonged, from the time of its organization. When she left it, several others left also, going to cast their lot with the little circle of those who rejected all creeds save the one divinely given. Thus weakened, the Baptists had found it difficult to keep together and at work; and for a year or more had met only irregularly. The debate had turned the minds of many away from the difficulties of a

Calvinistic theology and toward the plain teaching of the word of God. One after another among the Baptists began to inquire why their name and creed might not be cast away, and their forces joined with those of the people known simply as "disciples."

A visit from Stephen and Bro. Cady, just at this time, hastened the happy consummation. They were to hold what was vaguely called, in the shibboleth of the brethren, "a meeting of days," and were discussing the possibility of securing the town hall. Hearing of this, the officers of the Baptist Church came forward and placed their meeting-house at the disposal of the evangelist, and urging that there be no differences among us, but that henceforth the Lord's people walk by the same rule and mind the same thing.

It was a happy time for the little band of those who sought New Testament Christianity. Stephen had begun by this time to keep a very slight diary, which he called his "preaching-book." It contained little more than the names of the places where he preached, with his text and now and then a brief outline. But to me the little old leather covered book is full of romance, for it brings our youth back again. I find in it a few notes referring to this meeting of which I have spoken. A liberal deduction must always be made for Stephen's modesty, in anything quoted from him. He was ever inclined to underrate himself and to put others forward. Of Bro. Cady, in particular, he had an exalted opinion, as I have already said. Yet I distinctly remember that of these two good men, Stephen was the favorite in our little community. The home-grown prophet was not without honor in Blue Brook.

Stephen was a fine singer and the people were fond of the stirring hymns he taught them. I remember one of which they never seemed to tire:

> "Our bondage here will end
> By and by, by and by;
> Our bondage here will end
> By and by.

> "Our bondage here will end
> With our threescore and ten,
> And vast glory crown the day
> By and by."

Bro. Cady used to criticize him, and to say that "end" and "ten" did not rhyme properly; but Stephen always laughed at him, and told him that he should have remained in the East, where correct rhymes are of more importance than the spirit and the understanding.

"The hymn has a noble roll," he used to say, "and it can be sung without hymnbooks, which is the thing of greatest importance, in my way of thinking."

Here are some of the extracts from Stephen's little diary:

August 14. Meeting in Blue Brook Baptist Church. Baptist brethren anxious to drop all party distinctions and be known as Christians or disciples only. Would that the same spirit prevailed everywhere! Preached from I. Cor. ii, 2: "For I was determined not to know anything among you save Jesus Christ, and him crucified." Tried to urge that all put aside nonessential doctrines and unite in the service of Jesus Christ. Joseph led in public prayer for the first time. This gave my mother great joy. Two confessions.

August 15. Bro. Cady preached an admirable sermon on "The Love of God." His doctrinal strength is in correcting the evils of Calvinism, and his arguments tonight seemed to me unanswerable. Many expressed themselves as pleased and satisfied. I gave a short exhortation at the close of the sermon, and two more came forward.

LORD'S DAY, August 17. A day to be remembered. Our Baptist brethren met with us around the Lord's table, and we agreed henceforward to be one people. The sin of sectarianism seems to me so appalling that I must give my life to combat it. Why set up barriers which our Lord himself never set up, and keep God's people, in a community like this, from uniting to oppose the great enemy of souls? In the morning Bro. Cady preached and I exhorted. In the evening I preached and he followed. His subject this morning was, "The Healing Touch of Jesus." Mine tonight was, "The Truth that Makes Us Free." One confession at each service.

August 18. Preached on "The Simplicity of the Kingdom" not with enticing words of man's wisdom," etc. Tried to show how little the intricacies of theology belong to the preaching of that gospel which is meant for every man, however humble and ignorant he may be. After the meeting a tall, bearded man came up and held out his hand. It was a young Methodist preacher who once prayed for me at a camp-meeting. "I rejoice to know that the Lord heard my prayer in your behalf," he said. "He has indeed turned his face toward you." "He never turns his face away," I ventured to tell him. "It is we poor, willful mortals who go away from his love." I was perhaps tempted to admonish him to deal more in the spirit of that love, if he desired to convert the young men of our day; but thought better of it. No doubt he has learned many things already, and will learn many more if he continues to knock about this world until he is eighty years old. He asked me if it is true that the

Campbellites (as he called them) deny the ministry of the Holy Spirit. I did not believe at first that he could be asking the question seriously, but I soon found that he really inquired for information. I asked him if he had not heard that the Scriptures were our rule of faith and practice, and if he taught we could accept the authoritative teaching of the Scriptures and not accept their teaching concerning the Holy Spirit. It is strange that such wild statements about our position can be so readily believed.

August 22. Closed our meeting of eight days, with sixteen souls added to the saved. Bro. Cady and I each preached a short sermon, exhorting the new converts steadfastness. I should like to spend my life among these people, but duty calls elsewhere. Would that we might see many such triumphs of Christian love and loyalty over sectarian prejudice.

September 24. Visited Blue Brook again, and had the unspeakable privilege of sitting down with my loved ones at the Lord's table. M. was present with her husband. They invited me to take dinner with them, but I declined. Many outsiders were present. I can not but feel that the spirit of Christian fraternity, which had been demonstrated in this community, has greatly inclined the hearts of the people. Would that God's children everywhere might realize that oneness for which he prayed!

CHAPTER XXI

WIFE AND MOTHER

To almost every young man there comes a period of restlessness—a time when the monotony of his home life becomes suddenly intolerable to him. Often this follows his first great emotional experience, and is so much like a mania that the will seems powerless to shake it off.

I had always said that I would stay at home and help father. I had never considered any other plan of life. But in these last few months I had been able to put no heart or hope into the tasks which had hitherto satisfied me. I performed them mechanically, wished myself away from them, called myself a coward and again wished myself away.

Stephen saw my condition of mind, as I had seen his years before. He did not try to reason me out of it. He put his hand upon my shoulder and told me to go.

"Every boy needs to go away from his home at least once," he said. "He needs to look at his own life from the outside. I can very well make my headquarters here, and help father when he is especially hard pressed. It is best that you should go."

"But Rachel is here," I said. "You will be obliged to see her often, and I know what pain that means."

He scrutinized my face closely, as if he sought to find out how I knew. "Rachel and I are as far apart as the poles," he said. "I have not struggled for nothing. You must go away."

In my heart I knew that he was right, and I went. I saddled Queenie; made my way, through weary days of travel, to the Ohio River, and found employment in hauling and rafting logs.

It was a good work for me, though the surroundings were by no means such as my mother would have chosen. The men with whom I worked were rough fellows with little of real manliness about them. The work was laborious and monotonous, but it kept my mind employed, and taught me to look with a new respect to the farm tasks to which I had been accustomed from my childhood. Farm work was not the worst thing in the world, and it was worth something to have learned.

I found a little company of disciples, who had been gathered together and taught by Alexander Campbell. Their fellowship extended to me when I was a stranger, amidst uncongenial companions, was sweeter than anything I could have believed possible. They had no regular place of meeting, but held frequent services in the homes of their members. I have none but happy memories of those meetings, held in big, clean kitchens beside roaring log fires. There was no one in the number who was what we called "apt to teach," but we sang together and prayed together and read, turn about, long chapters in the Bible, evading the difficult proper names with such skill as we could command.

I was homesick, and I knew that homesickness was good for me. For the first time I knew that my own home was one in ten thousand.

My great delight, in those days, was in Stephen's letters. He wrote about all the affairs of the home and the neighborhood, going into particulars so carefully that I could almost see everything that he described. I wish I had preserved all of these letters. Here are two, thumbed with the many readings given it by a homesick boy:

BLUE BROOK, Oct 27, 18,

MY DEAR BROTHER:—We were glad to learn of your welfare, and especially to know that you have found a place and a welcome among the brethren. I suspect you of homesickness, but you have too good sense to be homesick for very long. Each one of us must take his little dose some time, and I know yours will be swallowed bravely.

Father and mother are very well. Father keeps busy and finds an odd job now and then for me. I have been away for but two days, and that was to pay a visit to Bro. Cady, who is preaching for a few days in

W——. He is having a fine interest, and is doing a great deal to build up the cause. On the first night of his meeting he was introduced to a young lady who is an ardent Methodist, and who berated him soundly for his doctrine. "I hear you do not believe in the Holy Spirit," she told him. "Do you believe in the Holy spirit," she told him. "Do you believe all you hear?" he asked her. And the lively young lady retorted, "I certainly don't believe all I hear from you." Bro. Cady was not in the least daunted, but asked if he might call on the young lady and explain our teaching to her. He did call, and, so far as I can judge, he continued to call daily. I told him to be careful, for a vivacious woman is never so interesting as when she tries to hold her own in an argument. "Oh I am in no sort of danger," he assured me. But in the evening, when he introduced me to her, I decided that he is in some danger. She has big blue eyes and brown curls, and is the prettiest young woman I know, always excepting Martha.

[I instantly resented this judgment, and told myself that it was only half meant. If Rachel was not called a "pretty woman," it was only because that word seemed too small for her. She was indeed less lovely than Martha, but her face had an expressiveness and her figure a supple grace such as are seldom seen. And Stephen knew it very well.]

Colonel Sylvestre and his son-in-law gave a dance in the new barn last night. It is hinted that both Rachel and Martha strongly disapproved of it, and that they were scarcely seen during the evening. Whisky flowed freely, and many of the young men were the worse for their dissipation. The Colonel does not care in the least for such company, nor, so far as I can judge, does Mr. Easton. Whatever he may be at heart, he is evidently been accustomed to associating with gentlemen. My only explanation of last night's carousal is, that they knew they were not held in favor hereabouts, and so made this attempt at a conciliation.

Another thought has come to me—one almost too horrible to be entertained. Is it possible that Easton likes to humiliate Martha, on account of her religious scruples? Perhaps I wrong him, but I can not help feeling that he is capable of it.

I met Ross Turner this morning in front of the blacksmith shop. He was the worse for last night, and very silly. "The son-in-law business is the business that brings in the money," he said. "Look at Easton, now! Just look at him! See how he has made it pay. But I never dreamed that the old man would take Martha back now, did you?" I let him go without a word, for he was half drunk, and not worth the tongue-lashing that he deserved.

My heart bleeds for poor little Martha. It is strange that so good a girl could ever have so blinded her conscience as to consent to such a marriage. But she was young, and she had no mother. It must be that she suffers. It can not be otherwise, with a nature as sensitive as hers. Contact with evil sends such a nature within itself, and to the endurance of unutterable agony. I wonder what Rachel thinks. I have not seen her.

Father and mother ask to be affectionately remembered. Let us hear from you often.

Faithfully yours,
STEPHEN ARRONDALE.

The other letter was written six months later, and must have reached me just before I started home:

BLUE BROOK, March 2, 18—.

DEAR JOSEPH: We are more than rejoiced to think you are coming home. To tell the truth, I think father considers that I make a poor substitute for you. "I thought Steve was the better farmer of the two, at the start," he said the other day, "but preaching has rather spoiled him. I shall be glad to get Joey back again." You know he is always in a softhearted mood when he talks about "Joey."

In truth, I have been at home very little for the past three months. The work seemed to call, and there was only me to go. Last week I saw Bro. Cady for the first time in months. He told me he was soon to visit his family in Albany. In the course of our conversation I casually inquired the name of the young Methodist lady to whom he introduced me when I saw him last. I was ashamed of having forgotten, but there had been nothing in the meantime to recall it to my mind. "Her name at present," he said, with a peculiar smile, "is Elizabeth Mather." "At present," I said. "What do you mean by that?" "I mean," he said, "that I trust it will soon be Mrs. Cady." "You are going to marry her," I exclaimed, in real surprise though I might have guessed. "But she is a Methodist," I objected. "No, she isn't, he said triumphantly. "I've brought her over."

So he is gone, and I shall miss my bachelor friend. But he will have a fine wife, and one who will keep him on his mettle. I wonder if Rachel will care. She will give no sign, for her pride is a coat of mail. I fancy that she does not altogether like her brother-in-law. Of course, I do not know this, but on the two or three occasions when I have seen them together I thought her manner toward him very distant.

Martha has a little daughter. Easton called up "the boys" at the tavern yesterday, and treated them in honor of the event. I was passing at the time, and when I thought of the saintly young mother, my heart turned sick. What a profanation of the sanctity of parenthood!

Where will it all end? In heartache and heartbreak, I believe, as I have believed from the beginning.

We long for your coming. It will not be long until the time.

Affectionately yours,

STEPHEN.

I had been anxious to get away, but I was more than glad to get back. I felt sure that I should never go away again. I had no such gifts as Stephen's. I could hold my own in common toils, and home was the place for me.

I was surprised soon after my return, by a rather formal invitation to dine with the Eastons. Ordinarily, in our neighborhood, we "dropped in" to one another's houses, and ate meals wherever meals came in our way. The Sylvestres had always been more ceremonious than the rest, and had become much more so since the advent of Charles Easton.

The Colonel received me quite warmly, and even alluded to my services on the night of the fire. Easton shook my hand with the air of good fellowship, and I liked him less than ever.

Martha floated into the room presently, in a soft white gown, with her baby in her arms.

"I wanted Joseph to see our little Rachel," she said, looking shyly up into her husband's face.

I have never seen a young baby before, and I remember I was greatly surprised that it was such a tiny thing. But something in its helplessness sent a strange thrill to my heart, and I said, quite honestly:

"It is beautiful!"

It was not the little lace-decked baby that was beautiful, though. It was the new look on Martha's face.

CHAPTER XXII

CLOUDS AND CARES

One evening Stephen returned from Rocksford with a strange story. It had just come to light—so Mr. Osburn told him—that Charles Easton owed large sums of money there. Some of the debts had been contracted before his marriage, but in all cases he had, since that date, given new notes, with his father-in-law's name added to his own. None of his creditors were impatient, but some had begun to ask questions, wondering why it was that a man with means at command for large investments should continue to accumulate debts.

"Debts," in those days, meant something quite different from what they mean now. The demands for ready money were few, and the amount in circulation small. People did not borrow money to advance great business enterprises. To be in debt meant in a certain measure to be in disgrace.

The fact that money had been so freely loaned to Charles Easton by these men was a kind of recognition of the fact that he belonged to another world than theirs. Something in the easy swing of his manner seemed to say that he would naturally need to handle a good deal of money.

But where was the money he had meant to invest? Stephen and I decided that it had never existed.

This was not the whole story. Mr. Osburn and others told Stephen that Easton's record in Rocksford, during the time of his courtship, had been correct enough. He had seemed to have no employment, but this was excused on the assumption that he was a man of means, looking about for a place to put his capital. He had seemed to be a man of the world, and some persons had expressed surprise that he should be drawn to a woman so intensely religious as Martha, but in reality there was nothing strange about this. Martha's beauty of face and charm of manner were quite sufficient to account for the attraction. That her father's property was also an attraction, we were but just beginning to guess.

But since his marriage, his manner, on his occasional visits to Rocksford, had been altogether different. He had fallen in with some men of questionable reputation, and went to their houses to drink and play cards. This was the more noteworthy because, in our own neighborhood, he held himself aloof from this class of persons. He did indeed, "treat" freely, but he always avoided bringing those to whom he dispensed favors to a social equality with himself. In Rocksford, however, some restraint seemed to be withdrawn, and he allowed himself free rein.

But that upon which Stephen's Rocksford friends dwelt most had happened only a few days before. Mr. Osburn himself had come upon Easton on the road near Rocksford, mercilessly beating a high-spirited horse.

"I would not have known him for the same man whom I had been used to seeing," was Mr. Osburn's comment. "The man has a cruel heart. He has played a part with the Sylvestres, but sooner or later the evil in him will come to light."

"Poor Martha!" And Stephen groaned aloud. "Coarseness, cruelty and dishonesty joined to purity and sweetness such as hers!"

"Rachel will never let him ill-treat Martha," I said confidently.

How do you know? There are a thousand cruelties which a husband can practice upon a sensitive woman, besides actual physical ill-treatment. And Martha would die rather than tell it of the man she has married."

Two or three days later Rachel came by our place on Dolly and halted before the field where I was at work. I went at once to the road, and urged her to go into the house.

"No," she said, "I must talk to you alone, and do it in such a way as not to attract attention. There is no one in the world whom I can talk to but you, and I come to you because of the conversation we had long ago, before"

"Before Martha was married," I said, boldly.

She nodded. "Joseph," she said, "I would rather suffer torture than to tell you what I am going to. I despise myself for it, and yet there is no other way. It is a choice of evils. You are the soul of honor. I would trust you with anything, and trust you with Martha's secret. She has married a man whom she fears and can not respect."

She drew a long breath. "I shall not tell you what he is, or what she suffers. I dare not leave her for a day, for to me he seems to be afraid." I did not bother wonder, for as she drew herself up, with dilating nostrils and flashing eyes, she looked like a creature who would inspire fear.

"I must not waste a moment's time," she went on; "I shall soon be missed, and called upon to give an account of myself. As you have seen, Mr. Easton has acquired a great influence over my father. He bends all his efforts in this direction, and carefully keeps back anything that father would oppose or disapprove. He knows very well that Martha would die rather than complain of her husband. I sometimes go to my father, but he thinks I am prejudiced against Mr. Easton, because I was opposed to the marriage. But this is what I wished to speak to you about: Mr. Easton has persuaded father to divide his property, and give Martha her share immediately."

I saw the danger instantly. But what could be done? I was a man, but I knew no more of law at that time than my Queenie did. (I served several terms as justice of the peace, later on in life, but I never thought that my talents especially adorned the position.) It seemed to me that there ought to be some power to restrain the old Colonel from an act that could not but prove disastrous. But I knew of no help, and I had a strong feeling that none could be found.

"What put the plan into his mind?" I asked.

"Mr. Easton seems to have filled him with the idea that he could greatly increase the property, if he could have the handling of it now. Father talks constantly of what astonishing things 'my son-in-law' is sure to accomplish."

"Is he planning to divide the farm?"

"I hear only a little of the talk, but I judge that they are not quite agreed on this point. As nearly as I can tell, father's plan is to divide the farm into equal parts, and to use what a ready money he has for another set of buildings. Mr. Easton seems to be weighing this, but in reality I think he is opposed to it. Perhaps it interferes with some plan of his own. At any rate, I notice that he never wants more money put into the property."

"For the best reason in the world, Rachel. He owes heavily, and your father has signed his notes. Ready money may be needed at any time."

Rachel looked puzzled. "Are you quite sure about this?" she asked.

"It came from Mr. Osburn," I said. I was as independent as ever, and did not care to have her know that Stephen had been concerning himself with her affairs. Somehow, I was always wishing to punish Rachel for the way she had treated Stephen. "Do you believe it possible," I ventured to add, "that your father really put his signature on those notes?"

"I dare say he did."

"I can't see why such a careful business man as your father could put such complete confidence in one who was almost a stranger to him."

"Neither can I, except as my observation is that every cautious man now and then does something venturesome. But father must be blind, to go on placing more and more power in his hands. Don't tell any one you have talked with me, Joseph. I am not in the habit of discussing family affairs."

I could bear witness that she was not. As she rode away I stamped to and fro in my impatience, longing to help my old playmates, and not knowing how I could be of the slightest use.

I learned afterward from Stephen that Rachel went to Rocksford and learned from Mr. Osburn all he knew concerning the notes. He really knew little more than he had told Stephen, save the names of some of the men to whom Easton was indebted. No doubt Rachel thought this knowledge might be useful to her in an emergency, and so I believe it finally proved to be.

But her opposition did not prevent her father from deeding the north half of his farm to Martha, as Ross Turner, our village newspaper, duly reported that he had witnessed the deed, and intimated that he was "clear beat" to think Martha had come out ahead of her father, after all.

"I heard her say she didn't want no land," he condescended to inform us. "But the old man told her she was lucky to have a husband that knew business, and would take care of her property and make her a rich woman some day. He said he was going to manage Rachel's half, and see which would come out first best. Then he and Easton passed a lot of fine talk back and forth, and each one let on that the other was the greatest man on earth. I guess them two swap considerable soft soap back'ards and for'ards."

No doubt they did. Others might have but slender respect for Charles Easton, but his father-in-law's confidence was certainly unshaken. A little after the transfer of the land, a carpenter from Rocksford came to confer with the Colonel concerning the buildings to be erected on Martha's part of the farm. Charles Easton, it was said, was liberal with suggestions, and intimated that he desired his home to have many comforts which those of his neighbors did not possess. But he seemed willing to defer the work of building, and it was finally decided that he and Martha should remain in the Sylvestre home for one more year.

For the first time in several years, I worked for Colonel Sylvestre during harvest. Naturally, I observed the life of the household somewhat keenly. Rachel led in the management of the household, as she always had. Martha was devoted to the care of little Ray. When she played with her baby the sunny joyousness which was natural to her seemed to break over her face.

One scene which I witnessed then I shall certainly never be able to forget in this world. I wonder if I shall forget it in the next! I can feel the pain and the misery of my own helplessness all be as keenly now, in my tottering old age, as I felt it then.

Little Ray was at that interesting period of infancy when she was, as good aunts and grandmothers say, "beginning to take notice." Martha's innocent delight over her daughter's accomplishments was quite unbounded, and she was never so happy as when the baby "took notice" of things in general, and we older people took notice of the baby.

Perhaps it was because the rest of us were inclined to make much of the baby, that Easton began to pay some little attention to it. Up to this time, I had thought he showed small signs of affection for the little creature.

One day, when he spoke to the infant, Martha, who seemed greatly pleased, held Ray out to him. "See, Ray," she said, "that is Daddy! Go to Daddy, Baby!"

A shade of annoyance crept over Easton's face. "I must beg you, my love, never to use that word of me," he said. "Daddy is vulgar and disrespectful. Never teach the child to call me by that name."

Martha winced. "It isn't a very pretty word, I suppose," she agreed. "But I never thought of it, because Rachel and I used to call our father by that name. But I certainly will not teach it to Ray, if you do not like it."

It may be that he had thought he had shown unnecessary vexation, and wished to cause his wife to forget it. At any rate, he took Ray on his knee—a thing which I had never seen him do before. But the child was frightened, and began to cry.

"I had best take her," Martha said. "See, she wants to come to me. She is getting so timid!"

For answer, Easton tried to bend the rigid limbs of the baby. She only cried harder. In a flash, the red blood flew over Easton's face, and then, shameful sight, in the eyes of such a wife! he struck the child a smart blow.

"I will manage this child as I please," he said, with an oath. "If you want to make a fool of her I will not. Here, take her!" and he threw the trembling, screaming child into Martha's arms.

The cry of horror which she had raised is still ringing in my ears. All had been done too quickly for me to make my escape, but I did so now, tingling with shame and dread. If Easton could fall into such a cruel rage with the presence of a neighbor to restrain him, what must he be when he and Martha were alone! And still her father trusted him!

CHAPTER XXIII

THE YEARLY MEETING

The great event of the season was to be the yearly meeting—the annual convocation of the disciples of the county, to be held this year in Blue Brook for the first time.

The spiritually well-fed believers of our day can not understand what these gatherings meant to the starved believers of that time, many of whom never heard a sermon except at their great annual feasts. In their separate communities, they met "on the first day of the week, to break bread." Their sense of obligation in this was imperative. There might be excuse for neglect in other matters, but there could be none in this.

If there were in the congregation a man gifted in public speech, an address, more or less formal, preceded the Lord's Supper. Otherwise, the elders "gave thanks," and the eloquence was in the great fact commemorated, and not in the speech of men.

All the time, however, the longing to hear the good word grew within the hearts of the people. They came up to the yearly meeting careless of everything except that great opportunity. At other times these shrewd sons of shrewd Yankees were mindful of their stock and their crops. Now their minds were set upon hearing the great fundamentals of their faith again rehearsed.

The meeting this year was held in father's woods. Stephen was at home, and we all worked together, hauling planks from the mill and making benches of them. We constructed a rude pulpit, too, and cleared out the lower spring, so as to make sure of plenty of good water.

My mother had her full share of the burden of preparation. She sewed sheets together, two and two, and bade us boys to be ready to fill them up at a moment's notice with the clean sweet-smelling straw from the newly built stack.

"Ten extra beds!" I said. "Where can you put so many?"

"Never you fear!" she told me, as she gave a loving pat to the last improvised mattress-cover. "There are the two rooms upstairs for the women, and the front room and two bedrooms downstairs for the men. Fourteen beds—we can keep twenty-eight, but that isn't any more than our share."

"But there are four of us," I objected. But I could not upset her calculations as easily as this.

"There is the kitchen floor for me, and the new hay in the barn for you men folks," she said. "You didn't suppose you'd get a bed to sleep on, did you?"

Her preparations did not end here. A prime beef must be killed, and bread, cakes and pies baked. At first she kept account of the number of each class of articles provided, and repeated it to us joyously when we came in at mealtime. But as the frenzy took possession of her more and more completely, she simply baked and baked and baked, without any attempt at mathematical calculation. I wonder that the old brick oven did not burst with its sense of responsibility.

"Do get someone to help you," Stephen begged, one night when mother looked more weary than usual.

"I can't have any one around in the way when I'm in a hurry, and that's what 'help' amounts to. There's only one person that I'd give two pins to have around, and that's Rachel Sylvestre. And I dare say she'd rather burn her hands off than to cook for Campbellites."

And Stephen made no answer.

When our dear Maude Arrondale gives a dinner to six or eight, even with the cooperation of a *chef* and his aids, I am sure she takes it more seriously than my mother took her preparation to feed fifty persons for three or four days. And I am perfectly certain it is more serious business.

My part in the occasion was a humble one, but it kept me from enjoying the meetings to the full. I looked after the horses of the guests, who sometimes come from long distances, and were glad enough to turn the tired animals over to me for water and food.

It was not until Sunday morning that I was able to enter into the full enjoyment of the meeting. Such a meeting as it was! Such hungry, expectant faces as those of the worshipers, I can never hope to see again. The penalty of abundance is the sense of satiety.

The platform was filled with preachers, and I was conscious of a slight sense of importance in seeing Stephen among them, and in noting how his fellows seemed to respect and love him. Except on public occasions, I never thought of Stephen as a preacher.

My mother, who had been with father to the yearly meeting of the previous year, pointed out her favorite preachers to me.

"That plainly dressed man is John Henry. He is full of wit and eccentricity. Once a man told him he could not go to hear him preach, because he had no shoes. Bro. Henry sent him his own shoes, and went into the pulpit barefooted. That strongfaced man with the hymnbook is William Hayden. You will hear him sing—there is nothing like it. Ah, there comes Mr. Campbell!"

I bent forward, as did many another, to get a glimpse of the great leader to whom the religious world of his day owed so much. Tall of figure and stately of bearing, with boldly cut features and keen eyes, he would have been a marked personage anywhere.

John Henry started the "Bondage Hymn," which I had often heard Stephen and Bro. Cady sing together:

> "Our bondage here will end
> By and by, by and by;
> Our bondage here will end
> By and by;
> And our sorrows have an end
> With our threescore years and ten,
> And vast glory crown the day
> By and by."

I do not remember anything more about the service until it came to the sermon. I wish I could set that down. But I fear I should make a sad failure of it, for nothing is more disappointing than an attempt to put down in black and white that which has profoundly moved one's inmost soul. I should like the Arrondale children of today to know what that sermon was like, but in order for them to know that it would be necessary for them to know the age in which it was preached, to know the crude religious teaching of the day to which its calm reasonableness was in such striking contrast and to know the striking personality of the speaker. None of which can ever be. For in those days no one seemed to remember that history was being made, and much that we should count precious now has passed from memory forever.

Never, before or since, have I seen a man with so much real dignity and so little affectation of it. He impressed me as a man who was naturally very great, and who had been so fortunate as to have found a mission large enough to express all that was in him. He was quite without tricks of oratory. He made no gestures, he never declaimed or gave expression to personal emotion. The truth!—this was his passion. Calm in manner, majestic in thought, he looked as a younger Moses might have looked, coming straight from the Mount of Divine Communication.

His text I remember. It was, "God said, Let there be light; and there was light;" and when he had read it he added these words: "This was the first speech ever made within our universe. It is indeed the most sublime and potent speech ever made."

Then, with the quiet confidence of one who knows, he preached his sermon. He did not hasten, he brought forward truths apparently unrelated, and stated them clearly, yet in stately terms. By degrees, these truths began to assume relationships. We began to see a central meaning in them all. The work of creation, of providence and of redemption became alike the expressions of divine and gracious Fatherhood. We saw the light of the stars pale in the light of the moon, the light of the moon herself fail at the rising of the glorious Sun of righteousness. No longer was our world one of mischance and confusion, for in it we were allowed to see the benignant workings of that love which at all times does its best for man—that love which creates and sustains, and will eventually glorify us all.

A sermon two hours in length, and nobody weary! The speaker closed, but the first notes of the invitation hymn had not yet arisen, when a woman, tall and slender, walked with firm step down the middle aisle. My mother gave a little choking cry, and put her hand on my arm. It was Rachel.

I remember the first thought that came to me was that all the world had been converted now; that the work of the church on earth was done. Rachel! Why, that meant all that counted, in the way of opposition and difficulty, suddenly removed. It meant all alien powers turned suddenly into allies.

The preachers came down from the pulpit, and gave Rachel the welcoming hand. Stephen had been stricken with sudden pallor, and his face was that of one who hears news too good to be trusted as true.

Perhaps it was because the surprise had such full possession of the people's minds that there were no other converts. The hymn was sung through, but Rachel remained alone, standing in perfect quiet, with her hands clasped and her head bowed.

It fell to Stephen's lot to take her confession. When he asked for it, he remained silent for just a moment with her head still bowed. Then she raised her eyes, and repeated the words solemnly, in a clear, emphatic tone:

"I do believe—with all my heart—that Jesus is the Christ, the Son of God."

Then she spoke in a low voice to Stephen. He seemed to assent, and then said to the audience:

"Our sister requests that she may be baptized without a moment's unnecessary delay. Those who came to Christ in the olden time had the joy of obeying him in the same hour. We will go at once to the place of baptism, praying in our hearts that God may attend this act of obedience with his Spirit."

Some of the people brought out their horses and carriages, but most of us went on foot. My father and mother borrowed one of the neighbors' buggies, and took Rachel with them.

As the procession wound slowly through the woods, we sang again the old, old, song:

"How happy are they who their Saviour obey."

To think that we were singing it for Rachel!

We had but just reached the road when we were overtaken and passed by a carriage containing two figures. One was Colonel Sylvestre. He was leaning forward in the seat, his hands resting upon a cane, his long hair blown about by the wind. The other occupant of the carriage was Charles Easton; and his driving must have been like unto the driving of Jehu, for he was driving furiously.

CHAPTER XXIV

THE PRICE OF DISCIPLESHIP

Traveling on foot, I was slower than some of the rest in reaching the place of baptism. But my mother and Stephen gave me a full account of what transpired, so I tell it as it was:

When Rachel got out of the carriage, Martha slipped up and put her arm about her.

"Why did you come, dear?" Rachel whispered, kissing her tenderly. "It would have been better for you if you had not."

"I couldn't stay away, Rachel. Last night, after you told me, I couldn't sleep at all, for gladness. This morning I didn't have a moment to speak to you. I couldn't go to the meeting, so I came here, and waited for you. I wanted to tell you that Mr. Easton was at the meeting. He will hurry home and tell father."

"It need be no surprise to father. I told him that, if the way should be made clear to me at any time, I would walk in it without a moment's delay."

"He did not believe you would ever do it, though—he had such faith in his own teaching. I'm afraid he will be very angry."

"I never expected anything else, Martha. You were not afraid. Why should I be?"

At this moment, Charles Easton came up, with Colonel Sylvestre puffing after him. At the sight of his wife, an angry glitter came into Easton's eyes.

"Go immediately and get into the carriage," he said. And she obeyed him—this gentle Martha, upon whose sensitive ears no harsh word ought eve to have fallen.

The Colonel came up, and faced Rachel with lowering brow and flushed cheeks.

"You may get into that carriage and go home this minute," he said, "or you may stay away forever."

"I will stay away forever, then."

"Ah! you may think I will take you back, because I took your sister back. But I will not—I swear I will not! Martha was a child, and an easy prey for fanatical fools. They persuaded her, and frightened her with the idea that she would burn everlastingly if she didn't join them. "But you, you"—his anger almost choked him—"you knew better. You disobeyed me deliberately. You have made your bed—you may die on it. I will never forgive you—I swear I will not."

"Goodby, father," said Rachel, very quietly.

Evidently he had expected her to argue the case, but she did not. She stood very still, her lips white, her hands trembling just a little.

He turned and strode away. As he did so, he encountered Stephen.

"Put her under ten fathoms of water if you want to," the old man said. "You will never wash the willfulness and ingratitude out of her."

He clambered into the carriage, and sat down beside Martha. Charles Easton sprang in after them and drove them quickly away.

The morning had been cloudy, but as Stephen and Rachel walked down into the water the midday sun broke forth, and its light seemed to envelop them. I am sure that no one who looked upon that scene ever forgot it.

Rachel sat between my mother and me at the solemn communion service that afternoon. She had begun to know an actual fellowship with Christ in his sacrifice, yet I am sure that this fact brought no diminution of her joy.

After the service, she asked if I would bring Dolly to her. "I rode her over this morning," she explained.

"Rachel!" said my mother, reprovingly, "you will not go away from us—now?"

"I shall find a place." I had never before understood what a troublesome thing such pride as hers can be. To all of us it seemed the most natural thing in the world that she should stay at our house until she could decide upon some plans for the future. But I could see that she was keenly sensible of having a favor offered to her, and that the sensation was by no means agreeable. She was a new Rachel, no doubt, but the new Rachel was made out of the old materials.

However, mother kept her for a time, and Rachel made herself useful about the house while our company remained. I well remember how astonished the preachers who were of the number seemed, at the quality of her conversation, and especially at her knowledge of the Bible. It surprised me, even, to find that she had been studying the Book for many months, never expecting, indeed, that she could accept its teachings, but feeling that simple justice demanded this of her. She felt that she had not dealt fairly with others, especially with Martha, and that she ought to base her objections to Christianity upon nothing less fundamental than a knowledge of the Bible itself. She could not herself tell when she first felt the longing to find the gospel of Jesus true. She had told this longing to no one, until the day before her baptism. Then she had told both her father and Martha of her intention to hear Alexander Campbell preach.

"And," she had added, "if he, or any one else, can answer for me the questions that are in my heart, I will instantly follow my faith."

Her father had stormed, then had mastered himself and tried to call up the arguments which had been effective with her in the past. She was surprised at their weakness, surprised that the faith that she had felt to be so imperfect was proof against them. In her surprise and thankfulness she was silent, and perhaps her father believed that he had triumphed.

The meeting on Monday morning was a wonderful occasion. It was a time of that precious exercise known in those days as "exhortation." I think the preachers of that day did better preaching than those of today can do, but in this noble art of exhortation I know they were a long way in advance. I sometimes hear it asserted that the teaching of the pioneers was coldly logical and intellectual. Ah! but those who so assert have forgotten about the exhortation! True, the logical gift and the gift of persuasion did not always dwell in the same man, but there is no need that they should. The Pauls companied with the Barnabases, and God was glorified through all.

These men who were born sons of exhortation did not scorn the ministry of tears. They themselves wept, oft-times, as they described the glories of the new Jerusalem, or the joy of reunited households. Their rhetoric was largely Scriptural. Death was "the Jordan;" heaven was "Cannan;" sorrow was "Marah's bitter stream;" joy was "Pisgah's shining mount." They differed one from another, as strong men differ; but they held together the vital, elemental truths of Christianity, and united in pressing them upon a needy world.

There was a great stirring among the people, the Monday morning, as these men pleaded. Again and again the hymn of invitation broke forth. Again and again earnest men and women crowded forward to declare their faith. Now and then a Christian wife led her husband to the place of confession, or a Christian parent whispered an appeal to a wayward child.

To a mere observer it might have seemed that the audience was under an unnatural excitement. Yet nothing could possible have been more natural or more reasonable. The preaching of the past few days had convinced the people; the time had come for them to act upon their conviction.

At last the closing moments came. There was a hymn of farewell, and the preachers went up and down through the audience shaking hands with the brethren and sisters and bidding them Godspeed. There were many tears, though they were no doubt expressions of joy rather than of sorrow.

That afternoon, after the last of the visitors were gone, Rachel wandered down to the beautiful grove where the meetings had been held. No doubt she felt that there, better than elsewhere, she could call up the resolution necessary to face the future.

I was not surprised to see Stephen follow her. There was plenty of work to be done, but I could fix my mind upon nothing. So I strolled up to the house, and helped mother to put things in order here. I fancy she was a nervous as I. She kept watching the old clock, as she briskly folded away quilts and emptied straw pillows; and at length she asked:

"Are Stephen and Rachel together?"

"I think so."

"I wonder if anything will come of it?"

"What should come of it?"

"You know what I mean. I love Rachel as if she were my own daughter, and yet I often wonder if it is in her to make Stephen happy. Perhaps he has never cared for her as much as I think, but certainly he seems to care for no one else. As long as she held on to her skeptical notions, I was very anxious. It would have ruined Stephen's life. But now, I don't know! I don't know!"

Neither did I. I merely waited, and watched the clock, as mother did.

Stephen came in first—a good sign or a bad one, as one might choose to call it. He spoke kindly to mother, telling her not to be disappointed that he must hurry away this time. He had an appointment, and would have to leave early in the morning. Then he went out to the orchard, and flung himself down under a tree.

I went out and sat down beside him. As you have no doubt noticed in the course of my story, I was of a curious nature, and always interested in the affairs of others.

"Well?" I said.

"I have blundered sadly; I couldn't help it, Joe—I was so sorry for her. I couldn't let her go out and fight her way in the world alone, without even stretching out a hand. She is brave and strong, but what woman is brave enough for such a battle? She will make her way, but her heart will cry out for love and home."

"She hasn't as much heart as other women," I said, all my bitter feeling toward Rachel returning at the thought that she had scorned Stephen once more.

"Hush, Joe! She has more heart than any woman I ever saw, but I can't touch it. Heart! the ordinary little butterfly woman doesn't know the meaning of the word, as it applies to Rachel. Listen to me, Joe: she has not one word of fear for herself, of complaint at her lot. Her only regret—the one she can not shake off for a moment—is that she can not watch over and protect Martha and her baby. She seems to fear that they will come to actual physical harm."

"No wonder," I interrupted. And then I told him how I had seen Easton strike the baby.

"Horrible!" was Stephen's comment. "Think what those two women have suffered from those two men who should have lived to make them happy!"

My heart began to soften toward Rachel, as it usually did when I remembered her devotion to Martha.

"Did Rachel absolutely refuse to marry you?" I asked.

"Absolutely. She said, 'Do you think I could accept marriage as a refuge? That would be impossible."

"Perhaps it would, to a woman like Rachel. I don't like her pride, but it's a part of her, and one can't reckon on her and leave it out. Perhaps she couldn't bend it enough to accept marriage now, especially from you. It might even cheapen her own sacrifice in her eyes."

"Nonsense, Joe; if she loved me"—he spoke these words reverently, as if it were a kind of profanation to use them—"if she loved me, she would not hesitate. She knows I have always loved her; that I can never love any one else. Why should she care what any one might think? She is too brave for that."

"She may fear herself, though, especially if she really does love you. She is quite capable of questioning her own motives, and asking herself if her love for you had not influenced her course in becoming a Christian."

"No, she does not care for me. Sometimes I think she must care for some one else, but I do not know. At any rate, it makes no difference. I was a stupid blunderer to trouble her now, and I shall never speak to her of the matter again."

CHAPTER XXV

STRANGE GUESTS

Almost immediately after the close of the yearly meeting, Rachel went to Rocksford. She wished to teach school there during the coming winter, and in the meantime a warm welcome awaited her with the Osburns.

Before she went away she exacted from my mother that she would keep her informed concerning Martha's welfare.

"I have not forgotten that you took her in, too, when her own home was closed against her," she said. "I was grateful then, though I was too proud to say so; and I know better how to be grateful now. Let me have this one more thing to thank you for. Try to be a mother to my sister, as far as you can be. She is very young to be left alone."

"Alone" was a strange word to use, of one who was to be left with her husband and her father, but my mother understood, and promised.

Just as Rachel was about to enter Mr. Osburn's carriage, we saw Martha hurrying down the road, with her baby in her arms. I went to meet her, and took little Rachel from her.

"How nicely you carry her!" she said, with something of the artless gaiety of her childhood. "Mr. Easton never knows which end to pick her up by. Oh, I am so glad I shall be in time to see Rachel!"

Her hurried manner, and the fact that she was walking instead of riding, told me that she had watched her chance to slip away for a goodby. She threw herself into Rachel's arms in a perfect transport of affection, saying over and over: "I am so happy, sister—so happy!"

"Happy to have me go away?" asked Rachel, patting Martha's cheek lovingly.

"Happy that you have found the right way. That means happiness for both of us. Being apart in body need not matter so much, when our souls are so close together. See, Rachel, I have brought little Ray, for you to tell her goodby. Give her to my sister, Joseph."

Rachel took the baby, and laid its soft, dimpled face against her own. "I shall miss you, little one," she said. The mouth whose proud curve I had once disliked softened and trembled. Rachel was a woman, after all.

Martha would not let me drive her home, but said a brave goodby and hurried off before the carriage started. Rachel turned to me and held out her hand.

"You have been a good friend to me, Joseph," she said. "You have been a good friend to Martha. I have only one thing in the world, and that one I am going to give to you, begging you to believe that to take the gift will be to do me a favor. I can not take Dolly with me, and I will not sell her. She has been mine since she was a colt, and she seems to me almost like a human creature. You saved her from the fire for me, and now she is yours. Only, I want you to keep her as long as she lives."

"I will do nothing of the kind," I said. "I'll take Dolly, and take care of her as well as I know how, and keep her sleek and handsome until you can use her. But as for owning her—you know very well that I'll do nothing of the kind."

She saw that I was in earnest, and did not urge the matter. But you may be sure that I took good care of Dolly, and petted her so much that Queenie became a trifle jealous.

Strangely enough, the only member of the Sylvestre household whom I continued to see, after Rachel's departure, was Charles Easton. I fancy that he found life in our quiet neighborhood decidedly monotonous, and feared to seek his old haunts in Rocksford, lest he should encounter by the way. So he used to drop in on us now and then, and to treat us with something like cordiality.

The Colonel did not go out, and we heard from several sources that his health was wrecked. It seemed more than likely that his violent outburst of passion had shortened his life. The very day after Rachel's departure he made his will, taking care to read it to his witnesses, that they might publish its contents. (There were no newspapers.) By this will, all of the Colonel's property went to Martha for her lifetime, and to her child or children at her death. Rachel was not even mentioned.

It was in the early afternoon, not more than a month later, that we were surprised to see a woman riding up to our door, with a little boy mounted behind her. Strangers were seldom seen among us, and my mother was at once in a flutter of curiosity. "Do go out and take her horse," she said. "Poor lady! how pale and ill she looks!"

I went to the turn of the lane, and found that our strange guest had halted there. She was a worn-looking woman, of about thirty-five, well dressed, and with the air of good breeding.

"Will you kindly tell me if Mr. Charles Easton lives here?"

"No, madam," I said. "He lives with his father-in-law, Colonel Sylvestre, on the next place."

"Thank you," she said, and was about to turn and ride out. But I saw that my mother was right, and that she was very ill or very weary. So I begged that, unless her business was pressing, she would dismount and take rest and food. She accepted my invitation almost eagerly, and I did not wonder, when I lifted her from her horse and found how near she was to complete exhaustion.

The boy raced into the house merrily, delighted with the prospect of supper. His mother started to follow him, but tottered so that I hastened to support her. More and more heavily she leaned upon my arm, and when we were just across the threshold she sank upon the floor.

She had not fainted, though she was quite beyond speech or effort of any kind. My mother threw a blanket over the long settee by the stove, and between us we managed to lay our guest there. Presently she rallied sufficiently to take the hot milk which my mother brought for her. She even smiled a little to see the eagerness with which her little boy devoured his supper. But she was too weak for more than this, and presently she fell into a heavy sleep.

Little Mark—he had told us his name after much coaxing—seemed entirely happy in his new surroundings, but for a lively child he was very uncommunicative. I have ever had rather more than my natural share of curiosity, and you can imagine that I wished to know more of this strange pair who had landed at our door so unexpectedly. We had none of the newspaper sensations which feed curiosity in our time, and you may believe that the sight of a sick woman and a six-year-old boy, riding through the woods together, was enough to set all my inventive faculties in motion. So I questioned the little boy with the persistence of a detective. Don't call me ill-bred, young people. *You* have the daily papers.

"Did you ever ride on horseback before?" I asked of Master Mark.

"Yesterday I did, and the yesterday before that. I like it when the horse goes fast, but now the horse is tired, and mother is tired, and we can't go fast any more. I'd rather sleep here tonight, only I s'pose there wouldn't be any room. Say, was that last apple you gave me all the apples you've got?"

I was obliged to make a pilgrimage to the cellar for more apples, and when Mark's appetite was partially appeased I began again:

"Do you have apple-trees where you live?" I asked him.

"We don't live anywhere. We just stay 'round. Sometimes I stay at my Uncle Ephraim's, but he hasn't any apples on trees. He's got 'em, in barrels, but he'll box your ears if you touch 'em, 'cause they b'longs to the store, 'cause my Uncle Ephraim wants to sell it. You're nicer than my Uncle Ephraim. You don't want to sell your apples, do you?"

"No, indeed," I hastened to assure him. "I want you to eat them—as many as you can, at least, without getting sick. Where does your Uncle Ephraim live?"

"In"—he stopped short, "I guess my mother wouldn't like to have me tell you. She said it's bad for me to tell things, and I don't like to be bad, for fear I shall make her cry more. Does your mother cry a great deal?" And Mark cast an admiring glance at my mother's sunny face.

"I don't believe she does."

"My mother cries all day, sometimes. I wish she wouldn't, 'cause I have such a funny lump up in my throat. But mother says I mustn't cry, 'cause I'm a boy, and boys must be brave, and take care of their mothers. She says I'll soon be a man, and then I can take care of her for sure."

"Why doesn't your father take care of her?" I asked boldly. (I have no excuse to make for myself, except that the temptation was great.)

"'Cause he's bad!" broke out the boy, with sudden vehemence. "It's about him that my mother cries so much. If I was a big man, I wouldn't make my mother cry—would you? My daddy used to be good to me sometimes, and bring me sugar-plums. But sometimes he was awful bad, and my mother would cry to him to stop, and he just wouldn't. And one time he whipped me with a big whip out of the buggy, and I screamed, and he whipped me some more, and mother cried, 'Oh, he is killed!' and then my Uncle Ephraim came, and made daddy stop. And mother put me in bed, and I cried some more, and said I'd kill my father when I got old enough. I will, too," added Master Mark, confidentially.

I glanced at the sleeper by the fire. She was in the heavy stupor of exhaustion, and there was no possibility that the child's chatter would awaken her. With the shortness of memory characteristic of childhood, Mark, having once begun to talk, forgot all injunctions and restrictions.

"Once he whipped my mother," he resumed, the horror of the recollection in his tone. "My Uncle Ephraim says nobody but a brute whips a woman. She can't whip you, you see, and it's no fair. He cut a big hole in her cheek, and it nose-bleeded all over her dress. And then my Uncle Ephraim came in, and took him by the collar, and said a lot of awful swearwords. And that night my daddy went away but "with a sudden return to himself—"mother doesn't ever let me say anything about *that*."

By and by, when my little man had eaten all the apples he could manage, he grew drowsy, and dropped his head over on my shoulder. My mother came, and asked me what could be done for the comfort of our guest. It was a pity to shorten the sleep so sorely needed, but the settee was hard, and it would never do to leave her there for the night.

"Let her sleep a little longer," I advised, looking at the pale, drawn face, and noting for the first time a scar on the left cheek. "It will be easier to rouse her, after the first heaviness is past."

"I will make my bed ready for her in the meantime," said mother, with that delight in an emergency which is instinctive with women of her type. "Slip off the little fellow's shoes, and presently I will come and put him into your trundle-bed."

I did as I was bidden, and managed to remove the shoes so carefully that little Mark did not waken. It all came back to me an hour ago, when little Sylvestre Arrondale, who had been spending his aftersupper hour in my den, begged me to take off his shoes and carry him up to bed.

There was a knock at the door. I could not but say "Come!" and Charles Easton entered.

"Good evening!" he said, with that slight condescension which I fancied I could always detect in his tone. "Ah! what little fellow have we here?"

He came forward into the light, and he saw little Mark's face, he frowned as if he were mystified. Then he turned, and caught a glimpse of the drawn, scarred face on the settee. In an instant he was as pale as death.

"Excuse me!" he muttered. "I didn't know you had company," and he strode out of the room.

I felt a stir in my arms, and looking down, I found Mark sitting bolt upright, his eyes wide open and full of dangerous fire.

"That was my daddy!" he said; and the hatred in the child's tone was something terrible to hear.

It seemed to me I had known it all along. That was why I had dared to ask the child such intrusive questions. Yes, I had known ever since she came that this woman was the wife of the man whom Martha called her husband.

CHAPTER XXVI

THE STRANGER'S STORY

How to save Martha—this was the one thought in my mind. To hide the woman, to threaten the man—to do anything that would break the blow for this gentle girl, seemed at first the thing most desirable. How could she, who had sacrificed so much to wifehood, bear to be told that she was no wife?

Yet presently I knew that she must know. This poor, wronged woman had rights, and would maintain them. The truth must be told, and Martha must suffer. The left hand of the sleeping woman had slipped from under the cover, and on the third finger I saw a plain gold ring. Martha, too, wore one. What blasphemy were the words with which it had been placed upon her hand!

I longed with an unspeakable longing for Rachel. She could be told. She would know how to help.

But Rachel was not here. I must think what to do if, indeed, there was aught to be done.

Mark soon fell asleep again. I laid him in the little trundlebed which had been Stephen's and mine long ago, and which mother had hastened to drag from its place in hiding. Then I went to my room, and paced up and down until morning.

Before daybreak my mother was stirring in the room below, preparing our early breakfast; but I did not go down at once. I dreaded to see her and to listen to her innocent guesses about our visitor. I would speak first to my father. His shrewd sense might help me. I slipped down the stairs, and joined him as he went to his early tasks.

But he was as completely nonplused as I. Of one thing he was very sure—that Martha must know all very soon, and that she must bear her trouble as best she might.

"You think only of Martha's side," he reminded me. "But you must remember that this other poor soul has been shamefully treated, too, and that she has a child to think of, the same that Martha has. Poor little Martha!"

I saw his heart was as tender as mine toward Martha, though perhaps he saw the other side of the case more plainly. But he could suggest nothing, except that we keep our visitor with us for a few days, and examine closely into the proofs of her claim.

"Then do you bring her and Easton together and let them have it out," was my father's advice. "The tongue of woman is the only weapon that will ever punish that scoundrel as he deserves. Let 'em have it out, I say!"

I went into the house, little comforted, and still afraid to face my mother. To my great confusion, the first person I encountered, on entering the kitchen, was Martha Easton.

The first glance told me that she was in great distress. Her hair had been so carelessly coiled that already it was beginning to fall about her shoulders. Her eyelids were reddened, either from tears or watching. She was standing before the fire, drawing a shawl tightly about her shoulders.

"Good morning, Martha," I said. "Why, how cold your hand is! I am afraid you are not well."

"I am frightened about—about Mr. Easton. He went out last night, saying that he was coming here, and he has not come back. Your mother says he did not come here at all. I am afraid something has happened to him."

"Oh, don't think that," I said, foolishly, trying to think whether I should tell her of Easton's hasty visit. "I—well—he was in here for minute, last night."

"He was here? For how long?"

"For only a minute. He saw we had other company, and went away at once."

She looked into my face with eyes that pierced my soul. I knew that I had blundered. "Your mother has told me about the woman and her little boy," she said. "It is very strange. Are you sure they were never in these parts before?"

"I am sure I never saw them before. But you must not be alarmed about your husband, Martha. He probably went further on to spend the evening, and was induced to stay all night."

"That is not likely. He would not have gone so far that he could not get home. I—I am afraid."

While I wondered what to say, the door opened, and Mark's mother walked into the room. A night's sleep had evidently brought refreshing, and her step was far steadier than it had been on the preceding night.

Before I could speak, my mother had bustled forward, with goodnatured hospitality.

"I'm glad enough to see you up," she said. "I was calculating on giving you your breakfast in bed. This is my son Joseph—you met him last night, you know. And let me make you acquainted with Mrs. Easton—Mrs. Charles Easton. Mrs.—I don't believe I got your name."

"I am Mrs. Redding," the stranger said, looking at Martha and no one else, and, perhaps, maddened into cruelty by the girl's beauty. "And if you are known as Mrs. Charles Easton, ma'am, I've come to tell you that I am the lawful wife of the man that you call your husband.

Martha staggered and cried out, but my mother gathered her tenderly into her arms.

"His name is not Easton," the woman went on. "His name is Benjamin Redding. We were married in Albany nine years ago, and I have all the papers with me to prove it. He was poor, and my folks were well-to-do, and they were against the marriage. But he was good-looking, and had a way about him, and I was bewitched; so at last they gave in. Before we had been married very long I found that he was a very demon of cruelty. I have seen him wring the neck of an animal, for pure pleasure. He would have hurt me if he could, but he was afraid of my family, especially of my brother, who had always read him like a book. If I had known him as well from the beginning, myself, I believe I could have cowed him. After our boy came, things went better for a little while, and then a great deal worse. When he tried to torment Mark, it turned me into a fury. My husband began to get tired of my tempers, and I soon saw that he was ceasing to care anything for me. I found out other things about him, too. He had times of drinking heavily, and he made debts everywhere. At last there was a scene a little worse than the rest between us, and he went away. After he was gone, it was found that several honest men had undersigned him, and were ruined. I did what little I could do; I resigned my claim to my father's estate; and my share went in to help clear up my husband's debts. It did not go far, but it was all I could do."

She paused, as if waiting for one of us to speak, but we were silent. In spite of my prejudice, I could not help but see that there were many elements of strength and nobleness in this injured creature. In happier surroundings, she might have made a happy and useful woman.

"At first," she went on, "I did not care what became of him. I did not want to know. It was a relief to be free, and I did not think beyond the day. After awhile, though, I began to wish I knew something about him. I was afraid he would come back, and try to take Mark away from me. He did not love the child, but he loved to be cruel, and he knew I could be hurt through the child. Strange as it may seem, I never once thought that he might try to marry again.

"My brother and sisters have taken care of Mark and me, and I have worked in their homes as much as I was able. There was no way by which I could earn a living for both of us, but I helped what I could.

"Last year a man who had always lived near my brother moved to this part of the country, and settled a little way beyond Rocksford. Three months ago he wrote to Ephraim that he had seen Benjamin Redding on the Rocksford road; that he had inquired about him, and learned that he was married and living with his father-in-law near Blue Brook.

"When I heard this, I vowed that I would come here and face him. My brother opposed it. He said I was rid of bad rubbish, and ought to let well enough alone. But I could not rest. I suppose I had some idea of making him suffer for his sin, but I had another idea with it—I wanted to keep him from more mischief than he had already done.

"So I came. The journey wore me out, and these people had to take me in and care for me. Perhaps it was because I am weak and ill that I could not bear to see you, ma'am, so young and beautiful. But you will suffer all the more, for the time to live will be longer. And now, ma'am I am very sorry for you."

Martha did not accept Mrs. Redding's sympathy. She lay quite still for some time in my mother's arms. Then she suddenly aroused herself, and sat bolt upright.

"He saw her last night, didn't he?" she asked, with terror in her eyes. "Didn't you say, Joseph, that he came in and found her here? He may—oh, Joseph, don't you see that he may have done some dreadful thing?"

Her meaning flashed over me. I started to reassure her, then stopped short. Perhaps two horrors were easier for her to bear than one.

"We will have search made," I said. "We shall soon be able to find out all about it, I am sure."

"I must go home now," she said. "I have left father and Ray. I can not stay here any longer. I must go." She spoke almost petulantly, as if some one had opposed her wish.

Mother brought some breakfast to her, but she would not taste it.

I put Rachel's saddle on Dolly, and let her up to the door. "Shall I go with you?" I asked.

She nodded. I flung myself upon Queenie and rode after Martha, wondering what would happen when the Colonel heard the news.

Martha did not wait for me, but slipped from the saddle and hurried at once into the house. On the threshold she paused, and mechanically shook hands with Ross Turner, who was just leaving the house.

"He is not there, father," Martha called, the dread aroused by the man's disappearance still uppermost in her mind. "Joseph says he was there for just a little while last night and went away—"

"I have later news," the Colonel said. (Either he did not see me, or he did not consider my presence worth noticing—probably the latter.) Ross Turner called to impart some very singular facts. He says that he started out hunting very early this morning, and met Mr. Easton who was on horseback. Ross expressed surprise at seeing him abroad at such a time, and Mr. Easton explained that he had been called away on important business, and might not return for several weeks. Mr. Turner being, as—ha!—you may recollect, of a somewhat curious disposition—called, ostensibly with relation to the sorrel colt, but in reality to learn the nature of your husband's business. It is quite unnecessary to say that I—ah!—did not enlighten him. But I must say that the whole affair is quite extraordinary—quite extraordinary!"

In spite of his elaborate English, I could clearly see that the Colonel was much excited. I remembered what I had heard of Easton's—or Redding's—debts in Rocksford, and what his wife had said of his dishonesty. It seemed more than likely that the Sylvestre fortune was involved in the action of this man.

But a fortune seemed like a poor thing just now. Would Martha tell her trouble to her father? To ask sympathy from such a man would seem like commanding water from the rock.

A bundle in the cradle stirred, and a child's cry roused Martha to the full meaning of her sorrow. With the groan which has sounded in my ears from that day to this, she flung herself across the cradle. "He will never come back!" she cried. "He had a wife before he ever saw me, and he will never come back!"

For the first time, the Colonel seemed to see me. He was trembling from head to foot, and a purplish flush seemed to overspread his face.

"Do you know what she means?" he asked me. Something in his appearance alarmed me, and I answered, guardedly:

"There may be some mistake, sir, but a woman has appeared who claims to be Mr. Easton's wife."

Martha gathered little Ray into her arms, and stood erect. The womanhood within her seemed to speak as it had never spoken before. "There is no mistake," she said. "There are many things beside her words that tell me so. The woman is his wife."

Slowly the purple flush on the Colonel's face deepened. An expression as of awful hate settled in her eyes. "Curse him!" he said. Then he fell forward heavily upon the floor.

Martha was kneeling at his side in a moment. I thought at first that he had fallen through sheer weakness, but soon his heavy breathing told me that the attack was serious, if not fatal. What could I do? It seemed heartless to leave Martha alone at such an hour, yet help must be had, and that as speedily as possible.

I started out, and met my mother in the lane. Dear mother! I might have known that she would not stay long away from Martha, in such a time of need.

"Does the Colonel know?" she asked me.

"He has known. I doubt if he will ever know anything again."

"What do you mean?"

"The Colonel has had an attack of some kind, and is unconscious. Stay with Martha."

I remember how Queenie neighed when I mounted her.

"Good speed, my girl," I whispered. "You must do your best today."

I went by the village store, and sent a messenger for the doctor. Then I rode like mad for Rachel.

CHAPTER XXVII

"AS THE TREE FALLS"

Colonel Sylvestre never regained consciousness, although he was still living when Rachel reached him.

I do not know, at this day, how I managed to tell Rachel the horrible story of Martha's trouble. My memory of the earlier events of the day are as keen as if all had transpired but yesterday; but I suppose that in time one's power to feel and remember is exhausted; and I recall only Rachel's set white face, and her self-accusing cry, "And I left my darling to bear it alone."

I fancy that Rachel's keenness of perception must have saved me from the necessity of going into details. She had always distrusted Easton, and now she saw clearly many things which she had only suspected before. I believe that she suffered for Martha almost as severely as Martha suffered for herself; for at this instance, she was able to take in more fully all that was involved for the future.

Of her rather, I remember that Rachel spoke only once. Then she said, "I suppose he would not forgive me, even if he could."

Whether or not he would have forgiven her if he could, we never knew, for the opportunity did not come. He died at midnight. Rachel, my father and I had been watching beside him. Martha was lying, very ill, in the adjoining room, and my mother was caring for her. The doctor had given her an opiate, which had not induced sleep, but had brought a semi-delirium which was perhaps better than consciousness.

There had been little change, from the first, in the Colonel's heavy breathing. The doctor had said that the end might come in a day or a week, but that there was no chance that he would rally. Yet, in spite of this, I think Rachel hoped for something—for a word or the pressure of her hand—to tell her that she was forgiven.

She was too just and reasonable to dream of tardy repentance. She knew that her father had willfully, all his life long, mocked at God and his offers of mercy, and that, even if his mind should come back to this world, he would die as he had lived. A passage from the Book of Ecclesiastes came into my mind. Perhaps it was in Rachel's also: "If the tree falls toward the south or toward the north, in the place where the tree falleth there shall it lie."

At half-past seven, I thought I noticed a change in the breathing. The others did not see it, and I said nothing. Rachel sat as silent as stone. Father dozed lightly in his chair. In the next room, Martha muttered in her delirium. The strain was almost intolerable. I had not slept at all the night before, yet never had I felt more sleepless.

All the strange scenes of the past few hours moved again and again through my mind. Never before, in my simple life, had I realized what sorrows and sins there are in the world. Now, naturally enough, it may be, I was inclined to go to the other extreme, and believe that evil and heartache were everywhere. If not, why should Martha, innocent and gentle as she was, be obliged to suffer so?

Yet Martha had done one great wrong—the partiality of my heart could not blind me to that fact. She had sinned against her womanhood in marrying a man whom she did not love, and this is one of the sins for which the present world brings its punishment.

Some one was riding into the lane. I thought it must be the doctor. He had promised to come back before morning, if possible.

Rachel did not seem to have heard the sound. She was sitting, as she had been for an hour, with her head bent forward a little and her hand resting upon it. The door opened and Stephen walked quietly into the room.

I had grown so used to strange things that it did not then occur to me as anything out of the ordinary that he should be there. I knew only that I had unconsciously wished for him, and that he was here.

Afterward, when I thought to ask him about the matter, I found that he had arrived in Rocksford soon after I left, had heard of my hasty summons to Rachel, and had followed us to her home.

I suppose Rachel was no more surprised to see him there than I was. She gave him her hand, without rising, and motioned him to a seat beside her.

He looked quickly over the little group, then the incoherent murmurs from the next room reached him.

"Martha?" he whispered.

"She is ill—she is worn out—we have made her lie down," Rachel said. There was no time now for Martha's story.

The sick man gasped convulsively, and stopped breathing. Stephen leaned forward and felt for his heart. "It is the end," he said, solemnly.

Rachel did not sob or cry out. She stood erect, while Stephen closed her father's eyes, and smoothed the covers about him. Then she sank on her knees beside the bed, whether to grieve or to pray I could not tell.

Stephen knelt on the other side, with father and myself. I wish I could recollect the words of the prayer that Stephen poured out at that moment. I can bring back only the opening sentence: "O God, our Refuge and our Strength, our very present help in trouble!" With those words, I began to feel that God was there, in that house where hearts were breaking; and I felt that he would not allow his children to suffer uncomforted.

Rachel did not rise after the prayer, and we slipped softly from the room, leaving her alone with her dead.

Stephen and I threw ourselves down on blankets in the kitchen, but I knew that my brother would not sleep, and presently I crept close to him and told him all.

He sat upright, a kind of sick horror in his eyes. "Where is the man now?" he asked.

"I don't know. Making tracks, I suppose. There has been no time to think about him, and no one to say what should be done."

"Perhaps it is just as well. We can think more clearly in a day or two."

"Maybe it would be the easiest way, to let him get away altogether. Mrs. Redding might be induced to keep quiet, and no one else knows but us."

I saw from Stephen's face that he had thought of the same thing. It was a sore temptation to save Martha from one added humiliation. But he put it away quickly.

"It would not be right," he said. "It would not be Rachel's way, nor Martha's either, when she understands. If the legal wife had been more watchful, Martha would not have been so injured. Now it becomes the duty of them both to protect some other woman, whom he would injure if he could. But we will think and pray, and try to know what is best."

Perhaps after that we slept a little. The morning found Martha no better. The doctor was puzzled. We lived before the time of "nervous prostration," which is, I believe, the easy name given nowadays to a pressure of work or joy or sorrow too great for the body to endure. So he shook her head, and bled her freely, and promised to come again the next day.

Rachel was with her sister all the morning; but toward noon she came out, with little Ray in her arms, and asked Stephen to make arrangements for the funeral.

"Please tell me just what you wish, Rachel," said Stephen, quietly, giving her a seat beside him. "You wish it to be here?"

"I wish it to be here, and as quiet as possible. Martha does not know, yet. The time may not come to tell her. There must be nothing that will disturb or alarm her. I think I can manage that."

"But here is something else. You wish to have a preacher?"

"I wish to have *you*, Stephen—just you. It is not for him, you understand. He would not have wanted a preacher, and there must be no make-believe. He did not believe, and you will not say that he did. But I think it is right that we should have you for our sakes—Martha's and mine."

"It *is* right," said Stephen. I could guess that the task which had come to him was one of the hardest he had ever attempted, but he could not let Rachel know that it was hard.

When I said this to him that night, he answered: "That is not all. It will be a hard thing to conduct Colonel Sylvestre's funeral, but think of letting some one else do it, and say what he might to wound those poor women!"

Ross Turner's version of Charles Easton's absence had gone abroad, and many of the neighbors expressed their regret that Colonel Sylvestre's son-in-law could not be present at the funeral.

"It's too bad," said one of them. "He and the Colonel were so took with each other, and the mourners is so few, anyway."

Unconsciously, the old man told the truth. The "mourners" were few. Colonel Sylvestre had exerted a masterful influence in our community for years, but he had never been loved. His neighbors had stood in awe of him, and had given him the semblance of respect; but they did not mourn for him now.

Martha was not present at the funeral service. She was conscious now, but very weak. It had fallen to Stephen's lot to break to her the news of her father's death, and she had received it with a pitiful apathy of one whose emotions have been drained dry.

So Rachel sat as sole mourner. The service was a brief and simple one. Stephen read the Scripture and offered prayer, and the neighbors looked their last upon the hard old face. It was hard, even in death, and if Rachel looked into it for the forgiving tenderness she had missed in life, she certainly never found it.

A tall monument towered above the mound where Mrs. Sylvestre slept, and in the open grave beside it we laid the body of her husband. It was only after we turned away that we remembered in the loneliness the two whom he had left behind must henceforth walk.

Mrs. Redding and little Mark remained at our house until after the funeral. At first, in my sympathy with Rachel and Martha, I rather resented the presence of this woman, who had brought them sorrow. But by degrees I became accustomed to her presence, and even learned to give a share of my sympathy to her. The moment's resentment which her first glimpse of Martha had brought, gave place to real pity, and now she was eager to do something for the woman who had suffered through her husband. She even asked my mother if she might go and say this to Martha.

My mother shook her head. "Martha has lived—that is all," she said. "One thing more, and she may die. If the time for it ever comes, I will tell her how you feel toward her. That will be better than that you should try to see her now."

The one thing that seemed to rouse Martha from her apathy was the thought of little Ray. My mother told us that she always remembered the child's bedtime, when she seemed unconscious of everything else. Except for the little girl, she seemed to have no hold upon life.

CHAPTER XXXVIII

THE LOG HUT BY THE ROAD

It was impossible that such a curiosity-loving community as ours should wait always to know the cause of Charles Easton's sudden departure. While his easy habit of dispensing hospitality in Colonel Sylvestre's name had made him some friends among the rougher class, there had always been a few of the more sensible persons who looked upon him doubtfully, and wondered that Colonel Sylvestre should have accepted his claims so readily.

People were not in the habit, in those days, of starting upon journeys abruptly. Nowadays, a business man slips across the continent without bothering to kiss his wife goodby; but when travel was difficult and slow, no sane man wished to miss the importance which a leave-taking gave him. That a man should disappear before daybreak, without a word to his friends, was preposterous.

It began to be whispered about Rocksford that Charles Easton had left his home unceremoniously. There was immediate alarm. His creditors began to compare notes, and to see the seriousness of the situation. They asked each other openly—so I was told by Mr. Osburn, who kept us posted concerning Rocksford affairs—whether Easton was supposed to have quarreled with his father-in-law. At all events, they said, it was time that their claims against the Sylvestre estate were pushed.

Colonel Sylvestre's will, as I have said before, gave all of his property to his daughter Martha. What I had not known before was, that Charles Easton was made sole executor of the will. This fact made it the more necessary that the cause of his absence be known.

Nor was this all. We had tried to keep the presence of Mrs. Redding at our house a secret, but in the hurrying to and fro which followed Colonel Sylvestre's death she had been seen by several persons, who were but poorly satisfied with such embarrassed explanations as we could give them. We feared every day lest she should be connected in the minds of the people with Charles Easton's disappearance.

"It would be better to have it all over," Rachel said, in a tired voice, one day when I called to bring my mother home. "Hushing things up never brings any good. The only thing I fear is the shock for Martha. Her life hangs by a thread. Sometimes I think we can save it, and save her reason too. For her sake we must be careful how we move."

I came home and told Stephen what she said. Next morning, when I came downstairs, his horse was saddled and at the door.

"I must go and hunt that man," he said. "I have thought it over, and it is the only way. If I need the authority of the law, I will get it; but the first thing is to find out where he is and what he is about. I can do this quietly, and as quickly as any one. Tell Rachel."

I told Rachel, and it seemed to me that the message should have evoked some expression of gratitude form her. But it did not. She merely walked to the window and looked out, as if she expected to see Stephen riding away to his hard task.

The days went by. I began my term of school in the new schoolhouse which had replaced the slab-floored structure of my childhood. Mrs. Redding and little Mark went back to their friends, the other side of Rocksford. Rachel nursed Martha, cared for little Ray, and put off the men who came to her to discuss business matters. Thus we waited for Stephen.

One day, just as I was starting for my school, a rough-looking man rode up to the door and gave me a note. It ran about like this:

DEAR BROTHER: Bring Mrs. Redding and the boy and follow this man. Put into the wagon some quilts, and such food as mother has ready. *Do not wait.* I have found Charles Easton in a sad condition.
STEPHEN.

I wanted to go to Rachel, but the words "Do not wait" seemed to deter me. I hurriedly harnessed the horses, and bundled Mrs. Redding and Mark into the wagon.

The woman was sad and silent, and her mood affected the boy, so we had a quiet journey. Once Mark slipped his hand into mine and whispered, "Are we truly going to see daddy?"

"I think so."

"You won't let him hurt me, will you, Joseph?"

"No, indeed, Mark. He won't want to hurt you, though."

"Not the first thing, maybe. But he always gets tired of being good, in a little while. Mother would keep him from hurting me if she could, but she can't—can you, mother?"

Mrs. Redding smiled sadly, but did not answer. I wonder if the ghost of her mad love for this man still walked in her heart. Did she dream of that long-past time when, in reckless defiance of the judgment of others, she had flung her life into his keeping? I could not guess.

The place to which our guide led us was almost new to me, although it was not more than a dozen miles from our home. The road for the last few miles was a lonely one, and, in bad weather, must have been impassable. Even now, our light wagon made slow progress.

We stopped before a little log hut at the side of the road. It looked uninhabited, but a thin line of smoke rising from the chimney told of the presence of human life within.

Our guide had dismounted, and disappeared within the cabin. Stephen appeared, and beckoned to me.

"He is still living," he said, "but very far gone. Did the man tell you how I found him?"

"I didn't ask him—didn't know whether it was safe to discuss matters with him."

"It is safe enough, I dare say, though I think he has little knowledge of the situation. When I left home, I had only one idea about Easton's whereabouts. I felt sure he would avoid Rocksford, for he is so well known there. So I started out in the opposite direction. I rode for days. I have friends in nearly every town, and I was able to make my search a thorough one without awakening suspicion. Nowhere did I get the slightest trace of him, or even a hint that I could imagine might point toward him. At last I got thoroughly discouraged, and started for home. I took this road because it was a strange one, but without any real thought of getting my clew here. As I passed this cabin, I saw Easton's horse tied to the fence. I should have known him anywhere. I came to the door, and heard a groan inside. I did not risk knocking, but walked straight in. Easton was lying on a miserable bed on the floor, in the most excruciating pain. I learned afterward that he had left the road on which Turner met him, and had kept in hiding until dark. Then he tried to cross by this road, but it was new to his horse. Somehow, the horse stumbled and threw him. He lay by the roadside until morning. Then he was found by the man who brought you here. In spite of Easton's suffering, he refused to let the man Stoney go for a doctor. Stoney managed to drag him into the house and has taken care of him ever since. At last Stoney got so frightened that he went for a doctor without leave. I don't know what the doctor thought, but he kept his own counsel. He said that there was little to be done; that Easton's spine was injured, and though he might live for some time in helplessness, he would never recover. He left morphine, and told Stoney to get more if it was needed. Since then, Easton has been under the influence of opiates most of the time. He recognized me soon after I came, and I got the whole story from him. He has paid Stoney well to keep him here, and to hold his tongue."

"Does he know he is going to die?"

"I have told him so, but he will not believe it. His heart is hard toward every one, unless it is his little boy. When I told him that I had seen his wife and child, he asked quickly whether Mark was well, and added, 'Poor little chap! poor little chap!' He has never seemed to think once of poor Martha's child."

"Does he know that you expect his wife?"

"Yes. He did not know until half an hour ago. We must not delay, for I think he has not long to live. He is conscious now, but weak and irritable."

Stephen motioned to Mrs. Redding, and she and little Mark went in before us. The woman knelt beside the wretched bed, and drew over it carefully one of the warm quilts we had brought with us. Easton looked up, and cried out excitedly:

"Emily!" he said. "My God, it *is* Emily."

"Here is Mark, Benjamin."

"Mark? So it is, poor chap! Know your daddy, little man?"

"Yes, sir," said the child, in an agony of shyness.

"You've found me in a bad fix, Emily. I never meant to go back on you and the boy altogether. I got tired of your tears and complaints, but I wouldn't have gone back on you, if I hadn't got into such an infernal mess about money matters. I never meant to marry any one else, but I was in a tight place, and the girl *was* a beauty. Is it true that the old man is dead?"

"Yes, it is true."

"Martha will get it all. The other one is a Tartar—*she'll* get her deserts. But it'll do me no good, now you have found me out. The preacher says I'm going to die, but I don't believe it. If there is a God in heaven he wouldn't be so cruel as to take me now." "Cruel!" repeated little Mark, with sudden recollection. "That's the thing daddy was when he whipped me, isn't it?"

The sick man winced. "Send the youngster out, Emily. I'm too tired to talk any more. You've no idea what this cursed pain is like. It is ten thousand irons, burning me at once. Oh, a dog deserves better than this."

"A dog may, but you don't," were the words which came into my mind. Yet I could not but soften toward the man, as I saw how pitiable was his condition.

Stephen came close, and bent over the bed. "Benjamin Redding," he said—and I saw that the man shrank from the old name—"you have only a short time to live. If there is anything you can do before you die, to make restitution to those whom you have injured, I advise you to do it at once. Do not add to your sins by withholding now the little you can do to right these wrongs."

"I am *not* going to die," cried Easton, with awful vehemence. "Curse all your praying, sniveling crew—I'm not going to die."

"Hush, Benjamin," said Emily Redding, sternly. "You are going to die. You have been a bad man, and I—God forgive me!—have not been a very good woman. I have been passionate and headstrong, and often I have left God out of the account. But I want to do one good thing—I want to do one good thing—I want to forgive you before you die. Not many women have more to forgive than I have, it seems to me. But I can't forgive you unless you repent and want to be forgiven. You *must* repent."

"I won't. I'm not going to die. I'll get out of this, yet. Oh, the pain! Give me some morphine, quick!"

"Not yet," said Stephen. "You may never return to consciousness again. I can not let you leave this world until you have faced your past, and asked yourself whether there is any of its wrong-doing that you can make right."

"Curse you, I must have the morphine. I suppose it's about the old Colonel's money that you are making all this fuss. Here, then, Joseph Arrondale, you are an honest fellow, and no preacher. Unbuckle this belt, will you? No one has found it except the doctor, and I soon shut his mouth. What there is sewed in there belongs to Martha. It's all there is left, and you may take it back to her. The rest I spent, and this would soon be gone, so she might as well have it. Now get me the morphine—I won't stand this pain—I won't stand it!"

He began to curse and rave, and Stephen gave him the morphine. He closed his eyes, than opened them again, and sought his wife's face.

"Emily," he groaned, "don't tell the little chap how bad I was."

If there was in his heart any sorrow for his sin, these words were the only evidence he gave of it. That night he died, and his wife was denied the comfort of offering him forgiveness.

CHAPTER XXIX
THE SECRET PAGE

In a long lifetime of observation I have noticed that evil news always travels more rapidly than good. Stephen and I questioned much as to whether the whole story of Charles Easton's life and death need ever be told. There was no one to be injured by our silence. Mrs. Redding was now full of pity for Martha, and would gladly have saved her if she could. If Martha should rally, she would have enough to bear, without this last humiliation.

But we soon found that our silence would not avail. The story was abroad, as if the wind had carried it. We afterward learned that Ross Turner had been full of curiosity about Easton's whereabouts, and had not ceased to make inquiries concerning him. In Rocksford he heard the stories—now freely told for the first time—of Easton's debts and dishonesty. To Rocksford, ere long, was brought the account, through the relative with whom Mrs. Redding had stayed, of Easton's first marriage and his desertion of his wife. It did not take much effort to piece the different parts of the story together; and Ross was prompt to put his discovery into circulation.

Slowly, after long weakness and many relapses, Martha came back to life. The necessary facts concerning Easton's end were gently told to her by Stephen. She asked no questions, but listened with a pinched and piteous face. When he finished, she buried her face in her hands.

"My poor, poor baby," she murmured. "My poor little Ray!"

After that, it was a long time before she walked again. But by degrees she began to go about the house, and even to venture out a little. For a long time she shrank from meeting people, and I was much surprised one Sunday, in early summer, to see her sitting in the little church, beside Rachel, who held Ray on her lap.

After this, she was seldom absent from her place, on Sunday morning. We had preaching only now and then, but church-going in those days meant something besides attendance at a literary lecture or a sacred concert, and those who believed kept faithfully their tryst with the Lord, on the first day of every week.

We soon found that the financial affairs of the Sylvestres were in sorry shape. My father was appointed administrator of the Colonel's estate, which, according to the terms of the will, belonged to Martha. One-half of the farm was already hers, and, when she came to learn the conditions of the will, she refused to accept anything beyond this.

However, as Rachel well knew and as we all soon learned, it mattered little what the conditions of the will were, or what were the wishes of the two women with regard to the property. Easton had already squandered a large part of Colonel Sylvestre's ready money. Whether he had made a pretense of borrowing this, or whether he had helped himself to it, of course we never knew. Rachel told me that her father made a practice of keeping large sums about the house, and that she had often protested against this habit as involving the family in danger. The Colonel had been wont to laugh at her fears, and in his ridicule Easton had always joined. The probabilities are that, when he found flight necessary, he took whatever he found in the strongbox. If so, this was the money he gave me to return.

The notes which the Colonel had signed with Easton were paid as they were presented. That this might be done, all of the farm was sold except forty acres of the east part, which included all of the buildings. Rachel would have sold the whole and gone to seek a home for herself and her sister elsewhere. But against this, Martha, usually so acquiescent, protested.

"I could not bear to have strange eyes look at me," she said. "I could not bear it, Rachel."

So they stayed on in the old home. Rachel managed the little farm with wonderful skill, and saw that Martha lacked none of the comforts to which she had been accustomed.

A year passed quietly. It has ever seemed, in my life, that surprising events are closely crowded together, and succeeded by periods of calm, in which all days are much alike. I taught the district school in the winter, and helped my father in the summer. Stephen went on longer journeys than heretofore, for the circle of his influence was widening, and he was sent to preach in distant places. There was little to mark the year, except the growth of little Ray, who alone, of us all, the time seemed to change.

But other changes were before us. I come to write of them with a pen which often falters, for I feel that I have dipped it in my own heart's blood.

One sunny morning I called at the Sylvestre home, and found Martha looking brighter and stronger than she had looked since her sorrow. Ray was in her lap, cooing out the pretty baby talk which it puzzled every one but her mother to understand.

Martha greeted me kindly, as she always did. I took Ray from her, and the little one played with the buttons on my coat while I talked to her mother. Little children have ever been my friends, and I should lose much out of the memories of my long life if I were to forfeit the happy hours I have spent among them.

I can recollect that June morning far better than I recollect the events of yesterday. I can see Martha's looks, as she sat there by the window, as plainly as I see the pretty Maude Arrondale who sits beside me as I write. She wore a dress of some soft, dark stuff—she was ever plain in her dress, as it becomes so beautiful a woman to be—and about her neck was a collar of some sort of fine needlework. Her soft, dark brown hair was parted, and allowed to fall in its own natural waves.

The miniature of Martha Sylvestre, painted in her school days, does not do her justice; yet I heard the artist who painted Maude Arrondale's last portrait say of that quaint little old picture, "This is the American Madonna! I have searched for her all my life, and I have never found her until now!"

Little Sylvestre Arrondale has eyes like Martha's—like, save that his are the eyes of a handsome child, and hers were the eyes of a saint.

We talked of many things that morning. I had not meant, even when I began to fill these pages, to write down what we said. The story has been sacredly kept in my heart through all the years, and I meant that it should die with me. But as I have written on there has come to me a desire to have those of my name, who may read these pates, know the secret of my lonely life. As we grow old, the desire to be kindly remembered by the world we are leaving seems to grow upon us. I would have those who will sometimes think of me when I am gone think of me as neither a cynic nor an alien from life's common interests, but as one who had and kept a human heart. So I tell the story of that June morning, concerning which I had meant to be silent.

I told Martha how glad I was to see her stronger.

"I am stronger," she said. But her voice lacked the old ring, and she looked out across the hills, as if seeing there something that others did not see.

Then she turned quietly and looked at me. "I have changed a great deal since the days when we used to be together," she said. "I have lived, oh, so much, in such a little while. I do not blame any one except myself, but I hope that, when Ray is a woman, those who care for her will keep her from knowing the dark side of life while she is as young as I was."

I remembered afterward how strangely she spoke of Ray's future, as if it were a thing in which she was to have no share. But at the moment my mind was fully of the past, and I did not dwell upon the words.

"I wish I could have saved you from it all, Martha." I felt that my words were bungling enough, but they were from the heart. "I have always loved you, Martha—you must have known that. I was so unworthy that I dared not tell you. I was always hoping to grow more worthy. I felt sure you did not care for me except as a friend who had been your playfellow from childhood. I thought you cared for me even a little less than for Stephen. Was I not right, Martha?"

"Perhaps you were right," said Martha, with a little blush. "But why do you tell me all this now? It is all past—all past."

"No," I said; "it is not likely to be all past for me. I have few virtues, but constancy is one of the few. If such a thing be possible, you are dearer to me because of the past; dearer because of what you have suffered. I did not mean to startle you. I did not mean to tell you this today. But sooner or later I must have told you. I will not ask for an answer. Indeed, I do not want an answer, for I know what, in your surprise, you would be sure to say. I have nothing to offer you. I am not good, and I shall never be great. But if you will let me try to serve and comfort you, and be a father to little Ray—oh, Martha, the world will not hold another man as blessed as I."

Two or three times she had waved her hand as if she would stop me, but I paid no heed. When I was done she leaned back in her chair and shaded her face with her hands.

"It is all past now," she repeated wearily. "I am so weak and tired"

"I would take such care of you," I broke in, eagerly. "Perhaps with care you would be well again in time. If not, I could at least wait upon you and watch by you when you suffer."

"I can not—you are so good—but truly I can not, Joseph. Don't think I don't feel it all. I am sorry you care, because I cannot give anything back, and yet I am a little glad, too, because it is a comfort to know one person would take me, poor, bruised creature that I am. But I can not. All such things are in the past now."

She did not remove her hands, and her attitude showed such utter weariness that I reproached myself for having stayed so long.

"Goodby, Martha," I whispered. I was not sure that she heard me. At any rate, she did not answer, and I stole out softly and left her alone.

A few days later, as I was leaving the house after a talk with Rachel concerning business affairs, Martha slipped this note into my hand. It is yellow with age, and worn with much handling. I shall copy it here, and then burn it, for I could not bear the thought that it might fall into irreverent hands:

DEAR JOSEPH: If I should think it over for many years, it would make no difference. What you ask for can not be. Sometime—I hope and pray it may be soon—you will know the reason why. Till then, you must be content to trust me.

I know what you have offered me, Joseph. I pray every day that you will be rewarded for your goodness. And you will be, for God remembers.

MARTHA

CHAPTER XXX

THE HEAVENLY GATES

I do not know how it was, or just when, that we accepted the fact that Martha was going to leave us. I am quite sure that it was Rachel who first mentioned it to me.

"She grows weaker every day," she said once, when I inquired for her sister. "She will never rally. Joseph, she is going away."

"Going away!" I repeated, with lips which seemed to be frozen.

"Going away—to God."

"Rachel—don't be so sure! She is young—she may get well."

"Do you suppose I would be sure, if I could help it?" She bent her eyes upon me, and in them there was the prophecy of a loneliness almost unendurable. "No woman could suffer as she does, and go on living long, unless she were terribly strong, like me. I could not die of mental suffering, I suppose. I am like a tree, that gets strong by battling with the wind. But Martha is like a delicate flower that has been ground down by somebody's heel. It is not possible that she will ever hold up her head again."

"She is better suited to heaven than to earth," I said, with a feeble attempt at comfort for us both."

"She is eager to go—so eager that I think she hastens the time. She is only sorry—for Ray and me."

"Oh, Rachel, how can you bear it?"

"God gives strength. At first I thought I *could not* let her go. At times, I feared my old doubts would engulf me. But I held on—just simply held on. And then, I began to see. I saw that I could never make life over for my darling. God could, but even he needed a new world for it. Then I took my hands away, and gave her up to him."

After this, I could not but notice Martha's rapid decline. Each time I saw her she seemed to have grown more frail in body, more heaven like in spirit. Rachel was right. She was going away—to God.

What I am to tell you now was told to me by Stephen. He will not mind my setting it down, for it is the last scene in that life so unspeakably dear to us all.

Stephen remained with us during the last weeks of Martha's life, for his visits were a source of great comfort to her, and he would not deprive her of them. With him, more than with any one else, she allowed herself perfect freedom in the expression of her religious faith; and my brother told me that often, when he was with her, he felt himself to be on the very borderland of the upper country.

One day, when they were alone, she followed his prayer with a short petition of her own. She prayed for the salvation of sinners, for a higher life for Christians; then, in a trembling voice, she asked God to make her ready for her presence, and to take care of Rachel and Ray. She seemed to be in a kind of ecstasy of happiness and anticipation.

Her emotion seemed to exhaust her and she lay quiet for a time. Then she opened her eyes and fixed them wistfully upon Stephen.

"You have been very good to me," said she. I should be glad to think, when I go away, that you will always be happy."

"I shall be happy, I believe, Martha—happy in the work I love."

She looked at him curiously. "I have a strange desire to see those I love happy," she said. "I know happiness is not the highest thing, yet surely we ought not to put it out of our lives needlessly. Stephen, I am going to die, and you will let me talk to you as I could not if I were going to stay here. Have you ever loved any one—I mean, in the way people love each other when they would like to spend their lives together?"

For answer, Stephen bowed his head upon his hands and groaned aloud.

"Poor Stephen! I did not mean to hurt you so. Do—do I know her?"

Stephen nodded. "Did Rachel never tell you?" he asked.

"It *is* Rachel, then. I thought it was. No, she never talks about such things. We never chattered foolishness as other girls do. Perhaps it would have been better if we had. But—did you never tell her, Stephen?"

"Many times. I have promised not to do it any more, for it only brings unhappiness to us both."

"Rachel is proud and reserved by nature, and it could never be easy for her to learn how to love. But, can't you see that if she ever did care for a man, it would be more than any man was ever loved before?"

Stephen smiled. "I have never doubted that for one moment," he said.

"Listen—I can not talk to her about such things. It has never been our habit, and she would guess that I had talked with you. I may be mistaken in my thought about it, but I want you to tell her just once more.

Stephen shrank back. "I can not, Martha. It will grieve her, and to no purpose. I have her friendship now. It has been won through a hard fight, and it is worth a thousand times more than the love of any other woman. I can not forfeit it."

"You will not. Rachel knows that you are the best man in the world. I told her the other night that you were, and she said it was true. Such friendship can not be forfeited.

"No, Martha, I can not speak now. If a promise will comfort you, I will make this one: If there should come in the future a time when I can speak without hurting Rachel, as I would hurt her now, I will speak once more. I can not do it yet."

"But I want you to do it now, persisted Martha. "If harm comes, I shall be more sorry than any one, but something tells me that you must not wait. Go and find Rachel, Stephen. She can not be far away. Please go quickly."

He started out, more because the tension of his feeling had become too great than because he really meant to do Martha's bidding.

In the orchard he found Rachel. She had a book in her hand, but she was not reading, and there was upon her face the look of sadness that she never allowed to rest there when she was with Martha.

That look was more than he could bear. In simple words he told his love, and asked her to let him try to comfort her. She lowered her head for a moment; then she raised her brave eyes to his, the greatest joy of her life shining through its greatest sorrow.

"I don't deserve it," she said humbly. "I have been so hard and bitter—I don't deserve it!"

Stephen never told me how he answered.

Presently they went in to Martha. She was asleep, and they sat down together beside her. When she awoke, she looked from one to the other with a question in her eyes.

"Martha," said Stephen, gently, "will you trust me to take care of Rachel?"

Her happiness was beyond words. She drew Rachel's face to hers and kissed it. Then she took from her hand an old-fashioned cameo ring.

"It was my mother's," she whispered. "Now it is almost too loose for me to wear, but Rachel's fingers were always slimmer than mine. Put it on her hand."

Stephen slipped the cameo on Rachel's finger, then raised the firm, slim hand to his lips. "Till death shall us two part," he said, solemnly.

Martha was silent for a moment, as if in deep thought. Then she said: "If it is not too much to ask, I want to see you married, before I die. Don't be vexed with me for saying so, Rachel dear; it will make me so happy to know that Stephen will have the right to take care of you and Ray. It is the only thing that will make me happier than I am now."

"You will surely live till then, Martha. You are wonderfully bright and well today," Rachel told her.

"When is 'then'? I mean now—at once. It would make me so happy!"

It was strange how she dwelt on this word "happy"—she whose short life had been so full of pain.

"Why should we wait, Rachel?" Stephen asked. "We are not young any more, and we know each other. Martha has spoken the truth. I ought to have the right to take care of you."

Why should they wait, indeed? Rachel had no heart for guests and gowns. There had been one fine wedding in the Sylvestre home, and no one wished to revive the mockery of it.

I was dispatched for Bro. Cady, and found him in a neighboring town, debating with an Universalist.

"You are too hard on that poor fellow," I told him, after listening to the argument for half an hour. "You must have forgotten how lately you came over that road yourself."

"I have forgotten nothing of the kind," Bro. Cady assured me. "But I'll have him understand that he needn't waste his time arguing against Calvinism when he's debating with me."

The debate was nearly over, and in the afternoon Bro. Cady returned with me, enlivening the journey with accounts of the pranks of his baby son, John W. Cady.

"My wife was firm about the name," he said, "though she is rather less of a Methodist now than I am. Her father and grandfather had both been 'John Wesley,' would never do, so we compromised on 'John Washington.'"

At ten o'clock the next morning, Stephen and Rachel were married. They chose this hour because it was the time of day when Martha felt her best. She was propped up in her large chair in the livingroom, and her face had in it more joy than I had seen there since the time when she first showed little Ray to me.

There were no guests present except Bro. Cady, my parents and myself. I think this day was the consummation of many a secret longing on the part of my dear mother. Even in the days when she had feared

Rachel's influence over Stephen, she had loved the girl, and felt that the two were somehow intended for each other.

I do not think Rachel had a new gown for the occasion. She looked to me just as she had always looked, except more gentle and womanly than ever before. Perhaps I have said somewhere that Rachel was one of those women who have the gift of looking perfectly neat at all times and in the midst of all kinds of work, and who never, even on the most formal occasion, appeared to be elaborately dressed. Today, as she came out and held out her hand to me, I said to myself what I had often said before, that she was the most beautiful woman in the world, except the one who was soon to leave it forever.

After the ceremony, Stephen and Rachel knelt together beside Martha's chair. She folded their hands together between her own, and said tenderly, "God bless you, and make you very useful together, my dear brother and sister!"

Then she asked my mother, who was holding little Ray, to put the child in Rachel's arms.

"She is yours, dear," Martha said, "yours and Stephen's. It isn't often that a mother can leave her child and feel so sure that all is well. She is a little willful, but you will understand, and will make a noble woman of her. I pray every moment that she may give you love and complete obedience, in return for all the sacrifice she will cost you. If you should sometime feel like giving her your name, please remember that it would have made me very glad. The name of Arrondale is a good one, and has never brought us anything but happiness. But tell her about her poor mother, and that she prayed for her baby until the last."

We were all in tears except the speaker. Her eyes were dry, and heavenly bright. As she raised them, she caught sight of me, and I fancy that a great wave of pity came over her.

"Let Joseph love Ray a great deal," she said. "Ray is very fond of Joe."

She had not used this little nickname since our childhood. It was the last word I ever heard her speak. The strain was too great, and I slipped away to be alone.

Stephen and Rachel carried her to her bed. She never left it, though she lived for nearly a week after this. During this time she seemed to be conscious, although she seldom spoke, and never expressed a wish of any kind. All the eagerness of the past few weeks was gone. The things for which she had continued to live were accomplished, and she was done with life.

One evening, just at sunset, she opened her eyes and looked into the radiant west.

"Ah!" she said, "it is sweet to die when the sun is going down."

Rachel bent over he in sudden apprehension.

"Kiss me!" Martha whispered.

The kiss was given quickly, but none too soon, for already the dear lips were turning cold.

CHAPTER XXXI

THE LAST WORD

I am near the end of the big book in which I have been writing, and the story of fifty years must be put into a few pages. And I am well content that it should be so; for it is upon the days of our youth that we old folks like best to dwell. The age at which life is new is the age at which its events make the greatest impression upon us.

My father and mother lived to a good age. Dear mother held the eldest grandchild of Stephen and Rachel in her arms before she was called hence.

"We are going to name the baby for you, grandma," said Rachel's son, Sylvestre Arrondale the First.

"Nonsense!" said mother, with her old spirit. "I never thought Abigail a pretty name, and I'm not going to have this dear baby burdened with it. Why not honor Joseph this time and call the baby Josephine?"

And Josephine was the baby's name.

Mother went away two years before father. She had thought it would be otherwise, and when asked if she were ready to go, answered, "If Samuel can spare me for a little while, but I always thought he would need me at the end."

Then he laid his face against hers, and whispered that it would be but a very little while, and that he would bear the loneliness, for her sake. So the two white-haired lovers parted.

After my mother died, the look of girlishness that we loved came back into her face. "She looks as she did when we were little children," Stephen whispered to me. And I knew that it was so.

Father bore his loneliness bravely, as he had said he would. He kept his interest in life to the last, and his shrewd humor never failed. But when a slight illness came he lay down, quietly content, and sure that it would be the last. So it proved to be, and, remembering the love that had never grown old, we could not grieve for him.

After this, my home was with Stephen and Rachel. Indeed, it is with them still, and we three share a happy old age together.

Rachel's five children are all sons, and all Arrondales. They made men of my father's type—men who loved God, wrought righteousness, and turned up fortunes by their thrift and shrewdness. They are the best gift given to the world by a father and mother whose lives have been full of unselfish benefactions.

The best gift, perhaps I should say, except one. Strangely enough, the only one of the children of this home who resembled Rachel was the child who was not her own. At first we watched little Ray for a likeness to Martha, and were disappointed when we did not find it. But by degrees we grew used to her as she was, and content with a charm which could scarcely have been greater. As she grew older, we saw in her Rachel's mental powers, and Rachel's strength of will. With the atmosphere of love and admiration about her, there might have been danger that such a nature would become assertive and domineering; but Ray was guided by a loving woman who read the girl's heart through her own.

"I want to have Ray a happier girl than I was," said Rachel. "But I do not want to have her a spoiled girl."

She had her wish. Ray's intelligence and vivacity had added to them, as years went by, a gracious womanliness which drew to her every heart. Inevitably and immediately, she became the center of every social circle she entered. The children of the several Arrondale households know that their beautiful Aunt Ray has been fairy godmother to them all. They have heard of her early and romantic marriage to a man high in the counsels of the nation. They have been told how, first in Columbus, and then in Washington, she used her social gifts to confer happiness, and especially to honor the religion of Christ. They know, too that her great tenderness for them, and for all children, is partly because of a little grave where her only child sleeps.

The little grave is in the old graveyard at Blue Brook; and beside the slender shaft which marks it is a simple stone with this inscription:

"MARTHA:
"Blessed are the pure in heart, for they shall see God."

Ray early learned her mother's story, and I remember that once she said, as if in self-reproach, "I wonder if I do not hate my father's memory—just a little!"

But, naturally, the story of the past seemed vague and far away. She was near to middle life when an incident made it real.

In Washington, she came to know a Congressman from a Western State, by the name of Redding. She asked her husband to learn the Westerner's first name, and found that it was Mark. The discovery saddened her at first, then she learned to be grateful, that this man, whose blood was so closely allied to hers, wore the stamp of manhood and usefulness. She invited him to her house, and she and her husband made themselves useful to him in many ways.

"Some day I shall tell him who I am," she said to her husband. "Some day I shall tell that he is my brother, and that he has my real love and interest."

But she never did. His gratitude to her was unbounded, and, in return for her interest, he one day confided in her the sad story of his childhood. From this story, Ray found that he had never been told of his father's marriage to Martha. It was thus that poor Emily Redding had fulfilled the dying wish of her scapegrace husband.

"Since she did not tell him, I shall not," Ray said. "She deserves that from me—poor lady!"

Stephen, Rachel and I! The young folks come and go, and their interests are our chief concern, but, after all, we three gray heads have some things in common that the present generation can not share. Was there ever an old man blest as I am, in being the third in such a trio?

Stephen is bent, as well as gray, but Rachel's erectness is the pride of her granddaughters, with whom "as straight as grandma" is the ideal of elegance in a womanly figure. Her eyes are keen, and look out from under jetblack brows, although her hair has been snow-white for twenty years.

Stephen seldom preaches now, but his talks at the communion table are a feast to the soul. He is a veritable Gamaliel to a circle of young preachers, who delight to sit at his feet and listen to his teaching. Among these are two of the Sylvestre-Arrondale boys, and this is compensation to Rachel, who long grieved in secret because none of her own sons chose the calling of their father.

Stephen has many times told me that to him it is a marvel all but too great for comprehension, that the people with whom he allied himself in those early days of hardship and persecution, should have grown, during his own ministry, to such numbers and influence.

"But I am glad I lived and worked when I did," he always adds. "We are growing a bit comfortable and complaisant, and comfort and complaisance would not suit me as well as the old heroic days. I am glad I lived when I did."

In heroic days, Stephen surely has lived heroically. He has kept back no part of the price of a noble ministry. He has spent and been spent, asking for no man's gold or silver or apparel, but often in cold and hunger and weariness he has preached the gospel of simplicity and power.

His reward has been great. Thousands honor him as their father in the gospel. He has taught a multitude who have themselves become teachers, and thus the power of his life has touched a host of those whom he has never seen.

Few men have done as much, but I am inclined to think that no man has ever had such a helper. Remembering my dear mother, remembering too, the pure saint who has been in glory for so many years, I still say deliberately that Rachel is the best woman I have ever known. What she has been to the needy, the sorrowful and the wayward is written only in heaven. What she has been to me, the lonely pilgrim, I dare not trust myself to say. Without her counsels and her ministries, the pilgrimage would have been a weary one indeed.

I have shown many of these pages to her, and we have laughed together over the story of her perversity. But I shall not show her this page, for she has ever been chary of praise, except when it comes from Stephen, from whom she has learned to regard it as a matter of course.

For a perfect surrender to the man she loves, commend me to the woman of strong will and strong character. When she makes a choice, her reason is behind it, and she will stand by it to the uttermost. However, this is merely a piece of an old man's moralizing, and you need not read it into the story unless you choose.

"When I loved you so long," I once heard Stephen say to Rachel, "did you believe that I would win you in the end?"

"No," answered Rachel, with her wifely smile (indeed, now, she has quite a different smile for her children and grandchildren, and one which they know well). "No, I did not think so. But sometimes I was terribly afraid you might!"

*   *   *

Maude Arrondale just came in and put her pretty hands over my eyes.

"Uncle Joseph, you must stop writing," she commanded. "Why, your poor eyes will be put out altogether if you go on in this light!"

Now, I usually mind Maude, because I like her. And I like her for several reasons. She is a dear young thing, to begin with; then, she is the wife of Sylvestre the Second and the mother of Sylvestre the Third. And, by no means least, she is the granddaughter of that staunch old friend of our household, Bro. Cady. (I tell her this is why she is uncompromisingly rigid in her orthodoxy.)

"I am almost done," I told her. "Let me finish this page, and I promise you I will write no more for many a day."

So she has left me, and I must keep my word. What, then, shall I say at the end?

I can only repeat what I said at the beginning—that my long life has been encompassed with mercies, that I am glad I have lived, and that I shall be glad to die.

THE END